THE SONG
OF THE
BLUE BIRD

THE SONG OF THE BLUE BIRD

ESTHER GOLDENBERG

100 BLOCK

BY ROW HOUSE

For all inquiries and usage requests, please contact
rights@rowhousepublishing.com or write to
Row House Publishing, PO Box 210, New Egypt, NJ 08533.

ISBN:9781967182084 (Paperback)
ISBN: 9781967182091 (eBook)

Printed in the [United States]
Distributed by Simon & Schuster

Library of Congress Cataloging-in-Publication data
available upon request.

Edited by Gina Frangello
Typeset by Iram Allam

First Edition
1 3 5 7 9 10 8 6 4 2

To our children and descendants
and all the people who will come after us.

The edge of the wing is laced with blue.

NUMBERS 15:38

CONTENTS

IN THE BEGINNING

In the Beginning — 3

I Was Born — 13

Memory — 22

The Three of Us — 34

Before — 44

We Returned — 58

Sickness — 69

Shade — 75

We Traveled — 88

NAMES

Names — 99

Every Woman — 110

My Father — 119

Carried — 128

Walking — 144

Oilers — 150

Bathing — 157

Life — 166

Baby — 171

Other — 177

Suf — 185

The Children — 197

We Learned — 209

HE CALLED OUT

He Called Out — 221

Midian — 231

Tzipporah — 238

Moses Led — 247

Moses and Aaron — 257

Final — 272

Go — 278

First — 291

CONTENTS

IN THE WILDERNESS

In the Wilderness — 301

Refidim — 309

Amina — 316

Days — 324

We Passed — 328

Years — 337

Together — 342

Out of Egypt — 347

Moses — 359

New — 368

WORDS AND THINGS

Words and Things — 379

Author's Note — 388

About the Author — 393

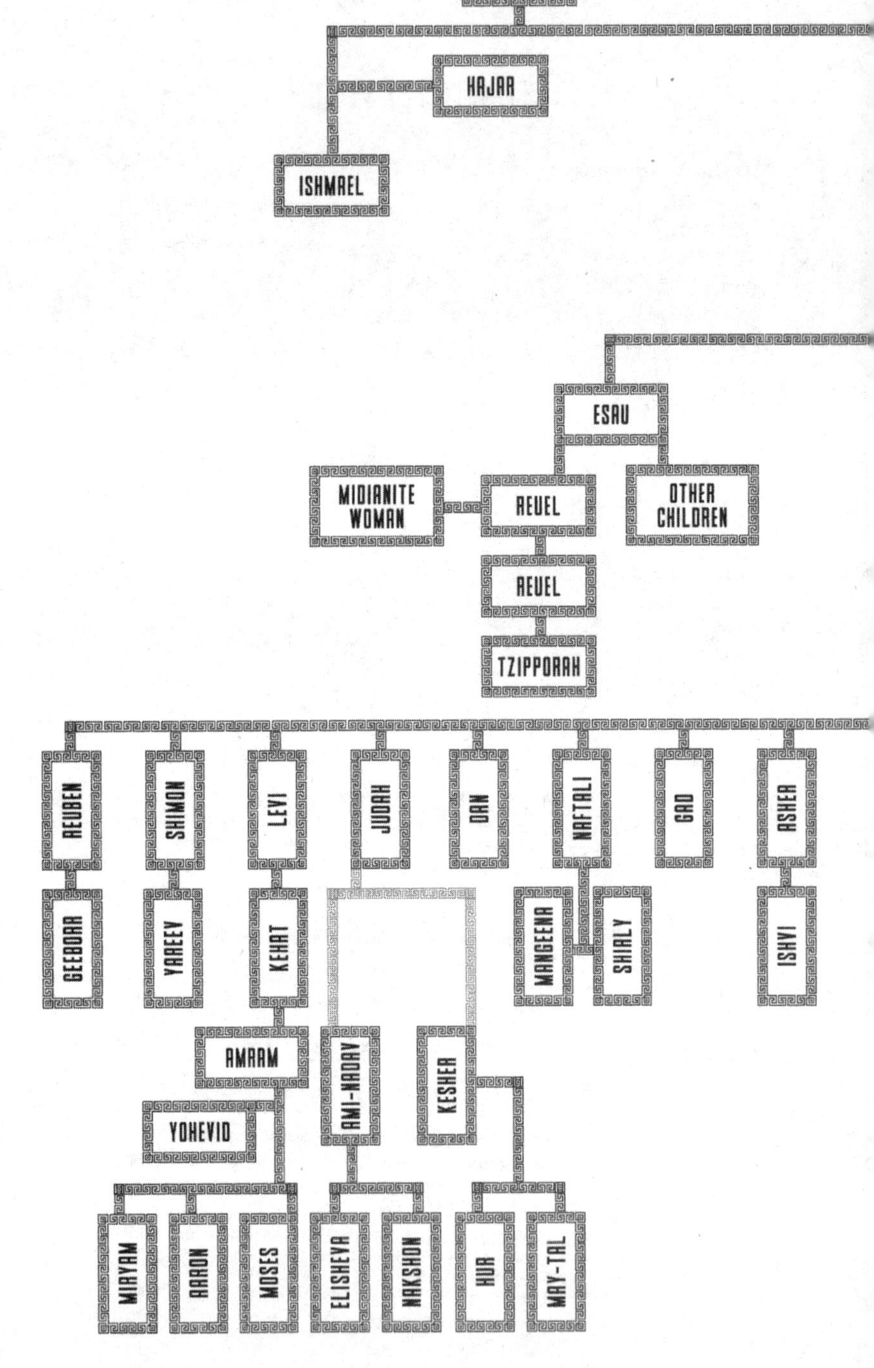

ABRAHAM
HAJAR
ISHMAEL
ESAU
MIDIANITE WOMAN
REUEL
OTHER CHILDREN
REUEL
TZIPPORAH
REUBEN
SHIMON
LEVI
JUDAH
DAN
NAFTALI
GAD
ASHER
GEEBORA
YAREEV
KEHAT
MANGEENA
SHIARLY
ISHVI
AMRAM
AMI-NADAV
KESHER
YOHEVID
MIRYAM
AARON
MOSES
ELISHEVA
NAKSHON
HUR
MAY-TAL

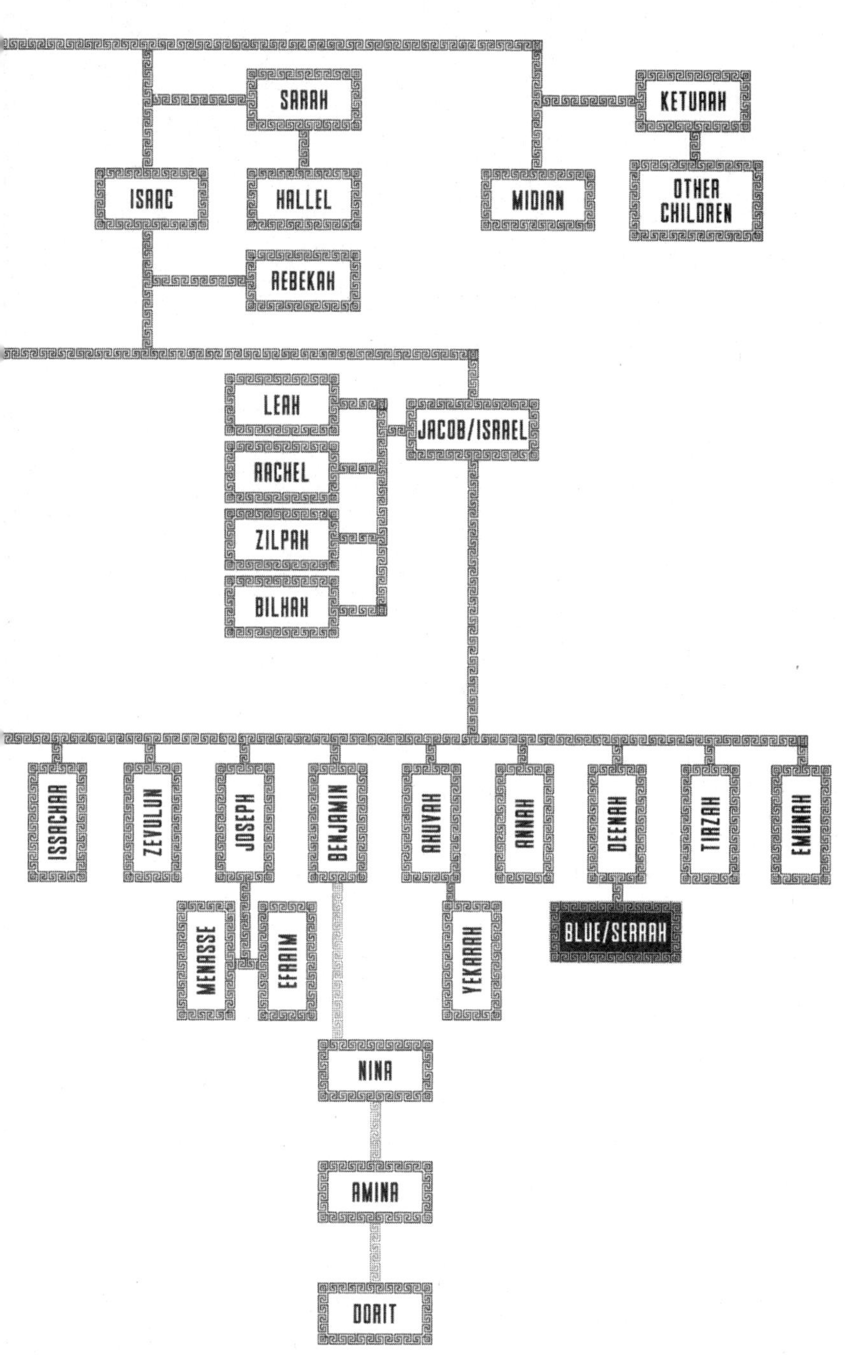

SARAH
KETURAH
ISAAC
HALLEL
MIDIAN
OTHER CHILDREN
REBEKAH
LEAH
RACHEL
ZILPAH
BILHAH
JACOB/ISRAEL
ISSACHAR
ZEVULUN
JOSEPH
BENJAMIN
AHUVAH
ANNAH
DEENAH
TIRZAH
EMUNAH
MENASSE
EFRAIM
YEKARAH
BLUE/SERRAH
NINA
AMINA
DORIT

IN THE BEGINNING

IN THE BEGINNING

n the beginning of Rabbi Yohanan's class, all the eyes in the
room were on me—including the rabbi's. Thirty-six pairs of
wide eyes—most of them brown, many of them tired, some of
them familiar, and all of them surprised—were fixed on my face.
I had been there only long enough to say, "No, it wasn't like that
at all," and I was just as shocked by my appearance in the study
hall as the students were.

In my experience, men don't like to be told that they're wrong,
especially by a woman. But in this case, that wasn't what had
stunned this roomful of them. The students had been deep in
thought and discussion about the Israelites' experience crossing
the Reed Sea after having just left Egypt, and one or two of the
men had offered their ideas. Then suddenly, there was a young
woman standing before them in strange clothes and contradicting
them, having entered unannounced, and not even through a door.

When Rabbi Yohanan recovered himself, he asked me who I
was. I sighed. This was my fourth time reappearing unexpectedly among people, so I at least knew a few things that I hadn't
known the first time. I was thankfully clothed—in fact, wearing

the exact robe I'd worn before. I appeared to be a young woman of around twenty years, even though I had lived so many more. I was frustratingly going to be questioned extensively; and then, ultimately, I would be both revered and detested. However, I also had an important task, and I would find out what that was, hopefully soon. In the meantime, I would be as honest and efficient as possible. With any luck, my identity would mean something to them.

"I am Blue. Known in Israel as Serrah, daughter of Asher," I said.

At that, the jaws in the room dropped to twice the width of the eyes, and the rabbi sat down, seemingly to prevent himself from falling.

As nobody there looked prepared to speak, I went on, "I was born in the land of Israel, the land of my grandfather, whose name was Israel. I went with him and his tribe to Egypt when famine threatened our demise, and Joseph sustained us with the stores of food there. Generations later, I helped lead the Israelites back to the land of our forebears. This is how I can tell you with certainty that the Reed Sea did not look like sprouting bushes on either side of us when we crossed, as one person here said. Still, more generations later, I returned to my birthland to help King Solomon with the building of the temple in Jerusalem. Now, I would very much like to know where I am and when I am so that I can get my bearings while I learn why I am."

Rabbi Yohanan stood again, then bowed before me. He stayed that way long enough for his students to follow his example. Then he quietly dismissed them. The young men, all dressed in clean but rather ragged-looking robes that had white fringes neatly tied on the corners, walked out of the room backs first, still gaping at me. Once they were gone, Rabbi Yohanan opened a cabinet and pulled out a bottle of wine, two cups, and a small bowl of dried almonds. He poured us each a glass, then said, "Praised are You, Master, Our God, King of the World, who created the fruit of the vine. Praised are You, Master, Our God, King of the World, who enabled us to be alive, to exist, and to reach this time." He looked at me expectantly for a moment, then drank his wine, and I did the same.

The liquid going down my throat felt at once strange and familiar. I hadn't had anything to eat or drink in some time, so the sensation was shocking at first. The taste, though, was smooth and tangy and felt almost playful in my mouth. I enjoyed a second small cup when he offered it. Ready to add food to my experience, I copied the rabbi's motions as he reached for an almond.

"Praised are You, Master, Our God, King of the World, who created the fruit of the tree." Again, he looked at me expectantly as he paused after speaking. He seemed to be both waiting for me to say something and judging me for not doing so. But when he ate his almond, I ate mine.

I ate it slowly, first feeling its bulk between my back teeth on the left side of my mouth, then letting the right side have a turn before biting down. *Splat!* The almond broke between my teeth and burst its sweet, nutty flavor through my mouth. I chewed the pulp with satisfaction and gratefully accepted a second almond and a third when they were offered. The bowl was then empty.

"Thank you for your hospitality," I said.

Rabbi Yohanan bowed his head in humility. "Of course. It is an honor to be here with you. The honor of a lifetime. Serrah, daughter of Asher, the eighth son of Jacob." He shook his head in disbelief. "But," he quickly went on, "I try to welcome everyone in this way. I try to offer a warm and welcoming space for people to feel comfortable and appreciated and respected. This is a longstanding tradition and value . . . Well, I don't have to tell *you* that," he concluded.

I smiled.

"You mentioned that you would like to know where and when you are. Shall I tell you now?"

I nodded my approval.

"This is my humble study, in the city of Jerusalem. The temple that you helped King Solomon build was also in this city, of course. But that was long ago. If you walked these streets and alleys at the time of Solomon the Wise, that was a thousand years ago. The temple stood here for centuries, a proud and beautiful home for the Master. I'm sorry to say that it was destroyed some five hundred years ago when the Babylonians came to our land, conquered it, and took many of us captive in exile. Some Israelites were able to stay here and were rejoined by returning exiles, and together they built a second temple that is still standing. I can show you, if you'd like. Praise the Master, we need only step outside to see its glory."

"I would like that," I said. "But first, who is that master of yours?"

"Why . . . well . . . ," he stumbled as he tried to get the words out. "The Master," he said, as if I should know. "The Master. The One and Only God of Israel. Of . . . your grandfather, Israel

. . . Of Abraham . . . Of Moses. Of all of us. The Master. The one with the ineffable name."

Ineffable? How disappointing. In my lifetime with Moses, I had seen signs that the people were drifting away from Yah, but I didn't think it would last. In my lifetime with King Solomon, I was disappointed that the Israelites had appointed a human king for themselves, but they still seemed to appreciate that the temple they were building was for connecting with Yah, praising Yah, *dwelling* with Yah in that place and beyond. I hoped this second temple was the same. But Rabbi Yohanan praised the Master. I would show him that YhWh—while a name more complicated to say than Yah—is not ineffable, but a name that brings us closer to the Oneness it holds. Also, I would calm myself at the same time.

"I would very much like to see the Second Temple," I said. "But first, I must tell you that I do not know this 'master,' and I must cleanse myself of the anger and sadness I feel in hearing that my nation has drifted from Yah. If you like, you may join me in my people's—*our* people's—traditional way of connecting with Yah." Without waiting for his decision, I closed my eyes and put my hands on the table where the bowl of almonds had been. I briefly drummed my fingers there to echo my heartbeat. Then I took a slow inhale of all that was around me. *Yhhhh.*

I took in the stale air of the room, the presence of the kind rabbi, and the lingering musk of his students. I took in the temple he'd told me was out there and the dust from the beautiful rolling hills I knew were just beyond—the hills my feet had first touched. I took in the sheep I believed would be grazing not far away, and I took in the birds in the sky, especially the ones with blue on their wings, that I was certain flew above us sometimes, even if not at that exact moment. Then *Whhhh*, I gave myself to all of that. *Yhhhh. Whhhh.* I repeated that "ineffable" name over and over, receiving from the All, giving to the All. Receiving, giving, receiving, giving, turning myself into Yah, and turning Yah into myself in the holy process.

When I opened my eyes, I could see that Rabbi Yohanan had chosen to join me. After he opened his eyes, he graced me with a serene smile. We remained quiet for a while, then he said, "It has become our tradition that only the High Priest says The Name, and only when inside the Holy of Holies in the center of the Temple, and only on the most sacred day of the year, Yom Kippur." He paused for a moment, before sharing his next thought. "Perhaps it is time that we reexamine that tradition," he said.

The rabbi escorted me out of his study. From the balcony just outside, we had a stunning view of the Second Temple. The sun shined on the stone, making it look like gold. Its beauty and size took my breath away. It was larger than the First Temple, and it seemed that there was a crew working to make it even larger at that very moment. My eyes began noticing other differences, and I wondered, *if it was so important that I help King Solomon build the first one correctly, why wasn't I here to help with the second? Was I here now to guide changes?* I didn't find out that day.

For the rest of that day, I enjoyed Rabbi Yohanan's hospitality, if not his news. While walking me through Jerusalem's streets and to his home where he would host me, he told me that the city was under siege by a people called Romans. That was, he explained, why he had only a token bite of food to offer me in the classroom. Food was scarce in the city; fear was abundant. Still, he worked for peace and hoped for peace. But he suggested that I stay by his side as we walked and not roam the city on my own. I also thought that best, for otherwise I would have surely gotten lost.

The temple wasn't the only thing that looked different to me. The city walls that had been built by Solomon's father, King David, had clearly already fallen and been repaired in many places in the thousand years since I had last been in Jerusalem. The streets looked to be made of the same stones, but as they wound around and over the hills, they marked paths between buildings and houses that I had never laid eyes on. There were still wells where I expected them, but the ovens had been moved to a location that we didn't pass on the way to Rabbi Yohanan's home.

He gave me his bed in the sparse room where he slept in the city. He insisted that he would sleep on a blanket on the floor, and he hung a curtain for my privacy. He shared his food with me. He accompanied me on tours of the city and ascensions to the Temple Mount. He watched over me from a distance while I sat on the rooftops and gazed at my homeland and breathed it in and breathed myself into it. He brought me with him when he taught his class so that I wouldn't be alone. Rabbi Yohanan told everyone that I was his niece, though a couple of his students whispered other news. And still, I didn't know why I was there—until the fifth day.

Every morning, I had been thoroughly delighted by the Levites singing psalms from the temple. Their harmonies floated through Jerusalem from the highest point in the city, and the music reminded me of the joy that is possible in the world, even in a city that is captured. Of course, not every moment was a joyful one, and our trip to the market that morning was a clear reminder.

We'd gone to buy bread and whatever else we could from what would be available that day. The rabbi warned me to expect little due to the siege. But he also told me that I could look forward to hearing a section of the Torah chanted in the marketplace. Twice a week, a short section was chanted in the market, and a longer piece would be sung on the sabbath.

He beamed with pride as he told me, "This week, we'll be hearing about the Israelites crossing the Reed Sea and the song they sang on the other side. That's why we were discussing it in class. Surely, you must remember the song."

I gave him a noncommittal smile. They had not been correct about what the crossing of the sea was like. I would have to hear the song before I could know whether it was the one that I remembered or not. Together, we eagerly walked to the market. I enjoyed the crowd of my tribe around me. I looked for signs of my grandmothers in the wise faces of the elder women. I looked for glimpses of familiar smiles or walks in the children. I made my way to the front of the gathering so I could hear the words well.

Soon, a young man whom I recognized from Rabbi Yohanan's class stepped onto a crate. "Praise the Master, the praised one!" he shouted.

Idle chatter in the marketplace changed to an obedient response from the crowd as one: "Praised is the praised Master, forever and ever."

The student then called out, "Praised are You, Master, our God, King of the World, who sanctified us with commandments and commanded us to involve ourselves with the words of the Torah." Then, in a strong and lovely tenor voice, the student chanted a very, very long song. It held remnants of what I had experienced, and yet it was all wrong. I insisted on leaving that gathering at once, and Rabbi Yohanan reluctantly followed me, clearly wanting to remain until the end, but likely fearing for my safety if I were alone.

We stepped onto a side street, and I asked him, "Where is this song from?"

He stammered a moment, then said, as if it were the most obvious answer, "It's from the Torah. Moses received the Torah at Sinai and transmitted it to Joshua, Joshua to the elders, the elders to the prophets, and the prophets to the men of the great assembly. We practice memorizing it, but we also have it written down on scrolls so the students can review it that way and make sure they know and say the words exactly. Korey, who you just heard chanting, has memorized it perfectly."

"What I just heard is written down?" I asked.

"Yes," he answered. "In the Torah. The teachings. The Five Books of Moses."

"I must read them," I said.

Rabbi Yohanan made the arrangements, and for seven days, I took only a few breaks from reading to eat and sleep. I read the Torah from the first word to the last, but long before I was finished, I knew through and through why I was there. These words had been written on scrolls by dedicated scribes. Each one had copied a scroll from a scribe before him, making sure the teachings were identical. It seemed that the original words hardly mentioned me. Thus, each copy had all but erased me from the story! Me and so many others. Understandably, it is impossible to include every detail, every experience, every perspective in any story, but these writings were being treated as holy and complete.

In fact, they had omitted so much, I was lucky the rabbi had even recognized my name!

Continuing with his generosity and hospitality, Rabbi Yohanan worked to get me supplies so that I could write the missing pieces of the story of the Israelites, especially mine and the stories of the other women. Not knowing that I could do the writing myself, he assigned his student Ezra to help me. But I would write each word. Yesterday, the Levites sang, "Master, open my lips and my mouth will sing Your praise."

Today, I say, "Yah, guide my hand, and I will write my song."

I WAS BORN

was born one hundred paces outside of my grandmother Leah's tent. She shared that tent with her two unmarried daughters, Deenah and Emunah, with her handmaid Zilpah, and with the matriarch of the family, Grandmother Rebekah. When I was born, Grandmother Leah shared it with me too. My mother, Deenah, had hardly left that tent or the safety and comfort of her mother, Leah, during her entire pregnancy. But when she felt me trying to exit her womb, she fled that tent and the whole camp, trying to get out before my birth. She was afraid her brothers would kill us if they found out about me. They had murdered before with no remorse.

Every day of her pregnancy, Mama was filled with fears that her brothers would discover her round belly and attack her, running their knives through us both. Or maybe she would deliver me after all, and then, once they heard my first cries, once they saw in my tiny face, the face of her husband whom they had slaughtered, then they would kill us side by side. Although my uncles spent most of their days in the fields, my mother hardly left the tent for fear of being seen by them.

Blessedly, my mother's terrifying daydreams did not follow her into the nights. She had peace and calm while she slept, even joy and excitement. When she closed her eyes and drifted away from her brothers in her dreams, she heard birdsong. It was special birdsong. She could understand what the bird was singing, as if she and the little bird were speaking the same language. And it also felt as if the bird were singing from inside of her. For these reasons, my mother was able to take comfort from both the words and the melody and have respite from her fear-filled days.

Here I am,
Prepared and invited
To live, to exist, and to be brought
To this moment
Hallelu Yah

Though my mother found peace at night, when it was time for me to be brought into the world, her labor pains began during the day, when her usual fears were already heightened. So, when her delivery time grew close, she walked away from the camp where her family dwelled, away from her mother's and grandmothers' tent where she had found company for her grief and refuge from her brothers. She walked alone into the wilderness to a place where her cries would only be heard by the hills and where our bodies would be buried by the dust brought with the breeze and picked apart by vultures, not brothers.

But it was not to be that way. Thankfully, Deenah's mother, my grandmother Leah, followed her out of the camp. And so, when Mama began laboring, she had her mother to hold her, encourage her, and sing to her. When I finally arrived, Leah was the first one to see me, and when she did, she gasped. I don't remember that, of course. But she told me many times, and Mama did too. Grandmother Leah told me she was glad that she had not uttered her first thought, instead letting it simmer in her mouth, though it burned her tongue.

Rachel.

That was my grandmother Leah's first thought: *Rachel.* When she saw my face, she saw the face of her own baby sister, Rachel. Rachel had died only a few months before my arrival. She was not a baby at the time but a woman who had recently died while birthing a baby. Rachel was Leah's little sister, whom she'd loved, adored, and squabbled with all her life. And there was Rachel's face—baby-sized—on her daughter's daughter.

My grandmother Leah held me in her arms and let her tears fall on my new little face. A face that would save my life because it would make it clear to everyone that I was a member of the tribe, not a reminder of the man from a foreign tribe whom my mother had briefly been married to. Looking at me, nobody would suspect that my mother bore the child of the prince of Shechem. In fact, I was not the child of the prince. Well, not the child of *that* prince. When my grandmother Leah saw my face, she could see that her sister, Rachel, was my other grandmother. She realized that my father was Rachel's son, Joseph. Though she was surprised, she was tremendously grateful. She knew her daughter and the new baby would be safe.

Indeed, I was safe and well and thriving on my mother's milk and embrace and love. On the thirtieth day after my birth, my mother, Deenah, wrapped me in a blanket and carried me to her father's tent. My grandmother Leah walked behind us. And Mother's grandmother Rebekah walked behind Leah. We were four generations on our way to Grandfather's tent like a little parade of royal women, decked out in our finest cloaks—and blankets, in my case.

I don't remember the day, but I do remember the blanket, because I had it for many years. It was small, just right for a baby who would grow into a child and want to carry it places—which I did. The wool was soft from so many uses, and the blue dye faded with time. I was told that what I saw as brown circles in each corner had started as white full moons, but the desert dust had stained them long before I had a chance to commit the white to memory.

Deenah was an expert weaver. Not as skilled as Leah, but, of course, Leah had many more years of experience than her daughter did. This was most clear in the embroidery on the blanket. If you looked very closely, you could identify which stitches belonged to Leah and which were done by my mother. The blue bird, singing happily in the center of the blue sky, was all my mother's work. The green stem of the hollyhock she sat on had been stitched by her mother, Leah, and Grandmother Rebekah had even done some of the violet flower petals. But my mother, Deenah, had made most of my blanket. Almost all of it.

Sadly, there had been days and weeks of her pregnancy when she just couldn't work on it. She couldn't see well enough through her tears. And there were many, many days when she didn't even think I'd be born.

I was born, though, and being presented as a new member of our tribe on the thirtieth day of my life was the first noteworthy thing after my birth. It was the custom in our tribe that if a baby girl lived for a whole month, she would be brought to the head of the tribe to have her name written on the parchment that recorded all the births of girls.

The boys' names were written down on their eighth day of life. Whether that was because it was the day they entered the tribal covenant by circumcision, or whether it was because a boy meant more hands and more prestige and more riches for a father, or whether it was because a mother wanted to bond with her girl longer . . . it's impossible to know *how* the custom began. It's easy to know that's *what* it was.

So, on the thirtieth day of my life, my mother wrapped me in the little blanket she had made mostly herself and escorted me to have my name written on the scroll: Serrah. She'd only decided that would be my name the day before the ceremony. She had been calling me Blue since she first saw me. At first, she had been afraid to look at me, to see the face of the baby she had brought into the world to die in the desert, but with her own mother's reassurance and insistence, she finally did. Then her whole body relaxed with relief. She smiled at me and stroked my cheek and kissed my fingers and said, "Hello, Blue."

She put her cheek next to mine and closed her eyes, smiling about the dream my father had told her he'd dreamt on what turned out to be the night I was conceived. There were ten all white birds and one more that had blue on its wings. My mother recognized me as the blue bird who had been singing to her from within. She stood slowly with me in her arms and let her mother help her back to our tent.

But she felt I needed another name, a name to be called in the tribe of Israel. So, she chose Serrah. "Because you are a princess," she told me, "and not just any princess. You fly beyond the palace walls into freedom. May you have not only what you need but even more. Excess." That was how she decided that Serrah would be the name she wanted added to the list of Israelites.

When my mother, Deenah, arrived at the entrance of the tent of her father, Israel, for my naming ceremony, she paused. Her grandmother, Rebekah, went from the end of the little procession to kiss Deenah on the forehead, and then do the same to me. Then she walked in first. "Jacob," she addressed her son, "mazal tov. Congratulations. You have a beautiful new granddaughter." Jacob kissed his mother's hand and invited her to sit on a cushion to his right.

While that was happening, Leah kissed me on the forehead, then my mother, and then entered the tent. "Israel," she said to the same man, using his newer name, "mazal tov. Our daughter has given us a new granddaughter. She is beautiful. You will think she is the most beautiful of all our granddaughters, and you will probably be right." Leah sighed at that point. I'm quite sure she did. "And it is not just her face that radiates with beauty but also her voice."

Grandmother Leah said that last part after I let out a long coo. While Leah had been speaking to her husband, and while the two of them had been looking at each other, my mother had walked in quietly and bowed her head to the ground just inside the entrance of the tent. She waited silently and nervously. While fully prostrated, she took a deep breath *Yhhhh*, bringing the calm of Yah into her body, and then *Whhhh*, breathing her fear away.

I, still in her arms, decided that was the right moment to sing.

Israel, who was Jacob, who was my grandfather, looked at his daughter with her forehead on the entrance rug. He surely would have been perplexed if he had been in his right state of mind. Why was a daughter of his here? Any child of a daughter belonged to another man's tribe—her husband's tribe. But he had been trapped in grief for months and couldn't notice much outside of that. Though part of his grief was in having a daughter whose husband had been slaughtered by his own sons, he tried not to think about that much.

"What is the girl's name?" he asked.

"Serrah," my mother answered, still low on the ground. My grandfather took his reed and dipped it in ink. He didn't do much of his own writing anymore, but he kept up the list of members of the tribe. *Serrah*, he wrote. Then he wrote *daughter of*, and in a moment, he would write my father's name, thus recording me the way I would be called in the tribe of Israel. Serrah, daughter of . . .

He hadn't heard the name of the father—it hadn't been said—but he didn't realize. "Rise, daughter," he said, "and tell me her name so that I may hear it and write it." When Deenah rose, she saw the shock on her father's face. He had not even known she'd been pregnant. The men and women didn't often mingle. Add to that the fact that Deenah and Jacob had each been steeped in mourning and secluding themselves from others, and it was no surprise—or accident—that they hadn't crossed paths.

Jacob's face stayed in shock so long that my mother wondered what she should do. But just when she thought they might all be there forever, his face reconfigured to anger, and his voice matched it.

"This newborn is not my responsibility," he said. "The baby should be living in the town of Shechem with her father. I wanted a peace treaty with the Shechemites. I acted honorably, but my sons did not. Take this girl to one of them. Let them bear the burden of their wrongdoings."

My grandmother, Leah, put her hand on her husband's. "The baby is not a Shechemite," she said softly. At this point, Israel's expressive face moved to confusion. While his fists were still clenched in anger, his forehead was wrinkled as he looked to his wife for more clarity. Deenah had been married to Prince Shechem before he'd been murdered by her brothers. Who was this baby?

"Israel," Leah said softly, "the baby is an Israelite. She is Serrah, daughter of *asher* . . ." She paused. Israel picked up his reed and wrote *Asher* after the words *daughter of*. Israel had a son named Asher, and Leah realized the miscommunication as soon as it was happening. She'd just been having a hard time saying *asher ayn-aynu* . . . the one who is no longer with us.

For a moment, Leah had a dilemma. Would she let the mistake stand, or would she let her husband know who the baby's father was? For thirty days, she had been wondering how her husband would react to the news, and now she had the opportunity to avoid it. But she moved ahead. Leah motioned to my mother to bring me closer. My mother knew her father wouldn't approve of her having had a child with Joseph while married to another man, but she was grateful to have this little piece of her beloved. Joseph had been her father's favorite son. Maybe he would feel the same. With tears in her eyes, she placed me on her father's lap. He looked at me and saw what Leah and Rebekah and Deenah had seen the first time they'd laid eyes on me. He saw the face of his recently buried, favorite wife: Rachel.

"Rachel," he almost whispered.

"This is Serrah," Leah corrected. "She is our granddaughter. She is the daughter of our daughter Deenah and . . . *asher ayn-aynu*." Nobody had said the name Joseph to my grandfather since the day he'd had to identify his treasured son's bloodied coat. When Joseph was referred to at all, it was delicately said that he was *asher ayn-aynu*, the one who was no longer with us. Hearing that from Leah, Israel handed her the baby—me—and left his tent in tears, without writing my father's name on the scroll.

That is how it came to be that my name was known as and forever called in Israel: Serrah, daughter of Asher. As it turned out, Asher's wife Yonah was pregnant. In an act of quick thinking, my grandmother Leah went to Yonah and told her to claim me as her own. Leah told her that when she delivered her baby, she should declare that she had twins. So, when her son Ishvi was born, it was said that I followed him out of the womb. Yonah was not at all pleased but really had no choice in the matter. Leah promised her that my mother, Deenah, would become her nursemaid and feed both the babies. But that didn't actually happen. Yes, it's true that I was called Serrah, daughter of Asher, and that my mother was called Yonah's nursemaid, and that I was given to Asher to hold on the eighth day of Ishvi's life. I was sleeping, and Asher was attentive to his son Ishvi's circumcision. But Yonah then took Ishvi back to her tent to nurse him and raise him while I continued to live with my mother in my grandmothers' tent.

MEMORY

My first memory is of meeting my first love. Not a romantic love like the one between my mother and father, but the first deep and lasting love that came from someone new in my life. I met him in an onion patch. He was missing his bottom two milk teeth already, but one of mine was wiggling a *lot*. I saw him digging between the rows, then watched as he lay down on the loose soil and sprinkled bits of it over himself.

When he stopped doing this, I called out to him. "What are you doing?"

He hadn't seen me and had to lift his head to look to where the words were coming from.

"Why did you do that?" he asked. "Now I have to start all over again."

"Start what?"

Without lifting his body again, he said that he had to go under the dirt. Like the onions. So he could grow. Like the onions.

"If you lie down in the dirt, you're going to grow tall and spicy and green?" I asked.

"Green? Spicy? Of course not! Don't be silly. I'll just be tall."

I wasn't sure this plan would work, but it seemed worth trying, and this boy seemed worth knowing. So, I made myself some room in the next row by digging down a bit, then I sprinkled the loose soil over myself. I watched the clouds floating in the sky. It was the beginning of the rainy season, and I'd already decided that was my favorite time because I loved the clouds so much.

This might have been the first time that I felt myself knowing Yah, becoming one with everything. It was as if I were floating with the clouds. Not my body—just me. At the same time, it was as if I were floating like the land. Yes, the land-me also felt like I was floating. And the me in my body was becoming more cloudy and more land-y, and the land and clouds were becoming more me-y.

That was abruptly interrupted when the boy asked, "Now what?"

"I don't know," I said. "It was your idea."

"I'm tired of this," he said. "I'm going to stand up. You watch me and tell me if I'm taller."

In one quick motion, he stood up and looked down on me from beside my head. "Woah," I said, startled by how much higher up his head was than mine. "You're so tall." He nodded his head and reached out his hand for mine.

"Come on," he said. And I did. He started running, and I ran after him. He was older and faster than I was, but he would stop and wait for me, and he didn't tease me like Asher's son Ishvi did.

When I caught up, the boy motioned for me to follow him. Soon, we were sneaking into Grandfather's tent. I had been there many times but only with Grandmother Leah and Grandmother Rebekah. I had never even been there with my mother since my naming, let alone . . . alone. But we went in quietly. Nobody was there to notice us tiptoeing along the side of the tent that sheltered us from the morning sun. Nobody was there to stop us from opening a small basket of dried, pitted dates and helping ourselves to two each. And nobody was there to notice us run out, our mouths so stuffed that our laughs were muffled.

Once I'd swallowed all the sweetness, including the sugary saliva I shoveled back in from my chin, I said, "We shouldn't go in there; that's Grandfather's tent."

"What grandfather? That's my father's tent."

"You should go to your mother's tent."

"I have no mother," he said.

No mother? "Of course you have a mother," I said. "Where do you sleep?" How could he have no mother? Surely, he was wrong.

"In Bilhah's tent," he said.

"Then she is your mother," I told him.

"No," he said. "Father says that my brothers need to be kind to me because I have no mother."

"Well," I said with my hand on my hip, for this was something I knew about, "Yonah says that she and my brother need to be kind to me because I have no father."

"No father?" he asked. "Of course you have a father. Who provides a tent for you and your mother to sleep in?"

"I do have a father," I said. "Just Yonah *says* that I don't. Asher provides for me, but he is not my father. Joseph is my father. But he's gone. My mother says that his brothers probably killed him."

I had never shared that sentence with anyone. It felt exciting and important. Until it felt like the sharp pain of a fist coming down on my head followed by screeches in my ear. "I did not kill my brother!"

I ran from my new friend. My first friend. I ran from the wonderful adventure I was having. My feet carried me fast out of fear and determination until I reached the onion patch, went back into the little ditch I had dug earlier, and sprinkled soil on myself again.

I had run faster than him the whole way, fear motivating my feet farther and farther. When he caught up, he stood above me and asked me what *I* was doing.

"I'm going to grow taller than you and hit you on the top of your head!" I yelled.

"No, you won't," he yelled back, taking his place in the narrow groove he'd dug for himself earlier. But I didn't look at him over there. I just looked up at the fluffy clouds. Then I fell asleep and dreamt of those clouds coming down and hitting him on the top of his little head. When I woke up, he was sleeping, and I went to get something to eat.

Grandmother Leah was sitting outside our tent weaving in the shade. She offered me a barley cracker and a seat beside her. After I ate, I told her I wanted more. She said I could get it myself from the sack. So, I took out as many as I could carry and brought them back to the shade.

"Why so many?" she asked. "Can you be that hungry?"

"I'm not hungry," I said, "But Mama said that eating makes me get bigger and stronger. When I eat all these barley crackers, I'm going to be big enough and strong enough to hit that boy right on the top of his head."

"What boy?" She asked.

I told Grandmother Leah all about the boy in the onion patch, the sweet dates from Grandfather's tent, the hitting and the yelling and the clouds. She listened attentively, then gently took the barley crackers from my hands and placed them in the basket she set beside her.

She took me onto her lap and said, "Blue, that little boy is Benjamin, and I will talk to him so that he won't hit you again." I hugged her tightly in gratitude. "First, there is something I must tell you—and I will tell him too. Something important. Are you ready?"

I nodded that I was.

"You do have a father, Blue. In fact, you have two. Joseph was the father that placed the seed in your mother so that you could grow inside her until you were ready to come out here. And Asher is the father who provides you with a name and place to belong." I nodded. I knew all this already. I was going to get off her lap, but she went on. "And Benjamin, he does have a mother. In fact, he has two. Rachel was the mother who held him in her body until he was born. And Bilhah is the mother who nurses him and soothes his cries and gives him food and a mat beside hers.

"She has worked his whole life to keep him safe and protected, for he's now the only child left of Rachel, and now he's his father's favorite son. But if you two have only seen each other for the first time today, perhaps she is protecting him too well. The secret should be let out too. I'll speak with her." With that, Grandmother Leah slid me down from her lap and walked toward Bilhah's tent. I was glad she was going to have a talk with this head-bopping boy named Benjamin. And I was curious to learn of this secret.

I realized when we got to Bilhah's tent that I had never been there before, nor had I even wondered about who lived in the tent. It was larger than the servants' tents, but smaller than Grandmother Leah's, or even Yonah's. The fabric by the windows and entrances were adorned with colorful threads, but the other areas were plain. Inside, there were a few gorgeous cushions and beautiful rugs, but all were worn thin. And most surprising of all, there were two boys in there. One I had just learned was Benjamin. And the other?

He and Benjamin were wrestling when we entered. They stopped in surprise, and Bilhah was no less surprised by our presence. Grandmother Leah looked at her and walked out, and Bilhah followed. When they went to talk outside, I went to see who this boy was. He seemed to be about the same age as Benjamin. He was much quieter, though. In fact, he said nothing and did nothing other than stare at me.

"What's the matter?" I asked him. "Never seen such a lovely girl before?"

"You're not supposed to see the secret," Benjamin said about the little boy. "He's a secret."

On the rare occasions that this boy was called anything, he had been called Sode among the people of our tribe who knew the secret. But in his mother's arms, he was called Geeborr, a name that means hero. I learned that day that Geeborr was the son of Bilhah, my grandfather's fourth wife, and he was also the son of Reuben, my grandfather's first son. I learned that Sode was born from the love of two people who had felt overlooked until they'd found each other. And yes, that baby was called Sode—secret—and kept hidden due to the shame. But before he was a year old, he was called Geeborr by his father and mother, for his life allowed her to also nurse Benjamin when his mother Rachel died.

Once Geeborr got over the shock of being seen by someone else, he told me all of this on the day that I met him. I think he would have talked and talked endlessly had we not been interrupted. But the women came back in with tears in their eyes and their arms around each other. Grandmother Leah walked over to Geeborr and kissed him on the head and told him she would come and visit him in the morning.

"I'll bring you sweet treats and tell you stories, like a proper grandmother," she paused for a moment, "and you may tell me stories too," she continued. "I hope you will tell me your favorite stories and your hardest ones and the ones you wish will come to pass one day."

I wasn't there to hear those stories when she went back the next day. I didn't know what Grandmother Leah said to Bilhah about Benjamin hitting me, so I promised myself that in the morning, I'd go back to the onion patch to get a little taller, just in case her talk didn't help. It seemed he had the same idea, for the next morning, I hadn't been there long enough to finish sprinkling the soil over myself before he came and started doing the same.

After, we lay side by side for a while, with only the short green sprigs of new onions growing between us, Benjamin turned to me and said, "Bilhah has told me that when I was born, my mother called me BenOni. Bilhah calls me Benno as a reminder of the name my mother chose."

"My mother calls me Blue," I told him.

"Come on, Blue," he said, getting up. And we went back to Grandfather's tent for dates.

When we finished our sweets, I wanted to be the leader. "Come on, Benno," I said, and took him to my grandmothers' tent. All the women were there when we arrived. My mother and her sister Emunah were pitting and drying dates. Zilpah was massaging Grandmother Rebekah's feet with oil. And Grandmother Leah put down her weaving to take us into her arms together, and then released us so we could kiss Grandmother Rebekah on her small hands. I was hoping to give Benno something from our tent, but we weren't alone, and I didn't know what to do. Luckily, Grandmother Leah invited us to hear a story.

She gave us some peas to peel and kept her hands busy with the same task while she talked.

"Your mother, Rachel," she said to Benno, "was the mother of your father, Joseph," she looked at me, "and I knew both of them when they were your age. Rachel was beautiful. She was so much more than that, of course, but that was what everyone remarked on. All the time. Once, when she was small like you, Benjamin"— Benno sat taller and peeled faster when he was called small—"she was tired of all the attention and wondered how she might make herself less noticeable. So, she went to find a dirty sheep. She rubbed her face in the wool, sneezing and coughing as the sheep's dirt went onto her face and up her nose. Then, instead of looking beautiful, she looked like a child who had been playing in the dirt.

"Her plan didn't work, though," Grandmother Leah sighed. "Everyone still noticed her. And her beauty. You look a lot like Rachel," she said to Benno. He smiled broadly. "You do too," she told me. I had been just about to say that, but she'd said it before I'd had a chance.

Then she asked us whether we'd like to hear a story about Joseph. We eagerly said that we would. I saw my mother's body stiffen and wondered whether I should have said no. As it was, I had no time to change my answer, for Grandmother Leah immediately agreed to tell us while we kept peeling the peas.

"Your father, Joseph," she said to me, before turning to Benno and saying, "Your brother, Joseph, was a sweet boy." We both smiled at that. "He always wanted to help. He wanted to help with the sheep, but Israel mostly kept him to himself. Much like he does with you, Benjamin. So, Joseph didn't learn to be a shepherd, but he learned to be a scribe. He wrote our most important scrolls, *The Scrolls of Deborah*, our Auntie. That's right, Deborah was our Auntie. She left this world while you two were preparing to come into it, so you never met. But she knew you were on the way. In fact, Benjamin, it is thanks to you that Auntie Deborah and Grandmother Rebekah came to our camp. They wanted to be here for your birth. Now, Deborah is gone and Emunah is the one called Auntie, even though she is my youngest child. She takes care of everyone now.

"Long ago, Joseph, Emunah's big brother, took loving care of her. He carried her around when she was a baby, and even when she had a hard time walking. He laughed with her. He lit up when he received her smiles. One time, Emunah found Joseph's pile of shards that he used for practicing his writing. She took them to a wide, flat stone and laid the shards on top. Then she took a rock and smashed all the shards. She later explained that if it was good to have small pieces of clay, it must be even better to have more small pieces of clay. She was proud to have worked out how to do that."

"Look," Grandmother Leah said, "you get to have a story about Emunah too." I smiled at Auntie. Emunah was everyone's favorite auntie. So much so that we really didn't call her Auntie Emunah, just Auntie was enough to know who we were talking about. But since she was Grandmother Leah's own daughter, Grandmother Leah didn't call her Auntie.

"Joseph saw the pieces of clay, some of them so small that they were ground into dust, and he saw Emunah's excitement. He told her that some clay was good to have in bigger pieces, but that it looked like it was fun to smash them. He asked whether he could do it with her. Together, they chose a rock for him, and then, together, they smashed the rest of the shards into dust, the sounds of rock against rock and joyous laughter rang through the camp."

When Grandmother Leah finished her story, I waited for more, but Benno jumped up and said, "Come on," and he started to run off, with me right behind him.

Grandmother Leah stopped us before we got too far. "Wait," she said. "From now on, take Sode with you. That is, Geeborr." Benno was shocked. "I've spoken with his mother and father," Grandmother Leah said. "He is to be allowed out of the tent now."

So, together, Benno and I ran back to Bilhah's tent, where Geeborr was inside drawing pictures on a patch of dirt. He immediately covered the spot with a rug and sat up, startled to see us.

"Come on," Benno said to him. Geeborr didn't move at first, so we went and took his hands. "Leah says you're to come with us," Benno told him. Geeborr smiled what was perhaps the biggest smile ever to grace the face of a child. As we walked out of the tent, we passed Bilhah, who gave him a teary nod and a quick hug before watching us run off.

Benno had the idea to gather some rocks and bang them together to make music. When we did that, I had the idea to put them in order according to the different sounds each one made when hit. It was much nicer to be hitting rocks than heads.

From that day, the three of us met every morning in the onion patch. I don't know how long we kept up the habit of lying down and covering ourselves with dirt so that we could grow. It was long enough that we saw the sprigs turn into strong green shoots that grew taller than our horizontal bodies. Maybe it was then that we decided we could skip the ritual and go about our day.

Benno, Geeborr, and I spent as much time together as possible. We started by having fun with rocks and running, but we also often did chores together, like gathering sticks for the fires or chickpeas for the stews that would cook on them. We grew the peas and picked the plants, letting them dry in the sun until we could easily remove the leaves and have dry peas for making hummus and stews all year long—except for the few dry peas that we threw at each other or into the hills to see who could throw them the farthest.

It was *me. I* was the one who could throw them the farthest! Geeborr was the oldest of the three of us, but he was also the weakest from having spent so much time sitting around. Benno always took a running start and said he released the chickpea at the starting line, but I saw him cross it every single time, so his throws didn't count.

We were competitive at times and cooperative at times. Over time, we were most things together, since we were always together. We were happy to have companionship. I had been almost exclusively with my mother and grandmothers—whom I adored, but they treated me like a baby. Geeborr had been confined to his mother's tent, often alone, but when he wasn't alone, he'd only spent time with Benno and Bilhah and, occasionally, his father, Reuben. Since Benno's brothers were all married before he'd even been weaned, Benno had mostly spent time with just Bilhah and Geeborr and Grandfather. My brothers were Yonah's sons, but I was her extra work. So, it was me (Serrah), Benjamin, and Sode. Or as we liked to call ourselves and each other: Blue, Benno, and Geeborr.

THE THREE OF US

The three of us were always together. Though we had long since stopped covering ourselves in the onion patch, we often played in the barley. When it was planting time, there was no playing, of course. The men would yell at us for coming to the fields for any reason other than bringing them cold drinks or warm food. But there was no fun to be had there during that season anyway. When the stalks grew tall and waved this way and that with the wind, that was when the fun began.

Benno, Geeborr, and I would walk through the tall barley grass and try to find each other using just our voices. If we would sit or lie down just right, the barley could provide us shade from the sun, and we could comfortably stay there as long as we wanted. We'd share our thoughts and dreams, our hopes and imaginings with each other. There was very little, if anything, that we did not tell each other. Whenever we ran out of something to say, we would sing or make up stories or even nap so that we could have more dreams to talk about.

One afternoon, Benno, Geeborr, and I were playing hide and seek. This was after the harvest, after the sheaves were bundled, and after the ground where the grain had once grown looked so bare that it was a shock every time we saw it. The only barley remaining was what had already been picked and hulled and stored in tightly woven baskets. Even though the baskets were so tightly woven that hardly a bug could get in, the mice managed somehow. I suppose that with their little claws and tiny sharp teeth, they could make their own entrance. And wherever the mice went, cats would follow. We saw the cats walking around the camp, enjoying scraps and sunshine in their leisurely ways. Usually, when they had kittens, they made themselves little nests for nursing. The mamas would go out and get food but come back.

That was always the intention, anyway. Parents do go back to their young. Usually. We knew, though, that it doesn't always happen that way. So, when I was hiding among the barley baskets waiting to be found, I ended up doing some finding of my own. Three little kittens were in a nest. They were all much smaller than my hand and were so young they had almost no fur. Two were crying—whimpering, really, which was all they could manage. One had already died. These two would die, too, without a mother.

I ran out and called for Benno and Geeborr. Geeborr kept hiding, but Benno came out because he was happy to tag me.

At first, he teased me for not being difficult to find, but then he saw my face. "What's wrong?"

"There are two kittens in the barley," I said. "Their mother is gone. We need to help them."

Benno came with me, and we each picked up one of the tiny little lives. I whispered to the kitten we were leaving behind that we would be back for her. And we did go back the next day and give her a proper burial. But first, we needed to urgently take care of these two. We ran to Bilhah's tent, just in case Geeborr had gone there. He hadn't, but Bilhah was there.

"Go and get Leah," she said to Benno. "Leave the kitten with me. I'll take good care of her, don't worry. Just go get Leah." As he handed her the kitten, she said, "And bring back a cup with milk." Benno ran to do his errand and come back as quickly as possible. I was still humming to the kitten when Bilhah told me that when Emunah was born, they thought she might not live through the week. She could not latch on for milk, and getting it in her in other ways wasn't easy, either, but with lots of trying, she got enough.

"I don't know if that will work for these kittens," she said. "But we'll try." I nodded my head. I had some hope. Grandmother Leah came in and supported that hope, though she also cautioned us not to feel certain that the kittens would live.

Benno and I decided to name the kittens anyway. We said it was so that we could better talk to them and tell them how much we loved them. The one I held was nearly all black but had a white patch on her neck. That little spot reminded me of a raindrop. I called her Rain because of all the life that the rain brings, but also because I thought it would be fun to say things like, "I'm holding Rain," or "Have you seen Rain today?" or, on the very dry days of the summer, I could say, "I see Rain coming!" Benno decided to name the kitten he held Barley. She was golden brown like the barley sheaves, and I had found her behind the barley.

That was how we got the little kittens who became part of our lives. Mother even made a tiny sling and showed me and Benno how we could carry the kittens by our skin. But within a few days, she herself was carrying Barley that way almost all the time. Most of the time, I wasn't jealous.

Whenever my mother saw me, her face lit up. But unlike when she was with Barley, the light would leave her eyes. I tried to keep it there with songs and laughter and cuddles. Sometimes I succeeded, and sometimes I didn't. Grandmother Rebekah told me that I was wonderful, and my mother thought so, too, but Yonah would tell me I was extra and a burden to both her and my mother. Too often, I believed Yonah, but when the moon was full, I believed my grandmother.

Sometimes, even the night before the full moon, my mother would begin to feel happy with anticipation. Those were my favorite times of all. When just she and I were together, Mother would smile and tell me stories of visiting Grandmother Rebekah and Auntie Deborah in Hevron.

"Tomorrow night the moon will be full," she'd begin. Whenever she said that, she'd be lying on her back on the mat, not curled up small, but with a body wide enough for me to snuggle under her arm. And when I did, she asked, "Would you like to hear about my celebrations under the moon when I was a girl just like you?" I always did.

"It was just us women," she'd say. I knew that her grandfather Isaac was there, and my own father, Joseph, too. Grandmother Leah had told me. But my mother was referring to her brothers, the murderers, not being there. "It was so relaxing and free," she'd say. "And joyful." I nodded along as if she hadn't told me before. I didn't want to interrupt her. Even if the story didn't change, I hung onto every word, just to hear her voice.

"When we arrived at the camp, Grandmother and Auntie would come out to greet us with water and sweets." I knew that when she said *Grandmother* she was speaking of Grandmother Rebekah, and when she said *Auntie*, it was Deborah, not Emunah. Emunah was even younger than my mother, so she was just a child when they used to go. I imagined the two of them and their other sisters eating crushed almonds made into sticky balls with date paste. I thought it would be nice to eat sweets with sisters—to do anything with sisters, really. I would slip into a moment of feeling sorry for my sisterless self, but soon I was attached to Mother's voice again.

"There was always water waiting for us so we could wash our feet after the long journey. It wasn't so long, really, but it was nice to have clean feet. Auntie and Grandmother always put fresh herbs and oil in the water to make it extra special for us. Grandmother would say, 'Finally, we're surrounded by women.' But I knew she meant us girls too. They always included us in the singing and laughing, the stories and conversation."

I wondered what it would be like to have so many girls together at once. I spent time with the women—my mother and the grand-mothers. Otherwise, I was usually with Benno and Geeborr or alone. But my mother had two older sisters and two younger ones. What fun it must have been! But Ahuvah, Annah, and Tirzah were married and off to their husbands' tribes before I was old enough to even wave goodbye to them, so I had never danced with them.

"And on the nights when the moon was full, Auntie put a copper bowl of water outside to reflect its light, and we sat in a circle around it. There, we shared with the moon and with each other about our deepest feelings. Sometimes fear or sadness, sometimes joy or gladness. It could be anything and everything that we had been waiting to share with the moon and with each other. We knew it was time to sing when Auntie and Grandmother picked up their drums.

"Everyone started tapping on their own drums then. I was eager for the drumbeat to enter my body. It started with slow, soft sounds, then would move to a rhythm that brought me to my feet. Mother would follow me quickly, and Tirzah, too. Then the others would join along, and we would dance and sing over and over and over again:

"Sister, Mother, Daughter, and Friend,
You shine with love from beginning to end.
We give you our hopes, our dreams, and our pain,
You keep them safe, until we meet again."

Mother would whisper-sing this song during her story. I knew it well, but it was such a treat to hear it from her voice alone while we were happily lying together in our tent. When the verse ended, I joined in with her, always hoping but never sure, that she'd sing it a second time if I sang with her. She did, but still, the breath before the first word brought me a pang of uncertainty each time.

When we finished singing, I could feel the smile in her body even in the darkness. Then she would whisper, "Blue, my little bird. You have such a beautiful voice. You always have. Auntie knew you'd be a singer. Do you know that?" I did know, because she had told me one hundred times that Auntie had known I was growing in her and that I had a song to sing. But her voice was so soft and her words were so sweet that I always responded with a request that she tell me.

"Auntie knew you'd be a singer. She said your song is one that will uplift the tribe of Israel to higher abundance. You certainly do have a lovely voice. Auntie would have enjoyed hearing you sing in the circles. And when the singing ends, you know what happens next," she said. And I did know. So, I took an inhale with her. *Yhhhh*. Just as if we were in the circle. Then we exhaled together. *Whhhh*. The two of us became One as I drifted off into Yah, where I felt all the love and where I knew my mother did too.

The next night, we would live out the story. Well, not exactly. I think that in my mother's heart, she was living out the story. I don't think she was really with us when we danced and sang with my uncles' wives and daughters. Her feet were there, but her heart was safe in Hevron, dancing around the old copper bowl under the moon's light far away.

I had never been to Hevron, and I enjoyed our circles. I loved dancing with my mother, even if it was only with a part of her. It was exciting and kind of funny to see the grandmothers playing drums and singing with loud voices. Mostly, I liked having the other girls around me. Mangeena and Shirly were my favorites. They were the daughters of Rakdanit and Naftali. Of course, my uncle, Naftali, didn't come to the moon circles, but his wife and daughters were there every time. Mangeena and Shirly were only a little older than I was, and they never shooed me away from them. Their mother loved to dance, and they loved to sing. And so did I.

The three of us harmonized often. Sometimes we took the words of the moon chant and played with them. Sometimes we brought our voices together without words, humming or lalala-ing beside the fire. They told me they did that on other days, too, not just under the full moon. "Our father plays the flute on dark nights," Shirly once told me. "Mother dances, and we sing along. Even when it's not a special night." I, of course, sang any day or night that I pleased. But never with the luxury of a flute.

Drums were the only instruments we used at the celebrations. Grandmother Rebekah and Grandmother Leah got the two biggest ones. Theirs were carved with scenes of plants and rivers. They said the drums were made by Auntie Deborah and her husband long ago. They still looked and sounded beautiful so many years later. The grandmothers had the fanciest drums, but we could all have one. Even the babies. And we could stomp with our feet and clap our hands and sing as loudly or as quietly as we wanted. Until, eventually, one of the grandmothers told us it was time to lie down.

It was hard to lie still with the sound of the drums still beating quickly in my heart, but I did. And I followed the breathing leader, even when it was hard to get started. Usually, I was beside my mother but not always. Mangeena and Shirly were the only other girls who came every month, but sometimes other girls and their mothers came. When they did, I would often lie on the biggest blanket with everyone else. It was really three blankets that were stitched together so that many of us could sit or lie on it at once.

Grandmother Rebekah would shake her head in disbelief whenever we took that blanket out. She said that when she was a girl, Auntie Deborah told her a story about music, so the two of them decided to make music together under the moon each month. "Many times," she said, "it was just the two of us. Now look at how many daughters of Deborah there are!" I thought it was strange that she called us daughters of Deborah. When I asked Grandmother Rebekah about it, she said that Auntie Deborah was just as much of a mother to Jacob and Esau as she was, and so her daughters were really *their* daughters. It took me many years, five children, and a barren womb of my own to understand what she meant.

It really was lovely to be with so many of us under the moon. The harmonies we could create together were fuller than any two or three or even four of us could do in a small group. Just being close to all those girls and women gave me a warm and safe and loved feeling, even though most of them paid me no attention most of the time. They were my tribe, my clan, my family—like it or not.

And under the moon, I think they did like it. Under the moon, we all liked everything. Even if there were tears, we liked it, because there were hugs and words of comfort. But most of the time, there were more laughs than tears and more singing than talking, and there was always lots of dancing and lots of dreaming. I don't remember exactly which night was the first time that I slipped into the other world through the door of the breathing and the beating of the drums. But my memory of being a toothless child experiencing the awe is vivid.

I struggled to get my breathing just right at the beginning. But when I did, I felt myself float-flying. That's what I called the feeling of becoming a part of Yah, of becoming the breath that goes in and out, in and out. Sometimes it felt like zooming up into the stars and then floating down back to Earth. Zooming up, floating down. *Yhhhh* was the zoom. I got closer and closer to the stars, but at the same time, I actually was the sky. And *Whhhh*. I was still the sky, still surrounded by stars, but I was floating, not zooming. The only things I saw was light and darkness, yet I felt more than that. I felt shapes and colors, heat and cold, and sound. It was all one. It was all me.

It is all one. It is all me.

BEFORE

efore Grandmother Rebekah died, she asked to have *The Scrolls of Deborah* read to her. "I am an old woman," she said. "I am the only old person here. Being around so many young people makes me feel tired. I want to be reminded that I was once young. I want to be reminded of the life I had before now. Emunah." Grandmother Rebekah asked, "Do you know how to read?" Auntie dropped her head and looked to the ground, as if the answer might spring forth from it. "Do not be ashamed," Grandmother continued. "I do not know how to read. Deborah did. Neither is better. I know you have been making sure that Benjamin practices his learning. Did you learn to read as you helped him or not?"

"I did," Auntie said.

"Then you shall read to me from the scrolls of my Deborah," Grandmother said. "Do you remember hearing them before? Back in Hevron?" Auntie lit up with this question and nodded and assured Grandmother Rebekah that she remembered them well. "Come when the sun sets. We will light lamps. Everyone is welcome."

And so, that evening, Auntie began reading the scrolls. It was a wonderful way to be together. Some of the other children came and listened sometimes too. The children of Judah and Batshua were there most nights, but I was there every night. I would not have missed it for anything. Bilhah and Geeborr and Benno always came too. Grandmother Leah told Benno he had to come in case Emunah tired from the reading and he needed to take a turn. It never happened, though. Auntie read for as long as Grandmother wished.

Auntie didn't read every night, though. There were some times when Grandmother Leah kept her away with busy tasks. They were all meaningless, as far as I could tell, except that they prolonged the reading. None of us wanted to come quickly to the end of the scrolls. I think Grandmother Leah least of all, for she knew that at the end, Grandmother Rebekah would die, and Grandmother Leah didn't want to be the only old woman left.

My mother came to the reading every time the scrolls were opened. She had heard them read aloud by my father at the time that he was writing Auntie Deborah's words. My mother's body was with us in the tent, but though she was surrounded by Grandmother Rebekah and Grandmother Leah and Zilpah and Bilhah and Emunah—all of whom had been with her in Hevron—her mind was in a different place. I could see on her face that those nights brought her back to the happy times of Hevron. When she wasn't lost in her thoughts, she would sometimes encourage me to go look at the scrolls and the words and memorize the markings.

What fun it was to have Auntie read the words of the moon chant! She pointed them out to me to prove that she wasn't just singing the song but reading the words that my father had written at Deborah's request all those years ago. That was how I learned to read the words *sister*, *mother*, *daughter*, and *friend*. Auntie also showed me the scrolls every time the name Deenah or Joseph was written in there. I loved learning to read some words, and I loved hearing the stories of my ancestors. I loved every part of the reading, though my favorite part was when I was mentioned.

My father wrote in the scrolls that just before Auntie Deborah died, she'd told my mother, "You think that I do not know, but I do. You carry a song inside you as beautiful as that of a blue bird. It is one that will uplift the tribe of Israel to higher abundance." When Grandmother Rebekah heard Emunah say those words, she stopped the reading. She called my mother to her side.

"Deenah," Grandmother Rebekah asked her, "Auntie knew? She knew you were carrying Blue?" My mother nodded. I even nodded, because my mother had told me that many times. But nobody had told Grandmother Rebekah. When she found out, she began to laugh. "Oh, Auntie!" she said. "My Deborah. So full of blessings. What a blessing it is to still get to learn something new about her all these years later."

It was a great joy to hear Grandmother's laugh and love. And it was funny to think of Deborah as being called Auntie and funny to think of Grandmother Rebekah and Deborah as the young women in the tribe. In most of the story, Grandfather was not even born yet. It made me think of the children and grandchildren I thought I would have one day. And their children and grandchildren. And theirs. Of course, I didn't know at the time that I would never once birth a baby. I never could have guessed that I would someday meet descendants of my siblings and cousins down past the twentieth generation. In those moments, my thoughts were still uninformed, mostly left to imagination. Deborah's scrolls made it easy for me to imagine myself as a fly on the wall in her tent, in her life.

It was Grandmother Rebekah's life, too, for they had shared many more years together than not. This was why Grandmother Rebekah wanted to hear the story. She said ten years had passed that she had been living without Deborah. She then guessed that she had lived ten years before they had met, and she was now finished with what she called "this foolishness" of living without Deborah. She told us that we were all wonderful but that Yah had given her enough time to enjoy her son and his wives and their children and grandchildren, and now she knew that her day to die would come soon.

She was correct. She did not die on the day that Auntie finished the reading as Grandmother Leah had feared, but less than one moon cycle passed before she did. It was a time of mourning for our whole tribe. Grandfather was called in from the fields before she died but was back out there when she took her last breaths, and it seemed that at least as much of his weeping was from missing her final moments as it was from her death itself.

"I should have made her more comfortable," he said. "I should have been with her."

Grandmother Leah put her arm around him. "You were her baby," she said to her aging husband. "She wanted to be your mother, your elder. You did not need to take care of her. She took care of you." This wasn't the only truth, of course. Grandfather took care of our whole tribe. Everything was his. Everything we had was because of him. But it was Grandmother Leah who put oil on Grandmother Rebekah's lips to keep them from cracking, and it was Auntie who came out of the tent to tell everyone when she died, and it was one of Judah's sons who blew the shofar to call everyone in from the fields.

Grandmother Leah was at least as sad as Grandfather, but she did not sit around crying. She organized Zilpah and Bilhah, my mother and me, Emunah, and Judah's wife Batshua and all the tasks she had for us to do. Together, we bathed and anointed Grandmother Rebekah's body and wrapped it in a rug she had brought with her from Hevron. It was not the fanciest one we had, but she'd said that all the green reminded her of the leaves of her childhood, and she wanted that around her when her body was buried.

We made quite the procession bringing her body all the way to the cave where her husband, Isaac, had been buried. At the front of our line, it was quiet.

Grandfather stood before us and led us in prayer before we left: "Praised are you, Elohim, for guiding us as we leave, watching over us along the way, and returning us safely." After that, he didn't say another word while we walked. Sometimes Grandmother Leah walked beside him. Sometimes he requested Benno's company. Most of the time, he walked alone. As alone as one man can be when followed by his wives and his eleven sons with their wives and children. A few times, I caught myself looking for Grandmother Rebekah and needing a moment to remember that she wasn't walking but being carried in a rug in a cart pulled by an ox who was following his handler. I hoped she was happy and comfortable, even though I wasn't sure if such things were possible for her.

As for me, I was having a wonderful time. It was my first big journey, and I was excited to see what was over the hills. Even when I found out that it was just more hills, I didn't mind. I enjoyed the walk and the change in routine. I found Mangeena and Shirly, and we sang together for a while, until some of the mothers gave us a look that made it seem like it was the wrong thing to do. I tried quietly telling stories and making them laugh, but after being scolded, they walked with their backs straight and their eyes forward.

Back with Benno and Geeborr, we were able to have fun together. We were used to each other's ways and able to talk and laugh quietly without gathering attention. We pretended that the hills and the bushes were different animals and told each other about all the giant backs we were climbing over and all the little furry creatures that watched us walk with admiration. Nobody interrupted us for lessons or chores, since everyone around us was busy in their own conversations or thoughts.

But after a while, in the distance—the far distance—we saw some city walls.

Mother told me about the first time she had seen a city: "I was younger than you are now," she said, "when we left Haran and came to this land. Along the way, we stayed the night in a city. Joseph and I got to have cinnamon on our wrists, and it smelled wonderful for days." She called my father by his name because Benno was there and because she knew he missed having his brother as much as I wished I had my father. But Benno took two steps back and started following behind us, closely enough to still hear, but far enough away to let me hold hands with Mother.

He knew how I cherished the times when she could be happy with me.

Mother continued her story, saying, "Your father and I walked through the city streets with wide eyes and wonder. We had never seen houses before. Nor had we seen people confined to walking in the narrow spaces between houses."

I had never seen any of these things before, either, even though I had nearly all my teeth by the time Grandmother Rebekah died. I always listened intently to my mother's stories, but this time, I listened for details that could help me imagine what it was like to be in a city.

"We could have gotten lost there," Mother said, "but we were together, so we didn't think about that. We just admired the fancy sandals we saw and the unfathomable number of bricks. Imagine the number of bricks that needed to be used to make a wall the size of a tent wall!

"When I was older," she continued, "I went to another city. Shechem. I went there by myself, though I wasn't really alone because the girls of the city were there too." Mother's eyes lit up, but she didn't share many other details about Shechem. She only said, "That city was so much bigger and brighter and better than the first one." Then she was quiet again, reliving the sadness or fear from when her brothers had invaded the city and stolen her from it.

Luckily, just as she finished talking, we both heard a little noise coming from her satchel. It was Barley! She had brought Barley with her! I was surprised, but Mother wasn't. She winked at me and said, "I told you I brought Barley for the journey."

"I thought you meant grain!" I said.

"I know," she said lightly. "I wanted you to think that." She squeezed my hand.

I took Barley in my arms for a little while, but she was ready to walk on her own legs. She always stayed close to Mother, and that day was no exception. Especially with all the feet around and with what must have been an abundance of new smells and sounds. She was very happy to walk beside us or be back in Mother's satchel.

Walking with Barley was the last thing that Mother and I did together. Certainly, we both made the journey to Grandmother Rebekah's burial, but I spent most of my time with Benno and Geeborr. And, of course, we were both there when Grandfather took the body into the cave and when, much later, he came out alone. And we were even both there when Grandfather began the mourning ceremony in the little temporary camp that had been quickly erected near the cave. We were both there. Everyone was there. Including Grandfather's brother, Esau.

In my tribe, the name Esau was known but not spoken often. I knew more about him from hearing the words in *The Scrolls of Deborah* than from any lips of those around me. That was how I knew as soon as I saw the man who looked just like my grandfather except for his red hair that it was Esau. Grandfather must have sent word of their mother's death. By the time Esau and his tribe arrived, Grandfather had already buried their mother's body.

Esau's disappointment about that was palpable, and though he and my grandfather did not fight or have a formal greeting, I saw Grandfather bow his head in a meek apology. Then my uncle began to set up his camp. It was just as large as ours, if not larger, and side by side, our size was something I thought Grandmother Rebekah would be pleased about. I know that I was.

I did not think that her husband, Isaac, would be proud of his numerous descendants. Having not met him, I didn't give him much thought. We were gathered that day to think of Rebekah, not Isaac. But when we began the ceremony, I did have cause to think of him. Bilhah was passing out the finest goblets to the elders. Everyone else had to share or use a regular clay vessel that we had brought. But Bilhah took a fancy cup to Grandfather, another to his eldest son, Reuben, one to Esau, and one to Esau's eldest son. Then she brought one to Grandmother Leah. Auntie and I walked behind her with the strong wine, filling the cups.

Esau did not look at me as I poured wine for him, but he'd fixed his gaze on Auntie. "Emunah," he said, while lovingly stroking her cheek, "you wear my father's face, but it looks much prettier on you." It was only then that I thought of Grandfather Isaac being buried in the cave, now with his wife finally beside him. For just a moment, I wondered who I might lie beside when I died.

Once Auntie and I had finished pouring for the elders, one bottle was given to a woman in Esau's tribe to pour the drink for them, and one was given to Zilpah. She poured for the rest of us, then went to sit by Mother. Zilpah had always tended to my mother. She was Grandmother Leah's nursemaid. A second mother to my mother. They were together often. Geeborr was with Bilhah. I sat with Benno. The fire was already strong and warm. No drums were taken out, but I heard soft humming coming from somewhere in the darkness and joined along.

As the smoke rose to the sky, our bodies sank to the ground, heavy with the drink—or maybe I should say, relaxed. I let the earth cradle me as I began the breathing. The sun had only recently gone down, and the fire kept me warm enough. I was eager to begin. I spread my arms and looked up at the sky and breathed the emerging stars into me. *Yhhhh.* I held them there for as long as possible, then returned them, along with as much of myself as I could. *Whhhh.*

With my breaths, I dreamt of my mother and father. I dreamt of them breathing *Whhhh* while I breathed *Yhhhh.* I dreamt of them becoming part of me in that way, thousands of little Fathers and thousands of little Mothers becoming part of me, all swirling and twirling, skipping and dancing in their tininess inside me. All the little Fathers gathered into one adult-sized Father and flew far, far away as a rainbow that covered a land full of colors. At the same time, all the little Mothers gathered into one elephant-shaped, adult-sized Mother who wrapped herself in a blanket of the very hills I had walked upon. And even though Mother and Father were gone, they were also not gone. Because now they were the land and the light that was in me and below me, above me and around me.

That is how dreams are, isn't it? Confusing, yet seemingly so important. I'm not sure whether I was asleep during that dream. I may have been awake during the ceremony, though oblivious to what was happening beyond my own experience. When it ended, I know that I slept a comforting and comfortable sleep. I felt as if I were cradled in color and wrapped in a blanket softer even than the one that Grandmother Rebekah was just buried in. I remember having that thought: *I'm all wrapped up in a blanket that's better than Grandmother Rebekah's, because I have light inside it, which is my father, and because the blanket itself is my mother.*

When I woke from that peaceful night, I went to tell Mother all the details of my dream. That's when I found out that she was gone. Nobody had seen her leave, but her satchel was nowhere to be found, and neither was Barley. In the place where her mat had been, there was a sketch in the dirt of an elephant, head held high, trunk, even higher. Of course, none of us had ever seen an elephant, but we had all seen my mother's elephant sketches. I had heard many times about how much she loved the beauty and exoticness and power of elephants. They represented freedom and possibility and joy for my mother.

When we searched for Zilpah to ask her, we found that she was gone too. When my uncles got word that my mother, their sister, was missing, they gathered and began planning search parties in all directions. However, these big men with beards, shepherding staffs, and children of their own were still the sons of Leah, so they came to an immediate halt when she screamed, "No!"

Never before that moment had I heard my grandmother make so much noise, but there was more to come. She growled like an animal, a sound that seemed to come from a place hovering just above the ground. Her voice could have drowned out any drums and was colder than a winter wind: "Don't. You. Dare." She went to each man and stood with her face in his, making the men bend down to her height while she bore into them with her eyes and repeated her command to each one of the ten hairy men individually: "Don't. You. Dare."

"Even if you plan to go and bring her back kindly this time, for Deenah it will be a fate worse than death to have left her brothers behind only to have them conquer her once again. She has endured your not-so-subtle whispers of 'whore' and your judgmental stares long enough. You leave her alone! Do you hear me?" The men were silent, heads bowed, but their stillness was not an acceptable answer for her. "You leave her alone! Do you hear me?" she yelled.

Grandmother Leah's body was shaking, but it was clear she wouldn't fall. Could she burst? Maybe. Hit someone with his own staff? Very possible. But she wouldn't fall. She was as steady as a boulder. I was never told by her or my mother or anyone else exactly what had happened when my uncles dragged my mother back from her wedding to the prince, just that she had kicked and screamed and was fierce and fighting back as they tore her away. But that was enough detail. My mother had never gotten over it, and neither had her mother.

"My Deenah was a happy girl," she said, still holding her sons as a captive audience as she yelled. "She was vibrant! And curious! And joyful! I would have missed her when she was in her new home in the court of the king. But I would have made the short journey often! Now I live far from my daughters Ahuvah and Annah and Tirzah, and the farthest from Deenah, wherever she is. But in that place, she is far from her brothers. And there she shall remain, unpursued by you. I will not ask you again if you heard me. You heard me. Do not pursue her."

I started to cry while she yelled. I was sure that my mother would not have wanted to be chased down by her brothers, and I was proud of my grandmother for protecting her. But why wouldn't she also protect me? Protect me from becoming a girl with no mother? I didn't wish to be a girl with no mother! My mother was wonderful! She told me stories and taught me to weave and count and skip. She seasoned the oil for the bread I ate. She held my hand and stroked my hair and tickled my toes. Even if my mother was too sad to sing with me or talk with me or even sit with me sometimes, she was still there. She was still my mother, and I wanted her.

Grandmother took my hand and reached for Emunah's, and together, we walked to her temporary tent that had been set up for the funeral. Grandfather began to follow, but she looked back at him and shook her head no. Bilhah stepped behind us, and Leah gave her a slight nod of her head. So, the four of us went into the tent and wept until we slept.

When the sun finished rising, I sought out Benno, my first love, my friend whose mother had left when he was born. I told him that if only I had sung the right song for my mother, she would still be there. I told him that if only I had been cheerful enough or maybe quiet enough, she would still be there. I told him that I was sure that if Joseph were with us, she would be too.

Benno didn't say that maybe she would come back. Neither did Grandmother. Nobody said it. I wished so deeply that anyone would have said it! Benno didn't say that maybe she had gone to one of her sisters or to look for a brand-new place. He didn't say that Zilpah would take good care of her, or that she would have Barley for comfort, or that they would be okay. When I told him I hoped for those things, he said that they were nice hopes and that he would hope them with me. But we didn't know for sure. What he knew for sure, he told me, was that it wasn't my fault she had gone.

That just made me cry more. But the cry was a little bit

better than the one before. A little calmer. When my tears finally stopped, I remembered something. I hugged Benno and went back to find Grandmother Leah. Bilhah and Emunah had left the little tent as I had, but Grandmother was there alone, sitting on a cushion in the shade, staring at the hills. I took her hand and kissed it and sat beside her. She put her arm around me, and we were quiet together for a while. Finally, I asked her, "What is a whore?"

Grandmother squeezed me close and kissed me on the top of my head. "*Whore*, dear Blue, is a word that men use to describe a woman who makes choices for herself instead of her husband or her father or her brothers owning her body." I already missed my mother terribly, but I sat taller with how immensely proud of her I felt. At that moment, I knew that I wanted to be just like her. And I thought that maybe Grandmother Leah did too.

WE RETURNED

No sooner had we returned from Grandmother Rebekah's burial than people started getting sick. My first thought was to be glad that I wasn't sick. My second thought was to be glad for a moment that Mama wasn't there. Maybe she was well with one of her sisters. But I didn't need that trick of the mind to take my thoughts away from her absence. So many others got sick that worrying about them kept my mind very busy.

First, it was some of Issachar's sons who got sick. I didn't know them, but I heard that they were burning with fever and vomiting even the smallest drops of drink that their mothers tried to give them. Their mothers were the next to fall sick. A tent was set up outside the camp to keep the people who got sick separated from everyone else, and many of us took turns bringing food and water to those who were sick and bringing back news. Within a few days, there were more than twenty people in that tent: babies and their mothers, mostly, but also a grown man or two.

In the healing tent, there was enough room for the ones who were sick to spread out but still stay sheltered from the weather and away from those of us who were still well. Fewer than half of those who went into that tent came out alive. There was sadness throughout our camp, but it didn't touch me personally until Geeborr had to go in. Bilhah had kept him in her tent as long as she could. She wanted to stay with him, but she also wanted to stay with Benno. She eventually had to admit that he had the sickness—and she did too. Benno briefly came to stay in Grandmother Leah's tent with me, and we thought it would be fun to get to spend more time together. However, Grandmother Leah wouldn't really let us be together; she was worried that Benno was already sick, even though he looked well. It turned out that Grandmother Leah was right. After only one night, he was reunited with Bilhah and Geeborr.

That was how it was in that time. Every day, more people went out of the camp to try to keep the sickness away, but they ended up doing more dying together than recovering together. Those of us who could still walk around did so with tears in our eyes. We went through our tasks without noticing.

Graves were dug, bodies were buried, prayers were said. Many, many prayers. I'll admit that most of mine were for Benno and Geeborr, though I also included Auntie and my grandfather and Grandmother Leah and Bilhah, praying that they would stay well. After a while, it occurred to me to include myself.

I didn't only pray, though. I also went to visit the sick tent. I knew I wasn't supposed to, so at first, I went when nobody was around. As soon as Benno saw me, we waved to each other from a distance. I called out to him, but he was too weak to call back. For a long time, we just sat together, though far apart. One morning when I went, he wasn't sitting outside in the usual place. I waited and waited for him, but still he didn't come. I was worried and went closer. I went to where I had seen him sit or lie in the sun so many times. There, instead of Benno, I found words scratched into the dirt.

Bilhah says no . . . There were two more words after that. Oh, how I wished I knew how to read as many words as Benno. At that moment, I became determined to learn all the words. Bilhah says no *what*? I waited longer to see whether he would come out of the tent, but eventually, I stomped my feet in anger and frustration—and more than a little fear—all the way back to my tent.

The next day, I went to my usual place to wave to Benno, and again, he wasn't there. I went to see whether at least his words remained. I would copy them over and over until they were just right, then I would go and ask Auntie. But when I got there, the words were replaced with these: *Go home.* Go home? I stomped on those words until they became boring, message-free dust again, then wrote my own word: *No.* Sadly, after writing that I wouldn't go home, I went home. I left my word there, though, for Benno to see. He would understand that I would be back.

I continued to go back every day. Though we couldn't see each other, we left words for each other. That was almost as good. Auntie helped me with the ones that I didn't understand, and she helped me learn new words to write to Benno. One day, I wrote to him that Rain was coming, and I drew a picture of a round cat face with two pointy ears next to my message. I hoped this would make him laugh.

Rain often helped me laugh. She didn't seem to be mourning the losses or even noticing them. She went about her cat day, lounging in the sun or shade, and following around anyone who she thought would give her some scraps. Of course, she chased the mice and lizards that dared to enter her territory, and it was fun to watch her pounce. I made a little toy for her with a long twig and a bunch of wool that I dipped in some broth. She chased that thing as if it really were a mouse, and she wasn't even disappointed when she caught it and couldn't eat it. She just enjoyed tearing it apart and chasing the stands as they scattered in the dust.

Rain brought some smiles to my face and tunes to my throat. When her warm body curled up on mine during her quieter moments, it was then that new songs came to my lips. When I felt the vibrations of her purring against my heart, I hummed along, and then sang, making up words as I went. Parts of me felt guilty. Should I really be feeling relief, and even comfort and joy, while so many others were suffering and dying? I told myself that yes, I should. I was not heartless. I had compassion for them, fear, too, and immeasurable grief. But it was okay to also be light and happy when I was able. After all, I was wishing that for everyone who was sick; why not wish it for myself?

After so long of writing notes and not seeing Benno, I jumped with delight when I went to write more words and found him in the place where our messages had been. He wasn't writing, just sitting there like he had before. I almost ran to him, but instead I called out. When he looked up, I saw his face was covered in dirty smudges, seemingly from him wiping away tears. What could be so bad now that he was allowed to see me? I went closer to find out. He still wasn't strong enough to yell, but I got close enough to hear him say that Geeborr had died yesterday and that Bilhah had died last night.

It took only those few words to yank me from my relief back to sorrow and fear. But Geeborr had been a hero! He had saved Benno's life! Why wasn't anyone there to save Geeborr when he needed it? I wanted this for him, but also for myself. I wanted to still hide with him in the tall grasses and leap like frogs with him in the wadis. I wanted to see his smile. And I wanted so desperately to hug Benno. I wanted to tell him that it would be alright, but we both knew that it would not be alright and that I could not hug him. All we could do was cry our tears. Would we never stop having sorrow? Would we never stop losing fathers and mothers? Not wanting to be apart, I stayed until the sun was almost down before finally going back to my tent.

There, the tears continued. When I told Grandmother Leah where I had been and what Benno had said, I at least got to be held while I cried. But she was little comfort, for she, too, was devastated. "I am the only wife now," she said, "and the only mother. We started as four. Then one by one they left me. First Rachel, then Zilpah, and now Bilhah. Deborah had Rebekah in her old age, and Rebekah had me. And now I have nothing but loss and grief."

"I will stay with you, Grandmother," I said quickly. "And Auntie is here." However, Emunah was not in the tent. Just as I began to fear that she'd gone to the sick tent, she entered, and I exhaled with relief. For a moment, I had felt what Grandmother had felt: the weight of being the only one left. But I would not be the only one to care for Grandmother. Auntie would be there too.

We had many days of mourning, all of which were days that I visited Benno as best as I could. Finally, there was the good news that he was getting better. I could see it when he could smile.

When I told him of Rain's latest antics and he gave a little giggle, I knew he was going to be okay. Every day, I got a little closer and nursed him as best I could with stories and songs. He said that my being there with him was doing more good than the herbs and the broth he'd been receiving. While I could see that the remedies were helping him, I knew he was right about the company too. It was good to be together again.

It was good for me too. He comforted me when I told him I was still sad about my mother. I had cried many times already, and others had tried to console me. But it was Benno's arms around me that allowed me to sob until I slept from the exhaustion of it. He still didn't tell me she might still be all right. He still didn't remind me that my mother loved me or that it wasn't my fault. He only sat quietly with me. At most, he'd say "yes" or give my hand a gentle squeeze.

The next day, he was a little stronger, and we both wept with relief. We had both been so scared that he would die. We both felt the deep losses of Geeborr and Bilhah, though I understood that this was a deeper loss for him. In Bilhah's death, he had lost the only mother he'd ever known, but it stung like the loss of losing a mother a second time. And though Geeborr was Benno's nephew, he was far more of a brother to Benno than any of Grandfather's other sons had been.

I tried to comfort Benno as best as I could, mostly just by holding him and listening to him, as he had done for me. We were both still scared that the sickness would come to me. It never did, but we couldn't know that at the time. All I knew was that Benno was getting better and better. When he was well enough to walk back to the camp, which was the test for being allowed to return, I was filled with so much joy that I couldn't contain it.

"You're doing it, you're doing it!" I applauded every step. I trilled my tongue and clapped my hands and leapt with joy. Benno laughed at me, but I knew he was appreciative. He really had tried to stay alive, and it really hadn't been easy. So many people had tried, but so many had died. Some had lived, though, and Benno was one of those.

Even though it was for sad reasons that he'd be joining me in Grandmother Leah's tent, I was excited that we'd be together. Mostly, I was glad he was well, and I couldn't contain my relief and excitement. I ran ahead to get Grandfather. He knew Benno was getting better, for he, too, had been having distant visits. But he was still so afraid.

"Grandfather, come!" I pleaded. I could see he was torn. "Please, please," I added, though he didn't answer or move. "Grandfather," I said, more softly this time, "Praise Yah! Benno . . . Benjamin is well!" I quickly corrected myself and called him by the name Grandfather used. I took his hand. "I'm also sad about Bilhah . . . and the others."

Grandfather had lost others that weren't even known to me. He had many to grieve. But still, Benno was well! "Hallelu Yah!" I said that aloud again: "Grandfather, Halleu Yah!" What could he do? Would he refuse to praise Yah?

He whispered a quiet word of praise.

"Grandfather! Hallelu Yah!"

"Hallelu Yah," he answered, a little bit stronger.

"Hallelu Yah!" I yelled.

"I did," he said. "Serrah. I am old; I am sad. I praise Yah that Benjamin has lived. His brother died long ago, and I still mourn losing that son of mine. At least Benjamin has not died. Hallelu Yah." He moved to walk away, but I would try once more.

"Yes!" I said. "Benjamin has not died! Hallelu Yah! Praise Yah not just with a private whisper just for yourself. Praise Yah loudly for all Yah's holiness! Praise Yah all the way to the distant edges of Yah's strength!" I saw him considering it. "Hallelu Yah! Hallelu Yah!" I sang out to him.

And he echoed me back: "Hallelu Yah. Hallelu Yah!" He was starting to feel the depth of the miracle of Benno's life—starting to.

"Hallelu Yah! Hallelu Yah!" I sang out again.

And Grandfather echoed me louder: "Hallelu Yah! Hallelu Yah!" It was known that Israel could not resist a song. Music moved him to his feet. I kept encouraging him.

"Yes, Grandfather! Praise Yah for the mighty miracles! Praise Yah's greatness!"

This time he sang out: "Hallelu Yah! Hallelu Yah!" and I was the one to echo him. By now, we were walking toward Benno who was still approaching us. He didn't have the strength to run, but he was steady and determined and smiling, and he was close enough for us to hear him echoing the praise: "Hallelu Yah! Hallelu Yah!"

Hallelu Yah! While the two of them sang, I threw my head back and my hands into the air in gratitude and praise. "Come on everyone! Praise Yah with the blast of the ram's horn! Praise Yah with the harp and lyre!" I was making a ruckus, and I was glad for it. Shirly appeared with her lyre, and Naftali came with his flute.

They began playing music as I sang out, calling for even more praise. "Praise Yah with the clash of the cymbals and the beat of the drum! Let every one of us, with every breath, praise Yah!"

With that, women appeared with drums, and voices sang up in praise together: "Let every one of us, with every breath, praise Yah!" We repeated this line, Grandfather and I and the tribe that surrounded and joined us. Grandfather's feet were never able to be still when there was music, and even now was no exception. He danced, holding hands with the toddlers and showing them his fancy footwork. Every one of us was smiling and grateful for the reprieve from fear.

Yes, we were mourning. Yes, many people had died. And yes, the grief in the camp was immeasurable. But on that day, yes, we celebrated what we were glad about: those who *had already returned* to our camp and the health of those who *would soon rejoin* us. For that, we praised Yah. In the remaining light of the day and when the first lamps were lit, we celebrated what we had. It was a glorious night.

The next morning, though, was very difficult. Even before the sun was up, I woke to the sound of a man's voice in our tent. Men had no reason to enter our tent. Grandmother Leah and Auntie and I were the ones who dwelled there, and Benno was with us now, but he was a boy. Even with all his teeth grown in, he had no whiskers and no deep voice; he was not yet a man. Sometimes my grandmother Leah slept in my grandfather's tent, but he never came to ours. So, when I heard a deep voice, I was surprised and alarmed and immediately alert.

My eyes took a moment to adjust to the darkness but were quickly drawn to a very small flame from a lantern near

Grandmother Leah's cushions. There was a man bent over her, shoulders shaking with sobs. I was just about to leap off my mat and run to her aid when I saw her sit up. The man gently helped her to her cushion, wrapping a blanket around her. He sat beside her on a rug and put his head on her shoulder and continued to cry. I stayed where I was, silent, motionless, and listening.

It was a long time before he was calm enough to speak, at which point he said, "I'm sorry, Mother; I'm so sorry, Mother," until his hiccups prevented him from speaking more.

In the silence, my grandmother said, "You're a good boy, Reuben. My firstborn. Kind, caring, and wise. I love you, baby." She really was holding him and speaking to him like a baby, though he was twice her size, covered in hair, and a father himself.

They stayed like that for a long time until my grandmother finally asked him what was wrong, and he started crying again.

When he could get words out, he said, "I have failed my father and Elohim. I've failed my wife, my beloved, my son, and my brother. I always tried to do the right thing, to show that I am worthy of the responsibility of being the firstborn. But I didn't. I failed. Now the god of my father has punished me by taking away Bilhah and Geeborr. This is what I get for finding comfort in my father's wife, Bilhah. This is what I get for losing my father's beloved son, Joseph. I told him I would go back for him, that I would always protect him from the others, but when I went back, he was gone! I didn't stop them from harming him, and now, nobody stopped the harm that came to Geeborr. Praise Elohim for not taking Benjamin." He had more sobs after that.

I think he may have fallen asleep on my grandmother's shoulder. I kept still on my mat. I don't know whether he knew they weren't alone. He had no reason to know that I slept in my grandmother's tent just as my mother had. If he had ever given one thought in his life to where I slept, he probably would have assumed that I was with Yonah, Asher's wife, the one who was called my mother. After a while of being in that silence and attempting to appear asleep, I might have also fallen back to sleep for real. But I don't think I missed anything said between the two of them, because I do remember hearing Grandmother Leah speak one more time before he left.

"My baby," she said. "I don't know what your father or Elohim think of you, but I love you dearly." She paused for a long time before she added, "And Bilhah did too. She told me. I'm sorry I didn't spend more time with her or Geeborr after he was born. You saved Benjamin's life, you know, because Bilhah had milk for him thanks to having had Geeborr. And Reuben, my sister, Rachel, complained to me every time one of my sons did so much as touch a hair on Joseph's head—and sometimes they did much more harm than that, I know—but I never heard a single complaint about you or Judah. I know it won't take away the sadness, but please remember that you have also done much good."

Reuben kissed his mother's hand then and wiped his face and left our tent as the sun began to come up. I closed my eyes tightly so that Grandmother wouldn't think I was eavesdropping; though, what I was actually doing was marveling at the wonder that even a grown man could be comforted by his mother, and, at the same time, I was feeling sorry for myself that I would never have that chance as a grown woman. I challenged myself to feel both this self-pity and this marvel at the same time, just as Grandmother had challenged Reuben to feel both sad and proud at once.

SICKNESS

The time of sickness was hard on all of us, but after a while, we did go back to our routine, and it somehow seemed like it would always be that way. But another hard part followed. I don't know how many years later it was, but the rain hadn't been enough to grow the crops we needed. We grew some, but not enough. In order to eat, we had to rely more on our flocks and our stockpiles. Within the next year, no crops grew at all, and our reserves were nearly empty. We drank milk and ate cheeses, but sparingly. Sheep and goats were slaughtered every day. My grandfather was a wealthy man, so he had many animals, but he also had many people to feed. Soon the food would be gone.

Word reached us that there was plenty in Egypt. We saw traders passing by with goods they had bought. Once or twice, some of my uncles tried to buy some of the goods from them, but the traders wanted nothing more than the food they had just bought from Egypt, so they would not part with any of it. One morning, Judah blew the ram's horn, calling everyone to gather. He and all my uncles—except Benno, who was my uncle, though not one of the men—were standing before Grandfather.

"Father," Judah addressed him. "You are a wealthy and honored man. You are Israel, someone who has lived with Elohim and with people. You know the ways of both. Thus, you know that our tribe cannot be sustained much longer on the flocks that we have. I ask you . . . *we* ask you . . . please send us down to Egypt. There, the food is plentiful. Let us take gold and silver and buy the means to keep our tribe thriving here on this land, even during the famine."

We all watched as Grandfather looked at each of his sons. Nobody interrupted his thinking, even though he took his time. After a while, some of the smaller children walked away, maybe thinking the meeting was over, though it wasn't. Finally, Grandfather nodded at Judah, and everyone started moving at once. Judah bowed before Grandfather and kissed his hand. Words were exchanged that I didn't hear over the noise of the preparations. Though I had known nothing of it, this plan did not come as a surprise to everyone, as was shown by the speed at which everything was prepared. Before the sun was high, camels were saddled, carts were loaded, and the men were on their way. Benno was a brother, but he was not yet considered a man, so he stayed behind with the rest of us.

We waited for their return for over a month. We knew that we wouldn't know how long the journey would last. It would certainly take them at least a week to walk there and at least a week to walk back, although these were just guesses. I thought to myself that Judah was wise to leave when they did, for we did still have food. If we had to wait in a completely desperate situation, lives would have been lost to starvation while we waited.

Thankfully, that wasn't what happened. The men returned some time later with more food than we had seen in over a year. They were greeted with cheers of gratitude and an abundance of helpers to unload the goods. I helped take down olives and dried melon, which was a treat I'd never had before. There was wheat flour and barley flour and baskets and baskets of almonds. I don't mind saying that I peeled a couple of them right there and popped them into my mouth. We all did.

When the food was put away, Judah gathered everyone again. He didn't need to blow the shofar this time, as we were already nearby. "Honored Father," he said, "You have blessed us with your permission to get food from Egypt, and we have come back with plenty of that and also plenty to tell."

Levi interrupted Judah and burst out, "But we haven't *all* come back. We're without Shimon! Judah left him there, as a captive! At the whim of the vizier, my brother is gone."

Levi and Shimon were thick as thieves. Even I knew that, and I hardly ever saw them. But my mother had told me that they were the ones behind the massacre of her husband and his town, and she'd also told me that they'd tortured my father so much as a boy that they'd nearly killed him more than once. She didn't have a kind word to say about any of her brothers, other than little Benno, but when talking about those two, she spit fire.

"What?" Grandfather asked.

"The vizier said he must keep a brother," Levi said. "He accused us of being spies. He said we could only prove our innocence if we came back with our youngest brother, and he kept Shimon until we do that. We don't even know where he was taken! We don't even know where he is!" Levi was standing and yelling at this point. Judah put a hand on his shoulder and backed him a little bit farther from Grandfather. Grandfather walked quietly into his tent.

It was not spoken of again for many months, but when our stores were getting low again, Reuben went to speak to Benno, and then Benno came to speak to me.

"Reuben says I should go back with them to Egypt. He confirmed Levi's story. He said they were accused of being spies and that we wouldn't get any more food if I didn't go back with them to prove their innocence. He said he went to Father and told him that he, Reuben, would personally care for me the whole time, in every moment and with every breath. He told Father that if he did not return me alive, Father could kill his sons as payment. Blue," he added, "it seems best that I go, so we get relief from the famine and from . . . death. But I do not think it would be wise for me to be in the care of a man who is willing to kill his own sons."

I agreed that Reuben having dead sons would not help anything and thought that surely Grandfather would want no such thing.

Reuben wasn't the only one to seek out Benno. Every brother went to him, one at a time. They had all spoken with Grandfather, and none of them could convince him to allow Benno to go to Egypt. He had already lost his son Joseph, and now Shimon was gone. It had been hard enough when Benno had almost died of the sickness, and to have him be in such peril again was unthinkable to Grandfather. But surviving the famine also seemed impossible, so each brother asked Benno to go with them, even against their father's wishes. They each told Benno that we would all die without him.

"I don't want you to go," I confided in Benno.

"But I'm afraid my brothers are right," he said. I had noticed that as he'd grown to nearly the height of a man, he'd started to include himself as one of the brothers. They still thought of him as a baby, that was clear, but when they came to him for help, Benno felt even more like he could be one of them.

"I'm afraid of that too," I said. "But I'm also afraid that you might be kept there, like Shimon and"—I paused for a long time—"and I would hate that. I want you to be here. I want to run in the fields with you and grow in the onion patch, even if it's too dry for onions to grow there. I want to go on great adventures together and on small ones too. I want to hide and find and play and laugh with you."

Benno hugged me. He wrapped his arms around me and lifted me off the ground and laughed. "I love all those things, too, Blue," he said. "But the fields have no more tall grass, just as the gardens have no more onions. And even if they did, when would we play in them? I spend much of the day writing and taking account of what we have left. You know that. I've been going with the sheep more and more. Not as much as my brothers, but I'm becoming a pretty good shepherd. And you are busy with the women's tasks. Those childhood adventures were wonderful, but my brothers need me now. We all need food."

I could not argue with Benno, for he hadn't said one wrong thing. I wish he had. I wish he'd been wrong about our childhood adventures and games being only memories. I had kept them alive so strongly in my imagination that I had hardly noticed them slowly slipping away. But he was right. Though we both slept in my grandmother's tent, we saw little of each other elsewhere.

How different would it be if he were to go to Egypt and come back with enough food to sustain us through the famine?

After some time, Grandmother Leah went to speak with Grandfather. She took me and Benno with her. She told me I should look like a hungry little girl, which was not so hard for me. I had reached the age of womanhood but had not officially started. At the time, we all thought it was due to the famine. Not having quite enough to eat was doing that to all the young women. Then Grandmother Leah told Benno he should look hungry, too, which he found just as easy.

Grandmother didn't hesitate. She went right up to Grandfather and said, "I love this boy. He's my sister's boy. Don't think I don't love him. I am the one raising him now. Don't think I don't want to protect him. Don't think it doesn't pain me to send him to Egypt. You think he won't come back. Maybe you are right, maybe you are not right. But listen, Israel, don't think that he'll live if he stays here. The food will be gone. He'll die. We'll all die."

That was it. Then she took me and Benno by the hand and walked away with us. We weren't really all that little, but we were unmarried and nearby, so she walked away with us the way she might do with babies. As we left, I saw her shoot a glance and a nod to Judah, who seemed to understand the unspoken message and then talked to Grandfather. The next morning, Benno and his brothers left for Egypt, with Judah assuring Grandmother that he would watch over Benno.

SHADE

was in the shade of the date palms working on my weaving when I heard my name floating on the wind.

"Blue, Blue."

Yah had called to me before, but this did not sound like that. This . . . this sounded like Benno! But was it really him? I placed my weaving beside me, not caring if the ants would claim it or if the wind would unravel parts. If it really was Benno, if he really was returning from Egypt safely . . .

"Benno?" I asked. Then I yelled into the wind. "Benno!"

"Yes! Yes!" he answered me at once. "Blue, where are you?"

At that moment, I followed the sound of his voice and saw him below the camp, still a distance away. He was alone and standing still, looking all around him, searching for me.

"Up here, here!" I yelled and waved my hands until I saw him turn in my direction. We both started moving as quickly as we could toward the other. Oh, why had I chosen the shade at the steep part of the hill? This was very inconvenient! I had missed him so terribly while he was far away, and now, there he was, close enough to hear him, and I still had to wait for our reunion.

After what felt like lifetimes, we finally reached each other in an empty patch of desert in the heat of the sun and embraced above the lizards that skittered away from our feet.

"Oh, Benno!" I exclaimed, "You're alive!"

"Yes," he said, "and I'm not the only one alive!"

Only when he said that did I give thought to his brothers. How strange that he was returning alone. For more than a month, we had worried and prayed. It had been so difficult for my grandfather to allow him to go, and I shared his fear. I had given so little thought to the other brothers. Even Shimon, who had been in prison all that time. But now, I realized they were not with him. I suppose since they had traveled together, Benno had given them thought and realized he should state their welfare.

"It is good that you are all well," I said.

"Yes," Benno said. "We are *all* well. *All* of us."

He was trying to tell me something, but I didn't know what. He took me by the shoulders and looked me in the eyes. "Blue, all *twelve* sons of Israel are alive and well. My brother Joseph is alive and rules over all of Egypt!"

My knees wobbled, and I fell right to the ground. It was the only time in my life that I fainted. When I opened my eyes, Benno was leaning over me, blocking the hot sun with his body and moving his hands back and forth above my face to create a small breeze.

"Tell me everything," I insisted, as soon as my eyes regained their focus.

He made me move to the shade and drink from his jar but was kind enough not to wait until we were resettled to begin his story.

"As you know, my brothers and I went down to Egypt to buy food for our family. As usual, my brothers largely ignored me, but they kept me close for my own safety. I heard them talk with anticipation of the abundance in Egypt. 'Towers of grain,' they said. 'Dried fish, dried figs, pickled melons,' they went on and on. My mouth watered with the thought of it. You know how many of our flock we've had to slaughter just to stay alive. Thanks to Yah, we have a large flock, but the talk of delicacies kept my feet going on the long journey."

Benno went on to tell me about meeting other travelers, making small trades, and other parts of the journey that were of no interest to me. I poked him in the ribs.

"Yes, yes," he got back on topic. "We arrived at the palace. Oh, what a place! Bigger than this very hill, only flat! The land is all flat! All of it! And the large palace, built on the flat land, is where we were taken to wait and see the vizier. He was the one in charge of distributing the food. The wait was long. For two nights we slept on the floor on the palace grounds. Even that felt decadent! Very uncomfortable, but fancy, and the floor itself was not dirt, but marble. And not marble as it once was in the ground, but marble made mostly flat. So much flatness."

I poked him again. I wanted to hear of his adventure, but even more so, I wanted him to explain what he was talking about when he mentioned my father.

"We saw that some travelers were leaving with filled sacks of grain; some even had carts pulled by themselves or donkeys and enough food to fill the carts. Still, others left empty-handed. We did not know the difference between those travelers—how some received food and some did not. We prayed we would be blessed to leave with full sacks.

"Benno!" I yelled. I could not tolerate another moment of this story. "You may tell me more later. Tell me of my father!"

His voice became as quiet as mine was loud. "Blue," he nearly whispered, "your father lives. My brother lives. He has been in Egypt all these years. He has been blessed by Elohim to become the ruler of the whole land. It is his own mouth that releases the orders to fill the sacks with grain—or not to. It is Joseph who sits on the throne, though he has an Egyptian name now. There, he is called Zafenat Paaneakh. He is the one who we bowed before when we sought sustenance from Egypt.

"It was our brother Joseph who kept Shimon in jail in Egypt, to ensure that I would be brought to him. While Shimon was there in jail, he heard rumors that Joseph had been there before him but had been taken to the pharaoh years before because he had a skill of dream interpretation. In the jail, they didn't know what had happened to Joseph next. But Shimon began to suspect. Once we had paid and had our goods and were departing Egypt, Shimon was released from jail and returned to us. He told us that maybe the man we'd been begging for food was Joseph.

"I lit up with excitement, but the others fought among themselves about whether or not to return to the vizier right away. In the end, the decision was made for us by soldiers who came after us and accused us of theft. We didn't know it, but our sacks were filled with the money we had paid, just like before when my brothers had gone without me and had come back with food and their money. This time, though, there was also a silver goblet, and it was in my sack. We were accused of stealing it and taken back to the vizier—back to Joseph. Only, we didn't know yet for certain that it was him. Now we are certain. I tell you. Joseph lives."

Joseph lives! Finally, Benno said it, the words I'd been waiting my whole life—and this whole extra-long story—to hear. I didn't need to know how, but I knew who and what. My father. Joseph. My father, Joseph . . . was alive! For a flash, I felt sad that my mother couldn't be here for this moment. And there were other times that I felt sad about that again. But that day, I was just focused on one fact: Joseph lives.

Benno talked a little more, but I couldn't hear him. *Joseph lives! Joseph lives!* That was all I heard. The words began swirling in my head, and then came out of my mouth in a tune and out of my toes with tapping:

Father, Father, Father lives!
My father lives in Egypt!

Benno laughed and danced with me and had to work very hard to regain my attention for the rest of his story. "Yes, Joseph lives. But we didn't know for sure yet. As we marched back in fear, heads hung low due to our surprise possession of the money and goblet, the brothers argued among themselves about what to do. Could they attack the vizier's guards? Should we flee? Would we all be put in jail? What if it was Joseph? What if it wasn't? Then Judah told us all to be silent. He said he had a secret with Joseph, and he would see if the man knew this secret."

What was this secret? Not a baby like Geeborr. No, it was rubbing his chin with his thumb. Benno told me that when Judah did this, Joseph revealed himself. I was torn between wishing to know more about my father in this way—what was this secret about?—and also wanting Benno to finish his story.

"You see," Benno continued, "Joseph was the one who had sent the brothers back with their full sacks and their money the last time. And he was the one this time. We were delayed in our return because he wanted to spend more time with us. With *me*. His brother. And Blue, when he revealed himself to me, he called me Benno—just like you and Bilhah and my mother. And just like—he told me—just like he had when I was first born and when he'd held me in his arms. He'd sung to me too, he said. I wish I hadn't been too little to remember. I was also too little to sing with him. I probably just said 'waaah waaah.'"

When I didn't laugh at his joke, Benno asked if I was okay. I had so many thoughts at once that it was like having none at all. I couldn't digest his joke. It was all so new that I could hardly hear him anymore. We sat in silence for a long time, simply staring into the distance. After a while, the other men came over the last hill, and with them were carts piled high with goods, pulled by strong donkeys, and led by men in strange, ornate clothing.

"Has he come home?" I asked Benno. "Did you tell him about me, and did he come to see me?" I began to stand, but he pulled me back down.

"No," he said, "the news is even more exciting than that." He paused until my finger approached his ribs, ready to poke him again. What could be more exciting than my father coming to see me? "Joseph has sent for us. He has sent gifts and provisions for our journey to Egypt. We shall be sustained and safe from the famine. We will go to the land of abundance, and *you* can tell him about who you are yourself." From the time Benno told me that my father was alive and that I was going to see him, until the time that we finally left for Egypt, I remember two things.

The first thing is that I was filled with song. Every part of me was filled with song until there was no room left in me and the song needed to escape. *Needed* to escape. So whatever else I was doing during that time, I was singing:

Father, Father, Father lives.
My father lives in Egypt,
And I'll see him soon.
Soon I'll see my father.
Joseph, Joseph, Joseph lives.
Joseph lives in Egypt,
And we'll see him soon.
Soon we will see Joseph.

My feet danced me everywhere. My voice bounced off the hills. My grandmother heard me singing and called me closer.

"What?" was all she could say. I took her hands in mine and danced around her and sang again. She put her hands on my shoulders to still me.

"Blue? Joseph lives? Why are you saying this?"

"Benno has seen him in Egypt!" I said. "And I will too!" I hugged her, and we cried together, and I carried on with my song.

"Blue," she said. "Come with me. You must sing this to Israel. But . . . quieter." I complied, of course, though it was hard for me to merely whisper my joy. When we didn't find him at his tent, instead of having someone call him in from the fields, Grandmother said we should go to him. I didn't mind. I was full of energy! We took two young lads with us to guide a donkey for Grandmother to ride and to help us find him. When they did, Grandmother dismissed them and waved to her husband.

He immediately came closer. "Leah, are you well? What is it?"

"Your sons have returned from Egypt," she said. "Eleven strong and healthy men. They have brought us food to sustain us—and good news, as well." She nodded in my direction, and I sang quietly while Grandfather gave us both a puzzled look. With each nod of Grandmother's head, I sang a little louder until I just couldn't wait a moment longer and belted out my song.

Joseph, Joseph, Joseph lives.
Joseph lives in Egypt,
And we'll see him soon.
Soon we will see Joseph.

I left my grandparents there in the field and danced my way back to find Benno so he could tell me the good news again and sing and sing and sing with me. We danced and twirled each other and only stopped when we were completely exhausted. As we rested in the shade, Benno told me the whole story again.

The second thing I remember was far less joyful and was, in fact, one of the greatest griefs of my young life—a life in which I had already suffered the loss of my mother and the deaths of loved ones. When the news had spread throughout the camp that we would be going to Egypt and when preparations had already begun, Grandmother Leah had me fetch Grandfather and bring him to her tent. I mostly gave them their privacy, but it was my tent, too, and I was not sent out. And so, I heard the conversation between them. I heard her share her joy that Joseph was alive. And I heard her say that she would not make another journey. She was too old and too tired and didn't want to leave the land where her daughters were living and her matriarchs were buried. Grandfather didn't want to leave her behind. She said that would not be a problem.

"You will stay here until you give me my proper burial in the cave where Rebekah and Sarah are buried—where you should have buried my sister, Rachel, so that we could all be in the cave together, but you didn't. You buried her in haste and disgrace by the side of the road. You will not do that to me on the way to Egypt. She did not deserve that dishonor, and neither do I." My grandfather hung his head. After all these years without Joseph, he wanted to see him badly, but he also held guilt from burying Rachel during travel. Before he could say anything else, Grandmother lifted his head so his eyes were looking at hers. "Israel," she said, "I am your wife. I have been your wife all these years. I cannot make this journey. I am not leaving this land. You will not leave it until you've done right by me." Grandfather nodded, and they embraced. He agreed to her request, and my heart that had been so full of joy about meeting my father sank.

"Now, one more thing," Leah added. "I wish to have my daughters with me again. Emunah is here, of course, and I will see her married before I die. You cannot bring Deenah back, but you can bring me Tirzah and Annah and Ahuvah and their children. Let me be surrounded by them under the moon." Grandfather agreed and then left. We did not see him again until the moon grew almost full. Early that evening, he made a grand gesture of presenting his wife with their daughters.

Grandfather blew the shofar to summon our whole tribe to come to the center of the camp. He placed a beautiful pale green rug in the middle, and on top of that, he placed a stool. The rug was one of Leah's best works. Nobody else among us could have made such a perfectly woven floor covering, and it had not ever been outside of Grandfather's tent before. The stool was wooden, with carvings of bunches of grapes on each leg, and was cushioned with soft leather. Grandfather took his wife by the hand and walked her to the stool.

"Leah," he said, "it was Elohim who gave me the blessing to be fruitful and multiply, and it was you who gave me the blessing of the multitudes. You bore me six sons and two daughters from your body, and you have mothered all seventeen of my children." Then he turned his voice away from Leah and toward the rest of us and shouted, "Sons of Leah, step forth!" Ten men and Benno all took a step forward. It didn't matter from which womb they had emerged. They all honored Leah as their matriarch. From oldest to youngest, they presented themselves before her, each one kneeling and kissing her hand and receiving a smile and a stroke on the head.

Witnessing this, I realized that Benno, even though he was so much younger than his brothers, was also a man now. His face had sprouted black whiskers that were short but clearly present. I would never stop loving him, though we had stopped our adventures together. Even when he shared his story with me about the trip to Egypt and seeing my father, it was clear that he was one of the brothers now.

After Benno honored Leah, my grandfather raised his voice again. "Daughters of Leah, step forth!" he said. And unlike the men who had lined up by seniority, three women exited a tent where they had been quietly waiting and came rushing at their mother who rose to take them all into her arms at once. Emunah had never left her mother, but her tears mixed with those of her sisters whom she had not seen in so long. The women stayed with their arms around each other for so long that Grandfather had to blow the ram's horn to get their attention. At this point, twenty children, some of them almost old enough to be married and some of them still young enough to be carried on hips, stepped into view.

Leah sat herself back on the stool and opened her arms. She had too many descendants to take in all at once, and those were just the ones she had newly met that day, the children of her daughters. The little girls came and stepped into her arms first, but the older ones were quick to follow. I joined in that embrace so that all the daughters of the daughters were with her at once. The boys lined up like their uncles had and kissed their grandmother's hand and let her pet their cheeks. Then those boys retreated to their own fathers who all followed the sons of Israel to a feast that the women joined much later, because all the women and girls, the daughters and granddaughters of Leah by birth or by marriage, stayed on the light green rug where we were served stews and sweets long into the night.

Most of these granddaughters of Leah were meeting her for the very first time—and the last. How blessed I was that I had seen her every day of my life! I could not imagine the life I would have had if my uncles had not dragged my mother back to our camp. I could only guess whether she would have been truly happy with the prince in the city. Would he have also taken one look at my face and known I was not a Shechemite and sent me back to my tribe? Or would I have lived as a princess in the city with a happy mother far from my grandmothers? There was no way to know. I knew that I was glad to be surrounded by the daughters of Leah, and I praised Yah that this was not the first time I had met her and that it was just another wonderful celebration together.

So many stories were told. So many songs were sung. So many tears were shed. The part for me that was at once most joyful and most sorrowful was singing the moon song with this tribe of women, with my mother's own sisters . . . but without my mother. I missed her terribly, and I was with others who felt the same—her mother and sisters. Yet, at the same time, she was with me, inside of me, and inside of Grandmother Leah, Auntie, and her other sisters. She was in our voices as we sang, our feet as we danced, our hands as we held on to each other, and our jubilation as we celebrated under the light of the full moon. That night, as the drums were brought out and the wine was passed around, the tribe of Leah was one.

For three days we had a holiday. We laughed and cried and got to know each other. When the celebration was over and it was time to part, we were a different tribe. That is to say, Auntie left with her sister Tirzah. The milk sisters missed each other terribly, so much so that Emunah was thrilled to become a second wife if it meant they could be together. It was terribly sad to say goodbye to Auntie, but comfort came in knowing how happy she was.

One woman left our numbers, but two joined. Ahuvah's eldest daughter, Yekarah, was betrothed to Benno and would become his wife as soon as she had her first blood. In the meantime, she was taken in by Yonah, because Yonah had also taken in Asifa, who would wed my brother Ishvi shortly. But scariest of all was that Asher nearly married me off to Annah's son Loh! If I'd married him, I never would have gone to Egypt! Thankfully, Grandmother Leah put a stop to it.

"Asher," she said, with me by her side, "you have a beautiful daughter." He beamed with pride. We didn't see each other often like he did with his other daughters, but he never questioned that. He knew I'd been nursed by Deenah and had always been in the grandmothers' tent. It was women's business that he didn't concern himself with. But marrying me to another tribe was certainly his business, and I didn't know how he'd take it when his mother told him not to.

"You're a good son," she went on, "a kind husband, and a responsible father. It was wise of you to choose kin for your son to marry and for your daughter as well. But Rebekah is gone. Zilpah is gone. Deenah is gone. And Emunah is leaving. I need Serrah to stay with me. When I die, you will depart for Egypt. Your brothers have sons. Kehat, son of Levi, is almost ready for marriage, so take Serrah with you to Egypt and arrange for her to marry kin there."

There was no reason for Asher to argue with Grandmother Leah, but even if he had wanted to, he could not deny that she spoke the truth. Asher agreed to allow me to stay with my grandfather's tribe, in my grandmother's tent. Once he left, Grandmother drew me closer to her. "When you see your father, Joseph" she said, "tell him that Leah loves him and that I'm happy for him. And . . . and that I'm so very sorry for the pain that my sons caused him." I promised, then I cried. It was in that moment that I fully understood that she would not be there with me in Egypt.

Of course, I had known that that was her request and the reason for the reunion with her daughters and the reason for our delay, but I had not yet imagined my life without her in it. Grandmother Leah had always been in my life. In Egypt, even if I would have a new person to sing me songs, a new person to tell me stories about my mother, and a new person to crunch on cucumbers with or to weave me a new blanket, that person would not be Grandmother Leah. I buried my head in her lap and cried about missing her on one of the last days that she was still there.

I don't remember how long it was until Grandmother died, but it wasn't that day or that week, and it felt like forty years while I waited to meet my father, though it probably wasn't very long at all, because we still had plenty of food left. When Grandmother Leah died, Grandfather did give her the proper burial that she deserved. She was wrapped in the very blanket upon which we had sat so recently with her—our matriarch—looking over us. When I saw that blanket rolled up around her, it was hard to believe how recent that had been. Shimon and Levi gently strapped her to a wagon that they walked beside. Reuben and Judah held Grandfather by each arm. Our whole camp went to the Cave of Makhpelah and witnessed her burial in her rightful place of honor. We slept under the stars that night, and first thing the next morning, we left for Egypt.

WE TRAVELED

We traveled for days to get to Egypt, and there were so many wonders to see along the way. Caravans of traders, shepherds with different traditions, and, of course, the sea. Benno said he wished we could stop there, but I was eager to keep moving. It was a blessing, really, that Benno was engaged to Yekarah. With my grandmother gone, I was under Asher's tent now, with Yonah. This meant I was also with Asifa and Yekarah, which meant I was still with Benno. Yekarah didn't like it, though, when Benno and I were alone. She got jealous. Benno said that when we got to Egypt, he'd talk to Asher about taking me as a second wife so that we could more easily be together. I didn't think that would resolve her jealousy, though, and I told him that.

"Aaaaaaand," I said, "there will be no need to discuss anything about me with Asher. I'll be with my father! Benno, I will not be your second wife and compete with Yekarah and get half of your attention. No, this will be our last adventure together." I hugged him tightly, fighting off tears. He hugged me back, less successful at fighting off his. "I was always meant to live in a palace, you know. So, instead of starting to do so at my birth, I'll be starting now . . . shortly . . . a new birth with my father, in Egypt, in the palace."

I spoke lightly and with laughter, and it was all true. But the other truth was that I was feeling somewhat jealous of Yekarah. She would get Benno's attention. She would be there if he had other adventures. She would be the one he would share his stories with and grow his life with. But even more than the jealousy, I was feeling sad. He was becoming a man, and our time together as youths would end with or without Yekarah. I did not long to cook Benno's meals or even chase after his children. As kind as he was, as much as I loved him dearly, I did not want to be his wife, whether first or second. I did not want to be his anything. I wanted to be my own person, like my mother.

I tried not to think much about jealousy or sadness or the fact that Benno hadn't even married Yekarah yet, so he certainly couldn't be ready for a second wife. I kept myself busy with thoughts of my reunion with my father. *Would he be glad to see me? Glad to know I was his daughter? Would he believe that I was his daughter? Would he question me about my mother?* All these thoughts vied for attention in my mind, along with some happier ones too. *Would he look like Benno? Would he marry me off to a prince and then I would have to be that man's wife instead of Benno's? Would I live with the great vizier in the palace?*

It took time to learn the answers to these questions and the thousands more I thought of. One of the many questions I hadn't thought to ask was whether we would see my father before we even arrived in Egypt. However, before we got there, my father, the dreamer, my mother's love, my grandfather's favorite son, the child who had been rumored to have been killed by wild beasts—or possibly by his brothers—the boy of our collective memory, the one who for so long was *asher ayn-aynu*—the one who was no longer with us—was announced by a parade of drummer boys and a crier who informed us that the vizier was coming.

After his announcement, we felt the vibrations before we heard the drums, then we heard the drums before we saw them. Our own feet marched more to their rhythm as they got closer. Then, there they were. Forty boys drumming in unison while stomping their feet. Each foot was bare, but each chest was draped with a belt that crossed it from one shoulder down to a short tunic of the same color. The boys marched in rows, the first row containing drummers with red belts and tunics, the next one showing boys wearing orange, then a row of yellow, green, blue, and, finally, violet.

After a big flourish of drumming, the boys stopped in unison. A man walked through their lines to the front, where he announced in a loud voice that carried in the new silence, "Bend your knees and bow to the decipherer of hidden meanings, the man who interpreted the pharaoh's dream and who oversees the vast stores of food, the grand vizier of all of Egypt, Zafenat Paaneakh!"

Everyone started bowing low. Even my grandfather and his sons, who were at the front of our caravan, were no longer visible from where I was because they had bowed their foreheads to the ground. Of course, the Egyptians who had announced my father were also bowing. And the women and children of our camp . . . everyone was bowing low to the ground. Oh, how I wished I were wearing a fancy tunic. Instead, I had my brown frock that was covered in dust from the journey. And I wished that I had not been in the middle of our caravan, so far from the front. And I wished to stay upright so that I could see over all the heads in front of me and see my father! *See* my father! Most of all, I wished to run to him. But of course, I could do no such thing. I bowed and breathed. *Yhhhh. Whhhh. Just a little longer*, I told myself.

And then, finally, just before I thought I would die from waiting, several blasts came from a horn, and the boys began playing a drumroll. A curtain was pulled back from a chariot, and a sandaled foot stepped from the platform onto a rug that was placed just beneath his foot. In a moment, he was standing on that rug, and I could see the beautiful, confident man that my mother loved. His face was clean-shaven, something I had never seen before, and he was dressed more finely than Mother—or I or anyone—ever could have imagined. He had a golden crown on his head that sparkled with jewels and a bejeweled crown that wrapped around his neck and descended down his chest—which was also without hair—toward his short, black tunic. Over all of that, he wore a robe that was striped blue and white from shoulder to ankle.

I thought of my grandmother, Leah. Oh, how she would have admired the weaving! And I thought of my mother. Would she have been thrilled to reunite with this handsome, regal man? Or would the sight of something like the coat that she'd seen covered in blood bring her to tears and hiding within herself? I wished either of those matriarchs had been with me in that moment. Both of them, really, but even one would have brought comfort. Instead, I gazed at my father not knowing what to think.

My grandfather rose from his knees to his feet at the front of the line, and that gave us all permission to do so. As I stood, I saw him walk toward my father and embrace him. The two of them fell on each other's necks and cried. Tears were covering my face as well, and my feet were carrying me to join the embrace. I wasn't giving it any thought. If I had, I never would have walked toward the front of the line, toward the vizier of Egypt, or even just toward my grandfather at the front of the line. But I was almost floating in that direction, drawn to the display of love and relief that I felt so deeply. I only noticed that I was doing it when what felt like a dream come true shifted into the feeling of a nightmare. My father was returning to his chariot. The curtain was being closed behind him.

I ran toward him. I pushed past women and children and bumped into uncles and called out, "Wait, wait!" as I went. But I didn't get far. Shimon grabbed me tightly around my arm and pulled me to Asher. I tried to break free of his grasp, but I wasn't strong enough. Even if I had been, he had two of his sons by his side to catch me.

"What kind of a father are you that you don't control your daughter?" Shimon asked Asher. I tried to break away from Shimon's grip, but I couldn't. His sons sneered at me as he handed me to Asher. Then Asher held my wrist—not as harshly as Shimon had, but firmly.

"Father," I whimpered. Asher saw that I was gazing after the departing vizier when I uttered that word, not addressing him. He looked at me, then the chariot, and then his face went white.

"Serrah," Asher whispered.

I heard my mother's voice in my ears: *Your father is Joseph, but don't tell Asher.* I hung my head. He released his grip on me, and I shuffled back to the women with the sounds of Shimon guffawing behind me.

Soon after, Benno came to find me. He simply walked beside me. The spring in my step was gone. When I started lagging too much, he gently took my hand, and I walked at his pace. *But why? For what?*

"You'll see him in Egypt," Benno finally said. Would I, though? I didn't get to see him now—didn't get for him to see me.

"I'll never see my father," I cried. "He'll never see me."

Benno let me cry, and we walked in silence again. When my tears dried, he said, "Maybe, Blue. Maybe you'll never see your father. Maybe he'll never see you. Maybe you're right. Maybe you're not."

I smiled. How many times had Grandmother Leah said those words to us? "Maybe you're right. Maybe you're not." Not about my father, of course, but about kittens and tents and crops and flocks and sweets and just about anything when we tried to convince her of why we should do things a certain way. *Maybe you're right. Maybe you're not.* Remembering that lightened my step a little bit.

"What is it that you hope will happen, Blue?" Benno asked.

"I wish I could see my father. I wish he'd hug me and say that he knew the dream he had of the white bird with the blue on its wing was a dream about a baby who would be me. I wish he would tell me he loved me, loved my mother. I wish he would look me in the eyes and be glad to be together."

"Okay," Benno said. "Those things didn't happen . . . yet. But you weren't even expecting to see him today at all. Even from afar. And yet, you did. Can it be that maybe something else unexpected will happen? Can it be that maybe you won't meet your father today, but that another time, you will?"

I nodded my head. Maybe he wasn't right. But maybe he was.

"I hope you won't be sad anymore," he said.

"I am still sad," I said. But after walking in silence a little more, I corrected myself. "I'm disappointed that we didn't meet today. But I can be other things too. I won't be only sad and disappointed." I smiled as the feeling of possibility washed over me. "I will also be hopeful and creative, and I will think of a way to meet him."

NAMES

NAMES

The names of the new places I lived in were Egypt and Goshen. That is, we settled in the land of Goshen, which was a part of Egypt that had grass for our sheep and room for our tents. As we put up our tents in the new land, many Egyptians visited us. They showed us where to find water and where to bake bread. They cooked stews and fed us. They tasted our stews and complimented us. Some words of theirs were similar to ours, and many were different, but because we all made an effort, we managed. We learned. They made our lives easier by accepting us into their midst and made their own lives richer at the same time.

While we were collectively receiving this welcome, I was personally being shunned. I was afraid that Asher wouldn't allow me in his camp after finding out that he wasn't my father, but he did. I still got shelter with Yonah and her children, and food, but nothing more. The brothers and sisters who had grown up not understanding why I slept in the grandmothers' tent became even more distant. The woman who had been forced to carry the title of my mother no longer put up a pretense.

Benno and Yekarah were wed. Grandfather threw a feast for our tribe and our neighbors. None of them spoke to me. Three times we had our celebrations under the full moon without one woman greeting me. Nobody sang along when I started a song, though they had always done so before. Everyone crowded together in a way that left me on a blanket on my own. When the fourth full moon came, I gave them what they wanted: my absence.

That night in the moonlight, I went to find Benno.

"I'm going to the palace," I said.

"Wonderful!" he responded. "I will saddle a donkey in the morning, and we will leave with the first light."

"I want to go by myself," I told him.

This was strange. He didn't even know how to respond.

"My mother went off and made her own life. I will too."

"But Blue," he said.

"No." I saw grief wash over him. "I'm going to my father," I said. "And he'll take me in. I know he will!" Benno didn't say that I might not be right. Surely, I was right.

"I can still take you there," he said. "We will go when you want and where you want. But you'll be protected. A woman alone crossing Egypt? How will you do it?" Benno sounded more and more like a man with everything he said. Little Benno was gone, and I missed him. It would be easier to miss him from farther away. He did not understand that the reason I'd gone to him that night was not to seek his help, but to part from him, and I couldn't bring myself to say it.

"The same way I crossed *to* Egypt. The same way you would if you accompanied me. I'll take a pack with food and drink. I'll follow the roads and ask the people I meet to point me to the palace."

"Blue," he tried again, "you are a beautiful woman. Any Egyptian man who saw you would take you to the harem for the pharaoh and profit handsomely."

"Then I'll be closer to my father," I answered.

"Shouldn't you be dancing with the women?" he asked. "I will meet you at your tent at first light, and we'll go together." I hugged him and thanked him and walked back to my tent, where I packed food and drink and a lantern in case clouds covered the full moon. But they didn't, and my path to the palace that night was well lit. Nobody knew I was going, and my journey was unimpeded. Would they even notice my absence in the morning? I did not know. I could only hope that they would call me a whore if they did, but I also hoped that they just would not come after me.

When I arrived at the walls, I found myself a dark corner to await daylight. I wouldn't steal into the palace at night like a thief. I would wash and prepare myself for an audience with someone more important than the pharaoh himself: my father. Of course, I didn't sleep at all that night, wondering what I would say to him in the morning. When morning came, I still wondered what I would say to him. I joined the line of people who had come from all over the world to ask for food so that I might ask for . . . for love, I guess. And all the while, I wondered what I would say.

My time was wasted, though, because I wasn't allowed to see him in the morning. Nor the following morning, nor the ones after that. Only the men were allowed in. With each change of the guards, I explained myself. "I am Joseph's daughter. I need to see my father." They didn't understand. Translators came, and I quickly learned how to say it in the Egyptian dialect myself. But it didn't help. Some passersby tossed coins at me, thinking I was a crazy beggar. I used those coins to buy myself a night of safety when I was mistaken for a harlot.

For seven days, I refused to leave. Then, finally, one of the guards came to me and took my arm. "Finally!" I said. "Finally!" But he did not start taking me to my father. Instead, he was pulling me in the other direction, away from my father. If I had waited for Benno to come with me, I could have gotten in by now. But I wanted to go by myself, just as my mother had, and I wanted to prove that I could do it, just as she had. I didn't need anyone to decide things for me, not even Benno. No. I would decide!

"I am not leaving!" I shouted. I resisted his pulling so much that a second guard needed to come and help him to drag me away. "I'm not leaving! I need to get in! For the love of Deenah, let me in!" I don't know why I said that. When I wondered about it later, I thought that maybe because my mother had told me that when she had been dragged away from the city of Shechem by her brothers, she had been so fierce, and I was in a similar situation. I don't know. I didn't think about it at the time, and I really can't say now. But I'm thankful to say that it worked. I was allowed in.

Not only that, but I was given water to wash my hands and face and feet. I did so, no longer thinking about what I might say to my father. I just walked into his chamber and without any thought began singing:

Praise Yah, praise Yah, my god and the god of my mothers.
Praise Yah, praise Yah, my god and the god of my fathers.

Grandmother Rebekah had taught me that song by singing it to me countless times. She said that Deborah had taught my father a similar one, and she liked thinking about Deborah and little Joseph and bringing us together in this way. It had been years since she'd last sung it to me, but that was what came out of my mouth and out of my heart when I walked toward my father.

Praise Yah, praise Yah, my god and the god of my mothers.
Praise Yah, praise Yah, my god and the god of my fathers.
God of my mother Sarah, god of my father Abraham,
God of my mother Rebekah, god of my father Isaac,
God of my mother Leah, god of my father, Jacob.

As I sang, I got closer to my father, and he to me. His eyes were wide, and his arms, outstretched. I do not know what I was like when I walked. I couldn't even feel myself walking. It was almost as if I, well, slid down a rainbow into his lap. And I say lap, because by the time I arrived, he was sitting on the floor and crying, holding me in his arms and whispering my mother's name.

Her name on his lips urged me to finish my song.

God of my mother Deenah, god of my father, Joseph.

This surprised him, and his surprise surprised me. I thought that when he saw me, he'd just known. But then I understood that he was thinking I was my mother. So, I held him tighter and extended my song a little bit.

I am the daughter of Deenah, who named me Blue.
Deenah is my mother, and my father is you.

I don't know how long we stayed in our embrace on the floor of the grand vizier's chamber in the palace, but I know that he took no more appointments that day, and by the evening, I was sitting beside my father at a table large enough for my whole clan but with just the two of us holding hands through our meal as his guard smiled at us from the corner.

"You look just like Deenah," he said. I smiled. I missed my mother so much. Here was someone else who missed her just as much as I did but who also saw her in me. I wished I had my mother and father together. I thought that if my mother had realized that my father was not only alive but that he was here in Egypt and that we would meet him and that they could have been reunited, she would have been happy. I thought that if she had been in Egypt to see her brutal brothers humbled before her beloved Joseph's power, she would not have fled our tribe. Regret and grief washed over me, and I had to compose myself so as not to lose out on my own joy at being with my father. I smiled when he said he saw her in me.

"She told me stories about you," I said.

My father nodded but said nothing for a long time. Then, he said again, "You look just like Deenah." He said it countless times that first evening and daily as our time together continued. "Did Leah ever tell you that? Or anyone else? You look so much like her. You look just like my memory of her."

"Grandmother Leah told me that I looked like her sister Rachel," I said. "And Grandfather thought so too. But once, not long ago, Grandmother called me by my mother's name. She must have seen the similarity," I said.

"Leah was always kind to me," my father said. "She was not my mother, but she was loving. And when her sons bothered me, she stopped them. She was kind to Deenah, too—to all the children. She must have been kind to you," he said. I assured him that she had been and relayed the message she'd told me about loving him. He was pleased. Once again, he told me how much I looked like my mother, and I came to understand things he did not say, things about the depth of his love for her. I even came to wonder whether, happy as he was to meet me, I might also be a painful reminder to him of things that had gone wrong and been lost.

I had grown up hearing of Joseph my whole life, but he was still adjusting to my existence. I could see it in his eyes every time we were together. He also still needed to attend to his duties as Zafenat Paaneakh, but every spare opportunity, he came to the chamber he'd given me so that we could get to know each other. He often found me there in my private garden, gazing at a flower or the sky, taking in the wonder of it all. Then we would talk until his guard Atsu reminded him for the third time that he must get back to his duties and that we could dine together in the evening.

We enjoyed feasts of such opulence as I never could have imagined, even before the years of famine. In all our dinners, I don't think I once had a meal that was the same. But, of course, as spectacular as sharing such a meal was, it paled in comparison to being able to share stories. After a couple of awkward evenings of speechlessness, floods of words were spoken between us.

My father told me he had two sons in Egypt, boys who were growing up as royalty. I told him about growing up with Benno and Geeborr. Mostly, we talked about my mother. I told him every single thing I could remember about her, and he did the same for me. My mother had never told me of the time when she and my father hadn't even lost teeth yet and they went to play a trick on their brothers out in the field. They'd hidden themselves amid a number of sheep and ducked down so they couldn't be seen. Then my mother had called out in a falsely high voice, "Look at me, everyone. I'm the most beautiful spotted sheep in this herd." To which my father had replied, also in a pretend, but much sheepier, voice, "No, I ammmmm. I ammmmm." After which, they both had to work so hard to stifle their laughter that they ended the joke and ran off before anyone spotted them and realized it was just them talking and not the sheep.

It was fun for me to hear about my mother when she was little. The thing my father told me the most often was that I was the moon. He would stare at me and shake his head in disbelief and wonder, and say, "It was you. You are the moon." It was because he'd had a dream long ago—when he was about my age—that the sun and moon and eleven stars would come to him and bow to him, asking for his help. The stars represented his brothers. Grandfather, who was clearly the sun, had thought that Rachel, my father's mother, was the moon, but she had died before my father had even had the dream.

It was this very dream that led to his brothers throwing him into a pit to die. "They tore my beautiful new coat off me and pushed me into the hole," Father said. "They had hurt me many times before, but I did not think they would kill me. But jealousy can cause a person to do terrible things," my father said, "and anger too," he added. "They were angry at me for not helping in the fields, even though I wanted to. My father said I was special and should learn different things. They were angry about that too. They were angry at me for telling them about my dreams, even though I just wanted to share with them. Of course, I was angry and scared in the pit, even when they pulled me out to make a profit by selling me to the Ishmaelites. But finally, years later, I understood that this was all part of Elohim's plan to bring me to Egypt for my rise to greatness. What I did not understand was who the moon was. The sun was my father, and the stars were obviously my brothers, but who was the moon?

"I thought Deenah must be the moon," my father told me. "Not at first, of course. But once I was here in Egypt and My God had taught me how to understand my dreams, I realized that she must be the moon. I also thought that in thirteen years, I would be in a position to help my tribe. Help them how? I did not know. I was curious, but I was more curious about the moon. She could not be my mother," he said, "because I knew my mother had died. So, I thought that the moon could only be Deenah . . . I hoped she was Deenah. I didn't even know that I could hope that the moon was you."

"Father," I said, "maybe Mother and I are both the moon. Or maybe the moon is still Mother. Grandmother Leah forbade her sons from going after her. But Mother would be glad to be found by you! And you are the ruler of Egypt! Perhaps you can send a search party? Or we could go together? We could bring Mother here." I felt ashamed that it had taken me so long to have this idea. I had been so preoccupied by everything wonderful and beautiful that I had only longed for my mother and hadn't thought to go and get her.

My father said he would ask Elohim. On my seventh day in the palace, he sent for me in the morning, rather than after he had finished his work for the day. "Blue," he said "I have dreamt. Last night I dreamt of an elephant. Her walk was strong and mighty. With her flapping ears and her wagging tail, she cooled herself and kept the flies away. She was comfortable."

"What does it mean?" I asked.

"Elohim has given me the meaning of this dream. The elephant is Deenah. She is strong and mighty and comfortable."

"And where is she?" I asked.

"I do not know."

"But you can find out," I said. "You can ask Yah, or you can send scouts. Or both." He shook his head no.

"I did not send scouts to My Father's tribe when I became vizier. My dream had already told me of what was to come. Elohim has shown me in this new dream that My Deenah has found comfort. I do not know whether that is in solitude or a husband or death. I do not wish to look for the answer to that question. My God has shown me that Deenah is comfortable. I am grateful."

My father and I did not see each other for the rest of that day, then we had a silent dinner that night. I wished Grandmother Leah were there, though she had not brought my mother back to me either. I was still grateful to have found my father, but the fact that he pronounced my mother more comfortable without me in her life had cut me badly. Even though I wished for her happiness, I could not help feeling both resentful of my father's words and sad that they might be true. I had been glad to be closer to my father, but this created a distance between us even while we sat at the same table. I felt alone.

I thought that perhaps it was time for me to go to Goshen, but Yekarah was Benno's wife, and I did not want to be another one. Asher would have a hard time finding someone else to agree to marry me now that it was known that I was the daughter of a whore and a woman who has shown that I will follow in her footsteps. I would like to be with the women and girls of my tribe, except they were shunning me. What was there for me in Goshen? What was there for me in the palace? Without Benno, without my mother, without my grandmothers to give me comfort and advice, I turned to my father for it. He made a surprising suggestion.

He said he could make arrangements for me to live in the pharaoh's harem. My father would give instructions that no man was to go to me, not even the pharaoh. No man would go to another man's woman, and my father made it clear that I was his property and under his protection. I would not be sold to the pharaoh or bound to a son of my grandfather's tribe. My father promised that I would be safe there and that we would still be able to visit one another.

I could be in a community of women again—not with my tribe, my grandmothers, mother, or auntie, but with new women. They did not yet love me, and they did not yet hate me. I thought of my mother taking charge of where she would live—sadly away from me, but a place of her choice. I thought of Grandmother Leah telling the men that they could not go after her. I thought of Auntie choosing to go with her sister. Now it was my turn to be a woman who took a risk, who made a choice. I agreed.

EVERY WOMAN

Every new woman coming into the harem went through a transformation. Kohenet, who was in charge of the harem, saw to that. For six months, we were kept mostly isolated so we wouldn't hear frightening stories from the other women who had already been to the pharaoh's chamber. While we were secluded, we had attendants whose job it was to prepare us. Of course, I wouldn't be going to the pharaoh, and Kohenet knew that as well, but I was still going through the rituals.

Every morning, I was brought a plate of fresh foods. The girl who brought them was kind enough to point to each one and say its name so that I could quickly learn the words for these foods in what would be my new language. It took me a while to discover that after eating, I could and should enjoy some time in the garden. This garden wasn't a place that was growing food, though, but flowers. It wasn't large since it was mine alone, but it contained countless multi-colored petals whose smoothness I delicately felt with my fingers.

When the sun began to set, a young girl would bring me a beautiful supper. It wasn't the same girl every evening like the morning girl was. Each time I received food, I pointed and asked for the name of that food. The evening girl stayed with me while I ate since it was her assignment to take me to stroll around in the harem courtyard afterward. I found that some of these girls were more willing to accept my offers to share the meal than others were. The ones who ate with me would come back more frequently, and they would teach me more words each time.

Despite how much personal attention I received and the proximity of all the young women, I was still lonelier than I had expected. Even though I was often alone with the flowers in my personal garden, I felt the sadness of loneliness more acutely when I was around others. The women who were already settled into the harem used that evening time to talk to each other, and I was still isolated and still only knew a few words—mostly for foods. Those women would stroll and chat, sometimes laughing together, and I couldn't do that. Whether I was with an attendant who I couldn't speak with, or by myself, I was alone. It was during those solitary strolls that I wondered whether I'd made the right choice.

It's not good for a person to be alone. Though I had every physical need handled for me and did not need to find food or shelter, it was still difficult. I felt compassion for the young version of my father who had been brought to Egypt and who had to learn everything new, just like I was needing to do. I developed more understanding of my mother, too, who must have felt alone in her feelings, even while she was surrounded by her tribe. I thought of the countless people who my father was selling food to during the famine. I was proud that he welcomed them to Egypt and gave them that chance at life. I was grateful for my chance at a new life, yet I had not expected it to be so hard, especially while I was being so pampered. How much harder it must have been for those who weren't. I was often dejected and questioning myself, even in the evenings, which were the most delightful times.

After our strolls, each woman went back to her own quarters. There, the ones being prepared for the pharaoh were treated by the oilers. Two women came in with fragrant oils. These women were always the same, but the oils were slightly different from week to week. They had a formula they were following. While some fragrances were more pleasing to me than others, each one was an adventure for the nose. And each oil was a luxury for the skin.

I was undressed and laid on a dark blanket on top of my sleeping mat. The women dipped their whole hands into the oil and then proceeded to rub it into every bit of my skin, from my feet to the top of my head and back again. They sang or hummed as they rubbed, and every night, I sailed into a state of bliss that had me sleeping before they'd even left.

The oiling was wonderful, but what was truly special was a visit from my father. The first time he came, I was overjoyed to see him! It was the first time the moon had been full since being in the harem. I thanked my father for his generosity in providing for me and told him I was receiving the most excellent care I could ever imagine—better, in fact, than I could even imagine. He said he was glad. I confessed to him that even though I was being treated well, I wasn't sure whether I had made the right decision to leave my tribe: I didn't speak the language, I wasn't able to mingle with the other women, and I was, even more so than previously, terribly lonely.

That night, my father told me a story. "When I was born," he said, "Elohim had a plan for me. I wasn't just the youngest son of a great man—I was to become an even greater man than he one day. I tried to tell My Father and My Brothers about this destiny, but they didn't understand or accept it. Sometimes it angered them. My Brothers even tried to alter what Elohim had set in motion by first throwing me into a pit to die and then, instead, selling me into slavery.

"Even with all their efforts, they couldn't interfere with what Elohim wanted for me. They had no way of knowing—even I had no way of knowing—that my destiny would still be fulfilled. Blue"—he looked deep into my eyes before carrying on—"My Daughter, daughter of Deenah, daughter of Rachel and Leah . . . Elohim will make you and your life whatever it is meant to be. Even if you need to spend some time being lonely. Even if you can't see now what will be later. Are you a dreamer?" he asked me.

I dreamt some nights, but I knew that wasn't what he meant. I shook my head no.

"My Son Menasse isn't a dreamer, either, but My Son Efraim is. Maybe you'll become a dreamer. Maybe you won't. It's for Elohim to decide. For now, you can take your pain of loneliness and give it to the moon."

We gazed up at the full moon together, and he began to hum the moon song. I joined him in humming one time through, and then we both sang to the moon together:

Sister, Mother, Daughter, and Friend,
You shine with love from beginning to end.
We give you our hopes, our dreams, and our pain,
You keep them safe, until we meet again.

"The moon will hold your pain until you meet again and until we meet again," he said. "All these years that I've been in Egypt, whenever I saw the full moon, I thought of My Auntie, My Grandmother, My Mother, and all the women of our tribe. Especially Deenah. But now, Blue, I also think of you, because now I know that you are the moon. Even when we don't appear to be together on the nights of the full moon, we are." His words gave me strength.

Slowly, I became more integrated with the other women. After the first six months in the harem, I was no longer isolated, and we had to interact. We were a small community, and we relied on each other. We cooked, cleaned, created, and cried. Some of the women were patient, open, and even curious about me. Through them, I became more fluent in their language and ways. Some of the women were resentful because I didn't go to the pharaoh and accused me of using the oil and the food for nothing and not deserving it. I became more fluent in their language and ways through those women too. I understood their resentments, as I would not have wanted to go to the pharaoh, either, even though I thought it would be better than being married against my will to one man for whom I would have to do everything. Still, I was glad to have been spared this by my father.

Eventually, I found a friend among the women. Habibti was one of the pharaoh's daughters who had been born in the harem. She had been hidden from him her whole life because her right nostril was squashed flat to her face and because below her nose, her top lip was permanently turned up, leaving one side of her mouth always open. She was her mother's first—and last—living baby, and her mother insisted on feeding and raising her despite this deformity. Habibti wasn't the only child in the harem born with a deformity, and those who lived were kept hidden from the pharaoh so he wouldn't know he had sired something so imperfect-looking. This protected not only the lives of the children but also the lives of the mothers and the Kohenet.

None of the other women wanted to be seen with Habibti. So, while we were shunned for different reasons, this common experience brought us together. Thanks to Habibti, I had someone to walk with in the warm breezes and someone to huddle with on stormy nights. I had someone to cook with and someone to eat with, someone to laugh with and someone to cry with. Though I did not love her the way that I loved Benno, I thought this might be what it was like to have a sister. We did not have the most fun, we did not have the deepest bond, but we always had each other and were always glad to have each other.

Sometimes in the mornings, Habibti would seek me out and tell me of colorful dreams she'd had the night before. Sometimes in the evenings, I'd share my pride with her about the new spice combination I had added to my olive oil for a delicious dip we would share with our bread. When she got her first blood, I celebrated her with henna and song, even though we both knew she would never be chosen for marriage or to become a mother. When it seemed clear that my first blood would never come, she celebrated my mastery of the language I had worked so long to learn.

Over the years, Habibti taught me how to ignore the sneers of others and appreciate what I saw as my faults. It wasn't just the privilege of not going to the pharaoh that distinguished me from the other women, or the time it took me to learn their language, but soon, keeping my youthful beauty was making me different. While the other women aged, I didn't seem to. My body was never misshapen by carrying a baby, but that couldn't be the reason for my continued youth since Habibti and others were childless but not ageless. This difference became most apparent as the women whom I had entered the harem with became mothers and grandmothers, while I did not. Even Habibti, who was also childless, still became bent and slow.

When this first became clear to me, I wondered earnestly whether the oilers, sleep, relaxation, and mild physical exertion was what kept me looking so young even as the years passed. But, of course, other women who received the same treatment eventually went on to bear children—or died trying—while I didn't. All the young women who surrounded me in those years developed wrinkles and slack skin. Some died. As relaxing and rejuvenating as the special treatments were, they could not be the reason.

The harem became divided into two groups. One group of women was amazed and awed by my unchanging appearance. The other group was angry and mistrusting and began to blame me for their own sagging skin and aching bones. What all the women had in common, though, was that they saw me as different. Whether I was to be appreciated or attacked for this difference was the question that most faced, but not Habibti, nor the Kohenet in charge of the women.

I believed that Kohenet saw me as neither awe- nor hate-worthy, just as extra work for her. She was the one who had to break up the occasional fight when women started yelling about me. She was the one who worked to keep the peace. And to Habibti, I was simply her friend. Even as her step slowed and her voice quieted, still her eyes always saw me as the friend she loved, no matter what I looked like. In truth, it was the same for me when I looked at her. She wasn't a woman with a flat nose and a hole in her mouth. I didn't view her as a new person when her ears started to struggle to hear the birdsong or when her back bent with the weight of age. She was simply my friend.

When Habibti died, Kohenet and her apprentice, Lomedet, and I were the only ones who buried her. If either of us had had children, they and their children would have been there. Though the other women I had entered the harem with reveled in their grandchildren, Habibti and I had none. I was the only one, then, to speak when she was buried. After saying parting, tearful words to Habibti, I apologized to Kohenet for the trouble I caused her. She laughed and waved me off. Since she never called me to go to the pharaoh and was busy overseeing everything at the harem, I didn't interact with her much, so her lightness surprised me.

"Blue," she said, addressing me by name, maybe for the first time, "I am an old woman. As are you, I believe, though nobody would know it by looking at you. You have been alive a long time and seen a lot in your years, I'm sure. I have too. I have been in this harem my whole life. I have heard the thoughts between the ears of every woman and child here and seen what's between their legs as well. I've learned that we're all more alike than different. We all have the same parts, even if they are organized in different ways. We all have differences, yes. Not aging is one of yours. If the women didn't fight about that, they would find something else to fight about. I am sure you haven't caused me any extra work at all."

Habibti's death gave me a lot of time to contemplate Kohenet's words and nobody to discuss them with. I missed my friend.

MY FATHER

When my father died, he left me with many gifts. Habibti had been the most recent loved one I had buried, but not the first. Every time someone special to me had died—my grandmothers, Geeborr, even Bilhah—I had felt sadness and loss. Of course, my sadness was profound when my father died, but with him, I experienced for the first time that death is not only a loss—it's a transformation.

In all the years that I'd been in the harem, my father had come to be with me under the full moon a number of times. I remember each visit, and though I won't recount them all, there are some that I will. There was my first full moon after we'd met, and there was the time he told me about how he used to race with my mother and how she always won. Next, there was the time he came because he couldn't sleep, and then, the time he told me of his first moon dance with Grandmother Rebekah and Auntie Deborah and the women and girls. He told me how he'd been so terribly disappointed to be separated from his father and brothers but also how warm he'd felt to be welcomed among the women. He told me about his sons, my brothers.

There was one time my father visited me when the moon was barely a sliver. It was one week after his personal guard, Atsu, had died. Atsu had been much more than a guard, I learned. He'd been my father's closest friend, his confidant, his beloved brother like no blood brother of his had actually been. My father had been left devastated by Atsu's death. He couldn't eat or sleep. He certainly couldn't work. And he couldn't find comfort. He had been telling the moon of his pain every night, even though it hadn't been full, or even close to full. He had been praying and breathing and begging for mercy. And one night, he'd been walking the palace grounds and decided to come find me.

"The moon isn't full," he said, "but then I remembered that you are the moon and that you're always here."

It was awkward to have my father crying in my room. He seemed to have a never-ending flow of tears, punctuated sometimes by hiccups and wiped away by his sleeve with golden thread. I was also not prepared for my parent or the ruler to be so vulnerable with me, but that was what I received that night and into the morning. My father told me what felt like every detail of his nearly lifelong relationship with Atsu: how they had laughed together and grown together and been there for one another from the first moment until the last. But now, my father's last moment had not yet arrived; and still, Atsu was gone.

I got to know my father that night in a way I had never even come close to on our other visits, in a way that few others ever saw him. Except Atsu, of course. It was plain how profound this loss was for Zafenat Paaneakh, as my father was known in Egypt, and for Joseph—for everything and everyone that my father was. Indeed, when he visited me on three more full moons over the years between Atsu's death and his own, his heavy grief was still notable.

On one of those visits, he told me that my grandfather, Israel, had died and that he'd be burying him in the Cave of Makhpelah to lie beside his parents and his first wife, Leah. My father still held sadness and disappointment, and perhaps even anger, that his own mother wasn't buried there. I noticed that only slightly, though, because upon hearing the news, I myself was then grieving the loss of my grandfather and all the years I'd been apart from my tribe. He was the last of the elders whom I had grown up with and the head of the tribe I'd been born into. He was the provider and the ruler, not of Egypt, but of everything I had once known. Though we had lived apart, I had never thought of him as absent. In my mind, he had always been a strong shepherd looking after his flocks of sheep and descendants.

My father told me that the pharaoh had arranged for the highest embalming and burial honors for my grandfather and would even allow for my father to bury Israel in the land of Israel, as he had sworn to do. "But"—my father hung his head—"I will need to come back. Only my brothers and I have been granted permission to leave. The women and children must stay behind, ensuring our return. My Pharaoh isn't ready to release me from his service. He never will be. I'm afraid that, like my father, the next time I go to my homeland will be in a coffin. But you, Blue"—he cupped my chin in his hand and looked at my face—"Daughter of Deenah, you will go back. My Auntie declared it even before you were born, and I have recently dreamt it, just last night. You will uplift the children of Israel and carry them back to our homeland on your wings."

I would?

He was right. His dreams were always right, even if they took a while to understand. He didn't give me the details of that one, nor did I ask. I was focused on the lines on his face. His makeup made him look younger than his years from afar, but staring at each other so closely, I could see the wrinkles that so many years of smiling and frowning had left behind. I wondered what my mother's face might have looked like if she, too, had had the opportunity to grow old with us. I wondered what my face might look like if I had the opportunity to grow old.

When my father went to revisit his homeland, I revisited many memories—happy ones and sad ones—of my youth among the Israelites, my tribe, my family. I'd become a different person since moving to Egypt. I wasn't sure how I felt about that, but I certainly was jolted into examining it when I heard the news about Grandfather. And I wondered: *What were Asher and Yonah doing? Did they ever think of me? Were they relieved that I was gone, or had they come to feel badly about the way they'd treated me when we'd first arrived in Egypt? Did they miss me? Surely my father had not told them where I was—did they believe me dead?* Only then did it occur to me to wonder whether they themselves were still alive after all this time. *Were Shirly and Mangeena the leaders of the song circles now? Would they harmonize with me if I were there?* And the most difficult thought: *Where was Benno? Did he still miss me, or had he forgotten all about me?* I had been so afraid of missing him that I'd blocked myself from doing it, not thinking I could bear it.

One of the gifts that my father's death gave me was a reunion with Benno.

After the pharaoh died, my father had a messenger come and fetch me. He'd never done that before. Since going to live in the harem, I'd never gone back to the palace; my father had always come to me. But that day, I was to go and meet my father in his chamber. I bathed and dressed in my fanciest robe and perfumes and makeup, then I followed my escort back to my father's private chamber. That is where and when and how I saw Benno again.

Benno saw me first and called out my name. His voice was that of an old man, but it carried the same love for me that it always had. We fell into each other's arms and wept and laughed.

"I missed the way you snort when you laugh," I said to him, only realizing that that was the case when I heard it again. "And I missed the smell of wool tunics and the sheep that provided the wool. I miss weaving with that wool—and with the women . . . singing and weaving and just sitting together." This all came back to me as I smelled the scents of my childhood on him.

"Blue"—his voice rose in question—"where have you been all these years, and why didn't you tell me? I was so upset when you left . . . like your mother . . . I've missed you too! I miss your voice and your smile and the playfulness we shared when we were younger. But how is it that you look exactly the same—not a day older than when I last saw you? My children have children, and you look like you could be one of them."

I laughed. Benno, a grandfather! And how did I look so young when he looked so old? I told him that I had wondered the same thing countless times and that I didn't know the answer to that question. I don't know whether he would have heard me even if I had told him because when I started to tell him about living with the women in the harem, he immediately interrupted me.

"You were in the harem? Like Hallel?" he asked. "And Sarah? Joseph sold you to the pharaoh?" He looked angrily toward his brother.

At that point, my father spoke up. "I did no such thing," he said and banged his scepter on the floor for emphasis. "I have ruled this land longer than My Pharaoh himself did. He kept nothing from me. But the same is not true of me. I kept My Daughter from him. She was safe in the harem: fed, clothed, cared for, adorned, and adored. I will not have you accuse me otherwise."

Benno bowed his head in apology and took my hand. As my father's anger cooled, I saw my brothers Menasse and Efraim for the first time. Their walk and clothing showed that they were high-ranking men of the palace, surely educated, wealthy fathers of many, though none of their children were present. The five of us sat at a circular table, and I was between Benno and Menasse, eating with one hand while the other one was securely in Benno's. We had an opulent, if mostly silent, meal. It was to be my father's last one, he explained. He would be entombed shortly so that he could accompany the pharaoh to the afterworld.

He asked us all to promise that after his death, when he was no longer overseeing the success of his brethren in Goshen, and when we went back to our homeland, we take his bones with us. He hadn't been allowed to leave his position before the pharaoh died, and Judah had sworn not to go without him, not to leave him again. Now, my father asked that we not leave him either, even in death. We all promised, but Menasse asked whether he really *must* be buried with the pharaoh, a question we all hoped my father would say no to. I was not ready to never see him again, and it seemed the others felt the same.

The pharaoh's vizier, even though he was also an Israelite, a father, a son, and a brother, had a duty. His status allowed him to choose *when* to take the poison that would take him to the afterlife, but not *if*. Efraim asked our father whether he was afraid.

"No," he replied easily. "Elohim is with me. I'm not afraid. Nor should any of you be. When we go back to our homeland, know that Elohim provides us with strength. It is always there for us."

We sat on my father's cushions in his grand quarters and breathed in each other and that which held all of us. *Yhhhh*. I felt the thousands of little fathers inside me mingling with the thousands of little mothers. *Whhhh*. I was ecstatic to have the thousands of little me's inside of my loved ones, no matter where they were or wherever they would go.

After the meal, he let all of us choose gifts, though I had already received the best gifts I could imagine: reuniting with Benno, meeting my younger brothers, and having known my father for so long. The only things I lacked were companionship now that Habibti had died, and the ability to age, which I'd seemingly lacked all along. My father could not give me either of those gifts. While my brothers and Benno chose special things, I didn't see anything I wanted to take with me. Benno encouraged me to choose something, anything, but I didn't know what to choose. After waiting long enough, my father proceeded with his plan for the evening. He showed us the way to his burial chamber so that we would know where to go to retrieve him.

We rose and followed him through a doorway. Lamps had already been lit so that we would be able to see. While the whole palace was filled with beauty and marvels—and it had been glorious to see my father's private chambers and to see that he was such an important and respected man with the pharaoh's favor—walking into his burial chamber was different. In there, the beauty wasn't just *for* him: it *was* him.

The first thing I noticed was the ceiling. It was painted the color of the night sky, and there was a large star shining brightly in the center. Surrounding that star was a circle of eleven other stars, a large sun, and a full moon. It was my father's dream. I stared at it until my neck hurt from tilting back my head so much. Then I lowered my eyes to the floor, which was a rainbow. Across the whole floor, front to back, right to left, there was a rainbow of vibrant colors for my father to walk on.

That wasn't all. The walls, with traditional Egyptian stories written on them, also had people carved into their stone. I walked to the one closest to me and reached out my hand to touch a person who was surely supposed to be me. For there I was, between my father and mother. To my father's other side were two boys. Above our heads was the moon with a white bird with blue on its wing flying by it. I looked at my father and smiled.

There, in his burial chamber, I knew what it was that I wanted. Not to take something but to be a part of something. I asked my father to let my name be written on the corners of his coffin. I did not know whether the scroll on which my grandfather had incorrectly recorded my name so long ago still existed, but I wanted that error rectified and permanently so. The chamber was beautiful beyond words, but it would stay here when we went back to the land of Israel. The coffin, however, would come with us. My father obliged with giddiness and wrote *Blue, daughter of Deenah and Joseph* on each corner of his coffin so that from every angle, and for all the ages, it would be known that he was my father and I was his daughter.

I parted with him for the last time that night. At least, I thought I had. But a few days later, a day that I would learn was the day he'd actually died, Joseph, son of Jacob, came to me in a dream. That was another of the gifts that his death had given me.

In the dream, my father was a golden goblet decorated with jewels, one in each color of the rainbow. I held that cup in my hand and submerged it in the river. Instantly, it was full of water, and in the dream I thought, *I have a goblet full of my father.* But then I realized that the water was flowing in and out of the goblet . . . my father was flowing in and out of the goblet. If I just removed the goblet, leaving all the water in the river, my father would be flowing everywhere always. But I didn't leave the water in the river. I filled the cup, and as I brought it to my lips, I heard my father's voice say, "Joyfully, you draw from the water of deliverance."

When I woke from that dream, I was surprised that there was no wet water in my mouth. But the word *water* was there. Over and over, the word came out of my mouth in song: *Water, water, water, water, joyful water everywhere!* That was my father now. No longer contained in—confined to—one goblet or one body, he was everywhere. We could never be apart.

CARRIED

Seven days after my father was carried out in a coffin before a cheering crowd of Egyptians, Benno came to the harem and made two requests of me.

First, he asked me to go back to my father's burial chamber with him: "A messenger came to me in Goshen the day after Joseph's funeral procession," he said. "He reported that Joseph had called out from his casket and begged for papyrus and ink. The messenger said that whether Zafenat Paaneakh was speaking from the next life or this one, he was afraid to disobey. I noticed he was also paid handsomely. Of course, I provided them at once, and he returned to complete the delivery. Blue," Benno said, "whatever it is that he wrote, let's go and retrieve it."

We knew the way, of course, as we'd just been there a few days before. I felt like we were children playing our games again, seeking and sneaking. I wondered whether we should bring Menasse and Efraim, but I was so glad to have an adventure with Benno that I didn't even suggest it. They would find out soon enough.

The chamber was guarded by the same man who had asked Benno to get the supplies. When we approached, they recognized each other. Whether that was why we were let in, or whether it was because it was still the mourning period, or whether for some other reason, I do not know. But the guard gave us no trouble. We entered and lit our lanterns. We found the scroll delicately bound with two golden ribbons and gently placed on a soft violet cloth, which we then used to wrap it to take with us.

Once we had my father's scroll, it was Benno who suggested that we find Menasse and Efraim, and I agreed. Our father wrote so that he could be remembered, or so that he could share what was important, or perhaps for another reason. It was too soon to know, as we hadn't yet read his words. But whatever the reason, it seemed right to share the knowledge with my brothers.

That day, I got to meet Menasse and Efraim's children and grandchildren. I held Efraim's little granddaughter in my arms as Benno began reading. Other than his voice, there was complete silence in the room while we listened with full attention to my father's stories of his life. When daylight turned to dusk, we paused for a meal, and Menasse had lamps lit for the reading to continue. Babies nodded off, and some mothers did too. Older children were given treats to keep their mouths busy so they could listen better. The cushions that had been used as seats became head pillows, but Benno kept reading.

When morning came and Benno had just read about the birth of Menasse and Efraim, we all agreed to take another small break. We watched the sunrise together—my brothers and Benno and I. Three old men, and an old woman who looked young enough to be betrothed, sat on a bench together in the palace garden, breathed in the colors of the flowers and the stillness of the air, and had a moment of quiet with our own thoughts. Then

Menasse said he'd like to take a turn with the reading, and Benno nodded. I would have liked to take a turn as well, but I was not yet an expert reader and would have slowed the story too much. As we headed back to hear more of my father's story, Benno wondered aloud where *The Scrolls of Deborah* were, saying he'd like to listen to them again and hear about when his father and his grandfather were young.

"I know where they are," I said. "Auntie . . . that is, Emunah . . . took them with her. They are with her and Tirzah. Or"—I paused for a moment and looked at Benno. Both Tirzah and Auntie were old enough to have been his mother. "Or," I said, "maybe with their daughters by now."

"I think we should copy our father's scrolls," Efraim said. "So that they cannot be easily lost."

"Deborah's scrolls aren't lost," I said. "I just told you that they are with Emunah."

"Yes," Efraim said, "but our father wrote those for her, and I wish I knew what stories were in there. Perhaps the daughters of Emunah will know, but I never will. Do you want the same for our father? Menasse and I both have sons who are skilled scribes. As soon as we finish the reading tonight, we should have them begin to make copies. Our father would like that very much, do you not think so, Blue?"

I did think he would like that very much, and I was glad there would be more copies, and I said as much. I just wanted them to know that Deborah's scrolls were not lost—they were sharing their stories with others.

When we finished hearing my father's stories, Benno made his second request of me. He asked me to go back to Goshen with him. Asher and Yonah had died, and so Benno invited me—requested me—to be a part of his tribe, his family. He promised to provide for me all the way back to our homeland and for the rest of our lives.

"I miss the wadis," he said, "and the rainy season, and even the dry season. I miss the way the sky meets the hills. The land here is wonderful, but we can go back home now. Come with me to Goshen, and we'll prepare for the journey together."

I didn't hesitate. Auntie Deborah and my father had both declared that I would help lift up the Israelites. Here was the chance for me to do so. I would help lead the children of Israel out of Egypt and back home. I could feel it in my body as plainly as I could feel my breath and my heartbeat that it was the right thing for me. My father had told me that Elohim—Yah—had a plan for me. When Benno asked me to return to our homeland with him, I felt what that plan was for the first time. This, too, must have been why I had not aged. I would be stronger and more capable for the journey. But I would need some time to leave the harem, not just leave Egypt. Though I had found no new close friend since Habibti, I wished to have my farewell with Kohenet and some of the kind women. The ones who would be glad that I was gone could learn later that I had left.

In the morning, a messenger from Benno arrived with a donkey and cart to carry my possessions, which, even though they felt like many, didn't even fill half the cart. I wasn't bringing pots or pans, a sleeping mat, or rugs or cushions. Even my loom would be replaced by one from my tribe, maybe one that Grandmother Leah's fingers had masterfully woven with. I could have taken more, but Benno had said he would provide for me, and I didn't doubt that for a moment. So, though the cart that carried my possessions was nearly empty, my heart was completely full.

Even before I arrived in Goshen, I was met on the road by Benno and a little girl who was missing her two bottom teeth and who was skipping ahead of him.

"She just couldn't wait to meet you," Benno explained. "And I was eager to see you too," he added with excitement. "Nina," Benno said, turning to address the girl whom I learned was one of his granddaughters, "this is Blue."

Nina's dark, tangled, bouncing hair and the giant smile she gave me made me think of my mother. By all reports, she'd been an energetic and enthusiastic little girl. And now, four generations later, here was someone who could be Deenah's great-granddaughter. She wasn't, though. Some women get to meet their great-granddaughters, but my mother was not one of those—except, with my first glimpse of Nina, it almost felt as if she got to.

Nina jumped up and down with excitement. "You're real?" she asked me. "I thought Grandfather was making up stories of playing with a girl when he was little so that I would believe he didn't mind playing with me." She slid her hand into mine. It was little but was already a hand with strong skin that had worked hard. She took a moment to spin the ivory ring around my finger, then she said, "Come on, Auntie! I'll show you my collections!" I ran with her, hand in hand, but for a moment, I looked back over my shoulder at Benno, whose face was covered in a big smile, maybe almost as big as mine.

Nina and I ran back to her home, where she showed me the stones she had collected and lined up according to their different shades, one slightly darker than the next and so on. Then she said, "Auntie, I can line them up by size, too, watch!"

I watched her put the smooth river rocks into a little pile in front of me and then take them out, one by one, each one smaller than the one she'd chosen before. Then she said that she has a doll who likes to play too. She took a little woolen doll out from under her cloak and then said, in what was supposed to be the doll's voice, "I will clap and cheer for whoever can count the stones first."

"I will, I will!" Nina replied in her regular voice. And then she counted the stones, all twenty-six of them. When she finished, she used the doll's voice again to say "Yay!" and clapped the doll's hands together.

"Now," said the doll, "I will clap even longer and cheer even louder for whoever can count the stones the fastest and"—she paused for dramatic effect—"also count a pretend stone after each real one."

I started counting the stones Nina had just counted, saying "One!" on the first stone, skipping the number two, then saying "Three!" when I got to the second stone. When I touched the third stone, I said "Five!"

Nina, who had been eying me winning at her trick, quickly blurted out "Fifty-one!" Then she immediately picked up the doll and made her hands clap and her voice cheer, this time having her doll specifically say, "Yay, Nina!"

Not wanting to risk the doll cheering for me, Nina then said, "I can do other fancy counting too. Watch me, Auntie." Then she counted by fives, sevens, and tens. This time, I was the one who clapped for Nina, though I'm sure the doll would have obliged had I not been there. Nina's eyes lit up with delight as I cheered for her and praised her counting.

Benno joined us just as I was hugging Nina and letting her twist my ring again. "She's a fun girl," I said to him. "I'm glad you still have someone to play with. I'd like to play with her again. In fact," I added, "I hope that she and I can spend some of the journey walking together and getting to know each other more and, of course, playing more."

"Blue," Benno said, "come and meet my wives and my children and my children's children. You know Nina, already. Maybe you'll find the rest of them to be just as wonderful." He hesitated for just one moment to add, "Yekarah is wonderful. She has been a strong wife for me and a wise mother for our children. She remembers you. And . . . she's not excited to have you back . . . especially because I told her you still look young. She does not. Please, be thoughtful around her."

Of course I would, and I assured him of that.

I followed Benno to a courtyard that was at the center of several brick houses, not unlike the ones we had at the harem. I had never thought of Benno or Asher or any of my brethren living in houses. When we'd first arrived in Goshen, our tents had been assembled the way they had been in Canaan. But over time, I guess they were set aside and replaced by these houses of people who didn't follow the weather or the flocks and could just live in one place.

Benno's daughters and their daughters served a great feast, accompanied by apologies that their cooking probably didn't match that of the harem. However, to my tongue, the foods I ate that night were far superior to the ones I'd grown to appreciate at the harem or even at the palace. When I tasted a cookie made of sesame and dates with carob in the center and a hint of salt, I burst into tears. "These are just like Grandmother Leah's cookies," I sobbed. "It is as if she's here feeding me. My grandmother, putting food in my mouth all these years later."

"She was my grandmother too," Yekarah reminded me. "I made those cookies a hundred times with my mother, who had made them one hundred times with hers." Yekarah, daughter of Ahuvah, daughter of Leah, had made the cookies my mouth had eaten as a girl. I had never made them with my mother, but I had helped Grandmother Leah do so at every feast, always sneaking in tastes as I stirred the sesame paste with the date honey.

"You are a dear woman," I said to Yekarah. "Benno is lucky to have you for a wife. Perhaps I should have married him after all. Then we could have been sisters and fed each other cookies. I did not think about that when I left. I was young and foolish then." My voice was light, but I truly did wonder whether I had been too hasty. I was glad to have lived in the harem, certainly glad to have known my father, and very glad to have not served anyone. But being back with my tribe showed me some of what I had missed.

"Well," Yekarah said, interrupting my thoughts, "you still look young. Perhaps you are still foolish too." She laughed, and I joined her. I had missed many years of that laughter, but I enjoyed it that day.

As soon as I finished eating, a parade of Benno's descendants came before me, kissing my hand, and telling me their names. Nina jumped the line and sat beside me and whispered each person's name to me before they said it themselves. Sometimes she'd add a little detail in her hushed tone, saying things like, "That's Maher. He thinks he can run faster than I can, but he can't!" or "That's Sayar. She's very patient at combing hair and won't just yank the knots out."

It was lovely to have little Nina by my side and wonderful to taste the flavors of my matriarchs' recipes and to see glimpses of their faces in their descendants. I relaxed inside the sounds of everyone around me speaking my mother's language, and I rejoiced while singing and dancing with women and girls whom I didn't know yet but who did know the songs and stories and ceremonies of my traditions. That night, I fell asleep beside Benno and Nina under the stars in the courtyard, surrounded by my tribe of strangers.

Soon, these strangers would become my traveling companions. Benno had sent his sons to spread the word among the children of Israel that we would gather that evening. This time, it would not be just Benno's tribe—everyone was invited, men, women, and children. The Israelites had prospered in Egypt. They were not—we were not—just the seventy souls who had left our land during the famine, but many, many more who were now ready to go and grow their own crops and raise their own flocks, and Benno was going to lead the way. The youngest son of Israel, but the oldest elder living, Benno would lead his people home.

When the sun made its descent from the heat of the day, Israelites began to gather in the square. I was overwhelmed by the number. They truly had been fruitful and had multiplied. My father had helped them prosper, just as he'd dreamt he would, just as he'd said he would. Benno stepped onto a table and addressed the others, opening with that very topic.

"Hebrews," he began, "our forefather Abraham came from the other side of the great river. Thus, he earned himself the title of Hebrew—Other. We, too, are called Hebrews in this land. Others. We came here as strangers. Thanks to my brother Joseph, we were welcomed, embraced, and sustained. The famine in our land has long been over. My father, Israel, has long been buried in his homeland. My brother Joseph is no longer bound by the pharaoh's obligations. He now lies in his coffin, awaiting his burial beside our father. At long last, we can return home."

Benno's tribe cheered for him. He was magnificent. He looked so much like Grandfather, his father. He was confident in his stance and clothed in his traditional tunic. His beard was long and white with wisdom. He was the leader of Israel, even if not the man Israel. I didn't feel like Grandmother Leah beside him. I still looked like the young woman who had come down to Egypt so long ago, but I tried to embody the authority and respect that she once held while I stepped up beside Benno and addressed the women.

"Women," I said, "daughters of Leah, Rachel, Zilpah, and Bilhah, in our homeland, these four foremothers raised sons to inherit the wealth of their father. Their sons are your sons now. They have an abundance of blessings awaiting them. I know that many of you do not remember the land from which we came, perhaps most of you were born here. There is work ahead of you to prepare for the journey, but the arrival will be worth your efforts."

Two young men yelled out from the crowd. "I am Yo-av," the first one announced.

"I am Li-av," said the second. Li-av continued, "Our grandfather, Judah, told us of the land of his birth, the land he and his brothers would inherit from his father, Jacob. Grandfather Judah described the beautiful hills and the grass for our sheep. He told us of the vast blue sky and the rush of the rains in the winter. We thought we were going to go there with him. He prepared us for the journey, but then he said we must wait until after Joseph's death, even though he knew it would be after his own. Now we are eager to go and claim our land and grow our tribe. We will have tents again and move with the seasons instead of being stuck in houses. We will have room to grow. Our wives are strong, our sons, wise, and our flocks, large thanks to Yah and Joseph.

"We have been counting the days of mourning for Joseph. We will be ready to leave when his mourning period finishes in seven days. We will honor Joseph's wish to return his bones to the land of Israel. We will take Grandfather Judah's bones as well. And we will take the bones of all the sons of Israel, all the heads of their tribes, for they are all dead except for Benjamin. We will listen to him."

"I am the head of my tribe, and I am not dead." This was spoken loudly by an old man who had his feet planted firmly on the ground and who had ten other, younger, men surrounding him, all in the same stubborn stance. I stared at the old man for a moment. His face was wrinkled, and his beard was long. He looked older than Benno, certainly angrier. Much angrier. His teeth were clenched, and his eyes burned with fury. I recognized him, his anger.

"Yareev?" I asked.

"You think you're so special because you're the daughter of the beloved Joseph," he sneered. "And through some trickery, you look the same as when I last saw you all those years ago when you danced and sang your way down to Egypt with glee to see *your* father while I coaxed *my* father's every step, begging him to let us go to Egypt so we would live. I looked every bit the pitiful, hungry little boy who was barely sustained by what was leftover once my older brothers finished the first morsels of food.

"My father, Shimon, would have rather died than be subservient to your father, but Shimon wouldn't disobey his own father. Now my father is gone and my older brothers too. I am the eldest of my tribe, and my sons will not disobey me. We came here to thrive, and we stay here to thrive. Show her," he ordered, and all the young women near him held up plump babies. This caused him to smile for a moment before he returned to his snarling announcement. "I would not follow the daughter of Joseph, or even his sons, or his favored little brother out of this land of plenty." Yareev spit on the ground to emphasize his hatred, and the men around him did the same before walking away, their families following behind them.

There was a lot of chatter in the group while Shimon's tribe walked away. Benno spoke loudly to bring the attention back to him and our task. "They will come around," Benno said to the Israelites. "But what will *you* do? I wish to go back to the land of my birth. The famine is over! We were there not long ago to bury our father in the Cave of Makhpelah. The date trees are so fruitful that the land flows with their honey. Our goats will have ample grazing ground, and we, their milk. We will dig our own wells and grow our own grapes. Before we lose our ways completely, we can go back."

"I've never been there," called out one voice.

"Neither have I," said another.

Before any further disruption could be made, Benno said, "That is why we must leave now. So that we can—*you* can—go to the land of your forefathers and inherit it."

"I remember it." This voice from the crowd also belonged to an old man. He wasn't stiff with stubbornness like Yareev, but his anger could be heard through his clenched teeth. "I was born there, too"—he paused and glared at me, then he finished his sentence with a sting—"Sister."

I gasped. Asher and Yonah had died, but I hadn't given thought to their children.

"I will go back to the land of my birth," Ishvi said, "but I will not follow *you* there. I will not follow you out of this land. Just like you did not follow me out of my mother's womb. You are a liar! My father took you in, my mother took you in, but they should have left you to be eaten by the wolves."

"They did not take me in!" I yelled. "I lived with my own mother and grandmothers. They shared their tent and their food and their ways with me. Yes, your father gave me his name and would have given me a dowry, but I saved him that expense, and the wealth stayed with you and your brothers."

"So, you admit, you are not one of my sisters." I was surprised by how much this old wound hurt. I hadn't paid it any attention in years, but now it boiled my blood. Before I could speak again, Benno wisely interjected.

"Ishvi, son of Asher, leader of his tribe, has also agreed that it is time to return home," said Benno. "We will leave when Joseph's mourning period ends. We have a week to pack and prepare. It is enough. Then we can be fruitful and multiply and grow our nation in the name of Israel in the land of Israel!"

"I will go," Ishvi confirmed. "But I will go when I decide that it's time. And when I do, I will not follow that whore!" His word was meant to hurt, but I smiled proudly at being compared to my mother—but only for a moment.

The first stone was a pebble that barely grazed my shoulder, but the next one was a rock the size of an egg that landed just beside my right foot. Looking into the crowd, I saw many angry faces. Some people were wandering off, including Yo-av and Li-av, but others were picking up more stones. Benno bravely put his arm around my shoulders and steered me away from the stubborn mob. We walked hastily out of the square, and by the time we looked back, we saw that there was a stone mound growing quickly behind us. Israelites were still bringing more to increase the border between us and them. Or was it between me and them?

"Benno," I said. "You should go back. Those stones are for me, not you. Maybe you'll be able to help them get back to the land of Israel without me, or at least you'll be safe among them here."

"And leave you to die alone? I won't."

"I won't die," I said. I hadn't died thus far, or even aged. I would make my way back to the palace; I would return to live at the harem. I would be safe and away from the Israelites, something they clearly wanted. What a stiff-necked people they were! They were alive thanks to my father feeding their forefathers. They had lived long enough to return to our homeland! Benno and I were ready to lead them there, but we couldn't force them.

Maybe we should have brought Menasse and Efraim. They were Egyptian elites and prepared to leave it all for their own inheritance. Maybe that would convince the others. I shared all these thoughts with Benno, urging him to go back and gather with his tribe and Yo-av and Li-av and anyone else prepared to leave. Even Ishvi—he can claim the credit for leading the way if he wishes.

"At least I will walk you to the palace this time," he said. "I won't let you go alone again." I took his hand in mine. It fit as comfortably as it always had, though it was calloused and wrinkled and a bit misshapen with age. I didn't mind. It held all the love that I remembered. I brought his hand to my lips to kiss it, but I gasped instead. Benno looked at me when I gasped, and then he did the same. He saw on my face what I saw on my hand: age.

The skin on my fingers was suddenly as creased as his was. My arm now looked leathery and had age spots and felt heavier and more difficult to lift than it had just moments before. My legs were suddenly tired, and my hips felt stiff. Was this why I had to slow my step so much to walk with Benno? Was this how it always felt for him to move his body?

"Blue, what's happening?" he asked. But I had no better answer than he did. In fact, for just a moment, I needed to work to remember who he was. Oh yes, Benno, my dear Benno. Youngest son of my grandparents Jacob and Rachel. My playmate. Look at us now, still holding hands! Still having adventures together! I smiled at him. Whatever was happening, I was glad that he was there with me.

"My feet hurt," I said. I looked down at them. They were still in soft sandals, but I could see my toes forgetting to bend as I took each step.

"Let's get you back to the harem," he said. I heard him as if he were whispering and moved my ear closer. He spoke up. "We're close already, look." I looked where he was pointing and could see the palace grounds, but the view wasn't as clear as it had been before. I saw mostly outlines without details, as if I were looking at it through a thick cloud. "The women there will know how to help you."

"Yes," I said. "They will. But who will help you? Who will help you lead our people back home? I am meant to do it, but I can't do it now." I could hardly walk the short distance in front of me. But the task was too much for one person. "After you take me to the harem, you must get Menasse and Efraim. I thought I was to lead our people home, but it seems . . . I am not."

I hoped the others would follow Benno and my brothers, but of course, I didn't know. And I didn't think about it much. I was consumed with the thought of putting one foot in front of the other without losing my balance. I was holding Benno's arm, not just his hand. By the time we reached the gate to the harem, he had his arm around my waist. He could not enter with me, of course. Already, there were women coming to take me in. I could see their bodies, but their faces were unclear this far away. Maybe when they got closer. The gate was open, but they could see that a woman as old and frail as I was would need help, so they helped.

Benno and I parted there with a final hug and very few words. "Oh, Benno," was all I could say. He knew me well. I know that he heard the love in my voice and all the nostalgia that hit me in that moment. I certainly heard it when he replied with "Oh, Blue." We stared into each other's eyes for just a few moments more. Then as he watched over me, I walked into the harem. And before any of the approaching women reached me, I walked with Yah.

WALKING

alking with Yah is difficult to explain but easy to experience. It is like the gentle peace you feel in a lush garden where there's beauty all around you and you know that you are a part of that beauty too. It's gentle, everlasting bliss and love. It's the Garden of Eddin. When you're there, you're not confined to limitations imposed by skin or judgment or thoughts. There is no *there*, really. It's nowhere and everywhere, no-when and every-when—which was part of what led to my confusion when I next found myself walking into the harem.

At first, I didn't know that time had passed. I just noticed that my body was back to the way that I was used to it being: smooth brown skin; thick, dark hair like my mother's; legs that were light to lift; and ears and eyes that easily detected the women who were about to greet me at the gate. I was wearing the tunic that I had worn when I first walked from the land of Israel to the kingdom of Egypt. The wool felt familiar against my skin even though I was readjusting to the skin itself.

Two women collected me from the entrance to the harem, each one taking one of my arms while they looked me up and down.

"An Israelite?" one asked me. I nodded. She shook her head and asked me how I had gotten separated from the other women. I didn't know how to answer this question, and while I was thinking of what to say next, she went on: "From now on, only go where you're told to go. We know that your people are selling their beauties in exchange for wealth from the pharaoh, and we understand your desire for the safety that might bring to your family, but we have ways of doing things here, and it will be easier for everyone if you follow them."

I didn't know these women or what they were talking about, but I let them escort me to a chamber like the one I'd first been given by my father. There was food and drink waiting for me, a courtyard, and a large basket of dates whose pits I was asked to extract. The women left me with instructions to stay there until my oilers said I could leave. I was more than happy to have the solitude and the opportunity to examine my thoughts while keeping my hands busy.

Thinking about my situation tied me in knots. *What was I doing there? How had I gotten there? Why was I back to my young self? Why hadn't the women recognized me, and I, them?* When the dates were pitted and nobody had yet come to me, I let myself sit in the courtyard without trying to find the answers. I appreciated the wide bright blue cloudless sky above me and the short new fresh green stems just peeking out of the earth, trying to reach that sky. Their green was beauty-full, life-full. Did they know they would one day grow even taller and even more color-full? I felt like one of them: something unknown and still growing. I breathed, taking them into myself and giving myself to them. *Yhhhh. Whhhh.* Since nobody came to interrupt me, I did that for long enough to let the breaths take me to my dreams.

Lying in the shade of the stone walls with my fingers delicately around a fresh stem, I let myself sink down, down, down into the ground. It was so solid, so supportive. The warm air that covered me like a blanket was also there to help me. I wasn't worried about the question of *what* I needed help with. I could feel the answer—whatever it was—already on the way. *Yhhhh. Whhhh.* It wasn't like being in the bliss of existing outside the confinement of my body that I had felt when I'd walked with Yah in Eddin, but it was enough that I felt the Oneness and my place in that. I was in my own body, but I felt calm, peaceful, and patient.

When I awoke, the sun was setting, and I still had not been visited by the oilers. My mind began to busy itself with thoughts once again: *Had Benno gotten Menasse and Efraim to help him? Were the Israelites ready to leave now? Ready for us to show them the way back home? Had my walk into the harem been a hallucination of myself aging, and was I now recovering from whatever had ailed me?*

Thankfully that night, two oilers came, and I was able to ask them some of these questions. However, they didn't know the answers. They didn't know much of anything, other than their task of preparing my skin with scented oils so that in a half a year I would be ready to be presented to the pharaoh—just like all the other new women. "But I'm not a new woman," I said, "and my father left orders that nobody was to seek me." They giggled but were curious enough to ask me about that.

"Who is your father?" one girl asked. "Only the pharaoh decides which women will go to him, and his decision is that all his wives will go. I don't know why you would be an exception."

"My father is . . . was," I corrected myself, "Zafenat Paaneakh." This clearly meant nothing to the oilers, even though I had used his Egyptian name. "He gave me a place to live among the women here in the harem. But I'm not for the pharaoh." I had already been through the oiling ritual long ago, so to prove that I wasn't new, I started to tell them some of the secret oil recipes and massage motions that were known only to oilers and the oiled.

"You best wait here," one of them said while they both stepped back. "You're not supposed to know the holy combinations. I don't know who told you, but Kohenet will be very upset to hear that a new girl speaks of these. You'll have to talk to her." With that, the women packed up their basket of fragrances and left me to myself once again.

It was three days before Kohenet entered my chamber. I wasn't surprised that I needed to wait, and though she had once kindly told me that I was not extra work for her because of being different, I was glad that she did not feel she needed to rush to me. She oversaw all the workings in the harem: everyone's comings and goings, whose turn it was to go to the pharaoh, who would become oilers and who would train them, who would attend the mothers of the princes, who would watch the princes themselves, and so much more. I patiently and happily enjoyed my little garden while feeling comforted by her upcoming arrival at my chamber and our reunion.

I was mistaken. The reunion wasn't a happy one, and this wasn't the Kohenet whom I had known but rather the apprentice I had met only briefly, Lomedet. "Why are you here?" she asked. "What magic have you done to return? Seven women saw you grow old in front of their eyes and disappear. Now you're in my harem looking younger than I am, though we both know you are not. How did you do such a thing? And why? Who do you spy for?"

"I'm not a spy," I said. "I am here because this is my home. You know me, Lomedet. I am Blue, daughter of Zafenat Paaneakh."

"And I am Kohenet now," she said. "No longer in training. And not to be fooled."

"Of course not," I agreed. "Did I ever fool you? I am not here to fool you or to fool anyone, Kohenet." I made sure to correctly address her as Kohenet, even though that was new to me, hoping it would help to show her that I had no negative intentions.

Kohenet held me by one wrist and used the fingernails on her other hand to dig into the skin of my arm. This caused me to cry out and jump back. "You're real?" she asked. This was not the first time I'd been asked that by someone, and it was a question I struggled with myself. Was I a real person? That wasn't what she asked, but it was what I wondered. No other person lived for generations without aging. No other person walked with Yah. Was I something else? But I didn't voice these doubts to Kohenet. I merely said that I was real.

"There are legends about you, you know," she said. But I didn't know. "'Blue, the woman who never went to the pharaoh and never aged.' And you should look older than I am. I was just a young girl when I started to learn from Kohenet. I was only a young woman when I met you. I have aged and you haven't. Kohenet said that you didn't. But then it was said that you did, all at once. Now . . . now what? You disappeared and you're back?"

"I suppose I am," I said. "And not to fool anyone," I added quickly. "Please, Kohenet, you know that I have never harmed anyone. I never will."

"I will get you two new oilers," she said. "If you're still here in a half a year when it's time to go to the pharaoh, you'll have to take your turn. There is no more Zafenat Paaneakh to protect you. Do not tell these oilers any of the things you know," Kohenet cautioned. "Your privilege sparked uproars before, and I won't have it. For now, the others in the harem will know only what they see: yet another Israelite woman who's been sold as a wife for the pharaoh, a beauty who might produce the heir to the throne instead of their son. This will create enough problems; we don't need more."

Kohenet paused for a long while, looking me up and down. "No," she finally said, "you never harmed anyone. But you're different from the other women—never showing your age, then disappearing. Who knows what else you might do?" When Kohenet finished her instructions, she rose to leave. I wanted to ask her so many things but didn't have time to ask more than one question before she was outside.

"How long has it been since my father died?" I asked.

She paused long enough to grant me an answer. "The Kohenet whom I learned from died seven years into this new pharaoh's reign, and then it became my role. The first babies born here under my care are over twenty years old now." When I heard that, I understood her surprise. Not only had I not aged, but I had also been gone for nearly thirty years.

OILERS

I n addition to oilers, Kohenet had sent Kesher to me to answer the many questions she was sure that I had. Kesher was an Israelite woman who had been sold to the harem to help get money for her family. When she came to me, she was very, very pregnant with a son of the pharaoh. She was tired and grateful to lie on my bed and rest her body and eyes. I started by telling her about the people I had loved, the ones who had been most important to me.

"Benno," I said, "usually known as Benjamin, youngest son of Israel, was my playmate when we were children. And recently . . . that is, just before I left . . . I thought . . . that is, we thought, that we were going to take the Israelites back to the land of Israel. Menasse and Efraim are my younger brothers. I hardly knew them, but I suppose as my brothers, I loved them. I am the daughter of Joseph, and they, the sons of Joseph who was second in command in Egypt, though he went by the name Zafenat Paaneakh. Do you know that name?" I asked her.

"Oh, of course," she said. "You can't go a day without hearing the name Joseph among the Israelites. "If Joseph were here, if

Joseph were here, if Joseph were here . . ." Everyone has their own ending to that sentence. "If Joseph were here, our food wouldn't be rationed. If Joseph were here, we wouldn't have to be bricklayers. If Joseph were here, the pharaoh wouldn't be taxing all our sheep. If Joseph were here, we would have to beg from him. If Joseph were here, he'd be so big-headed his body would fall over . . . Yes, I know the name *Joseph*."

If Joseph were here, I thought wistfully, *I wouldn't have to go to the pharaoh.*

Kesher had already been, of course. "It's not as bad as I feared," she said. "And it was over pretty quickly. Of course, I won't have to go again for a while," she patted her belly. "And I get to live here in the harem. I miss my mother and sisters, but I do live in the palace, which is lovely." Kesher paused before continuing. Then she sat up and looked at me. "Did you say that Menasse and Efraim were your *younger* brothers? And Benjamin, head of the tribe of Benjamin, son of Israel, was your *playmate?*" I nodded.

Kesher was silent for a while as she focused on me. My body looked like youth, but my words sounded like age. Then she closed her eyes again, and it was as if I had just told her that I used to have three heads or could breathe underwater. Was it different? Yes. Could it take some getting used to? Yes. But she was accepting of who I am and what I told her.

"Well, Benjamin," she said, "died on the same day that I lost my first milk tooth. I thought the gathering was to celebrate me. My brother quickly told me I was wrong. We are not from the tribe of Benjamin, I'm from the tribe of Judah, but all of us got together as one and mourned for Benjamin. He was the last of a generation, of an era. There were still some Israelites alive who were a few years older since he'd been born in Jacob's old age, but Benjamin was the last of the sons of Jacob, so his death was a milestone for all of us."

Oh Benno, I thought. I understood that some time had passed. He'd been an old man when I'd last seen him, and somewhere deep inside myself, I knew that he must have died. But I didn't want it to be true. Hearing Kesher speak the words made it final. How I wished he were with me. How I wished we could be young together forever. It saddened me that he had not made it back to our homeland, but I was more than a little relieved that he had died from old age, not stoning.

"And the sons of Joseph, I've heard of them, of course, because there are tribes who bear their names. But I never met either one. I'm not sure if I met any of their daughters. But I hear that they don't mingle much. Their tribes came to live in Goshen after Joseph died, and I heard it was a big change for them. I can see why, now that I've been to the palace. To go from living here to living in Goshen *would* be a big change. They were really your *younger* brothers?" she asked.

Kohenet had asked me not to tell the oilers, and Kesher was not an oiler. I knew that Kohenet didn't want to have to manage disruption in the harem, so I asked Kesher to not tell anyone.

"Who would I tell?" she asked. "The Egyptian women have already bonded over being similar to each other, and I'm too different. I didn't know why I couldn't both keep my traditions and befriend them. One woman tried to explain it to me when she heard me thank Yah for my food. 'People are seeing the real you,' she said. 'Think on that for a while,' she said, 'because if

I was anything like you, I would never want people to know the true me.'

"The other Israelite women must have gotten similar advice. They are pretending so hard to be Egyptian that they don't want a thing to do with me. One was considerate enough to tell me that if I knew what was good for me, I would do the same. None have spoken to me since. Whether it's because I was the newest one or because I'm not pretending, I don't know. Of course," she went on, "I don't know if I'm still the newest one. You know we're all kept separated for the first half a year until we can meet the pharaoh's standards. But now, I have been out and ignored for almost nine months. So, your secret is safe with me," she said. "What *is* your secret?"

"I suppose the secret that Kohenet doesn't want me to share is that I've been here before, in the harem. And that I'm older than I look, and that I'm . . . different." Kesher said she understood how different could cause disagreement, which could then make Kohenet's job harder.

When I was with Kesher, I felt comfortable, proud even, to be myself. Even if I was possibly the only person in the world to walk with Yah. Even if I was the only person in the world to not show my age. Even if I sometimes questioned whether or not I was real, Kesher never did.

"Who else did you know?" she asked. Over the next few months, while I prepared to go to the pharaoh and Kesher nursed her newborn son, Hur, Kohenet overlooked the isolation rule. So, Kesher and I were able to be in my private chamber and garden all the time, except for when the oilers came. One time while Hur was sleeping, I told her I'd known Yonah and Asher's son Ishvi, but Kesher didn't know him. That reminded me to tell her that I was known in Israel as Serrah, daughter of Asher, even though Joseph was my father. I told her about singing with Mangeena and Shirly. She didn't know either of them, but she did remember songs that begin with these words: *This is a song of Mangeena and Shirly.*

Kesher knew of Yo-av and Li-av because they were from the tribe of Judah, like she was. They were talked about often as the two rebels who had gathered seventy Israelites and gone to Israel even though the majority wouldn't join them. Like with Joseph, people talked about Yo-av and Li-av a lot. Some said they were crazy and dead. Others said they were brave and reclaiming their blessing.

"Did they take Joseph's bones with them?" I asked. Kesher didn't know.

Nina was another Israelite whom I had only met once, but I had so enjoyed our time together. When I told Kesher about this young granddaughter of Benjamin's, her face lit up.

"I know Nina!" she said. "She's always talking about numbers and noticing patterns. But she's fun to be with if you don't mind numbers and patterns. There were many times that she took us younger girls with her to walk through the squares and show us patterns in flowers and food. I learned a lot from her. She's made some exceptional cushion coverings with her embroidered patterns. Really, I haven't seen anything quite as beautiful as her patterned handiwork—even here in the palace."

In addition to telling me about the few people I knew, Kesher told me about her family and friends, even about her family's flocks of sheep, though they were dwindling as the pharaoh took more and more. She told me her past and her hopes, her favorite fruits and her biggest fears. And of course, I did the same. We sang songs that were familiar to both of us and learned new ones and sang those too. It was a rare and special time for both of us when we were free of any obligations—her because she had a newborn, me because I was in my preparation period.

I was grateful to Kohenet for granting us that gift, and I told her so when she visited me again six months after the first time. She was there to check me from head to toe to make sure I was to the pharaoh's specifications. "When was your last blood?" she asked me.

"Never," I said. My gratitude disappeared, and my shame replaced it. I had never gotten my woman's blood. This surprised her, but she shook it off quickly.

"Not every woman bleeds before she goes to the bed," Kohenet said. "The pharaoh will still accept you. In three days' time, you will bathe in the pool, that is, the quiet section of the Nile that has been made private for the harem women. I assume you know it?" She didn't pause for my answer. "You may take an attendant. You will choose Kesher?" This time she waited for confirmation. I hadn't thought about it, but yes, of course I would want Kesher with me.

For the three days before my bath, I breathed Yah into me and gave myself back each day. Kesher and I had been doing this under each full moon, usually after singing and dancing. We would lie down next to peaceful little Hur and breathe and be. The moon wasn't full as I prepared for my bathing day, but my worries were. Remembering to feel myself as a part of Yah helped, as did Kesher.

She told me over and over that it wouldn't be as bad as I thought. "You are like a plate of delicacies to him," she said. "When he's hungry, he summons food. He wants to be satisfied and to enjoy himself. When he wants to sire a prince, he summons a woman. You are a woman. He will be satisfied and enjoy himself. Whether a woman or a fruit or anything else, you are just there to please the pharaoh, and when he's done, he'll send you back here. Yes, it might hurt—it will probably hurt—but it won't be as bad as you think. Then you will return here and wait and see if you are carrying a prince."

Kesher's words soothed me while her hands bathed me. I enjoyed the feeling of the water. And though it was still just the two of us, for there were so many reeds surrounding the river-pool that we had a lot of privacy, it was nice and exciting to be out of solitude for the first time. It was nice and exciting to be dressed in royal robes and fancy jewelry. And it was very nice and exciting to walk through the palace, where I had been before, but long ago and not often enough. And when I went to pharaoh, it was neither nice nor exciting, but it was not as bad as I'd feared. I could even imagine that if that attention had been given to me by someone I felt safe with, I might enjoy it.

When I returned to the harem, as with everything else, I shared that with Kesher. She hoped I was carrying a baby to grow up with Hur. I wasn't, but it turned out that someone else was.

BATHING

athing in the river with Kesher had helped to calm me so much before my visit with the pharaoh that I wanted to do the same for the next girl who would go. Kohenet told me that this was common and said I, like the others, was welcome to attend any of the girls who wished to have me there. She also knew that I'd told Kesher all about myself and had realized that asking me to keep my secret only from the oilers had been a mistake. Now, she instructed me to keep it from everyone. There were other older women in the harem who had known me before, but there was nothing Kohenet could do about that, and since they were older, they rarely mingled with the young women, so maybe they wouldn't notice. She made sure to tell me again, though, that she thought that keeping my secret was especially important now that I wasn't secluded.

What Kohenet didn't know was that I had a second secret. Even Kesher didn't know that secret yet, but I told her as soon as I myself knew. It was just a few days after my visit to the pharaoh, a few days spent walking the harem grounds and enjoying the colors of the flowers, the sounds of the children, and the smells of the ovens, and thinking about how glad I was that I hadn't gone to the pharaoh when I was in the harem the first time. I was enjoying being in the harem again and was released from the concern I'd been harboring for months about having to go to the pharaoh. My heart was clearer than it had been under the ceiling of fear. When the full moon came and Kesher and I celebrated under it, I felt a clear connection with Yah and a knowing of what my purpose was. I was there, once again, to help the Israelites get back to the land of Israel.

Even while I questioned my worthiness for such an enormous task—especially after I had already failed once—Kesher didn't. Like everything else I had ever told her, she accepted it as a part of me. Kesher shared my chamber by that time, even though she and Hur occasionally went to hers, so I felt that I must be providing her with a feeling of acceptance as well. I was pleased. While I was going to face whatever lay ahead, I would have Kesher in my corner. I didn't know how I would convince anyone else to go or to follow a woman. I didn't know if I would lead them to my birthland alone, now, soon, or in a long time. I didn't know many things, but I knew what I was there for. I trusted that I would know more about guiding the Israelites to Israel when the time was right. In the meantime, I looked forward to helping guide my first young woman through her bathing ritual.

Her name was Suf, and she had lived in the harem her whole life, for she was one of the pharaoh's daughters. The pharaoh always had men searching for beautiful women for him, so this was how my foremother Sarah and her daughter Hallel had briefly spent time in the harem as well as how Kesher and the other Israelites had arrived. All throughout the land of Egypt, if a woman was beautiful to look upon, then the pharaoh wanted her. Suf's mother had been one of those women.

Suf had entered womanhood and her oiling time while I had been secluded, so we had not met each other. Her mother had died when she'd been in solitude (except for the oilers), so her mother could not accompany her to bathe. Suf was very sad and very nervous. Most of her former playmates were also in their preparation time, though some had already gone. She was scared by the reports she'd heard from them and did not want to choose any of those girls to bathe her. Kohenet suggested me, and Suf agreed.

We walked hand in hand to the river and sat on a bench by its edge for a long time before going in. I told her about the beauty in the palace: the sculptures, the tapestries, the fragrances. I told her that I had been scared, too, but that it had not been as bad as I'd feared. "The other girls said it hurt," she said. "They say it's bad. Are you saying it's not bad?" I could hear a mix of hope and doubt in her voice. I wanted to comfort her, but not by lying.

"It's not as bad as I'd feared," I said. After which, we entered the river and stood quietly together with just our toes in the water for a long time.

As a child, Suf had seen the older girls go there for their bathing day before being presented to Pharaoh. It was a little inlet with calm water and a narrow passage that brought the river to us in a stream too shallow and too narrow for a hippopotamus. There were no large fish, either, so there was no appeal for crocodiles to enter our pool. It was safe and secluded enough that when I had first lived in the harem, I'd often gone to the pool on nights of the full moon to float on my back and sing without fear of either beasts or men.

There wasn't much shade, only a few trees with a bench beneath. When the hottest part of the day began, I told Suf it was time to fully enter the water. I held her hand and hummed, and she hummed with me as we took our first steps into the pool. I gently poured water over her shoulders and combed her hair, letting the stray strands drop into the pool. I praised her strength and told her of the pride she would feel if she bore a prince who would become the next pharaoh. I told her that Ra, who came to this world to rule from the palace, could be her son.

I could hear in my own voice that this was not convincing, though. It was true that I did not think Ra to be a god, so I did not hold much respect for the idea. Regardless, I felt her body stiffen, so I returned to humming and gently pouring water over her shoulders. Then I held both her hands and told her it was time to submerge herself in the water. I assured her that I would not let go of her while she did. She paused for a moment, but the inevitable would come soon, so she plunged herself under. As promised, I did not let go.

Suf was under the water longer than I'd expected, but I saw bubbles rising above her mouth and didn't worry. Finally, she stood. She let go of my hands and wiped the water from her face. Then she wiped her eyes again. And again. After a third time, she pointed and said, "Blue! Look!" Following her gaze, I saw a small black basket wedged in the reeds. It hadn't been there just moments before when Suf was going under the water. But her eyes had been closed then, and mine had been on her, so we wouldn't have seen the basket appear. As we approached it, we could smell the tar that kept it afloat. Suf got there before me, and when she did, her hands went right to her mouth—but only briefly, for a moment later, she reached them into the basket and pulled out a baby.

"Tefnut has saved me!" she cried out. "Tefnut has sent me a baby! I have a son! The pharaoh has a son from me! This boy . . . is my boy! I don't need to go to the king! I can stay here with my boy. I shall call him Moses, meaning boy, for it was through a boy that I was spared: an ordinary boy, not a boy of Ra, but a boy from the river just for me."

I couldn't convince Suf to let me hold the baby, but I did bend down to kiss him and saw that he was circumcised. He was a Hebrew baby, an Israelite, but was not a newborn. He had been saved, maybe by Tefnut, but surely by Yah and someone wise and skilled enough to build a waterproof basket and put it close to the women's bathing pool so he would be seen and hopefully rescued. I looked around but could not see the mother. Then I stopped looking. I stood very still. Then slowly, I opened my arms and looked up to the sky, singing softly:

Thank you, Yah, for this baby.
Surely if he is to live, he shall need more than a home.
He'll need milk from a woman's body, and Suf has none.

Then I looked toward where the basket was still stuck in the reeds, though without the baby. Nearby, I saw a girl squatting behind the tall grass and watching baby Moses. I continued my song, but now in my first tongue. *"His mother will be safe here,"* I sang, *"and his sister too."*

Later, I learned that the girl's name was Yam, meaning sea. She told me her mother had named her that because her love for her daughter was as deep and wide as the sea—which was even deeper and wider than the Nile. That was later, though. With Suf, I just saw Yam by the river raising her hands to cover her mouth so that she would not squeal with the shock of having heard her own language come out of my mouth. I nodded to her, and she ducked into the reeds and then out the other end, where she immediately began running. In the time that it took for Suf to take Moses from the pool to the shore and have all the women have turns to ooh and aah over him, Yam had returned with her mother and a toddler in tow.

When I saw them coming, I was shocked and deeply saddened. There had been nothing noteworthy about how Yam looked when I'd first seen her, but when she stood next to her mother, I noticed how much care had been put into her appearance. Yam's clothes were plain but clean. Her hair was neat and plaited. She didn't look terribly out of place at the harem, and nobody would have given her a second glance since anyone who did see her would have assumed she was one of the girls that worked there. I learned later that giving this impression had been her mother's plan and hope.

When I saw Yam standing with her mother and brother, I saw a bigger picture than I had first seen. I now saw a little boy wearing scraps, whose bottom attracted flies, and a mother whose clothes were clean but had been torn and mended many times and now hung on a body much smaller than the one that had originally worn them. Her face, too, showed the thinness of a woman who fed her children before herself.

I rose to walk toward them as Yam pointed at me and whispered into her mother's ear. Then she stayed back and held her little brother's hand while her mother approached me alone. When she was close enough, she bowed before me with her head on my feet. "Please, rise," I said to her. "Tell me your name."

"I am called Vida," the woman said. "I am Yohevid, wife of Amram."

I then spoke to her in our mother tongue: "You are Israelites?" She nodded.

"Which son of Israel do you come from?"

"I am from the tribe of Levi," Vida answered, "and so is my husband."

"Amram from the tribe of Levi." I repeated the name as I thought of my father's scrolls. I remembered him writing about this boy. I wondered, not for the first time, where those scrolls were. I paused to think about that for a moment but then asked Vida about the details my father had written: "Is this the same Amram who is both a shepherd and a scribe and who trained with Judah and has only a few fingers?"

Vida was clearly surprised that I knew this about her husband. "He is," she said, "but he has all his fingers, just some are stuck together. It has never stopped him from anything, nor does it stop our son, Aaron, who has the same hands." She nodded in the direction of her son and daughter who were still waiting a few paces behind, and he raised his hand to wave. I could see that his first and second finger moved as one, and so did his third and fourth. Then Vida boldly added her own question: "How do you know our language?"

"It is the only language I spoke until coming to the land of Egypt with the Israelites. At that time, I was known as Serrah, the daughter of Asher."

Now it was time for Vida to cover her mouth, though she succeeded only in muffling her surprise, not stopping it. Nor could she stop her words. "You're real?" she asked.

I had the thought that surely, I must be real because only a real person would need to endure such a question so many times, but I said nothing. Vida told me that there had been legends about a woman from the tribe of Israel who was called Serrah, daughter of Asher, and who had come to Egypt with the Israelites but had such magnificent beauty that she was taken to the harem to be pharaoh's wife, which was why she was never seen again.

Vida said they hadn't been sure whether to believe this story or not. It could simply have been a legend, but it was similar to the story of their matriarch Sarah and her daughter, Hallel, being taken to the harem, though neither of them had become wives in the end, and perhaps this Serrah hadn't either. Maybe there were just stories of Serrah to help the Israelite women feel that we came from beauties.

"But then," Vida said, "there were rumors that Serrah had come back and that she claimed she could lead us again to the land of Israel. The Benjaminites said we should listen and that she was not a daughter or Asher but of Joseph. The Shimonites said she was neither, but a witch who wanted to curse us. And among the Levites, it was said that none of it was right and all of it was rumors."

By the time Vida told me about her tribe, the Levites, the newest member of that tribe—Moses—began to cry. He had been the center of attention as Suf told everyone that Tefnut had provided her with a son. The women passed him from arms to arms, but he wanted his mother's arms and, more so, her milk. While Suf looked on, he drank happily from Vida's familiar bosom and then drifted into the contented sleep of a baby with a full belly.

Vida smiled at her son, then lifted her eyes to Suf and addressed her. "You have a beautiful son," she said. "It would be an honor to feed him. I have milk thanks to my son," she glanced toward Aaron, "and Aaron's sister, Yam, will make sure that your baby is watched and cared for." Yam had not yet filled the empty gap at the top of her mouth with new front teeth, but it was clear that she was an attentive caregiver. "We will treat him like the gift from the gods that he is," Vida said, "while using very little room ourselves. What is your son's name?" she asked Suf.

"His name is Moses."

"That is a perfect name," Vida said. Suf smiled and kissed the baby on his forehead, then walked away. That was how it was decided that Vida, wife of Amram and mother of Moses, Aaron, and Yam, would stay in the harem. I took them to my chamber and gave them food and drink. Kesher had just finished nursing Hur to sleep. Vida put Moses and Aaron down on one side of Hur and nursed her boys to sleep while Yam snuggled against the other side of Hur's warm body and fell asleep there. The children slept well that night on the softest bed they had known, and Kesher, Vida, and I talked until the sun rose.

LIFE

ife in Goshen was difficult, dangerous, and depressing. It
was overcrowded with Israelites, many of whom begrudged
their parents' choice to stay in Egypt after Joseph's death.
Vida told me that the new pharaoh had become afraid that the
Israelites would join forces with his enemies in a rebellion, so he'd
worked swiftly to weaken them. The Israelites' taxes went from
one sheep in ten to one in two, one barrel of wine in ten to one in
two, and from one in ten men working to build the structures of
Egypt to one in one—every one. This, Kesher added, was what
had led to her wedding the pharaoh. Her father would receive a
much bigger payment from him than from any Israelite man, and
though he had wanted to find a husband for her in the tribe, he
needed the pharaoh's money to sustain his family.

While the men were busy building cities, the women were left
to watch over the sheep . . . and the children . . . and the garden
and the mending and the water hauling and the planting and the
drying and the goats and the donkeys and the broken carts and
the baking and the boiling and the healing and the weeping and,
on rare occasions, the singing. The Egyptian overseers wouldn't

allow any large gatherings, but the women quietly moved their celebrations from under the full moon to the darkest nights of the new moon so they wouldn't attract attention.

All month, the women saved the sweetest foods they could gather, and on nights of the new moon, they made cookies for each other. Each one was shaped like an eye, and each one was delivered to neighbors under the cover of a dark sky.

Women went door-to-door greeting each other with kisses and hugs and the phrase, "This is an eye," when handing a cookie to another woman. Then the receiving woman would smile and confirm, "This is an eye."

Kesher and I admired the creativity of the women in finding a new way to celebrate together, but we were confused by this new tradition.

"It's meant to be confusing if you don't know what it is," Vida said, pleased that even we didn't understand what was going on. "We love the cookies because they're a treat that we wait for all month while we make sure that our children eat, even if we don't. And we love that the cookies have taken on the meaning of us watching over each other during this difficult time. The eye phrase, though, comes from the song that we used to sing under the full moon: *This is a day that Yah has made, so we will rejoice!* Even the most challenging days are made by Yah, though that's easy enough to forget. So, when we took each of the first sounds of the words in that song lyric and put them together, it came out sounding like *this is an eye!*"

Kesher and I nodded in appreciation. Even with the weight of only hearing about the troubles in Goshen, it was easy to feel sorrow and no joy. But today was also a day that Yah had made, and on this day, Yah had brought us Moses and Aaron and Yam and their mother, Vida, whom I had already shared my secret with about having come to Egypt long ago. Now, I shared my other secret with her: "I will lead the Israelites out of this oppression and back to our homeland," I said. Like Kesher, Vida did not question this, though her reasons may have been different.

"Good," Vida said, "because I haven't even told you the worst part yet." Kesher and I were surprised.

"Why do you think I would give my baby to a woman of the harem?" Vida asked. I had wondered why there was a baby floating in the reeds of the bathing pool when we'd first found him, but everything had moved so quickly afterward that my mind had been busy with other thoughts.

Vida continued: "Moses, as his new mother calls him, was born three months ago, and his birth almost cost us our lives, but not in the usual way. When my pains began, I kept working. We needed the sheep. Without them, we wouldn't have had enough milk or wool or meat—and even with the sheep we did have, we were barely getting by. Eventually, I sent Yam for the midwives, but Moses was a fast little baby, slid right out before I could get in from the fields. He was born among the sheep. When he let out his first little wail, they all turned their heads to look in his direction. They were used to lambs, but not babies.

"He's not my first baby, of course. I let myself rest on a patch of warm grass and used my arm to shade him while he heartily drank his first milk. When Yam returned with Shifra and Pu'a, the midwives, they couldn't find me in the house, so they came to look for me in the field. And even though we were there, it was hard to see us because we were lying down and sleeping silently.

I woke to the sound of them laughing. It took me a moment to remember where I was, and it took an explanation to help me understand the laughter.

"Pu'a told me that when Yam had found them, they'd just been returning from the house of the pharaoh—he'd been questioning them about why they weren't following his edict to kill all the boys born to the Israelites," Vida said. Kesher and I gasped, but Vida was surprised by our surprise.

"You didn't know?" Vida asked. She then told us that in addition to sending the men to make bricks, the pharaoh had commanded that any newborn boy should be killed upon the birthstool. "He hadn't succeeded in crushing our spirit with work," she continued, "so he had to ensure we couldn't grow and raise an army against him. And though Shifra and Pu'a had been defying that order for months, eventually, the pharaoh got word. When he asked them why, they said that Israelite women were like beasts, birthing their babies in the fields before the midwives could even arrive. And there I was, unknowingly doing exactly what they'd claimed.

"I knew Moses wasn't safe, of course," Vida continued. "The new law is that any Israelite baby boy must be thrown into the river." Kesher almost threw up when she heard this. Hur was sleeping peacefully within her arm's reach, but she likely felt as if his life were in imminent danger. I had known Hur since the moment he'd been born . . . had felt him kicking to get out even before that. I could not imagine that dear little boy—any child— being so hated that he would be killed at birth. I felt even more resolute in my decision that we Israelites must leave Egypt.

"Nobody that I know of has had it happen yet," Vida said, "though, of course, we're all afraid. I started making the basket soon after Moses was born. It took months. Yam helped me, but there were still so many things that needed doing that I ended up doing most of the weaving during the times that I should have been sleeping. And the tar needed to be put on far afield so the guards wouldn't smell it and see what was happening. I thanked Yah every day for giving me a baby who was quiet, unlike my first two had been."

We all felt that gratitude in silence. As we drifted off to sleep, the back of Vida's neck was right in front of me, so close that she could probably feel my sleepy breaths with every exhale. *What a soft-necked friend I have acquired*, I thought, for even after all she had been through, she had so much trust in me that she could even expose the back of her neck without anger or fear.

BABY

aby Moses wasn't the only baby brought to us by the river. Two months after Moses arrived, another bathing woman found a boy in a basket in the reeds. He was pulled out and passed around and admired. I wouldn't have known right away except that Kesher had been letting Hur play in the grass by the water, so she'd been there when the other women started making all the sounds of excitement. She came and told me and Vida at once.

Vida handed Moses to Kesher and ran down to the water. As soon as she got there, she was handed the baby; after all, Vida was dressed as a wet nurse. She immediately put the boy to her breast, but after just a quick glance at him, she lifted her eyes and scanned the shore and the reeds for someone who would have watched over the boy. *Surely there was a child*, she thought. Finally, she spotted a young girl and smiled and called out to her, "Ra'ayva! Ra'ayva! Come!" The little girl jumped up and ran right into Vida's arms.

"Oh, Ra'ayva," Vida said, "you did a wonderful job. I'm so proud of you!" Vida hugged her again. "Look," she said, "your brother is well." Ra'ayva beamed. By that time, Yam had also arrived and embraced Ra'ayva, picking her up and twirling her around, for Yam, even with her top teeth only starting to come in, was bigger and older than this little girl. "Here, take this," Vida said, handing Ra'ayva some walnuts from her satchel. "Go home and get your mother. Tell her the baby is safe and that she can come and nurse him herself." Vida gave Ra'ayva one more tight squeeze and said, "Hurry back, I'll see you soon."

Vida was almost jumping out of her skin with excitement, and Kesher and I were eager to hear the words that spilled from Vida's mouth: "I wasn't the only mother to make a basket, of course. Ra'ayon, Ra'ayva's mother, was actually the one who'd had the idea. Ra'ayon reminded us of the story of Noah and Naama, our foreparents who had built an ark to survive a flood. Though their ark wasn't for a baby, it was for all their family and animals to have a safe haven from the water. Noah and Naama used wood and covered their ark in tar, so Ra'ayon thought that we could use reeds and cover them in tar.

"Four of us used the reeds and the tar and prayer . . . so much prayer. Yam and Ra'ayva found this place," Vida said. "They'd told us months ago that there was a place where the reeds were abundant and the water, still. They told us about the pool where the Egyptian women bathed, so we knew this was the right place to put the baskets. But still, we prayed. We didn't know whether our babies would be taken in. For all we knew, the women would have thrown the babies into the river themselves."

Vida began sobbing. It was plain to see how scared she had been for her son's life and for the other babies' lives. Soon her sobs were joined by Ra'ayon's—she must not have been far, for

Ra'ayva had pulled her toward us sooner than we'd expected. With Vida and Ra'ayon clinging to each other and sobbing, the babies quickly joined in, and there was a cacophony of crying. Hur calmed as soon as he was attached to his mother's breast; Moses calmed as soon as he was attached to his mother's breast; and the newest baby, Betzalel, calmed as soon as he was attached to his mother's breast.

"His name is Betzalel," Ra'ayon said, "because he was born in the shadow of Elohim. Surely Elohim has gone elsewhere, perhaps not able to stand the sorrow in Goshen, and left only a shadow." Ra'ayon paused and looked at me and said, "You cannot imagine how bad it is. With all the words in the world, I could not tell you how sad and scary it is to be an Israelite." My heart broke for her and my kin, and I was sure that she was right.

Kesher told Ra'ayon that she could have her quarters. Kesher had hardly used them in months since she was almost always in mine. Kesher's quarters would be plenty of room for Ra'ayon and Betzalel and Ra'ayva. Walking there, we felt like a little parade. Kesher and I were leading the way with baby Hur; Vida and Ra'ayon followed, each with a baby in their arms; and Yam, Aaron, and Ra'ayva skipped along laughing and playing, sometimes behind us, sometimes beside.

In Kesher's quarters—that is, Ra'ayon's new quarters—the children played in the courtyard while Ra'ayon shared with us news just as sorrowful as Vida's. The first words were shared in a whisper. Her husband had been beaten to death when he'd refused to drown the baby. Ra'ayva hadn't seen because she was slipping away with the basket, and Ra'ayon wanted to help her husband, but all she could do was help their children. In the moment she had to dash back into the house, she took only what she could fit under her skirt, then she ran to the reeds, praying all the way.

"It was terrifying," Ra'ayon said, "but I will tell it as a story of triumph. I am strong! *We* are strong!" She then told us about another mother who had saved her baby. "When Shokeret had her baby, she lied to the inspector and said her son had died. And when the inspector came to check, she buried her baby son in the floor and had her older children sit on the loose dirt and cry. They didn't need to fake their fear of the inspector, and their cries masked any sound from their baby brother. Many other women started saying that their babies were daughters, whether they were or not, and when inspectors asked to check the babies, the mothers asked whether Isis would approve of the inspectors laying eyes on the genitals of girls who were not theirs. Shifra and Pu'a even started rumors that the Israelites are such a weak people that we are not even able to bear sons anymore."

I marveled that the brave midwives who had defied the pharaoh before were still saving babies now. I wondered whether I would have had such courage, then I laughed at myself for a moment. Looking around, I was surrounded by babies—I guess I did not need to wonder whether I would be as brave as the midwives. It was good that I felt such confidence, because it was only moments later that Kohenet came to Ra'ayon's new quarters. Her body filled the doorway, and her displeasure was clear. Her eyes and words were directed to me.

"What is going on here?" Kohenet asked. I told her. She stayed in the doorway, though her body softened a little. She oversaw the whole harem. In her position—to rise to her position—she had to have compassion for women and babies. This was what she had been taught by the Kohenet who had come before her. I knew this personally. But she was also responsible for running a smooth operation, and it was always in her best interest to avoid the pharaoh's wrath—which was often done by avoiding his attention.

Kohenet sighed. Her voice was quiet when she spoke. "I feel your sorrow," she said. "And I share it. But I cannot save all the Israelite women and children. The harem would fall to pieces." I was going to protest, but she wasn't finished. "These women and their children can stay," Kohenet looked at Vida and Ra'ayon, "but no more. It is not in my position or my ability to rescue all of them." Even though she'd said those of us in this room were safe, we were stiff with fear for the others. "I will do what I can," Kohenet went on, "so that baby boys who arrive here may stay. We will find a place for them, but do not expect me to do everything. And I will not oversee this, do you hear?" Still her eyes were on me.

"Yes," I said, "of course, Kohenet. Your tasks are many; you do not need another."

Kohenet nodded and then stepped into the chamber, making room for a young woman to follow her. "This is Eemo," she said. "She is the lucky one who found this newest baby in the river. She will be his mother. Bring him out to meet his mother."

Ra'ayon followed these instructions immediately. Even not knowing what would happen next, she knew at least she and her two children wouldn't be killed. She smiled at Eemo when she handed her son over, and Eemo smiled at the baby.

"Besh," Eemo said, calling the boy by a name that means luck in Egyptian, "you have brought me good luck. You might one day grow up to be the pharaoh—without me even needing to go to your father."

"Eemo," Kohenet said, "give your baby back to his wet nurse now. You will get him in the morning like all the others." Eemo did as she was told and gave a little bow to Kohenet before leaving.

"I will not oversee this," Kohenet reminded me. But then her shoulders sagged, and she softened her voice. "I wish I could do more," she said. "I cannot do it all. It will not help anyone if the harem falls apart."

"I understand," I said. I bowed my head before her and added, "thank you for doing what you can," though she was already walking away as I said it.

OTHER

There was only one other Israelite baby boy who came to us. He arrived on top of his sister's head only a few days after Betzalel had joined us. Elisheva was his sister's name, and she walked into the harem with a water jug on her head. The top was broken off, but the bottom was intact. Girls often walked through the harem, and most other places, largely overlooked. And with ragged clothes anda large jug of water, there was no need to give this girl a second thought—everyone knew she was fetching or delivering water.

Later, Elisheva told us that when she'd first entered the harem, she did face a few challenges. There were women who wanted to direct her on where to put the water, and instead of listening to their directions, she'd reply, "No, this is bitter water. You don't want this." And it was true. Nobody wanted it. So she kept walking and looking for us. That is, she was looking for Vida and her children, who her mother had said were in the harem. Elisheva wasn't sure whether it was safe to ask after Vida, so she just kept walking through the harem, insisting that she was carrying bitter water every time she was told to put the jug down somewhere.

Yam heard her telling one of the women about the bitter water, so she looked toward where the voice was coming from. Recognizing Elisheva, she gasped, smiled, told us to follow her, and then went right to her old friend. The two girls were clearly happy to see each other.

"Guess what I have in the jug," Elisheva said.

"Bitter water," Yam said with confidence.

"Nope," Elisheva answered. "Guess again."

"Sweet water?"

Elisheva shook her head no. "Do you want another guess?"

We women didn't want any more guesses. Vida couldn't wait to hug Elisheva, so she moved the jug off the girl's head to do just that. When she moved the jug, though, she could feel that there wasn't water in it at all. Peeking inside, she saw a swaddled baby sucking on a milk-soaked cloth.

"I brought Nakshon!" she said, removing her baby brother from the jug. No wonder the top of it had been broken off.

Kesher reached in and brought baby Nakshon out of the jug. We weren't used to newborns anymore. He was so much smaller than the other boys. His face was all smushed up, and his eyes were closed, but he quickly smelled the milk on Kesher and opened his mouth wide, dropping the cloth and rubbing his face against her breast. Kesher happily started feeding him.

"You're so brave!" Vida praised Elisheva. "Coming here all alone and bringing your brother to safety, what a good sister."

"Hey . . . I did that too," Yam said to her mother.

"Of course," Vida said. A small cloud of regret crossed her face. She pulled Yam close for a hug.

"You think that was brave?" Elisheva asked. "Coming here with a jug of 'bitter water' was the easiest part! You should hear what happened before!" This girl made us giggle. Elisheva sat down, ready to tell us all, but we made her wait the few moments it took to get back to my chamber. She didn't even stop to look around—just walked right into my garden and sat on the ground, expecting that we would all sit with her, which we did.

"First," Elisheva said, "Mama was pregnant. Well, of course that happened before a baby. And you wouldn't *believe* how she got pregnant," she said to Yam, "but that wasn't the brave part for me. The brave part was when the baby started coming. Nobody was there to help! Only me! I said I'd run and get the midwife, but Mama said there wasn't time. Then I said I'd run and get Auntie, but she said there wasn't time for that either. And then I said I'd run and get some of the women out of the fields, but she said there wasn't even time for that. Finally, I asked her who she wanted me to get, and she said *me*! That is how I became a midwife!"

Elisheva beamed with pride. Her eyes lit up, and her smile was wide, showing that she had four full-grown teeth in her mouth and at least as many missing.

"But that wasn't even the bravest part," she went on. "Being a midwife was kind of hard. I held Mama's hand, and she squeezed it so much I thought olive oil might come out of it!" She paused. "I'm just kidding," she said. "I know olive oil only comes from squeezing olives. I'm just saying that my mama's very strong, and she squeezed very hard." We all nodded, and she picked up her story.

"Anyway, the baby was born, and then Mama said that I could go get the midwives. I had already done all the hard work, but I wasn't going to argue with her. I couldn't find Shifra and Pu'a, though, so I kept walking. It was close to evening, and I knew that my father and the older boys would be back from doing brickwork soon, so I kept walking. And then I saw an Egyptian midwife. She said her name was Massoot, and I said my name was Elisheva, since it is, and that my mama had just delivered a baby and I had been the midwife, but then Mama had sent me to find a midwife anyway.

"Massoot said she'd come and look at Mama. I had already looked at her, and she looked tired. But she had told me to get a midwife, so I knew she would be pleased. At least I thought so," Elisheva corrected. "She didn't say she was pleased when I got back. She didn't say anything. That was one of the bravest parts. I didn't like my mama not answering. Then Massoot opened her bag, gently poured a drink into my mother's mouth, and then less gently stuffed rags between her legs, even inside of her where the baby had come from.

"Exactly when Massoot's hand was all bloody from my mother's insides, a guard let himself into our home. He stood over all of us and saw the newborn boy. He reached down to take him and throw him in the river, but Massoot put her bloodied hand in his face, and he stepped back quicker than if she'd put a sword to his throat. He didn't leave our house, though. He announced very loudly, way too loudly, that it was his job to throw the baby in the river and that he was going to follow his orders and do his job."

Elisheva paused. She wanted to make sure she had all the attention, which she certainly did. This little girl sure knew how to tell a story. Even the babies had their eyes and ears fixed on her, and though they couldn't understand her words, they were captivated—Yam and Aaron and Ra'ayva even more so. And Vida, Kesher, and I were hanging on every word. Elisheva seemed satisfied, so she went on.

"And do you know what? This was one of the bravest parts," she said, "but it wasn't me being brave—it was Massoot. She stood right up and walked over to that guard and put her bloody hand right in front of his face again and said, 'I am doing *my* job. And I am not finished yet.'" Yam clapped and cheered for Massoot, and the rest of us quickly joined in even though she wasn't there to hear it. Elisheva was pleased by the reaction.

"Then my father got home," Elisheva continued. "He walked right to my mother and said, 'Oh, Ishti,' and when she heard him say her name, she fluttered her eyes a bit and said, 'Oh, Ami-Nadav.' And then Nakshon cried. Wailed, actually. The guard called out a reminder from just outside our door that it was getting dark and that he was still waiting for the baby. Mama was too tired to lift Nakshon, but Massoot put him on Mama's breast, and he sucked until he was satisfied.

"Massoot ignored the guard and spoke to my mother. She asked her if she had about one hundred different herbs and drinks. Of course, she did not have a single one. Most of our people's herbs had long since been used. We were lucky to have Shifra and Pu'a bring some when there was a baby, but like I said, Mama told me not to run and get them before he was born. So then, Massoot said things I had never heard in my whole life. Do you want to know what she said?"

Elisheva paused as if she were waiting for us to answer, though she was clearly just dragging it out. But we were all curious and waiting for what came next, so she didn't make us wait too long. "Then," she said, "Massoot asked me if I really wanted to be a real midwife." Elisheva folded her arms across her chest and harrumphed. "I already *was* one," she said, "I had already delivered my brother, hadn't I? But I didn't say that to Massoot; I only said yes. And then she took everything out of her bag and divided it in two and gave me my own satchel of medicines!" Elisheva exclaimed. She quickly added, "But they're not here; they're at my house. I really do have them! Massoot said that those herbs had been used by her grandmother Savta, and Savta's grandmother Tanqo, and Dorot before her, and now they could be mine. Then Massoot said that helping a mother and baby doesn't always need herbs.

"Now get ready, everyone," Elisheva said, "because here comes the best part." Satisfied that she still had our attention, she went on: "We helped Nakshon without herbs. The brave Ami-Nadav, the strong Ami-Nadav—that is, my papa—talked to my mama and to me and to Massoot and even to Baby Nakshon and said, 'I can swim. I can swim. I can swim. I can swim!' Then he took the baby bundle and ran out of the house right to the Nile yelling, 'If my son must go into the river, then it will be I who take him! He will not go alone!'"

I gasped, but Elisheva didn't care for the interruption where she hadn't planned it, so she went right on with her story.

"And before the guard could even think to chase after him, my mother used all her strength to yell, 'No! No! Don't take him! Don't help them to end our people!' But my papa didn't stop. He just yelled back, 'I am not helping them end our people. I swear to Elohim that I'm willing to risk my own life as an offering to help my people.' Then he jumped into the water and went under. Soon, only a small blanket could be seen floating downstream in the last light, leaving everyone guessing about what had happened to the father and son.

"But I knew," Elisheva assured us. "Because I was there when they had made the plan just moments before. My father had taken the baby bundle, but not the baby. Massoot had then wrapped Nakshon up, put him in her half-empty midwife's bag, and walked right out of the door with me beside her as her assistant. She took us to her house for the night. It was a big house with three rooms and . . ." Elisheva trailed off and was quieter and slower when she continued. "Well, it's not as big as this place," she said, looking around our quarters for the first time, "but it was still nice. We got to stay there for the night and eat and sleep, and then in the morning, she fed Nakshon one more time and wrapped him up again and put him in this broken jug for me to bring here, where my mother said I'd find you. See? That's how I saved my brother."

The stunned silence that followed was broken by Yam standing and clapping for Elisheva. Aaron and Ra'ayva quickly joined the ovation, and even Moses and Hur began clapping, happy to see others doing a trick they had mastered. That all seemed to suit Elisheva just fine, so she joined in the applause as well.

"You did wonderfully," Vida said. "You must be very hungry and tired after that. Let's eat and rest in the shade in the courtyard—."

"Oh no," Elisheva interrupted, "I'm not going to spend any time resting. My mama said I could stay one night with Massoot and one night with Vida, and then she wants me to come straight home. She says I'm always going farther and longer than she likes, and she wants to see me back home where she needs me. No resting for me. Yam, will you show me around this place?"

The two of them ran off together with huge smiles on their faces. Vida said seeing Yam with Elisheva made her realize that they had given up a lot in exchange for their safety. Yam noticed that too. When the girls came back, Yam said she felt like the bitter water that Elisheva had been carrying. It hadn't actually been bitter, just like her new life in the harem wasn't that bitter. But just like the water Elisheva had claimed to have in her jug had gone unwanted by the harem's women, Yam's new life wasn't what she wanted, either. That night, Elisheva began calling Yam "Miryam," meaning bitter water, and the name stuck.

Yam wasn't the only one to receive a new name that day. Kohenet kept her promise and made sure that the new baby would be cared for by bringing Umuhu to be Nakshon's mother. Umuhu named him Ankh, which preserved the sound of his original name while changing it to honor him in Egyptian as the key of life from the river. With his new name, his new mother, and a kiss from his sister, Nakshon, Ankh, was protected in the harem.

It was especially difficult for Miryam and Vida to part with Elisheva in the morning, but it was hard for all of us. We'd quickly come to adore her. She was ready for her next journey, though, and had promised her mother a swift return. We filled her broken jug with all the dried fruits and nuts we could fit, gave her a sack of flour to carry on her back, and then sent her back to Goshen. But that wasn't the last we saw of Elisheva.

SUF

Suf came to see Moses every morning. Each time, Vida would say, "Look, Moses, here's your mother." She would hand her baby to Suf, and the two of them would go to the benches with the other young mothers and babies until it was time for him to nurse again. I thought back to when Grandmother Leah had told me that I had two fathers and had told Benno that he had two mothers. One morning, I asked Vida whether it was difficult for her to part with her son each morning.

"Moses is Suf's son," she replied. "I may have carried him and brought him here, and of course I love him, but it should never be said that he is anything but Suf's son. She claimed him, she named him, she saved him. There should never be a question. As soon as someone thinks he's mine, his life is in danger again. No," she said. "I won't have that. He is a son of the pharaoh." I nodded. I supposed this was why she never called him anything but Moses. I didn't ask whether she'd named him before coming to the harem.

When Moses began toddling, Vida would pick a flower every morning before Suf's arrival, and then when she came,

Vida would say, "Go give this beautiful flower to your beautiful mother." Moses would do it, and Suf would smile and wrap him in a hug. They would then walk off together to enjoy the day until she brought him back to eat and sleep. Sometimes Kesher and Hur went with them, sometimes not.

When Moses was steady on his little legs, Vida began to worry about the day he'd be weaned and she would no longer be needed. Aaron, three years older than Moses, still had all his milk teeth, so she hoped that Moses would keep his for a long time, too, but that dreadful day was on her mind always. And what if Aaron were sent away when he stopped nursing, even if his mother was still there? So, one day, Vida tried something new. Before Suf came, she picked two flowers. When Suf arrived, Vida gave a flower to Moses as usual, but she also gave one to Aaron. "Go give this beautiful flower to your beautiful mother," she said, addressing both boys at once.

Moses ran right into Suf's arms, as always. Aaron knew what he was expected to do, but he hesitated a moment. He had known Suf for as long as he could remember. He saw her every day when she picked up and returned Moses. They had smiled at each other and laughed together. He had received sweets from her—and even hugs—but not mother-hugs. He looked at the yellow flower in his hand, then he handed it to Suf. Suf looked at Vida, who softly mouthed the word *please*. Suf brought Aaron into the embrace, which made Moses jump up and down with joy and Vida cry with relief.

"What are you doing?" Miryam asked her.

"Protecting Suf's sons," Vida said. "They are safe as Egyptian princes."

"Are we leaving the harem?" Miryam asked.

"No"—Vida paused—"not yet."

"Will you protect me?" Miryam asked with a tremble in her voice.

"I will always try to protect and help whomever I can," Vida said, "especially you. But you are safe right now; you don't need protection."

Before Miryam could say more, Kesher asked whether she would take Hur for a walk. Hur ran right to Miryam and took her by the hand and led her outside. He always loved to be with her, and she was wonderful with him. As soon as the two of them were gone, Vida's tears started flowing. Kesher and I just held her for a very long time. When Vida had exhausted herself so much that she needed to lie down, she stared up at the sky and asked how in the world she would protect Miryam.

"You were right before," Kesher immediately said. "Miryam is safe right now. She doesn't need protection. And if someday she does, you will always try to help her. As will I." I then repeated everything Kesher had said, for it was true for me, too, and her words were wise.

"Vida," Kesher went on, "you were brave and creative, and that helped you protect your sons." I agreed completely. And I was thankful that these two boys whom I loved so dearly were safe with Suf's help. However, to say that I was sad that it needed to be this way would not begin to describe my pit of sorrow.

Vida was lying in our courtyard with me on one side of her and Kesher on the other. She was scared, but she was also safe and strong. I didn't think there were any words that would help her feel that, so I simply took a long breath. *Yhhhh*. Kesher joined me when I exhaled. *Whhhh*. Vida was having difficulty slowing her breathing, but with us next to her, she was eventually able to join in. When I knew she was calm, I let myself dream.

I dreamt of going to the pharaoh. I was oiled and bathed and clothed and covered in fragrances and jewels. It was not my turn to go to him, but nonetheless, I was walking down a long corridor toward his throne room. When I arrived, he was surprised to see me. He raised his scepter and used it to wave me in. I bowed before him until I was given permission to rise.

"Why have you come here?" he asked me.

"I am here to help the Israelites return to Israel," I said.

This startled him so greatly that he burst into laughter. He clutched his side and shook and gasped for breath. He wiped away tears and was finally composed enough to say, "I do not know if I have ever laughed like that. You must come back and do that again tomorrow."

This was repeated nine more times. On my final time before the pharaoh, he was no longer amused. "Go!" he shouted at me. His voice was so loud that it woke me from my dream, and I was not as calm as I had been when it had begun—my heart was racing, and my hands were in fists. *Open*, I said to myself. *Open*. I convinced myself to slowly open my fingers and relax my hands, then my arms, my shoulders, and my back. I was able to breathe deeply again. I wished my father were there to interpret the dream for me. Without him, though, I would have to do my best.

No matter the meaning of the dream, I was not confident that I had been doing my best. After all, as I had told the dream pharaoh, I was there to help the Israelites return to Israel. I did not know how I was supposed to do that, but perhaps going to the real pharaoh was the way, so, I quietly got up and went to find Kohenet. She was as surprised by my request to be prepared to go to the pharaoh as I was, but she agreed to help me. She sent oilers the very next evening.

I had six months to make a plan. After days of worrying over one sure-to-fail idea after another, Vida suggested that we ask Ra'ayon. After all, it was her creativity that had brought about the idea of making baskets for the babies, so maybe she could help with this. We hadn't seen each other much since she'd come to the harem. When we did, she insisted that the pharaoh was the father of her children. Like Hur and Moses, Betzalel was running around and playing with the other boys, and she told him often that he was a prince just like them.

When I saw Ra'ayon eating on a bench outside one evening, I approached her. She didn't greet me, and she seemed unhappy that I was there. "I would like to ask whether you have an idea that might help me," I said. "How can we get the pharaoh to let our people be free?"

Ra'ayon gasped and covered Ra'ayva's ears with her hands. "Why would you ask me such a question? This matter has nothing to do with me."

"I, well, I . . ." It was clear that she had become one of the women who would deny that she was an Israelite and who didn't want her children to know that they, too, were from the tribe of Israel. I could see the fear in her face. "I heard that you are respected for your good ideas," I said. "That is all. It seems that the Israelites could benefit from a good idea." Her body relaxed a little, though she didn't lower her hands from Ra'ayva's ears.

"Look at my daughter," she said to me. "Do you see how well-fed she is? Look at my son. Do you see how he smiles? My days are busy with giving them food and joy. I don't have time to have ideas."

"I understand," I said. "If you do happen to think of one, please come find me. And," I added, "even if you don't think of an idea, I'd be glad to see you. We all would." With that, I left them to their meal. It seemed that Ra'ayon would not be helping.

From then on, I was consumed with trying to figure out how to approach the pharaoh. I had some relief from these worries each night when the oilers came. Since I wasn't new to the harem, I didn't need to be isolated, but Kesher and Vida and the children would leave while I had my skin massaged until I was supple and sleepy. When the oilers left, the women and children would come lie down, and we would all sleep.

But in the mornings, the worries would begin again. Suf would come and get Moses and Aaron. Kesher would take Hur out. Then Vida and I, with Miryam there, too, would start saying ideas, no matter how terrible. When Kesher got back, she would try to find some value in each one. Quickly, Miryam learned to examine these thoughts and mine for hope. But by the time the oilers would return in the evenings, we were all frustrated and full of despair until sleep relieved us.

To make matters worse, Elisheva came back to the harem with some bad news.

After not seeing her for three years, she was a lot taller, a little wider, and still filled with the drama, exuberance, and well-earned pride that she had demonstrated on her first visit. She carried no jug on her head but boldly called out, "Bitter water, bitter water, Miryam, Miryam!" until she found Miryam and hugged her tightly, only letting her go when she was ready to greet the rest of us.

Elisheva spent a long time telling us of her studies in midwifery and regaling us with stories of awe, courage, sadness, and some humor. She had come to the harem at this time mostly because she had officially become an apprentice, which meant that she could travel more easily and not have to pretend to carry water in a broken jug while actually delivering a baby. So, her mother had asked her to go to the harem and bring back word about Nakshon.

Elisheva had been to see her brother that morning and was pleased to see that he was well-fed, strong, fast, and thriving. He did not, however, know who she was. This had disappointed Elisheva, but since he had been a newborn the last time they had seen each other, she understood. She was just grateful that she could bring this hopeful news back to her parents, though the news she brought us about the Israelites was not so hopeful.

Elisheva had some sad news to relay to Vida about some women she had known and about Amram, Vida's husband. When Elisheva had returned to Goshon from sneaking baby Nakshon into the harem, she had told the older daughters of Amram that their family was well. The daughters relayed this to their mother, who then told Amram, who then told his sons; then Amram went back to his first wife to ask that a message be sent through Elisheva to Vida, his second wife:

"'Please tell her that I am glad that she and the children are protected. Please tell her that my first wife cares for me and the older ones. Please tell her that I look forward to them returning when it is safe for them to do so. Please do not tell her that my sons and I slave in the brickyard and are beaten regularly or that my wife and daughters are not given enough flour to make us loaves.'"

Elisheva covered her mouth after saying that last part aloud. She had been holding that message inside her for more than three years, practicing it often so that she would not forget. But when the time had finally come to deliver it, she'd said too much. It was Miryam who took it the hardest. She had been living peacefully in the harem without any concern about food or bricks. Even though she had been subjected to our worries about the Israelites and had been a child who was no longer in danger, Miryam now felt a burden of guilt. Elisheva was helping to deliver babies. What was she doing?

Of course, what Miryam was doing in the harem had value, and we reminded her of that. But now, Kesher and Vida and I felt the weight double on our shoulders too. I felt even more urgency to figure out how to help lead the Israelites out of this land. If only we had left when my father had died! If only we had gone back to our land with Yo-av and Li-av, we would not be serving pharaoh but building our own cities. That is, they would not be building pharaoh's cities and starving. I wasn't doing either, and I felt as guilty as Miryam did.

Before Elisheva returned to Goshen, I asked her to seek out Nina if she could, or anyone else from the tribes of Benjamin, Menasse, or Efraim. I asked her to tell them that Blue, daughter of Joseph and Deenah, is well in the harem and requests to receive a copy of her father's scrolls. Would they, too, ask if I was real? If I was really alive? Maybe if not confronted with my youthful appearance, they would not question the message. Nevertheless, I wanted the scroll, so I asked Elisheva to at least try, and she agreed. Then, we again sent her on her way with as much food as she could carry back.

In Elisheva's absence, we found ourselves overcome by both our good fortune and our helplessness. But when a full moon came, we were able to break this cycle. With Kesher and Vida and Miryam and the little boys singing and dancing with me under the round, glowing moon every month, I could not help but feel joy. Sometimes our evenings were so celebratory that other women joined in, but that night, it was just us. As always, I had given my hopes, my dreams, and my pain to the moon—we all had. As always, we brought out the drums and the wine and the blankets. As always, we breathed everything in. *Yhhhh*. Thus, I didn't hold only the pressures of what would happen when I went to the pharaoh, but I also got to hold the possibilities. I breathed out my worries and made more room for hope. *Whhhh*.

That night, I let the world hold me and the sky hold me and Yah hold me, and I let myself know that everything would be as it should be. I shared this with Kesher and Vida in the morning and was met with smiles of relief. "We do not know where the answer lies," Vida said matter-of-factly, "but we also know that we were not finding it the way we were looking."

Kesher nodded in agreement. "I'm glad we had the moon celebration," she said. "I did not tell you before, but I didn't want to have it. I didn't want to dance or sing or drum or relax. I wanted to use the night to figure out what you will say to the pharaoh. But thanks to our celebration, I learned that I already knew. It is like what Kohenet said. We cannot do *every*thing, but we can do *some*thing. I'm just afraid that I wasn't even doing *anything* when caring for Hur with my body—I feel like I was just ignoring him with my thoughts."

Hur, and all the children, could tell when we were more relaxed, and they became more playful. As Miryam was the oldest and the only girl, she was the natural little mother for the three boys, and they listened to her instructions, including when playing. She quickly created a little performance in which she, Aaron, Hur, and Moses acted out different roles. In one version, she was the pharaoh, Hur was me, and Aaron and Moses were Israelites.

"Let the Israelites go," Hur said as if he were me.

"Why should I?" Miryam the pharaoh asked.

Then there was a long pause. "Moses," Aaron said in a loud whisper, "now you say, 'we want to go home.'"

Moses didn't say anything.

"Come on, Moses," Aaron cajoled, "say, 'we want to go home.'"

But Moses was still silent. He wasn't much younger than Hur, and both of them were long past learning to talk; in fact, they could say all the words that Aaron could, but Moses couldn't seem to do it when asked.

"Don't you want to go home?" Aaron asked him.

Moses nodded that he did.

"Then say, 'we want to go home.'"

Moses tightened his lips.

Finally, Aaron asked him, "Do you want me to say it with you?"

With this, Moses's face lit up, and he recited the line together with Aaron.

Once they had said they wanted to go home, Miryam the pharaoh said they may leave. Then all three boys left, shaking their fists in the air with triumph and their butts behind them with joy.

If only it had gone that way when it was finally time for me to approach the pharaoh. When my six months were complete, Kesher and Vida both accompanied me to the bathing area. They both sat beside me as my makeup was put on, and they both admired my clothes when they were brought. They both helped to put on the jewels that I would wear to the palace, and they both hugged me and whispered words of strength in my ears as I was escorted first to Kohenet, who would then bring me to the pharaoh. My skin tingled with anticipation and nervousness. I still did not know what I would say or do.

When the guards opened the large doors of Pharaoh's private chamber, I bowed low to the ground until granted permission to approach. When I was within his reach, he placed both of his hands on my garment and began to remove it. I said, "Pharaoh, I am Blue, daughter of Zafenat Paaneakh who was—"

The pharaoh interrupted me with a yell while yanking my cloak off my body and throwing it to the floor. "How dare you!" he shouted. "You were not granted permission to speak. Guards! Guards!" Two men burst through the door while I stood there naked before the pharaoh. "Remove this woman at once! And do not allow another to enter who thinks it her place to speak to me!" I grabbed my clothes and ran from the room. I was thankfully not pursued as the three of them, laughing, remained together as I tried unsuccessfully to cover myself.

When I had put some distance between me and them, I dressed myself as best as I could and walked back to the harem. Kesher and Vida were surprised to see me so soon. We went to our private courtyard right away, where they tried for a very long time to both console me and learn from me what had happened. All I could do was hold them to me tightly. I had failed. Again. For a second time, I had not been able to lead the Israelites back to Israel as I fully knew that I was meant to do. I was devastated.

This time, I had a fear greater than the last time I'd failed. Perhaps it was selfish to not have my greatest fear be the continued oppression that my kin would suffer due to my failure. However, the cause of my deepest sorrow was knowing that at some point now, I would have to leave Kesher, who knew me better than anyone else at the harem, and Vida, my soft-necked friend, and the four beautiful children I woke up to every morning and sang to every night. I did not want to get old again and walk with Yah again and come back to try again and be alone again and be asked again if I was real.

When I was finally able to explain this to Kesher and Vida, we brought a mat into the shade in our garden and held each other as tightly as any person can hold another. They assured me that they knew I was real. They told me over and over again how much they loved me and felt my love. They promised they would stay and hold me as my body grew old for as long as they were able.

Three days later, after Miryam had been caring for the boys on her own and all the children had showered me in love and affection, Kesher and Vida broke their promise and let go of me. For I did not walk with Yah. I did not even grow old.

THE CHILDREN

The children grew older, and they seemed to do it so quickly. Aaron lost his two bottom teeth and proudly stuck his jaw forward to show the little tips of the new teeth growing in. Hur and Moses started asking everyone to look at their teeth to see if they were going to fall out. Of course, they were not even the slightest bit wobbly yet, but we indulged them by checking many times.

One morning, when Aaron and Moses had been out with Suf, she brought them back early so Aaron could show us that his first top tooth had just fallen out. Suf said that it was time for him to be weaned and live with her. Moses and Hur were suddenly no longer interested in catching up with Aaron.

"I will throw him a celebration, of course," Suf said. "I will need seven days to prepare that and to prepare his chambers. Then he will come and live with me and begin his lessons with the other boys." It was plain that she was proud of him. He had become her son over the years, just as much as Vida's—just as much as mine.

"And," Suf added, looking at Vida, "I am not used to taking care of a child. He will need to be bathed and clothed and fed. He will need to have someone oversee his practices and clean his quarters. The girl has probably learned all these things." Suf paused and looked at Miryam. It was a generous offering, and Vida nearly jumped into Suf's arms, for she was giving Vida a chance to keep her children safe and together, even if she herself would have to go back to Goshen when Moses lost his teeth. Vida stepped forward as calmly as she could manage and kissed Suf's hand in gratitude. Much to Vida's surprise, Suf kissed hers too.

When they left, Miryam spoke up. "I do not wish to go with her, Mother. She is not my mother. You are my mother. And you are their mother too! Why do you let them call that woman *Mother*?" Miryam paused for a moment, then softened her tone. "Why do you let them call Suf their mother?" she asked. Miryam had seen Suf every day. She had seen her kindness, her gentleness, her patience, and her firmness. She was even fond of her. She knew that Suf was the best protection her brothers could have, but she had never thought she would have to part with her mother, only with her brothers.

"I don't want to go," Miryam said, "I want to stay with you." She cried for a long time that morning. She knew she wouldn't be staying with her mother. She would go with Aaron, and they would be together. She would become a maidservant for Suf. Miryam had seen maidservants throughout the harem fetching water, cooking bread, shelling nuts, grinding spices, mending clothing . . . These were all things that she did with her mother. Soon she would do them for Suf. But she would not do so without telling her mother how bitter she felt about it.

Vida stroked Miryam's hair. "My love for you will always be as wide and as deep as the sea," she reminded her daughter.

"And mine for you," Miryam said. "But the sea feels even more bitter now that we will have to be apart. Miryam is truly the right name for me."

I left Miryam and Vida alone together while they lamented their parting. I was not looking forward to it, either, but I respected their determination to maintain their safety, even at high costs. I did not dare tell them how they could be thankful that they even had the opportunity to embrace and cry and mourn together before parting—three of the many things I had been unable to do before my mother had left. I consoled myself with the reminder that Miryam would have had to be married in a few years if she were not working for Suf and, therefore, would still have had to leave her mother. So, her opportunity to stay with her brothers and me and Kesher was probably better than that. Had my mother had those thoughts about me? Had she lessened her suffering by telling herself that I would still have Leah and Benno and the others?

As promised, Suf made a celebration for Aaron, showing everyone that she was his mother and that he was old enough to begin his studies. Vida helped her with the preparations, and the two worked cooperatively side by side. Along with the celebration, I wanted to give both Aaron and Miryam parting gifts. I expected we'd still be able to see each other, just as we crossed paths with everyone in the harem sometimes, but it was still a way of marking the occasion. I offered each of them a private story and a song just for them before they left to live with Suf. At the last moment, I thought to offer the same to Moses, as well, who was transitioning from having his siblings with him to having them elsewhere.

As the oldest, Miryam went first. We held hands and skipped together to a bench beside the river. She was almost as tall as I was, and I wondered whether she would still be able to find the joy to skip in her new situation. I almost laughed at myself. I was confident that Miryam would make joy wherever she could. That was at least one thing she had learned at our full moon celebrations in which she had always participated with exuberance. At the bench, Miryam put her head in my lap, and I stroked her hair as we watched the river flow. I asked her whether there was a specific story she'd like to hear. I had told the children—and Kesher and Vida—all my stories so many times, so I wondered whether Miryam had a favorite or one that felt especially meaningful to her.

Miryam asked me to tell her about my mother going on her own adventure after Grandmother Rebekah's funeral. "I went on an adventure like that," Miryam said. "My father did not know that I was living in the harem until Elisheva told him. You don't know where your mother is, but she might be living a wonderful new life." I agreed, but then I asked her who was supposed to be telling the story. She giggled. "You tell me, Auntie."

I obliged: "Once, there was a brave and adventurous woman named Deenah. She loved elephants, a cat named Barley, her brother Joseph, and her daughter, Blue—but not in that order. She loved her daughter the most. What she hated the most was feeling trapped and that she could be hurt at any moment. One day, when she knew that Blue was safe with others who loved her, she went and made a new life." I didn't know what had happened in that new life, but I hoped that it was something wonderful, just as Miryam had said.

"And what did her brothers call her?" Miryam asked, though she knew the answer.

"They called her a *whore*, a word that men use to describe a woman who makes her own choices about her body instead of letting them be in control of her."

"It is not exactly my choice to go with Suf and Aaron," Miryam said, "but I am almost a whore because my mother is protecting me by sending me there. Suf will protect me too. I know that if I didn't go with her, I'd have to go back to the suffering in Goshen or stay here and become a wife of the pharaoh."

"I don't think it was my mother's choice to go find a new adventure either," I admitted, just realizing it for the first time myself. "What she really wanted was to be married to my father. Since that wasn't possible, she wanted to be married to the prince. And since her brothers had killed him and dragged her home, she eventually just wanted to get away from her brothers for good, even if that meant she had to leave me behind."

"Maybe she thought it wouldn't be safe for her to take a girl with her," Miryam offered.

"Maybe," I conceded.

After a few moments of quiet, having told Miryam a story, I sang her a song. In that song, I sang to her about how strong and determined, wise and essential she was. I sang to her about how special it was that she was water. Whether bitter or sweet or a combination of both, she flowed with life. She had a special connection with water, and water had a special connection with her. They had already worked together to help Moses. I sang her praises for leading her mother and brothers to a new life and taking such good care of the little boys and for containing all the joy and sorrow that comes with having two homes.

I acknowledged her for holding the heaviness that came with understanding the suffering that her father and her friends and the others were enduring, for doing what was in her ability to help them, and for living with the knowledge that she couldn't do it all. *"You are a holy sister,"* I sang, *"and a holy daughter. I'm proud of you, your mother and father are proud of you, Kesher is proud of you—we're all proud of you."*

"Thank you, Auntie," she said. We watched the water flow in the river for a little longer, and then she went to tell Aaron it was his turn. I stayed on the edge of the bench, and when he saw me sitting there, he also put his head in my lap and stretched his body out to cover the rest of the seating area. I stroked his hair, as I had done for Miryam. I was a little surprised to see his feet at the end of the bench; after all, I had seen him every day. When had he gotten so tall?

I asked Aaron whether there was a story that he'd like to hear. He said he wanted to hear about Joseph having a secret signal with his brother Judah. "My father, Joseph, was the youngest of his brothers for a very long time," I said. "He looked up to them and wanted to be one of them. Two of his older brothers were nice to him: Reuben, the oldest, and Judah. Joseph thought that Judah was especially wise, even when they were both just little boys. My father was so surprised by Judah's wisdom that he reached up to Judah's chin to feel whether there was a beard growing there that he couldn't see. 'Surely someone that wise must be old enough to have a beard,' my father would say.

"Judah didn't grow a beard any younger than any other man did, so for many years, his chin was just as hairless as my father's. But the two brothers had developed this signal between them. The touch of a chin was an acknowledgment of wisdom—with or without whiskers there. So, after many years of being apart, when Judah suspected that Joseph was the vizier who had gifted the tribe of Israel with food, Judah put his thumb to his chin to show his brother that he knew him and thought him wise."

Aaron was pleased and, unlike Miryam, had nothing to add to the story, so I sang a song for him. I sang him a song praising his willingness to find fun, and, if he couldn't find it, his willingness to create it. Aaron often got in trouble for some of his trickery, but I'm proud that I praised it in him. It was a part of who he was. Should he be shamed for being himself? He was as much a part of Yah as anyone else. I know many people prefer the company of the parts of Yah that are obedient or predictable or helpful to them personally, but other people are no less holy, and Aaron didn't often receive that kind of acknowledgment. Aaron's heart was light, his laughter quick to come, and his thinking creative. I made my song a bouncy one, and he left my lap to wiggle and jiggle his body to it as I sang.

When I'd finished singing, he wrapped his arms around my neck and pressed his lips against my cheek and blew air, making his lips and my face vibrate. This sparked the laughter he hoped for. "Thank you, Auntie," he said. "That was a lovely song. I'll carry it with me forever." He pantomimed putting something into a sack and carrying it over his shoulder, then went off humming.

"Send your brother," I called after him, and he nodded as he ran off.

When Moses came, he ran right up to me and gave me a hug. "It was hard to wait for my turn," he said. "But I did it."

"Yes, you did!" I praised him. His little face beamed with pride in front of mine. His dark brown curls were askew on his head, and his fingers were sticky from something he'd eaten earlier. "Tell me," I said, "is there a story you want to hear, or should I choose?"

"I want to choose," he said. "I want the story of when your father saw you for the first time when you were already big, but he was so happy to see you." Moses had been taught by Suf that the pharaoh was his father, but the two had never laid eyes on each other. In addition, he knew that Amram was his father in Goshen, but he had no memory of either the man or the place. I knew he liked to hear of when I met my father, and I was happy to tell him the story.

"Miryam and Aaron put their heads on my lap while I sang to them. Do you want to do that too?" I asked.

I saw him hesitate for a moment but then he decided to make the same choice as his older siblings. I was all the way on the left side of the bench so that Miryam and Aaron could have room to spread their bodies out on the rest of it. Moses wasn't as tall as they were, of course, but there was no room to my left, so he had to lie down to the right of me. When he did so, he put his right cheek on my lap so that his face was in my belly. "Wouldn't you rather face the river?" I asked. Again, he hesitated, but he turned around and put his left cheek on my lap and faced the river.

I told Moses about the disappointment I'd felt when I thought my father was dead and about the longing that had replaced the disappointment when I'd heard he was alive. I told Moses about the day we'd met and embraced, and I even told him about how my father wrote in his scrolls about how special that day was. While I was speaking, I paid attention to the weight of Moses's little head in my lap. Though lighter than that of his older brother and sister, it was sure to catch up quickly. When I finished the story, I stroked his hair as I sang to him.

I sang a song about the joy he and his Israelite father would feel when they got to see each other again one day. I added praise for his patience while he waited for that, but I reminded him that there had been joys he'd experienced while he was small, like playing with Hur and chasing frogs and sleeping on the bed with me and Vida and Kesher and Hur. I reminded him, too, that though Kesher's belly was still small, she had been back to see the pharaoh and was growing another baby and that, soon, Moses would not be the youngest in the bed. I hoped this would make him smile. It made me smile to sing that special song just for him.

When I'd finished singing, such a long time passed before he moved that I thought maybe he'd fallen asleep. I enjoyed a few more moments of his little head on my lap, and then I gently stroked his chin to wake him so that I could start helping with food preparation. It turned out, though, that he hadn't been asleep. He'd been wide awake and now was sitting up beside me. I took his hand, squeezed it, and asked whether he wanted to keep holding hands and run back to the others with me. I thought he'd take off right away, but, instead, he started crying.

I turned to face him and took his other hand in mine too. "Moses, sweet boy, why are you crying?" I asked.

"I wanted a song," he said. "I wanted my own story and my own song. You said I was to have them even though I am not leaving. I waited and waited, and now you just want to go back? But what about my story and song?" He yanked his hands out of mine, not interested in being comforted.

I was confused. I didn't know what to say. He stood up in front of me and crossed his arms at his chest, wrinkling up his face and stamping his foot. "Sing me my song!" he demanded.

I stammered. "Moses . . . I just sang to you . . . remember? Just . . . right here . . . a moment ago . . . while you were on my lap . . ."

He stamped his foot again. "Why?" he demanded. "Whyyyyyy-yyyyyyyyyy? Why would you do that? Why would you make me close my people ear? Why would you sing to me when my people ear is closed and only my Yah ear is open? Was it a trick? Did Aaron tell you to do that? I want my song!"

"Moses, Moses," I said. "Take off your shoes." This is what Vida would say to all the children when they were overwhelmed. She would tell them to take off their shoes and feel the ground underneath their feet. The ground was special, she'd tell them, and could help to hold them and their feelings when things were difficult. Moses took off his shoes, and I took mine off too.

I was so confused, but I started to sing to him again, making up a fourth song. "*Okay,*" I sang, "*Moses, Moses, sweet little boy, you're such a delight; you're such a joy.*"

He let his arms drop to his sides, and I kept singing.

"*You're a comfort to your mother, and one day you'll be as tall as your brother.*" This made him smile, and he relaxed his body. He sat back down next to me and held my hand, listening while I made up another song for him. When I finished, he hugged me.

"Thank you, Auntie," he said.

"You're welcome, Moses."

He popped off the bench to put his sandals on and to start walking back, but I stopped him. "Can you tell me more about the ears?"

"I was just angry because I didn't understand why you would close my people ear before singing to me."

"What do you mean, 'people ear?'"

He giggled. "You know, Auntie. The *people ear*."

"I'm not sure I do know, Moses. Can you tell me? Just to be sure?"

So, he told me.

"This ear," he said, pointing to his left ear, "is the people ear. It's the one that hears people. And animals, of course, and music, and thunder, and the waves, and farts." He giggled. "I guess it's the people ear and the things ear. Is that what it's called, Auntie? Is it called the *people and things ear*? Is that why you didn't understand me at first?"

"I think I'm starting to understand," I said. "Go on."

"Well, this one," he said, pointing to his right ear, "is the Yah ear. It's for hearing Yah. Just like yours," he said. "You have two ears, too. Just like me, silly. When I close this ear"—he put his own hand over his right ear—"then I can hear only people, not Yah. And when I close the other ear"—he pointed to his left ear but didn't cover it—"then I can only hear Yah and nothing else. So, I thought you wanted me to listen to Yah before I listened to you sing. But then I thought you weren't going to sing to me at all."

I was pretty sure I understood, but I was stunned. How could we have not known this about Moses? How had he gone so long without us realizing that he could only hear us from one ear? It did suddenly explain why no noise ever aroused him from his sleep when he slept on his left side. And maybe it also explained why he didn't speak until long after Hur. We'd thought it was just because he was younger.

"Let me see if I understand," I said carefully. "This ear"—I wiggled his right earlobe—"is for hearing Yah. And this ear"—I covered his left ear with my whole hand—"is for hearing people."

"Yes," he said.

"Then how come you heard me when I covered your people ear just now?"

Moses rolled his eyes at me and crossed his arms in front of his chest. "Auntie, I'm not a baby anymore," he said. "I've already learned how to see the words on your lips. Do you think you can trick me? I know how ears work. We have two ears. One for Yah, and one for people. Have you ever seen someone with three ears?" He started to laugh. "Or four? Or five? Or six? Or seven?" He laughed to himself as he counted all the way back to the fig trees; then I sent him to gather fruit while I told Vida what I had just learned.

WE LEARNED

We learned so much in the years that followed.

Miryam learned that she could live in two worlds at once. As Suf's handmaid, she tended to all the food and water, clothing and furnishings, and other tasks and errands of the household. And as Vida's daughter, she was doted on and caressed and thanked and admired, though the same was also true in Suf's quarters. Miryam reported that Suf was kind and gentle at home, which was what we had all seen of her when she'd collected or returned the boys or when we'd see her in the gardens. Miryam learned to go back and forth easily; and though her duty and roof was with Suf, her heart was with her mother.

There were many mornings when it'd be Miryam who came to get Moses instead of Suf. But even when Miryam did not, it was still easy to see her often. We watched her blossom with her responsibilities and take pride in her accomplishments. She still danced with us under the full moons, and Suf began to join us as well. Miryam brought us cookies that she would bake on the mornings of the new moon. She held a cookie in each of her open palms as she handed them to us. "This is an eye," she would say, and we would respond the same. The plight of the Israelite women who performed this ritual not so far away from our homes was never, ever far from our minds.

Aaron learned potions and illusions with other boys in the king's court. With his fused fingers, he would never be chosen as the next pharaoh, but he would also not be raised as an ignorant commoner. He was still grouped with other boys according to the practice of teaching everyone a little bit of everything so that they could learn where they showed the most skill and where they could be of the most service. Shortly after his education began, Aaron was assigned to learn magic. It suited him well, giving him a place to apply his curiosity and wonder as well as his sense of humor.

The first trick that he showed us on one of his frequent visits was that of turning a snake into a staff. He brought the snake to our courtyard and laid it gingerly on the ground, telling us to step back so that we were not harmed by it. The snake was still, but it would only take a moment for it to decide it was angry enough to attack. Vida peeked through her fingers, barely able to watch, as Aaron grabbed it by its tail and, before we could blink, turned it into a stiff rod in his hand.

We all gasped and applauded, and Hur and Moses said, "Again, again, again, again!" until Aaron obliged and did it again and again and again and again. Knowing that he was safe, we all watched excitedly—Vida even used her hands to clap instead of to cover her eyes.

Then Hur and Moses both went from asking to see the trick again to asking to do it. "Absolutely not," Aaron said. Then he lowered his voice to a whisper and brought the snake to sit beside us. "Look," he said, "the snake is made of wood with metal hinges and all covered in paint."

Moses reached his hand out to touch it, but Aaron moved it away. "You must learn how to move your wrist and arm the right way to make it work," Aaron said. "I did not make it; it was made by the boys who learn to craft, then given to the boys who learn magic. Maybe when you're older, you can try."

Hur did learn to make such things when he got older. He weaned and began learning with the older boys before Moses even had one loose tooth yet, though he wished he did. Hur didn't need to depart from our chamber, of course. Since he was Kesher's son, he stayed with her—with us. Every evening, he came back filled with stories of carving or constructing, and he often spoke of Besh, who was quickly becoming the most admired artist in the group even though he was also one of the youngest.

"Besh is the son of Ra'ayon," Vida reminded us all, "though she had called him Betzalel when he was born and brought to the harem. Have Ra'ayon and Ra'ayva gone back to Goshen?" she asked. But Hur didn't know.

Later, we learned from Elisheva that they were, indeed, back with the Israelites. She hadn't come to bring us that news, but she shared it when asked. She had come back to the harem to check on her brother Nakshon, the one whose harem-mother called him Ankh. When she brought back word to her mother, she told her that he was learning to be a warrior and was becoming strong and mighty.

It was during this visit that Elisheva brought with her a copy of my father's scrolls, though it was actually Refa, a grandson of my brother Efraim, who had brought the copy. He'd been there on the day it was first read, and he'd been there when it had been copied. He would not release it easily and said he would only give it to me himself, for he needed to verify that his grandfather's sister still truly lived.

When he saw me at the gate of the harem, he knew it was me. While he had become a grandfather himself, I looked exactly the same as I had when he'd last laid eyes on me at the first reading of *The Scrolls of Joseph*. Without a word, Refa bowed his head, kissed my hand, and presented me with the scrolls wrapped in the violet cloth. My private life in the harem, where I interacted with only a few people most of the time, had allowed me to forget the shock that others felt when they saw me. For just as I was used to the signs of age on Kesher and Vida and Suf and the children, they were used to the absence of these signs on me. Refa's reaction to me was a reminder that I was different from the others.

Kesher learned that having a daughter was as wonderful as having a son. She gave birth to a girl she called May-tal, saying that Miryam contained the water of the sea and May-tal, the water of the dew that was on land—both as important to our family as all water. Though May-tal would never grow to become a prince, she brought Kesher the joy of a baby whom she would not need to part with for a long time. And though Miryam was living with Suf, Kesher wanted to choose a similar name for her daughter to help the two feel like sisters. May-tal brought all of us the joy that a baby brings with a coo, a smile, and the wonder of discovery and possibility. She also brought the reminder that there were still Israelite children being born into oppressive conditions. Though the order to drown the babies had ended, we knew our kin and their children were still living with many hardships.

Moses learned how not to be the youngest: he kissed and cuddled little May-tal; he sang to her and tickled her and waited impatiently for her to be big enough to run around with him; and he also learned that there were games that babies could play—he delighted in her laugh when he hid under a blanket and then surprised her with his face suddenly near hers.

Before May-tal learned to walk, Moses lost his milk teeth and gained an education. He learned to read and write and do accounting. Thus, he was assigned by his instructors to read the texts of the pharaoh's accomplishments and make copies of them. He was also assigned by me—that is, requested and gifted by me—to read my father's scrolls and learn about the history of our people. And, of course, Moses learned to live with Suf, which meant that we all needed to learn to live without Vida.

This was one of the most difficult things we had to learn to do in that period. Saying goodbye was tear-filled for everyone, but the tears were not only of sadness. While we were all sorry to part, Vida was happy that all three of her children were safe, thriving, and loved. She had seen to it that Suf was their mother, so they now belonged in Egypt. Her children were not surrounded by the tribe of Levi, but they were far from alone: they had Hur and May-tal, me and Kesher; they had Kohenet overseeing the safety of the harem; and they had each other.

There had been countless nights when Vida had cried in my arms or Kesher's, anticipating the departure and separation from us and her three children. But when the time came, it was the rest of us who felt the weight of that sorrow, for Vida had already accepted it.

"I will go and be with my husband now," she said. "Poor Amram, serving the pharaoh day and night; his only solace—I imagine—is that his family is protected. Now, I can bring him stories of the wonderful life we have lived and assurance that our children still live, and he will be strengthened. And," she added, "we will see each other again. Blue will reunite us when she helps all of us Israelites go back to our land. So, to pass the time until then a bit more comfortably, I have been setting aside a little food each day, dried fruits and small satchels of grain. This food was mine to eat, but I've saved it for Amram—for us. We will eat and be satisfied and think of how lucky we are."

Vida was not lucky among the Israelites. Her life was difficult. Elisheva brought us that news over the years. As a skilled midwife, Elisheva traveled in the clothes of her profession without ever meeting resistance or suspicion, so she continued to bring news between the run-down houses of the Israelites and the decorated halls of the harem. I did not know when or how to move forward with going to the land of Israel. Perhaps by setting aside food like Vida had, we could store enough for small groups to leave—as Yo-av and Li-av had so long ago—and slowly return home. Would just a few men be missed or worth pursuing if these groups left during the night every so often? Or maybe just one man could take some newly pregnant women and reunite them with the children of our matriarchs so that the next generation could be born free.

I eventually learned that none of the ideas I'd thought of were the ones that would be our path. I would like to say that I learned to patiently await the exodus, but I think it is more correct to say that I learned the longsuffering of not being able to make the big change. While waiting, though, we followed Vida's example and began to send food in Elisheva's medicine bag. She was even able to obtain a second one so that she could carry more. In that way, she began to carry more than just messages and news with her.

The most joyful news that Elisheva took to Vida was that she was to be wed to Aaron. Unlike Moses, who would also soon be old enough for a bride, Aaron did not need to ask the pharaoh for permission because he was an unknown son to his adoptive father. Thus, Aaron would not receive bride money or a home of his own. Nonetheless, he asked Suf, and she readily agreed to have Elisheva join them in her quarters. This delighted not only Aaron but all of us.

On the night of the full moon that came before the wedding, Kesher and I bathed Elisheva, massaged her skin with fragrant oils, and decorated her hands with henna. Suf gave her a beautiful robe to wear, and Kesher put a necklace around her neck that had small stones that glistened in the moonlight. Miryam brought out a copper bowl filled with water that she drew from the river, and May-tal arranged rugs and drums. That night, we danced and drummed under the moon with so much hope and happiness that we drew the attention of many other women in the harem. When Kohenet joined our circle, they also felt permission to do so, and our song flew as high as the moon herself.

"Sister, Mother, Daughter, and Friend,
You shine with love from beginning to end.
We give you our hopes, our dreams, and our pain,
You keep them safe, until we meet again."

That night, as so many of us lay panting on the blankets, I took it all in, *Yhhhh*, and felt my matriarchs with me. Then I gave myself to the circle, to the moon, to the timeless chant, and to the women and girls of generations to come. *Whhhh*. After others had joined me in breathing for a while, there was silence around me, and I told them of our mother Hallel.

"Hallel, daughter of Sarah and Abraham, lived in this harem, in this palace. She had five daughters and countless granddaughters. All of them learned about Yah; all of them knew Yah. All of them became one with Yah here in Egypt. All of them danced and drummed under the full moon. One of them was Deborah.

"After many years, these traditions returned to Hallel's homeland, even if she herself never did. And on this very night . . . right now . . . in Hallel's homeland, there are daughters of Sarah, Rebekah, Deborah, Leah, Rachel, Zilpah, and Bilhah who are dancing under the moon just as we have. These sisters are breathing in Yah just as we do. They are taking us in even while they are there, just as we are taking them in even while we are here. We are all one, tonight and all nights. One day, we will reunite in the land of my birth and have a celebration even bigger than this one."

That night, I dreamt of that celebration. I saw so many women that I could not count them. But since it was a dream, we did not look like women—we looked like bees. And we were not in a circle under the moon, but we were in a line leading to our hive where there were other bees making a sweet home for us. There was also a hand holding the hive, and when I followed the hand to the arm, shoulder, neck, and, finally, face, I saw that it belonged to Moses, though his face was not as I had always seen it, that of a clean-shaven Egyptian young man—it was that of a long-bearded old Israelite, much like my grandfather Israel himself.

In the morning, I wished my father had been there to provide the interpretation of the dream. He likely would have said that the meaning lies with Elohim, but I believe he would have been able to learn that meaning. I could only guess. I also, for a moment, wished he could be there to witness the wedding of Aaron to Elisheva. It was tiring, sometimes, to be of the eldest generation. Even though Kesher was an Israelite who looked older than me, she was many generations younger, and she did not hold the same memories of people or places as I did. My thoughts went back to Grandmother Rebekah saying that it was foolishness to live without Deborah and to Grandmother Leah not wanting to be the only old woman. I was often able to bring myself back to gratitude for my long life and many loved ones, but there was always a loneliness that stayed with me.

When I told Kesher these thoughts, she thanked me—not only for telling her but also for being the oldest. She thanked me for the wisdom I brought and the unique life that I'd endured so that she and others could love me and learn from me and, one day, leave Egypt with me.

"I'm not sure that 'endure' is quite right," I said. "I don't only *endure* you and the children," I said. "I love you all."

She knew that, though. She always knew, and I loved that about her. But soon, I would have one less child to love, for shortly after Aaron's wedding, Moses went to Goshen. Of course, I could still love him from afar, but I missed him too.

A position had become available to oversee some of the Hebrew work camps, and Moses had requested to be a part of that. There were ten men going, he said, and he wanted, finally, to see the place where he had been born and see the people he was a part of, even if secretly so. Suf was not pleased, for she feared he could be in danger. We had always thought that Moses would be fully protected because of his royal Egyptian status, but Suf was worried about what would happen to him if it were discovered that he had not been born an Egyptian prince. Moses, like so many young men who are ready to leave their mothers, assured her that he would be safe and return soon.

HE CALLED OUT

HE CALLED OUT

Moses called out to his mother as soon as he set foot back in the harem, but everyone but the guards were sleeping, and his exhausted voice didn't wake them. It was a dark night with only a sliver of moon, and clouds were covering many of the stars. Moses was having difficulty breathing. He was shaking. He was filthy. He was bleeding. He was carrying something that appeared to be a person under a blanket, and Vida was limping beside him and crying. The guard looked at him questioningly, but Moses ordered him to awaken one of the boys to fetch me and Kesher and tell us to meet him in his and Suf's rooms at once, and then he kept walking directly there.

We ran to their chamber and arrived just as Moses and Vida were stepping in. He looked strong carrying his burden. Vida looked small and weak, worn and slow. Moses laid his bundle on the bed, and Vida knelt beside it and lifted the blanket. It was a man. It was Amram. He wasn't dead, but he was badly beaten. There was dried blood in his hair, and blood still flowing from his mouth. His arms did not lie on his chest the way they would if they were intact. We all gasped at the sight.

Elisheva never went anywhere without her medicine bag. At night she even kept it beside the bed she shared with Aaron. It was as much a part of her hand as her fingers were—and a more permanent part of her body than the baby who was quickly outgrowing her womb. Still, none of us knew what had happened, but Elisheva knelt beside Amram, gently opened his mouth, and put a few drops of her oil onto his tongue.

Miryam brought water and began gently cleaning blood off her father's face. "*Yah, please heal him,*" she sang with each gentle stroke. "*Yah, please heal him.*"

I took a cloth and joined her in cleansing and praying: "*Yah, please heal him; Yah, please heal him.*" I don't know whether he'd have felt it if we had not been gentle, for he was completely unconscious, but we could only use our utmost tenderness. Soon Vida joined in the singing too. Kesher, tightly holding May-tal's hand, put her arm around Vida's shoulders and added her voice. Elisheva, mixing herbs into Miryam's water, softly hummed along.

Moses was crying into Suf's lap, and Hur had his hand on Moses's back. They, too, joined the prayer. Aaron then took all of them into his long, strong arms. I heard his deep voice join us in song. Moses was still gasping too much to sing, and it was hard to tell whether the prayer was for him or for Amram, but there was no need to narrow it to just one of them. We still did not know what had happened before, but we knew deeply what we wanted to happen next. Our whole family sang as one with every wish in our heart: "*Yah, please heal him; Yah, please heal him.*"

I don't know how long that went on. Sometime later, we were interrupted by Kohenet walking into Suf's chamber with a lamp.

We all looked at her, surprised. We had been so consumed by our prayer that it was a shock to see a person moving or holding light or staring at us. She looked at us long enough to know that she should speak softly, but she still spoke with urgency.

"What happened?" Kohenet asked. "Two armed men have come to the gate demanding to enter and retrieve Moses. I told them nobody would enter the harem in the dead of night and that they could come back and make their request again in the morning.

"One of the guards said to me, 'No request has been made. We demand that you bring Moses to us.' He wished to believe he was going to force me to do something, but I answer to nobody but the pharaoh himself, and I told him as such. 'If you will not open the gate tonight,' the guard said, 'we will wait here until morning and go in and get him ourselves.' And then the two of them grasped their swords and stood stiffly beside the gate, where I believe they plan to stay."

"I must leave," Moses said. "I'm bringing danger to everyone."

"Don't leave," May-tal said. She put her hand in his.

"Moses, Vida," Suf said, "tell us what happened."

"I was walking toward my father . . . toward Amram, that is," Moses began. "I had seen the Hebrews baking bricks, sweating in the sun and fire, carrying mud and muck, always being yelled at: 'Faster, farther!' The oxen have a better life. Grown men whose bodies were as skinny as straw were carrying bales of it to grow the pharaoh's buildings bigger and bigger. It is terrible. I knew it was terrible before, but I had not known exactly what terrible looked like.

"I was writing down the equipment at each camp. I saw when the overseers put extra food in their pockets to bring home to their wives and children. They were healthier than the regular workers, but no less subjected to the tight reins of the pharaoh's long-reaching whip and cruel restrictions. I did not write down their thefts; I looked the other way.

"But I could not look the other way when these very same men, who were, themselves, cheaters and thieves, whipped the Israelites for falling under the weight of their loads or tripping over their own torn shoes and then took those shoes away as well. I am higher ranking than any overseer in the fields—that is plain on my clothes—so they would not question me, but they would harbor anger. Still, what could I do?"

Moses hung his head. The room was still quiet, and Kohenet, though caring, had lost none of her urgency. "Is that why the men are here to collect you?" she asked.

"After seven days of this, I saw my father . . . that is, Amram. I would not have known him, but a young Israelite girl had been sent to the workers with apples. They were mashed and bruised and small, but she gave one to each man. As she did, she'd say the man's name and the name of the wife who'd sent the apple. When I heard her say, 'Amram, this is from your wife, Yohevid,' my head jerked in the direction quickly enough to see him take the apple.

"For three more days, I watched my father . . . that is, Amram. I wanted him to see me. I wanted him to know who I was. But I did not want the overseers to know. So when I was not bound to my tasks, I walked by him, carefully, without drawing attention. On the first day, I just watched him with my gaze. *That is my father*, I thought. On the second day, I praised him and said, 'May

Yah watch over you.' This caused him to look at me quizzically, though he did not stop his work—nor would I have wished him to. On the third day, he was working in an area separated from the other workers and overseers. *This is my chance*, I thought. So I walked closer to him. I was so careful . . ."

Moses trailed off and wiped tears from his face. Vida still had not said anything; it seemed that this was still Moses's story to tell. I held her hand, surprised and saddened by how small and fragile it felt from years of labor in Goshen. Moses breathed in. *Yhhhh*. He held that breath before giving it back. *Whhhh*. He was clearly not ready to go on, but he didn't have much choice as Kohenet, still standing in the doorway, was expecting more.

"I went and stood by him," Moses said. "I looked around. I didn't see any guards nearby. Really! I checked, and I checked again!" Suf stroked his arm to try to help him, but his voice was still raised and getting quicker with every word. "I stood in front of him with my legs apart and my hands on my hips. I looked every bit the Egyptian royalty that I am. It was clear that I shouldn't have been challenged, and I had checked, and there wasn't anyone there to challenge me. So, while Amram kept working, his back bent, his hands still digging clay from the mud that he stood in, I told him, 'I am Moses.'

"I was quiet when I said it!" Moses almost yelled these words. "I was so quiet! But he heard me, as I had hoped, and I didn't think anyone else had, for I'd looked around. But my father . . . that is, Amram"—he looked at Suf for just a moment—"Amram was so startled that he dropped his load. Then he also looked around and also saw that nobody else was there, so he whispered, 'My son?' I nodded, and he put his arms around me and embraced me. But before I'd even had a chance to embrace him back, an overseer was upon him, pulling him off me and throwing him to the ground.

"I yelled for him to stop, but he did not stop. He began beating Amram with his fists and kicking him with his feet. 'Stop!' I yelled again. 'I will deal with this Hebrew!' I shouted. But the man ignored me. He would not and did not stop until I pulled him off Amram. Then the overseer was going to strike me—How would he dare?—but before he could do so, I struck him in the nose with my staff and threw him to the ground behind me. I turned back to Amram. He was covered in blood, and his arms were broken from trying to protect his head from the blows. He was spitting up blood, too, from being kicked in the stomach. I immediately tried to help him up, and only then, when I was holding him safely in my arms, did I turn to tell the overseer that he would be punished for this. But . . ."

Moses trailed off, and this time he was not able to finish. His sobs overtook him, and he could not speak. Aaron wrapped Moses in his strong arms, and Vida took over the story, though she didn't leave Amram's side.

"The overseer had fallen face-first into the mud and didn't move," Vida explained, "even when Moses kicked his legs. Moses quickly took dirt and mud and covered the dead Egyptian, then helped his father limp—then carried him—back home, asking directions from Hebrews he saw along the way. Thankfully, no other Egyptians were around at the time to question his rank or actions. Now, imagine my joy at seeing Moses after all these years and then the horror that immediately replaced it when I saw my husband." This was easy for me to imagine, for I had just been glad to see Vida again before I took in the whole scene with Moses and Amram.

"Moses told me what had happened," Vida said, "and I praised his quick actions that probably saved Amram's life." Vida looked lovingly at her husband who was lying broken and unconscious on the bed but still breathing.

"I told Moses to hurry back to his duties, for surely the nine other men in his group would notice his absence, especially when it was time to gather for a meal or sleep. When he left, I tended to Amram the best I could. I was surprised to see Moses again the next day, but he returned to tell me that there had been Hebrews questioning him that morning. He'd seen two men fighting and had moved to stop them, but they challenged him, asking if he was going to kill them the way he'd killed the overseer—"

"I had really looked all around," Moses said, interrupting his mother to defend himself again, "and hadn't seen anyone, no guards, no overseers, no slaves. I was being so careful! I would never have revealed my identity if there had been others around. I would not have harmed anyone!"

Suf soothed her son as Vida finished the story, telling us how she, Moses, and Amram had stayed indoors until the sun was completely gone from the sky before setting out to come to the harem under the cover of darkness.

"You cannot stay here," Kohenet said. "I was able to keep the gates locked, but in the morning when they open, the men will force their way in. Even if I keep them closed a little longer, they cannot remain so forever. I do not want that kind of trouble in this harem. You will have to turn yourself in to them."

"Or leave," Suf said. "The pharaoh will not deal kindly with you."

As soon as Suf had made her suggestion, we recognized that she was right, and things began to move quickly. We needed to get Moses out before the sun rose.

"But how can he leave?" May-tal asked. "They're waiting by the gate. He won't be able to get out."

"He'll go out the same way he first came in," Suf said. Then she turned to Miryam, "You'll watch over your brother?" she asked. "And bring us the news that he was not seen on his way to the river?"

Miryam nodded.

"I want to go with her," May-tal said.

"And I will go with him," Aaron said. "He can't go out there alone. He's not going to the harem, like he did as a baby, to be scooped out of the water by a compassionate young woman . . . and he can't go and be among the Hebrews, either, for it's the first place that the Egyptians will look. Anyone found helping or hiding him will be punished too."

"You must go to our homeland, Moses," I said. "And Aaron, you cannot go with him. Your wife is going to deliver your child any day. She cannot make that trek quickly. If you take her, you will need to look after her and the baby, and Moses will still be on his own."

"Kohenet," I said, "will you arrange some clothing for a young lad to go with Moses? We'll pack a donkey with food and drink and provisions for the journey."

Kohenet nodded.

"Then I will go with Moses," I said. "I can wear the lad's clothes, and I will take Moses to the house of one of my mother's sisters in Israel. He will be safe there until the pharaoh forgets what has happened." These words came out of my mouth almost before I'd thought them. Finally, it would be time for me to return to the land of my birth. And finally, my youthful appearance would help.

Thus, before the sun had shed that day's first light, we had all the provisions packed for our journey tied to the back of a donkey and had different clothes on our backs. Moses's new clothes were clean and had belonged to Aaron. It would be helpful for Moses to be instantly seen as an important man from Egypt, even if he wore the garb of a court magician and not that of a court scribe. If he were chased, the Egyptians would be searching for a scribe. He removed the seal he wore on his finger and gave it to May-tal. I was dressed as an errand lad, too young to have a changed voice, and clearly subservient to Moses. We bade tearful, and far too short, goodbyes to everyone. Kesher hugged me close, then at arm's length, taking in my new appearance.

"Do you think this is it, Blue?" she asked. "Do you think this is why Yah has let you keep your youth? Why Yah had given you the life that you have lived?" Kesher wasn't the only one awaiting my answer. Even Kohenet, who had been rushing every move, paused to listen.

"Surely this must be at least a part of it," I said, "at least a step forward. We are going back to the land of my birth. I am going back, after so long. I thought I would be bringing all the Israelites with me, though perhaps I still will." That was all I could say. It was all I could think. It had been so many years of waiting, followed by so many years of my kin suffering as slaves while I had been unable to do anything—*no*, I thought to myself, *unable to do much.*

Miryam and May-tal walked in front of us, quietly leading us to the river, the bathing place from which Moses had first come to us. He and I followed a little behind them, with me pulling the donkey by its rope as if it were something I had done every day of a young life. Just before we turned the bend, Moses and I looked back at our loved ones: Miryam and May-tal watching us with the gaze of a hawk, Elisheva crying into Aaron's shoulder, Kesher and Suf holding tightly to each other. Vida was still inside by Amram's side—out of sight—but Kohenet had come out and was waving us to hurry along.

"Yah, please watch over us on our departure, our travels, and our return," I said. Then Moses, the donkey, and I entered the Nile through the bathing pool, exited through the reeds, and began our journey home.

MIDIAN

We got as far as Midian, which was a fourteen-day journey from the palace. We had plenty of supplies, and if anyone had pursued us, they did not reach us. There were several days in which we were each in our own thoughts, followed by more days in which we shared deeply about our fears and hopes. It was the first time that I got to know Moses the man. He was very similar, of course, to the boy I had cuddled and chased after years before, but he was no longer a child. He was now old enough to take a bride, and if I had not been dressed as a young manservant, we could have appeared to be a newly-wed couple.

Moses's memories of his youngest years were few, and the life that he had lived among the princes of the palace was more prominent in his mind. I believe this is the reason he was surprised when I reminded him that I felt it was my duty to help the Israelites return home. It was as if he were listening to my stories for the first time when I told him about leaving the famine in the land of Israel and then going down to Egypt to live in the land of plenty. I told him our time there was not meant to be forever, but the Israelites had settled into life on the lush green grazing land

and did not leave when the famine was over. Nor did they leave when Judah would have brought them back, since he'd promised not to abandon my father there. And nor did they leave when my father died and Benjamin, Israel's only living son, was prepared to take them back to their land with me. I told Moses that when I'd gone to ask the pharaoh to release them, I'd been stripped and shamed and sent away, leaving me with nothing else I could do. "Do you not remember?" I asked.

Moses said he did not remember my having gone to the pharaoh to ask him to free the Israelites, yet he knew immediately that it would not have worked anyway, even if I had been granted an audience. While he was probably right, I asked how he could be so certain.

"The pharaoh needs the Israelites for many things," Moses replied. "Yes, he needs them to build his cities that show off his greatness, but it is not only that. He also needs powerless people in order to show his power. If he were to free the Israelites, he would have to replace them with powerless Egyptians, and there are too many Egyptians with status who would not tolerate that. It is much easier to oppress a small group of people. That way the large group can think they are better and safe from harm. Of course, there are many oppressed people in Egypt, not just the Israelites, but the pharaoh is not the only one with power, just the one with the most power.

"It is well known that the Council also works to maintain the oppression of these peoples, for doing so allows them, too, to maintain their status and power. If the pharaoh were to release the Israelites, he'd risk the Council taking over. He would never take such a risk, even if he felt that he would win. Why go through the trouble? He would just lose men in the process. Auntie, it never would have worked to ask, nor even to cajole or bribe the pharaoh to let our people go. He would not only lose his labor but possibly his entire reign."

"What is this council?" I asked him.

"The Council of the Firstborns," Moses said. "It is the men who inherit the double portion of their fathers' wealth. The Council members work together to hoard that wealth and live off the fat of the land, enjoying luxuries that others cannot afford and protecting their wealth so that they can give it to their own firstborns. Auntie, when I read in your father Joseph's scrolls that he'd received the double portion from his father, even though he was not the firstborn, I was surprised. That is not the way in Egypt, even if he was the firstborn of his mother. The Council of the Firstborns is what they call themselves, but they do not include all firstborn Egyptian boys, only the ones whose fathers have enough wealth to give their firstborn a double portion of significance. Still, these men would protect any firstborn son before they would stand up for a lower born son or, especially, a slave of any sort."

I had always seen Moses dressed in the garb of a prince, for he was one. But he was a prince who had lived with me and learned to read with me, a prince who had still let me stroke his cheek, even there in the desert after it had grown prickly without his daily shave. So I had not stopped to think that this prince of Egypt had spent most of his days among other princes and people who had lives completely different from mine. Moses knew so much more about the workings of the palace than I did, even after all my years there, and him agreeing that I would not have been granted my request to the pharaoh—had I even been able to make it—helped me feel a little less guilty that I hadn't been able to do so. Thus, what I was learning from Moses gave me much to think about on our journey.

Moses and I both spent a great deal of time in thought and reflection and quiet as we walked. And after a while, it seemed like, somehow, we had spent too much time doing so. Regardless, I was grateful that we had seen only a few people on the roads as we traveled. I did not think we would be subjected to thieves, for we clearly had little to take, but I was eager to finally return to my homeland. I was surprised by how much I longed to see the cave where my ancestors were buried and to see the descendants of my matriarchs who still lived nearby. Finally, when we'd come to a well that was a gathering place for travelers, Moses asked one of the nearby men if we were close.

Much to our surprise, we were told that we'd gone too far south *and* too far east. And when we'd sincerely thought that we must almost be to the land of Israel, we learned that from where we were in Midian, we were still several days' journey away and would need to retrace our steps before correcting our course. Though we'd been appreciative of our solitary life, we thought by then that we would have already found my mother's sisters and be among kin.

In Midian, we were also among kin, just more distant kin. Moses had not realized that, so I had to tell him that Midian had been a son of Abraham and his wife Keturah, whom he had married after Sarah's death.

After learning that we were in the wrong place, we decided to stop our travels, spend the night where we were, and ask Yah to direct us on the right course in the morning. Once we had made our request, Moses wrote down the lineages that I realized I only knew thanks to having heard *The Scrolls of Deborah*. Though my father had been the scribe of those scrolls and knew all they had contained, he had not copied the lineages into his own scrolls, so Moses had never read them.

In the morning, Yah did indeed direct us on the right course, though not the one I was hoping for or expecting. When we awoke, there were seven women drawing water from the nearby well and filling the troughs for their sheep. The sun was only just beginning to show a hint of rising, but it soon became evident why the women had brought their sheep so early. Four men then arrived with their sheep and began to drive away the women and use the water they had drawn.

I began putting away our tent since it was something that Moses could not be seen doing due to his status. Even with a beard beginning to grow and some dust from the trip, he still clearly looked like a high-ranking man. When he walked to the shepherds, they stepped aside so that he could drink, but Moses did not use the water to quench his own thirst. Instead, he brought it to the women and let each take a sip from the ladle he held with his own hands.

Then he said to the shepherds, "I saw that these women arrived with their flock before you did. I will help them water their sheep, and then I will help you water yours, and only then will I draw water for myself and my lad."

And that is precisely what Moses did. He helped the women first, for which they thanked him by trying to give him a sheep, but he did not take it. Only once the women and their flock had left did he help the men. When they'd departed, Moses drew water for us to drink and water for us to take. Just as we began to leave that oasis, the seven women returned, this time without sheep.

"Master," one said, bowing before Moses, "we thank you for your help in caring for our flock. Likewise, our father thanks you. He has scolded us, asking why we did not bring you to him to have bread with him, for it is our tradition to welcome the stranger, the traveler, and anyone who needs help. We told him that you were still helping the others when we'd left, but he sent us hastily back to invite you to break bread with him. Our father, Reuel, is a priest of Midian and a generous man."

Reuel! I almost said the name aloud but was able to stop myself. And Moses, thanks to having read my father's scrolls, also recognized this name as belonging to a son of Esau and a friend of Joseph. With gratitude to Yah for what we hoped would be a reunion, we followed the women back to their camp. There, Reuel came out to meet us, and even though he was old enough to need assistance to walk and wrinkled enough that his eyes hardly opened, he honored his guest with this effort. I saw Moses and Reuel greet each other with respect and affection, and I heard Moses introduce himself as Moses, son of Amram of the tribe of Levi, who was the son of Israel, also known as Jacob. I also got to hear Reuel say that he was Reuel, son of Reuel, son of Esau the Edomite, brother of Israel.

I wished to rush to this man and embrace him. As the son of Reuel, my father's friend, I wanted to tell him of my father's dreams to combine our tribes or, perhaps, to hear that he already knew of those hopes. I did not run to him, though, or go to him at all. While Moses went to eat with this Midianite priest, our kin from two tribes, I was taken to a lean-to where I was allowed to relieve our donkey of his burden and rest in the shade. Oh, to be banished from such a moment! I tried to close my eyes and sleep, but I could not ignore that I was being ignored.

Eventually, Moses came and retrieved me. We would not be continuing our journey just yet, he explained, for we had been invited to stay with Reuel. In fact, the youngest of the women who we had seen at the well was Reuel's daughter of his old age, Tzipporah, and Reuel had offered her to Moses in marriage. The tribe of Jacob and the tribe of Esau would finally unite, even if only through two people. I surprised myself by how eager I was for Moses to marry, especially to marry a woman by the name of Tzipporah, meaning bird. I often felt so different from everyone else that this little similarity of a name—though I was named specifically for a bird with blue wings—gave me comfort.

Even as I looked forward to having this new bird among us, I was hesitant to remain in Midian. When I questioned Moses about delaying our journey, he said he felt he had little choice in the matter. Reuel was his elder and his kinsmen, and he did not want to disrespect him, nor did he wish to draw suspicion to himself. He was, he reminded me, still the object of much anger in Egypt.

I wished I could have disagreed with him, but my desire to keep going on our journey was not enough to make it happen. Indeed, Reuel was his elder and his kinsman, Moses was ready for a wife, and combining the tribe of Israel with the tribes of Esau and Midian was advantageous to all. We would need to stay long enough for that to happen, and neither my impatience nor my disappointment was enough to move us forward.

TZIPPORAH

Tzipporah was wed to Moses, but I did not see the wedding. As his lad, I at least was able to help him prepare for the day. I served him food and brought him water to bathe. I anointed his head, and, best of all, I blessed him. Amram was not there to see this day. Vida was not there to see this day. Suf was not there to see this day. Miryam and Aaron and Elisheva and Kesher and Hur and May-tal were all missing this momentous day. I, dressed as a servant, was the only one of us who was there. And even though Moses was cautious to only address me as Lad and never as Auntie, that did not change the fact that he had been my little boy and that I could bless him on his big day. I put my entire heart into it, and I also felt that the blessing was from the others who could not be present.

"You live in the blessing of Yah," I said, "and Yah is always watching over you. In Yah, you are whole. May you find wholeness with Tzipporah as well." In the privacy of the new tent that Reuel had given Moses, the little baby I had once held in my arms bent down and kissed me on the cheek and thanked me.

The night was a long one of merriment for the Midianites and work for me. Along with the other lads, I fetched food and drink, cleaned cushions and replaced bowls, fed donkeys and mucked their stalls. I did this and more for seven days following the wedding while the bride and groom were served in the privacy of their tent. The work was dirty and difficult, but the most disturbing part was the other lads. They banded together to tease me as the new one, laughing as I struggled with saddles and heavy jugs, and especially when I insisted on finding privacy for relieving myself instead of participating in the pissing contests they were so fond of. They showed none of the hospitality that Reuel demonstrated.

Once the wedding week finished, I told Moses that I would like to leave. I did not mind being his lad, but I did not want to continue to live with the other ones. And, after all, we were on our way to the land of Israel. With the festivities over, we could proceed with our journey. Moses said he would need to talk to Reuel. I suggested that we also each talk to Yah. Until we received word, Moses welcomed me into his tent. Tzipporah was not pleased, but she accepted me sleeping on a cot in the storage area. Moses kept me near him always, so I was mostly spared the torment of the lads for a while.

For one year, I lived in the relative quiet of Moses's tent. There were times when a lad would corner me when I was briefly alone, and not just the same lad, but each lad, one at a time, and always with the same mocking tone and twisted sneer. Even with different words, their intentions were the same: to scare me, shame me, harm me. Sometimes I was accused of lying with Moses on our journey, and sometimes I was accused of still doing so, even though he now had Tzipporah to quench his needs. Sometimes

I was accused of being there to spy on Moses's wealth so that I could steal it out from under his nose. But the scariest was when I was not only mocked for being so much weaker than the rest of them but also called a girl.

I had gotten used to the work with the animals, and I had become better at it over the year. But that did not stop the others from tormenting me. One morning, one of the lads called out, "You can't do better than that, can you, girl?" and I turned my head.

"I knew you were a girl," he said. "You have been here long enough to grow whiskers, but not one has appeared above your lip." He moved closer. "Not one," he repeated, directly to my lip.

"If it is lip hairs you seek," I said, "when mine grow in, I will pluck one out and present it to you on one of Reuel's shiniest platters. Maybe the smooth copper one so that you can see your reflection in it and admire your own hairs, the only ones you need look at."

He laughed. It was not as rowdy as the way the lads spoke to each other, but it was close enough that he dropped his accusation. I had wondered whether I should have revealed myself to Reuel when we first arrived, but since I had not done so, I never wanted them to question that I was a lad.

I suggested again to Moses that we leave, and he repeated my earlier suggestion that we talk to Yah. When we had done that the last time, neither of us had felt that it was time for us to go, as much as I'd wished we would. The same was true when we checked again. When we were truly connected with Yah, the knowing came easily, and neither of us felt a pull to leave Midian.

And so, I endured. While I had my daily life as a lad, at least I had peace in the nights. Meanwhile, Moses learned shepherding from Reuel. The elder gave him sage advice for sheep, for life, and for leadership, and Moses was becoming a wiser man every day.

The day Moses became a father changed him forever. I wished that I could be by Tzipporah's side as she labored, but, of course, a lad would never be nearby. Because she lived with Moses in his tent—which was different from the practice of my grandmothers, though it was the way in Tzipporah's tribe—I did get to spend some time near her even though we did not interact. My favorite times being near her were when she would remove the pits from dates and toss the pits into one basket and the dates into another—she'd purposefully put the two baskets out of reach so that she could toss them.

This reminded me of the fun that Moses and the other children used to have during the olive harvests. After the excitement of whacking the trees to get the olives to fall into the blankets, the children would toss the fruits into baskets, moving farther and farther away to test their skills. Moses must have had a similar memory, for when he saw his wife doing that with the dates, he sat down and joined her. Soon they were competing to see who could do the fanciest or farthest tosses. It was a rare moment for me to see them together, and I was glad it was one of such joy.

When Tzipporah's labor pains began, I was not allowed to be there, but neither was Moses, so he requested that I walk with him. Whenever he made a request of me, it relieved me from other duties, but even if it had not, I was thrilled to be with him as he awaited the birth of his first child. We returned just in time to hear Tzipporah's loudest wail and the baby's first one, and we rushed to the entrance of the tent to wait for admittance. When he was allowed in, I told him I would wait for him just outside.

The midwives came out and gave me no report. How was Tzipporah? The baby? Had it been a difficult birth? I had no idea, and it still surprised me how easily I could be ignored. But by the time that Moses had seen his wife was well and had held his daughter, he was unable to be concerned about the thoughts of anyone who might see him emerge from the tent with a baby girl and put her in my arms to hold and kiss.

"My wife allowed me to help name her," he told me. "I knew it was her privilege, but I asked whether we could name our daughter in a way that honors my sister. Tzipporah already knows that it was thanks to Miryam that I even lived to become a boy, then a man, then a husband, and now a father. She is grateful to Miryam for all of that, and so she agreed and named our daughter, Galeet, a little wave from the sea of Miryam." I let my tears of joy fall on Galeet's sleeping face.

I stole glances of Galeet whenever possible, though I never got to hold her again. Tzipporah, surely just wanting what was best for her daughter, questioned whether it was still wise to have me in their tent. A nearly grown lad with a little girl? Surely this was not safe for their daughter, she said. But after just another moment of thought, she asked Moses why I had not grown taller since our arrival. Why I had all my teeth but no whiskers? And did they really need a lad living in their tent, especially now that a nursemaid would be coming to care for Galeet?

It was then that Moses realized that he should have told Tzipporah about me. So he started to. He told her that I was not actually a lad, but . . . before he could say more, Tzipporah began to yell.

"A woman? This whole time you have kept a woman? I have been your second wife? You told me that I was the first wife! You accepted gifts from my father! You kept her sleeping in a corner in our tent?"

Moses told me all of this as we were walking. He had just finished the conversation with her. "No," he had said, "no." Then, realizing he had not yet said that I was a woman, only that Tzipporah had assumed so after he'd said I wasn't a lad, he told her that I was a eunuch.

"Auntie, I am sorry," he said. "You do not deserve to be treated this way. There is an area of the camp where the eunuchs live. My wife, the mother of my daughter, she will not have a lad in our tent with the baby. She will not have a woman in our tent. She insists that you leave our tent and live with the other eunuchs."

Moses said all of this as we arrived at the area where the eunuchs were kept apart from everyone. There was only one person living there, Lo-Mukar, who wasn't even known by the tribe since everyone kept so far away. "Auntie," Moses said, "you should not be treated this way. I am sorry. I don't know what to do. Maybe now that Tzipporah is no longer pregnant and that Galeet is born, we can go to the land of Israel. Maybe, at the very least, I can escort you there to join the tribe of Emunah and receive the respect you deserve."

I agreed with Moses. But, it was not yet time to leave. We both talked with Yah separately, and we both felt we should stay. So, Moses thrived. He became an expert shepherd and a father of two sons. A long time passed before I even learned their names.

During that time, I was not even permitted to work in the stables or clean latrines. Lo-Mukar and I survived on foraging and begging. There was a time that I stole glances at the children. Galeet was showing her little brothers, Gershom and Eliezer, how she could balance a heavy jug of water on her head without spilling it. Baby Eliezer clapped for her, and Gershom ran around her on his tip toes, squealing with excitement. I had not known I would see them, and after only the shortest glance, I looked away. I felt like a thief watching them, that even the sight of this joy was not mine to have.

I called out quietly on my mat that night. Not to Yah, but to Vida and Kesher. "Our little baby has babies," I said in a whisper. "They are beautiful and strong. I am filled with pride and sorrow. Because you are not here to see them, you might ask me whether they have a Yah ear and a people ear like Moses. You might ask me whether they take off their shoes to hear better. You might ask me whether they are curious or smart or scared or funny. You might ask me to tell you those things because I am here and you are not. But even though I am here, I am not here. I do not know Moses's children, a girl and her two little brothers, maybe just like Miryam and hers . . . but I do not know." I said all of that to them, but they said nothing, because they were not there.

Lo-Mukar was there, but he was not a good companion. Having been shunned and alone for years, he did not easily trust me. The most he'd confided in me was that his mother had loved him, but she had died long ago. Before that, he had been seen as one of the boys of the tribe. But when his voice did not change, they stripped him naked to see the truth of his birth, then threw him aside for being born different.

When he shared that with me, I knew it was important that I tell him about myself. So I said, "I, too, was loved by my mother, and I, too, was born different." I was grateful to not have received the treatment that Lo-Mukar had. Why had Reuel, a man who prided himself so in his hospitality, discarded a member of his own tribe? I was glad that my presence made him no longer alone, but it was a very sad and difficult time.

When I felt that I could not stand it for even one more night, I followed Moses at a distance when he took his flock out. Alone in the desert, I approached him and said I would need to leave if something were not done. Moses immediately bowed his head to the ground before me. When he rose, he vowed to make things better. In fact, that very evening when he returned to his tent, I was with him. He told Reuel that he wished to pursue wider grazing land with his flock, teach his sons the ways of the shepherd, and take me and Lo-Mukar with him to help him in the field. He got us fresh clothes and gave us many bags of food to pack in a cart behind a donkey.

"If you are going," Tzipporah said, "then I am also going. I cannot leave you alone with those two . . . two . . . I do not know what they are. But they could hurt my children, and I won't have it. Or they could tempt you, which I won't have either. Somehow, they have already tricked you into helping them. It seems you will help anybody, Moses." Moses smiled a humble smile with his head down when she said this, though her tone had made it clear that it was not a compliment.

Tzipporah insisted that the small tent set up for me and Lo-Mukar be at least one hundred paces from the one she shared with her husband and children. Thus, Lo-Mukar and I had little interaction with the others but plenty of food, shelter, and quiet. Sometimes when I talk with Yah, breathing and listening, giving and receiving, being in the Oneness, a new path becomes clear. But sometimes, a new path comes like a kick from behind when it's least expected. I did not expect that my mounting irritation at the treatment Lo-Mukar and I received would carry us to the next steps, but we were in the fields with the sheep for fewer than seven days before that was exactly what happened.

MOSES LED

oses led us and his flock to the same well where we had first
met Tzipporah and where he and I, as his lad, had drawn
water and filled the troughs for the sheep. His flock now
drank until they were satisfied. Then Moses began to bring them
toward the grazing land that was beside a wadi. Unlike in Egypt,
where the soil had been watered by the Nile, the grasses here
grew in the rainy season and were long and green and awaiting
the sheep. There were also small flowers that waved a bit of color
here and there, large bushes that bloomed in their full glory, and
beside the wadi, lines of particularly large bushes that had soaked
in so much water when it had flowed there last that they were
now magnificently orange and yellow—so magnificent, in fact,
that it had almost distracted me from admiring how much Moses
looked like my grandfather with his long beard, tall shepherd's
crook, and confident walk.

While I looked at Moses, I saw him stop to admire the blazing
bushes, and I walked to do so beside him. When I arrived, I discovered that he was not only looking but listening. Soon, I heard
what he'd heard: his name.

"Moses, Moses, Moses . . ." It was loud yet distant, gentle but insistent. It had been a long time since we had worried about the Egyptian guards tracking us down, and Moses did not carry a sword with him anymore, or even a dagger. But he had a sling-shot, so he gripped it with his hand while he walked closer to the bush and the sound of his name. I followed him but left a small distance between us.

After a pause, Moses removed his sandals. That was what Vida had taught all the children to do when they got too upset or confused or overwhelmed when trying to learn something new. "Moses, Moses, take off your shoes," she'd said to him on the days he returned from his first lessons so excited that he could not say his words fast enough. "Let your feet be held by all the land. It is so much bigger and stronger than your shoes. Feel that beneath your feet and know that you are held." He then calmed down with his feet on the ground and was able to tell us about what he had learned. Miryam and Aaron, Hur and May-tal, had each been helped by taking off their shoes in similar moments. As had I.

Moses stood that way for a long while beside the bush. It was truly an exquisite sight, bright like flames blowing in a gentle breeze, but neither emitting heat nor burning into nothing—just going on and on to both the left and right along the bank of the wadi.

I heard the voice again: "Moses, Moses, Moses." I breathed in the sound of Moses's name coming from behind the bush or, perhaps, from within. It sounded like Moses's own voice, yet he was not calling himself, for I could see that his lips were closed and hear that the sound was coming from elsewhere. *Yhhhh.* What was this? In the slow rise and fall of Moses's shoulders, I saw that he was doing the same thing. *Whhhh.* I gave myself to this mystery, hoping that as we became one, I would understand more.

I heard more. This time, I heard not just Moses's name, but many words. "Remember *Yhhhh Whhhh,* the god of your fathers, Abraham, Isaac, and Jacob." When I heard that, I thought of my grandfather Jacob hearing the voice of a messenger of Yah when he was traveling. Surely that was what was happening in the desert that day.

The voice continued: "My people have been crying out because of their slave drivers. I am concerned about their suffering, and I have come to rescue them from the hand of the Egyptians and bring them to a land that is spacious, flowing with milk and honey. Now, come with me, and we will bring my people, the Israelites, out of Egypt."

Moses sat on the ground where he was and put his face in his hands. I couldn't blame him. He sat like that a long time. I watched him. I watched the bush. I breathed. *Yhhhh. Whhhh.* I listened. It was Moses who spoke next.

"Who am I that I should go to Pharaoh and bring the Israelites out of Egypt?" he asked.

Moses would be a wise leader, I was certain. What was unclear was why I had not been born a son of Joseph. There I was, dressed like a lad, but without the power of a boy of even such a lowly status. All these years, I had been waiting and somehow growing more prepared to lead the Israelites out of Egypt, yet it was not me who was being charged with the role but Moses, who did not want to accept it.

"I will be with you," was the reply we heard to Moses's question. "And when you have freed the people from Egypt, you will all serve Yah at this mountain."

I lifted my eyes from the bush to the mountain that stood on the other side of it. I saw large boulders and small rocks, patches of grass and scraggly bushes pocking the side. I was not sure, but maybe there was a goat path too. This mountain looked no different from the other ones, other than the bush that blazed at the bottom.

My attention was brought back to the voice when it spoke again: "Go and gather the elders of Israel, and tell them that I have heard their plight and will lead them out of their misery in Egypt and into a land flowing with milk and honey."

There was a lot of silence. I wondered whether Moses and I were hearing the same things or if, perhaps, he was hearing more with his Yah ear in the times where I had only heard silence. I did not move for fear of making any distracting noise. Finally, I heard Moses say that he could not do it. Then he said it again, louder, and once more, with tears.

But when he settled, I heard the other voice respond: "Your brother Aaron, the Levite, he will help you. He is already on his way to meet you and will be happy to see you."

Aaron! Oh, I would be so happy to see him! Even with my excitement, though, I remained still so as to not miss any more of this conversation. I was so still and so connected through my breath, straining to hear, yet hearing nothing, that I fell asleep. When I woke, I saw that Moses had also fallen asleep and was being awakened by his brother Aaron. Moses jumped up and into Aaron's arms, and the two hugged and kissed and cried. It was all I could do to keep my distance so that they could have this moment to themselves, and as soon as they released each other, I ran to greet Aaron as well.

He scooped me up in his arms the way he might have greeted a daughter of his but then exclaimed, "Auntie! I am so happy to see you!"

He put me down and kissed me on my hand. What a fun surprise it was to feel a smooth face kissing my hand—I had gotten used to Moses's long beard and those of the men around us. But seeing Aaron was a sweet reminder of the homeland I'd had for many years, even though it wasn't my birthland.

"Vida and Kesher assured me that you would be well," Aaron said. "I was not worried, but I'm glad to see they were right. They are very much looking forward to seeing you, as are Suf and May-tal and Elisheva, of course, and our three sons."

"Three sons! Aaron, how wonderful!"

Moses clapped his brother on the back, and we began walking to the tent. The sheep followed us, as did Aaron's lad with his donkey and cart. I felt almost as if my feet were walking on the air above the ground, that was how happy I was to have little Aaron's big hand in one of mine and little Moses's big hand in the other. Moses then told Aaron of his years of living with Tzipporah and learning from Reuel. He told him how pleased he was to have fathered his daughter Galeet and his two sons, Gershom and Eliezer. Likewise, Aaron shared his pride in having fathered three sons: Nadav, Avihu, and Elazar.

"Perhaps," Aaron said, "one of them will become the husband of your Galeet."

It was nice to have that joyful thought before we'd heard the rest of what Aaron had to tell us about life back in Egypt. None of us had expected that life would have become even harder, but it had. Aaron brought us news of groups of Israelites who had been shackled for asking for food, not even for extra food, just for the food they were already supposed to be allotted, which was not being given to them. There were other groups who had tried to hire traders to bring them out of Egypt. Many Israelites still had the possessions they and their families had owned for years, but when the Egyptians learned that the Israelites were trying to use their possessions to leave, traders were attacked by Egyptian guards to send the message that it would not be good for their business to help the Israelites.

Likewise, merchants were ordered to no longer sell to Israelites. The Israelites had prospered when my father had ruled, and they'd been using their coins sparingly over the years, most often because they'd had little time to buy things and so had only purchased necessities. Even then, the merchants would charge them an extra fee just for being Israelites. Now, though, any merchant suspected of selling to an Israelite was beaten severely—as was the suspected Israelite. This had happened so many times, Aaron said, that even the Egyptian customers were becoming afraid to buy, so the merchants were faring very poorly.

There was no place in Egypt that a person could go and not hear the crying of those who were suffering. This was true even in the palace, for there had begun to be hushed murmurings against the pharaoh. Only the firstborns in the Council defended him, and they were prospering, buying goods cheaply from merchants eager to collect any money at all, and even expanding their wealth by buying their own brothers' properties and then kicking them off or charging them rent.

"It will not be easy to leave Egypt," Aaron said, "but we all believe that it is possible, and it is time. It was Vida, Kesher, and Suf who summoned me to come and find you, Auntie. They say that they need you—we all need you—to help the Israelites return to our land now. And Moses," he added, "Auntie will need our help. There are things she cannot do, people who will not listen to her. The heads of the tribes, the Council of the Firstborns, and the pharaoh will certainly not endure a woman coming to them. We will need to be the ones to show him that this is right with Yah. And I," Aaron added, "have talked with Yah. It was Yah who brought me to you, Auntie and Moses, so that we can bring our people home."

When we reached the tent and Moses told Tzipporah about all that had happened, her only question was about me: "Why do you call this eunuch, Auntie, and why is he . . . or am I supposed to say she . . . here in my tent?" While Moses struggled to find the words to answer this and Aaron sat in surprise, I was the one who answered.

"Tzipporah, honored Tzipporah," I said, addressing her for the first time ever. "I am Blue, daughter of Deenah and Joseph. The very Joseph, son of Jacob, who was your grandfather Reuel's true friend. I am real." I wanted to answer this question before it was asked. "I do not show my age. I do not know why. I came with Moses as his lad when he fled Egypt so that he would not be alone and so that we might go to the land of our forefather Jacob. When your wise father combined our tribes with your marriage as soon as we arrived, we did not tell you that I am Moses's auntie who had raised him and loved him since his infancy.

"It was wrong to keep this from you," I admitted, "but once we had done so, it also seemed wrong to reveal it. Now, I am grateful that you know. I have wanted to dance with you under every full moon. I have wanted to tell Galeet stories of her namesake, Miryam, when she was a child. I can tell Gershom and Eliezer about their father when he was a boy of their size—about how he loved to throw olives into baskets like Gershom, and how he sometimes had a hard time finding his words like Eliezer, and how he loved to run and jump and delight in the wind like all his children do. Now I'm so thankful that you know the truth and that I can tell them those things and so much more."

I moved to embrace this woman who was almost a sister, whom I had only seen from afar, but whom I'd held close in my heart for many years already. But Tzipporah moved her body aside. In truth, I did not know that she would be willing to take me into her heart the way I had already done with her. But I had been hopeful.

She ignored me and addressed Moses: "You have had a woman in your tent for years? You have been taking a woman alone into fields? You have had a woman since even before you wed me?"

I understood her surprise, though I wished she would not be so angry. She'd been angry when she'd thought me a boy, and now she was angry to learn that I was a woman. It seemed that she was simply angry about the presence of someone else, regardless of who I was. Though I was tempted to tell her that I had never had the blood of a woman, thinking perhaps I could say something that would appease her, she spoke again before I—or Moses—could say anything.

"I will return to my father's house now. I will be with my sisters."

Nothing else was said. Tzipporah was a good name for this woman. She was as graceful as a bird. Her walk was like a dance, so smooth that her movements evoked thoughts of flight. However, her small stature and ease and grace were not an indication of weakness. Birds have thin legs, but they hold themselves upright—and sometimes upside down—on those little legs. I'd never seen Tzipporah go upside down, but I had seen her lift water jugs and children, and even a goat one time. I saw her strength of leg and arm, and I saw her strength of will. What she wanted to happen was what she would make happen.

Moses put his wife on a donkey and his children on another and led them back to Reuel's camp. Aaron and I spent the night in the tent that Moses left behind. Aaron was tempted to go to the bush and cut some branches to bring back to Elisheva and the others so that they could see the magnificence of the bright flowers. He decided, instead, to simply tell them about the colors and the glory and let them enjoy the anticipation of seeing it themselves.

In the morning, Moses returned, and we dismantled the tent and packed the donkeys. Aaron had already drawn water for the sheep, and I could see that he could become a caring and successful shepherd, one who seeks to anticipate and meet the needs of his flock. As a man who had grown up in a palace, he was especially grateful for that compliment. He walked beside his brother as we went to return the sheep to Reuel.

I still did not have a reunion with this son of my father's friend, but it seemed he had heard who I was from Tzipporah. When Moses took his leave, Reuel made no attempt to have him stay. "Let me go back to Egypt and see how I can help my kinsfolk. It is too dangerous to take my wife and children. Please, let them stay cared for by your generosity until I return and can bring them to live on a land of my own."

"Go in peace," Reuel said.

It was more difficult to watch Moses part with his children. "It is most important that you and your mother be safe and cared for," he said to them. "I learned this from my own father when he was apart from his wife, daughter, and two sons so that they could be safe. When I return, we will be together again. And once we have reunited, you will meet your kin, your grandfather and grandmothers and your uncle's sons, and you will eat breads with seasonings you've never tasted, and then we will go to the land of Israel together, where you will teach the others how to be successful shepherds, just like Reuel." He took all three children into his arms. He did not say anything else to Tzipporah, but they nodded to each other kindly, having worked out their differences the night before.

We did not wait to depart the next morning since Reuel had sent two of his men to guide us on the most direct route. With them ahead of us and Lo-Mukar and Aaron's lad behind us with the donkeys and carts, Aaron, Moses, and I began our journey back to Egypt.

MOSES AND AARON

Moses and Aaron discussed ideas and plots for organizing the Israelites, appealing to the Egyptians, dealing with the Council of the Firstborns, and approaching Pharaoh himself. I listened attentively for a long time while they named people and places that I did not know. As men, and men of the palace, they were aware of so many goings on that I had never experienced. Without that inside knowledge, I could not follow all of their conversation, but I enjoyed hearing them talk. And I loved watching Aaron show his little brother how to turn a staff into a snake and back again. By the seventh day of our journey, we were almost back. They had a plan, and I had an overwhelming longing to see the women I loved and missed.

Not knowing when we would return, the women were all dispersed and immersed in their tasks rather than waiting at the gate to the harem as I had foolishly hoped. May-tal was the first to see me and ran from the garden to tackle me with a hug. She was as tall as I was and she looked the same age that I looked.

"Auntie," she finally said, "you must be so tired from your journey. And I see that you would like to bathe and change your clothes." She was right, though I had not been thinking about that. "Go back to our chamber," she said. "I will fetch Mother and Miryam and Vida. We all agreed that whoever learned first of your return would tell the others right away." I hugged her once more and followed her instructions to return to my chamber.

I saw that Kesher had added many things in the years that I had been gone. There was a bright new tapestry hanging on one wall and shelves with painted pottery. Hanging over the windows, she had placed new curtains made of beaded leather strands. The beads sparkled in the sunshine and made little bits of colored light dance on the walls and ceiling. I was watching this dance when Miryam burst in and buried me in a hug. Though I knew through and through that the woman in my arms was Miryam, she looked so much like my memory of her mother that I was startled for a moment that she wasn't Vida.

Vida herself was not far behind, though. She rushed into our room, right behind Suf, and pried Miryam's arms off me so that she could have a turn to greet me, but Vida was no more willing to let me go when Kesher entered than Miryam had been. Then Suf and May-tal could wait no longer, so, eventually, we were all in one ridiculous, uncomfortable huddle until we found the will to separate. What a joy it was to look into these women's faces again! I had missed them terribly while I was away, but I had not even realized how much until we were reunited. Seeing them again after so long, I wondered whether they had somehow gotten more beautiful. It was clear they had gotten older. Vida, especially, was looking very worn. I reached my hand out to stroke her cheek, and then rested it on the back of her neck. She did the same to me.

"You look well," Kesher said. "But your clothes are ragged and covered in scents I have never before had the displeasure of smelling." Everyone laughed. I had so much to tell them about how I had acquired that stench, and there was so much I wanted to hear, but the bathing needed to happen first.

"I will get you a new robe to wear when you come out of the water," Suf said.

"And I will bring oils," Vida said.

At the word oils, Miryam put her hand to her mouth and gasped. "I will bring Elisheva," she said. "Oh, how terrible that I rushed right here instead of waking her. Baby Elazar has not been well. She has been by his side all the time, but I know she will want to see you, Auntie."

Elisheva and I got to have our reunion when I was clean and smelled of thyme, and then I got to meet her babies. I had so wished to know Moses's children but couldn't, so holding Baby Elazar in my arms—a child of my child—felt like I was being crowned queen. Nadav, whose birth I had just missed when I'd left, had already lost teeth and declared himself too old to sit on my lap. His younger brother, Avihu, pointed out that two of his teeth were loose, so he was also too big. But we smiled and ate together, and it was the first day of us getting to know each other.

I did not return to only joy, of course. Less than a day later, Amram died. He had waited to see his son Moses again, longing to look at the face of the boy he'd saved who had then saved him. Amram had suffered every day since his blows and had struggled more and more from the injuries as the years passed. Suf had kindly provided him with safety under her roof, which was shared with not only Aaron and Elisheva and their children, but also with Amram and Vida. Elisheva nursed her husband's father every day that she was not at a birth, and she left instructions for when she was gone. After his injuries, Amram was never able to walk more than a few steps at a time or use one of his arms, but he sat in the sun, appreciated not working in the brickyards, endured his pain, praised Yah for the life he'd had with his wife and two of his children, and waited for Moses to return one day. The day after Moses returned, Amram took his last breaths.

Thus, being back in Egypt meant at once being in mourning and in rejoicing. Both were done in a community of love, rather than on my own. And I was not the only one who was not alone, for even before I'd bathed, I asked Kohenet to see to Lo-Mukar and bring him to the palace eunuchs. There, I trusted, he would find others who'd had similar experiences to his and could become seen and known.

I was surprised by the lack of urgency I felt after returning to Egypt. For more than a lifetime, I had longed for the day we would leave Egypt. For countless nights, I'd dreamt of returning to the land of Israel and helping the Israelites go, for their first time, to my home. Their home. Our home. Once I'd returned to Egypt from the years in Midian, leaving again felt close enough to taste. I think the surety of it released a worry that I had held for a long time. A worry that I would not help with an exodus. A worry that I had misunderstood why I was so different. A worry that I would go on forever.

Those worries left as the people around me began to embrace the exodus idea in wider and wider circles. Many of the Israelites had already cried out for help, and now they were willing to accept it from wherever it came—even from me. Elisheva, still able to travel anywhere as a midwife, took me as her apprentice. On the dark nights of the new moon, we spoke to the women in the camps.

"This is an eye," we said, bringing the traditional cookies on top of cloths that covered dried grains and lentils. "Conserve what you can," we said. "It will be a long time until we can go, but we will go, and we will need things for the journey."

I reminded the women of our matriarchs who had been brave, wise, and also scared at times. I told them of coming to Egypt to escape the famine and of my father, Joseph, feeding his tribe. I was faced with the question, "Are you real?" many times, but I was also embraced with gratitude even more often. I was told over and over about the horrors and losses they'd endured, and many women soaked my cloak with their tears. These women were grateful to have a matriarch among them, and I was honored to be considered one.

We could not visit all the women, but we did not need to. The ones we'd visited spread the word and worked with each other to collect supplies and, more importantly, hope. By the time of our fourth visit, it seemed that all the women were working together and that all the women had heard that Blue, daughter of Deenah and Joseph, called Serrah, daughter of Asher, in the tribe of Israel, was going to help them get home. And thanks to the women talking among themselves, I was greeted by one woman who gave me eye cookies.

She said, "This is an eye," and then said, "My eyes are overjoyed to see you again, Auntie."

What was this? Again? I had not yet seen this woman on these preparation visits held on the new moon, I was sure. Who was this? She was a very thin woman, undernourished as they all were. She was bent over, whether from work or age or both, it was unclear. Her eyes held the wrinkles of many years of laughter and tears, yet they were also very clear, and they even twinkled as if they had a secret behind them. As I looked at her more closely, she took my hand and twirled the ring I wore on my finger.

"Nina?" I asked. "Nina?"

She smiled.

"Nina!" I said, squeezing her hand. "Nina." That night, I was not the one introducing myself. Nina, the granddaughter of Benno, proudly introduced me as her auntie to the women who were gathered and, with tremendous joy in her voice, told them of the time we had spent together when she was young.

"I always remembered you, Auntie," she said. "I always knew you would come back. Grandfather told us that you died when you went into the harem. Not died . . . he didn't say died. He said that you disappeared. He died not long after that. But when I heard rumors told of an Israelite woman who was living in the harem and helping babies, and later, when I heard rumors of the same woman still being young years later, I just knew it was you. I just knew it." Even with her voice deeper, Nina still sounded like that playful, helpful, wonderful little girl I had gotten to meet. Benno's own granddaughter. She looked like she had become a grandparent herself. Still, she was Benno's granddaughter. I praised Yah for letting me see her again.

"Hallelu Yah!" I exclaimed, thrilled to be reunited with Nina.

"Hallelu Yah!" she repeated after me. "But Auntie, there is more," she said. "When you leave this land and go home, to the land where you and Grandfather Benjamin chased after lizards and threw chickpeas at each other, not only will *I* go with you, but so will my daughters and their daughters. And one of those little girls will grow to be a woman who gives birth to a daughter in Hevron, or Bet El, or Shechem, or Beer Sheva. She will nurse her babies where Deenah nursed you, and the birds with the wings laced with blue will fly above and sing with gladness."

"Are you a dreamer?" I asked.

Nina laughed. I could not help but see her as the little girl she had once been. "No, Auntie," she said, "but some have called me a poet."

My heart was soaring that night. Though we had needed to be quiet among the Israelites, the women of the harem indulged me in celebrating with song the next night. We sat on a blanket under the stars in the wide-open space that was beside the bathing pool. The moon was not full, but our hearts were. We were a large circle of women. It had once been only me and Kesher, but that night, it was us two and Vida and Miryam and May-tal and Elisheva. Our voices carried to the other women in their chambers, and Kohenet came to see what was happening, then joined us in song. Suf also heard and came to sit beside Vida and sing. Eemo came, too, though I did not recognize her at first as the woman who had mothered Betzalel. There were many other women who came and whom I did not recognize, but I was overjoyed that there were so many women.

Of course, the men were also preparing. Aaron and Moses had been making plans on their return to Egypt, and others had been planning in Goshen, even in their absence. The Israelite men were willing to fight their way out of Egypt, even if it meant that some of them would only have sons who saw the land. Moses told them that he hoped the way out would not be behind the sword, and Aaron said they hoped for the pharaoh to expel them, not fight them.

One evening, they came back home from a day in the field reporting that some of the overseers also wanted to leave Egypt. Aaron and Moses had hoped for that. It was in their plan.

"We had bribed some overseers to let us talk with the Israelites," Aaron said. "Though the Israelites were nervous, we all stayed within sight and hearing of the Egyptians who were in charge. When they overheard that the weaklings thought they could get out from under the pharaoh's rule, they laughed.

"'How can little slaves be mightier than our god?' they asked."

Moses then picked up the story for us. "'None of us alone is mightier than the pharaoh,' Aaron answered them, 'but all of us together, with the help of our god, can do anything. Yah has determined that it is time for us to leave our service to the pharaoh. We will only serve Yah.' Again, the Egyptians laughed."

Moses told us how pleased he was that it was all going as Aaron had said it would. He was also sure it would continue to do so, and he was right. "Then," Moses said, but he paused for a long time, keeping us in suspense before continuing his story only when we thought we could not wait another moment, "then I threw my staff onto the ground, and the Egyptians gawked and stepped back as it turned into a snake. They shrieked when I reached down, picked it up by the tail, and made it become a staff again." Moses looked at Aaron, who was beaming, and clapped him on the shoulder. They had enjoyed their performance, and

Moses had seemingly learned from his brother how to do the trick very well.

"The Egyptians were impressed," Aaron said. "That was all we had prepared for them for today, and we would have gone to the next group if one overseer had not said, 'Our god can turn the river, the source of life itself, into blood, death. I have seen it. No matter how many snakes you have, I will not believe you can overthrow the pharaoh, for nothing you can say will be more powerful than that.'

"But I know how to do that as well," Aaron said. After studying with the magicians, he had become one himself, so everything they could do, he could also do.

Continuing, Moses said, "Aaron held up his arm, and the next thing we saw was that the water was red as blood. We all stared at the water for some time, and then frogs were jumping out of the red, red river, trying to escape it as fast as they could."

Word spread quickly among the Israelites and the Egyptians that two Hebrew brothers could turn snakes to staffs and water to blood. When Aaron and Moses went out into the fields, they no longer needed to bribe the guards to let them talk to the Israelites. The brothers demonstrated that the rumors were true, and it wasn't long before it became known to all, even Pharaoh, that they could do this. Then they were called to have an audience before him.

The pharaoh made the meeting a public one. Surely, he wanted the people to see what happened to anyone who would think to compare themselves to him. Kesher and I went to witness what would happen, but Vida and Suf thought it best that they do not watch. They were right. The meeting was brief. The pharaoh asked them what they wanted. It was Moses who answered. He bowed respectfully, even if not sincerely, before he spoke:

"Let us go and serve our god in the desert."

I imagined Moses practicing that line over and over with Aaron encouraging him, helping him to get the tone just right. Or maybe Moses had grown the confidence for speaking to the pharaoh. I had done that once, and though I was willing to do it again, the idea scared me. Moses, if he was scared, did not show it. The pharaoh did not part his lips to answer but lifted his arm and used it to snap a whip once at Moses and then once at Aaron. Then Pharaoh signaled to his guards to escort him back to his chamber while Moses and Aaron were still on the floor, nursing their wounds.

Elisheva tended to them as soon as we returned. She was heavy with her and Aaron's fourth child, but she never rested when someone was in need. Aaron and Moses, though, would not let the wounds slow them down, and nobody, not even Suf, tried to dissuade them from continuing their mission. The very next day, they were out again, showing their powers and sharing their determination and hope.

I had learned with Benno that two people were not enough to do the job. Moses and Aaron knew that they could not do it alone either. Fortunately, Hur was connected to the Council of Firstborns through the brother of Zojto, his wife. And with Betzalel's help, Hur had also built a machine that could hold small insects and then blow them out. Betzalel and Hur had children help them collect lice and other small pests. Zojto told Hur what her brother had said about where and when the Council's next meeting was going to be held. On that day, just before the firstborns assembled, Hur and Betzalel filled the room with lice. The meeting ended early.

Hope grew stronger and stronger over the months. So did Pharaoh's wrath. But with the Israelites looking forward to leaving and with the overseers looking the other way, everyone felt that what had once been a dream could happen in their lifetimes. As the time seemed to be getting close, I asked Hur to find men to help him carry my father from his tomb. I wanted to go to the tomb with Hur, and I wanted to bring Kesher and Vida with me to show them the beautiful carvings and paintings in the special burial chamber that my father had worked for and designed. But just as I knew that Aaron and Moses could no longer go unnoticed or unharmed into the palace, I knew that we women could not afford to attract attention either. So, I drew Hur a map and explained the route, and a few days later, I was relieved and even a little amused to find that my father's coffin was now in my courtyard.

Looking at my name on the corners where we had written it so long ago, I spoke aloud to my father. "Soon, Father, we will go home. Your bones will come with us, and I will see to your burial in your land, just as you requested." The light from the beads that Kesher had strung chose that moment to dance across his coffin and create tiny rainbows all over it.

It was good that my father had been taken from his tomb when he was, because soon everything was locked down when a plague hit the cattle of the land. One cow was reported sick, then, suddenly, all of them. The Council of Firstborns said it was the Hebrews' fault that the cattle disease arose in the first place and for its quick spread from herd to herd. The Israelites, who had no cattle of their own and very few sheep remaining among them, became the focus of Pharaoh's wrath, for his wealth was decreasing. So, he called Aaron and Moses to appear before him again.

I thought back to when they were little and would pretend to demand that the pharaoh let the Israelites go. Every time they played out the possibilities, no matter what the pretend pharaoh said, they were still safe. I prayed that they would be safe this time too. The spectacle was similar to their first appearance before the pharaoh; the public was invited to stand around the room, and Pharaoh was in the middle, flanked by guards and witnessed by statesmen and anyone else who was early enough to get a seat.

"Why have you killed our cattle?" Pharaoh asked the brothers. "What is it that you want?"

"We wish to serve only our god *Yhhhh Whhhh*," Moses said.

"Yes," Aaron echoed, "*Yhhhh Whhhh*."

Pharaoh looked at them but did not raise his whip. "This is the name of your god?" Pharaoh asked. "*Yhhhh Whhhh*?"

Aaron and Moses answered in unison saying, "Yes, *Yhhhh Whhhh*." This was the fourth time that Yah's name was used in this meeting, and I could see that Pharaoh was calming.

"Alright," Pharaoh said. "You may have three days to go and worship your god in the desert. If"—Pharaoh paused his answer and banged his staff on the ground—"if your god is worthy of worship. If your god can put a stop to this plague, you may go."

I could see surprise cross Aaron's face briefly before he composed himself again. Then he and Moses both bowed before the pharaoh, who then left. Everyone was silent. Nobody had known what to expect, but this outcome had not been anticipated. The crowd dispersed quietly in confusion. I could hardly bring my feet to move and needed Kesher's help to walk back to our chamber. This was real, as real as I was, and we would be leaving soon. I had helped bring us to this day and this miracle.

Little happened other than prayer for several days. Countless people praying, breathing, beseeching for the plague to end. It did end. Just like the plague of sickness that had befallen our camp when Benno and Geeborr and I were children, it did end. But a long time passed before it did. The moon came and went, came and went, came and went. Buzzards picked the bones of so many dead cows that they became full and left other carcasses to rot or be buried. The growing season ended and the harvest season began before it was clear that some cows were surviving and beginning to thrive again.

Aaron and Moses went back to the pharaoh, but they did not get an audience. Instead, a guard instructed them to tell him their message. "The plague has ended," Aaron said. "Hallelu Yah. Let my people go." When the guard came back, he had one word from Pharaoh for Aaron and Moses: *No.*

A difficult time followed that decision. The hope that had been building for so long turned into despair. Elisheva and I were not able to go back to the camps to try to raise the women's spirits because the Council decided to place more guards throughout the whole land. Even with her midwife's bag, she was told she may not leave the harem. Even the princes of the palace had limited movement, needing to seek and receive permission from the Council for any errand. We were cut off from the rest of the Israelites.

The harvesting season passed, and the flooding season began. The relaxed certainty I had felt changed into fear and concern.

I should have done more. I didn't know what more I could have done, but as it seemed like we would now not get out of Egypt, I must not have done enough. And what would happen if we were not going now? Would I walk with Yah again? With Aaron and Moses leading the men and Miryam leading the women, even without me, I knew the Israelites *could* still leave Egypt, still arrive in our land, even if I were not to go with them. But *would* they even leave now? And what would have been my purpose in this strange body and time if they did not?

I gave these pains to the full moon, and she held them. Meanwhile, Kesher and Vida, Suf and Elisheva, and Miryam and May-tal, no longer girls but women, held me.

"If you had only taken Moses from the river and not brought us into the harem, it would have been enough for us," Vida said.

"If you had only brought us into the harem but not loved us like sisters, mothers, daughters, and friends, it would have been enough for us," Miryam said.

"If you had only loved us like sisters, mothers, daughters, and friends but had not helped us raise our children or told them stories of their forebears, it would have been enough for us," Kesher said.

"If you had only helped them raise us and told us stories of our forebears but not helped Moses escape, it would have been enough for us," May-tal said.

"If you had only helped Moses escape but had not come back with him, it would have been enough for us," Suf said.

"If you had only come back with Moses but did not help us leave Egypt, it would still be enough for us," Elisheva said. "No matter what happens now or next or ever, you have already done all of that and more."

"Blue, you are enough for us," Vida said, "just as you are."

The gratitude from the people who knew me the best helped me feel that being me was enough.

FINAL

That was our final full moon celebration in Egypt. Of course, we didn't know it at the time. But a few nights later, there was a day darker than any other, and that was the beginning of the end. Before the sun had even set, the darkness began. It was not right for the night to come, but it did. Rather than the sun disappearing behind the horizon, slowly a shadow began to cover it. Bit by bit, the blue sky turned dark until the sun and its light were completely gone and we were left with only darkness.

Aaron and Moses were swept away by guards who took them by lamplight to Pharaoh. This time, there was no public audience, so we heard about it only from their mouths when they returned.

"Pharaoh said that the darkness has shown him that Yah is a mightier god than he, so he will let the Israelites go if Yah will restore the order of day and night. Before we had a chance to speak, though, a messenger came to the pharaoh's chamber and announced that the sun was returning. When he heard that news, Pharaoh changed his mind and sent us away."

"I think we can still be hopeful," Aaron said. "Yah has shown us—me, Moses, Auntie, and perhaps others—that the time of our departure is getting closer. This is one more sign. Pharaoh is thinking of releasing us. We are still on his mind. He is wondering whether Yah is more powerful than his god, and he is afraid enough that his first thought is not only to blame the Israelites but to release us." Aaron was right, and we were encouraged. I thought that perhaps the other Israelites had hope, too, even if they could not have Aaron walking among them and sharing his thoughts directly with them.

Soon after the brothers' meeting, Hur brought word confirming that Pharaoh was, indeed, afraid—and that the Council of the Firstborns was as well.

"The Council will have a meeting in three days' time," Hur said. "Pharaoh is planning to send many generals and even soldiers to the meeting so that they can work together to restore his order once and for all."

When Moses heard about this meeting, he said he knew what to do. He had been hearing instructions that he did not understand in his Yah ear since the beginning of the flooding season. Now the instructions were clear. There was a bigger flood coming, he told us, and it would help us leave Egypt. Now he knew how, but he did not like what he knew. He asked me to walk with him.

"Auntie," I could hear sadness in his voice. "You saw me help Tzipporah and her sisters at the well."

Of course I had, though I did not know why he was talking about that now.

"Auntie, when the guard was beating my father, I did not want to kill him. I did not mean to kill him. I did not even know I had killed him. I told him to stop many times, but he did not. If I had not intervened, it would have been my father who had died, not the guard."

"Yes," I said.

"That guard was someone else's father, though. Someone else's father died instead of my father. I did not want either of them to die." He paused for a long time. "I did not even want to hit that guard or to throw him off my father. He should not have been attacking my father in the first place. It was cruel."

"Yes," I said again, acknowledging his words and agreeing with them but not wanting to say or ask more for fear of interrupting him.

"Auntie, you saw me at the well with the shepherds. I am not cruel. I helped the women defend themselves. And I did not raise a hand or my voice to the shepherds. It was just for the women to water their flock first, for they had been there first, and it was just for the shepherds to water their flock next. Do you see? I sought justice for both. Then I drew water for you and me. Do you remember?"

"I do," I said.

"I am not cruel," he repeated, "even if I did kill that Egyptian overseer."

Moses stopped for a long time, and I thought I should say something. I told him what was on my mind and in my heart:

"Moses, you are not cruel. You have never been cruel. You were a kind boy, and you have become a kind man."

"I am not like all the men," he said. "I am different, and I do not like it. I know it is the same for you—"

Then I did interrupt him. "It has been very difficult for me to be this way. I don't know why I do not age like others. I don't truly know why I am here, though it seems important. I do not always like being different, and I don't always dislike it."

"Yes," Moses said, agreeing with me that time. Then he continued. "Auntie, when I was a boy, I did not know that every person didn't have a people ear and a Yah ear. It was the way I heard . . . the way I hear . . . and I thought it was the same for everyone. But it's not. I get a lot of peace in my Yah ear. It has given me perspective and understanding that many around me lack. I am grateful for the Yah ear, for the peace, for the relationship I have with Yah. But now I have heard something with my Yah ear that I did not wish to hear. I know things that I do not wish to know, and I feel that I must do things that I do not wish to do."

We walked in silence until we got to the bench beside the river where we had sat so long ago for his special story and song. As a grown man, he was far too big to lie on that bench and put his head in my lap, so we sat side by side, holding hands and watching the water.

"Auntie," he finally said, "it is the flooding season. The Nile is higher than in the other two seasons, just like it is every year. The flooding is creating fertile ground for the farmers to plant the seeds that will grow into crops that will feed the people and livestock next year. The Nile gives life. It gave me life." Moses wiped tears from his face. "It was all a part of Yah, for we are all a part of Yah. And I am grateful to this river for helping me live. And . . ."

Moses stopped for so long that it seemed he might not begin again. Was he listening to Yah? Would I interrupt if I said something?

After a long while, I said, "Moses, take off your shoes. Put your feet on the ground. When you are ready, tell me what you are having difficulty saying."

With his feet bare and his eyes on the river, not me, Moses said, "Auntie, the Nile will have a larger flood than usual in three days' time. It is on the same day as the meeting with the Council and the generals. There are many chambers in the palace that are used for private meetings. They are hidden, and they were dug into the ground. If there is one with a weak wall—that is, there is one with a weak wall—the water will be strong enough to push through its cracks. If the door is locked, the Council of the Firstborns and the generals will drown."

That was what he had come here to say, and he cried once he had said it. With his head in his hands, he let me stroke his back. When all his tears were dry, he said, "I am not a cruel person. I do not wish to hurt anyone. But I know that if I say something, I will have killed the Egyptians, and if I say nothing, I will kill the Israelites. Why?" he asked. "Why must it be this way?"

The first thing I thought to do was to take the question to Yah. *Yhhhh. Whhhh.* I did not know what it was like to have a Yah ear. I didn't know what Moses heard or when or how. But I knew that when I breathed myself into Yah and took everything in, attentively repeating the cycle, I had knowings that I couldn't know without that connection. Still, I did not know the answer to his question.

"Moses, I wish I knew. Only Yah knows. But I have wondered the same thing many, many times." That was clearly not a good enough answer, yet it had to be, because it was all I had.

At first light, Moses gathered some men, and together they devised a plan for finding the chamber he knew would be there. Hur then took an agreed-upon message to Zojto's brother. News spread quickly that though the council and generals were meeting as planned, an elite group of them were going to be secretly meeting in a hidden chamber of the palace. This false rumor brought all the men—because they all considered themselves to be elite—to the room with the weak walls. Hur's brother-in-law volunteered to stand guard outside, easily convincing the others that only one guard was needed since the location was secret. With no other generals or firstborns who were willing to miss the meeting in order to guard it, he was able to lock them in.

Moses spent most of the day alone, walking with his bare feet on the ground, listening, perhaps, and awaiting the flood. When a heavy rain began to pour, those of us who knew what was happening watched it fall. There was thunder and lightning and hail. The storm continued for the rest of the day, through the night, and into the morning, but we did not sleep. Though we did not doubt Moses or Yah, we awaited news that the meeting had adjourned. That news never came. Another whole day passed. Then another. And then, finally, the news was heard that all the generals in Pharaoh's army and all the members of the Council of the Firstborns had drowned.

Aaron and Moses went to see Pharaoh. They had not been summoned. They did not bow before him as they had done in the past. They stood before Pharaoh with only his personal guards between them, and they did not get any closer.

Moses simply said, "Let my people go."

And Pharaoh did.

GO

Finally, it was time to go, to leave Egypt and return to the land of Israel. Everyone was busy preparing for a new life: those of us who were preparing to leave and those who were preparing to stay. Many more people were preparing to leave than we had expected, and by the time we were able to leave, the tribe of Israel had grown even larger.

However, it was not only Israelites who left. Countless Egyptians chose to join the nation of Israel. They, too, had suffered under this pharaoh and were eager to leave before he inflicted his anger on those who remained. Of course, there were many Egyptians who did stay. Some knew they would be the beneficiaries of the wealth and status lost by the Council of the Firstborns. Others felt that their lives were not so difficult that they wished to trade them for the unknown. And still others just did not have the strength to go. In the end, most of the Egyptians stayed in Egypt. Most of the Israelites left.

Nevertheless, life would be different for everyone regardless of whether they were an Israelite leaving or an Egyptian leaving, an Egyptian staying or an Israelite staying. Everyone was moving as quickly as possible, lest they get caught in the storm of Pharaoh's anger, which is why, at first glance, it wasn't simple to tell whether a person was preparing to stay or preparing to go. At one point, Miryam discovered that Vida wasn't planning to go. I don't know what had happened first, because I arrived in the middle of a loud argument.

"Mother, you have to come with us!" Miryam was shouting, pleading. "How can you not come? We've been waiting for this! Preparing for this! It's time! We get to leave this oppression and go home! *Home*, Mother!" It was not like Miryam to yell at her mother—to yell at anyone.

"Miryam," Vida's voice was quieter, more measured, but firm. "This is my home. This is where I was born. This is where I raised my children and buried my husband. This is where I eat, where I sleep, and where I bathe. This is where I walk among the flowers and where I drink from the wells. These are not things I take for granted. This is also where there is the wind that I know, the scents that I know, the birds that I know, the leaves, and the fish. This is where I—"

She didn't get to finish because Miryam cut her off: "I am the daughter that you know! We are the family that you know. How can you even think of not coming with us?"

"I love you—all of you," she said. Miryam had only named herself, though she knew that Vida had many people who were important to her. "Miryam, love, of course, I want to be with you. I am filled with pride each and every time I look at you. I am filled with awe every time I see you help someone else, as you do often. Whether you bandage a scraped knee or soothe a scared heart, I am so proud of you. And I am not surprised that you have become a leader among women. You are strong, Miryam.

"I am not. I am an old woman. You know as well as I do that the sons of Aaron and Elisheva are not little boys anymore; only their fourth son, Itamar, has an unchanged voice. The same must be true of the sons of Moses, whom I have never met. I would love to meet them and Galeet. One day, they will have babies in the land of Israel. I would love to hold those babies. This is why I did not tell you that I'm staying." At this point, Vida looked not only at Miryam but also at me and Kesher. "It is because I, too, thought that I would leave. But I'm so tired," she said. "My days are numbered. My bones hurt. My feet hurt. My eyes hurt. My head hurts. My knees hurt. My hands hurt. My back hurts. I wish to sleep both night and day—"

Again, Miryam cut her off, though she wasn't as loud or as angry this time. "Mother, we will take care of you. We took care of Father. And we took care of you as you cared for Father. Did you think for one moment that we wouldn't take care of you? There's no need to walk when that's too difficult. We'll cushion a cart just for you. Mother, I'm walking to Israel, and I'm taking the Israelite women with me—including you. I'll carry you on my own back."

The two women embraced for a long time. Their tears mingled. Their breaths slowed. Miryam was not a young woman, but she truly did look strong enough to carry Vida on her own back, and she was certainly determined enough to do so. And Vida did look tired. Her body was smaller than Miryam's and bent. I had known all along that Vida had aches and pains.

We were soft-necked friends, safe enough with each other to share everything without fear.

Vida had been living with Suf ever since Amram had come, and even after he'd died, she'd stayed with Suf. She had told Vida she could always stay, so the four women stayed living under that roof and had become a little tribe of their own. Vida, Miryam, Elisheva, and Suf. Still, I had seen Vida daily. I had known she felt unwell every day . . . but I hadn't really looked until that moment. I hadn't really seen all the ailments together that added up to Vida looking and feeling like a frail old woman.

"Miryam," Vida said, speaking with tenderness and pride, "Miryam, my daughter, you are a strong woman, a caretaker, a risk taker, a leader. I'm proud of you. And I'm proud of myself. I think I fostered this in you from the very beginning. You are so loving. Thank you." They embraced again, just for a moment, before Vida continued speaking. "You will use your caretaking heart to guide May-tal and all the women and girls—for they are all your daughters, all your sisters, all *our* daughters, and all *our* sisters—on the long trek through the wilderness. You will uplift their spirits and give them hope and solace. You will be their source of water, their gift of life. I know you will be there for them, whatever they need, just as you have been for me."

"And I will still be that for you, too, Mother. Of course, I'll still be that for you."

"I will be here," Vida said.

"No, Mother! What are you saying now? With everything we just said, I thought you were coming with us now! How can you still say that you're not going?"

"Because I want to stay, Miryam. Even though it breaks my heart. It breaks my heart to say goodbye to you, to my children, to my grandchildren, to Blue, and to Kesher. It breaks my heart to not see where Leah wove blankets and Rachel drew water, where Rebekah and Deborah raised the man called Israel, where Blue and Deenah and Emunah danced under the moon. It breaks my heart that I can't make the journey. But I can't. I will stay here with Suf and many others. Kohenet will keep the harem running; the pharaoh will want his harem. We will be safe here.

"Miryam, do you think I want to be carried on your back? Do you think I want to be jostled around behind a donkey's ass, bumping over rocks and rivets for endless days? I will die, Miryam. I will die. Hear me, daughter. I will die here, or I will die there, but I will die. So I choose to die here."

"Then I'm staying too!" Miryam shouted.

This was the part where Vida also raised her voice: "Oh, no you will not, Miryam, daughter of Yohevid! Miryam, daughter of Yohevid! Do you hear me? You are Miryam, daughter of Yohevid! That is me! I am Yohevid! I am the mother here, not you, and you, Miryam, will honor your mother! Listen to me. Listen to your mother. What I say is to give you a longer and better life."

"I am honoring you, Mother! That's why I'll stay here with you!"

"You are not honoring me; you are treating me like I am a child. I am a mother who has saved all three of her children! Just because you think that I'm making the wrong choice does not mean that I don't get to choose for myself. Is it any more acceptable for you to choose for me than when Deenah's brothers chose for her?"

Miryam gasped at the comparison.

Vida paused and calmed herself with a deep breath. *Yhhhh.* The crowd that had gathered around this scene all stopped and breathed with her. She closed her eyes and exhaled. *Whhhh.* We released our breath together, and there was silence.

"This isn't over," Miryam said as she walked away.

Vida and I left to sit on the benches beneath the date palms. We sat quietly for some time, just breathing together, just being together. I asked myself whether there was a difference in the scents between the bank of the Nile and the hills of my homeland. There was, of course. I might not have remembered every detail of the hills I'd originally called home, but the dust was unforgettable. And the smell of the flocks up north in Goshen might be the same as the smell of flocks anywhere, but there in the harem area, there were no flocks. As I was gazing at the sky wondering whether there was a difference even in the sky between here or there, Vida began to speak.

"My daughter is a strong woman, isn't she?" Vida smiled. "I'm proud of her."

"I am too," I said, "and I'm proud of you. You did help her become strong. And I think she learned her stubbornness from you too." Vida giggled and smiled and put her head on my shoulder. "So, let's think," I said. "How can we make the journey more comfortable for you?"

Vida sat up. "Blue, sweetie, I told you all. I'm not going."

"What? You know Miryam will be back with ideas. I just thought we could think of some too."

She was silent, but she gave my hand a gentle squeeze.

"You're really not coming?" I asked meekly. Tears began to pour down my cheeks, tears, snot, hiccups, shakes. It was the ugliest of ugly cries. My body was tearing apart like it had when my mother had left. Vida couldn't leave me too. "Don't leave me," I choked out. "Please."

"Baby," she said, "Blue, Baby Blue . . . I love you. When I said I will miss my children, I included you. You have been my daughter—you've been everything. You've been my sister, my mother, my daughter, and my soft-necked friend. Blue, *you* shine with love from beginning to end. And I love you from beginning to end. It is like your father said. You are the moon."

At that point, I was crying so hard that she stopped talking. I didn't want to be the moon; I wanted to be Blue, daughter of a happy Deenah, one who would have stayed with me.

Vida held me even as my shaking shook her body, even as my mucus and tears soaked through her clothes. We sat and sat. Together. Together.

Just when I'd thought I was empty, Vida spoke softly: "Blue, Deenah loved you from beginning to end too. And she had to do what was right for her. It had nothing to do with you. You were the greatest gift she ever got, and the greatest gift she ever gave. And you were enough and perfect and wonderful and real, and you couldn't have done anything differently, and even if you had, she still would have left, because it was what she needed to do. Look at how much I love you and Kesher and how much I adore my children. You know that I do. I'm not staying in Egypt because I don't love Miryam. You know I speak the truth. You know that I do. This was just as true for Deenah. I promise you."

I knew she was right. If Hur or Miryam or Aaron or Moses or May-tal were for some reason not coming, I would still need to leave Egypt for good, even without them. I would need to. Just, as it seemed, like I was going to be leaving Egypt without Vida. Grandmother Leah and even my father had us wait until after they'd died. Vida could have asked for, and maybe received, the same treatment. But she did not ask.

I cried so hard, I threw up. Then Vida helped me get clean, and she laid beside me on a rug and held me while I slept. When I awoke, there was still some light in the sky. I still felt completely empty, but not in a bad way. It was like I'd had a hole where my mother had been, and now that emptiness was clean space instead of a gouged void. And while I was still exhausted, I felt that I might somehow be able to get more energy. I felt hope.

I took Vida into both of my arms and hugged her with gratitude. And then I laughed for a long time. I thought about how many times I had thrown up, but it was a number too mysterious to guess. It was always so unpleasant, though. Always.

I shared these observations with Vida, then said, "Being a person is not easy."

"No, it is not," she agreed.

When Miryam came by later that evening, she was calmer. She hugged us both before addressing her mother. "Mother, I'm sorry I yelled before. I was just so surprised. Now I've had more time to think, and I sought out Betzalel."

It was well-known that Betzalel had an innate talent for inventions and design. Give him a challenge or a project or an idea, and he'd make something so beautiful or helpful that he would surpass all expectations.

"Betzalel said he can fashion a bed for you. He says it will be easy to fasten poles to it so that the bed can be carried smoothly by four men. They can take turns so as not to get overburdened—I knew you'd be worried about that—but remember that everyone will be carrying something, some men will just have the honor of carrying you or others who are struggling. Using cushions we already have and some wood and other materials, he can make several of these very quickly. He wants to carve them as well—his eyes lit up with designs that only he could see—but he understands it will have to be done later."

Vida smiled. "You are truly wonderful," she said.

I think Miryam had a moment of thinking that Vida really would leave with us. But by then, I was certain that she wouldn't.

"You're so very resourceful," Vida said, "and you're such an asset to our tribe. Miryam, you are truly a jewel in my crown. And you are so wise." Vida paused to breathe, to take in the moment, to take in us and give us some of her. *Yhhhh. Whhhh.* And, perhaps, she also paused to prepare Miryam for what was coming next.

"My wise daughter, what is it that you want most?"

"I want you to come with us. I want to go back to our land together."

Vida kissed Miryam's hand. "I think that what you want most is to have what you want. Yet, even if you want the sky to be orange, you accept that it's blue. And even if you want the pickle to be sweet, you accept that it's sour. But if you want something that you believe you can change, then you don't accept it for how it is. Like the Israelites serving Pharaoh instead of Yah—you helped change that. And right now, you want me to come with you. I understand, because you love me as much as I love you. My love for you is as deep and wide as the sea, and whether the water in it is sweet or bitter, the love will always be sweet." Vida squeezed her daughter's hand.

"Miryam, my strong girl, my brave girl, my helpful girl. All grown up . . . I know you do this with a kind and generous heart. You want me to be cared for. You want what's best for me. Now wise daughter, listen carefully. If you're truly being generous, then you must give me what it is that you want for yourself. To truly treat another person the way you want to be treated, you must not force me to do what *you* think is best for me; you must instead not hinder me when I'm doing what *I* think is best for me.

"Of course, I want to go with you. I want to see you rejoice in the births of the baby girls who will grow up to weave the tents that house the children of Israel in the land of Israel. I want to eat the wheat that grows on the ground that Sarah's feet once walked. I want to sit beneath the olive trees where Rebekah and Deborah once nursed their babies together. I want to drink from the wells that Leah and Rachel, Bilhah and Zilpah, and their daughters drew water from. I want all of that."

"So come with us, Mother, come with," Miryam pleaded. "Don't make me say goodbye to you again. It's enough to have to say goodbye to my home. To say goodbye to the only land I've known. To go to a new and strange place. Don't make me go without you."

"It will be hard to say goodbye to you," Vida said. "But I have said goodbye to you forty times already. Every time I see you, you are somebody new, for the former you is only a memory. You will take the former me with you. Our love will never end. But I am tired, and I have safety and comfort here in the harem. If I were your age, I would go. Maybe if your father were still alive . . . I don't know." Vida stopped talking for a moment. "There is no easy choice," she continued. "I will be safe here and loved. I don't want to go. Let me have what Deenah had, what Leah had at the end, what Blue has had sometimes, and even what you have had sometimes, though not as much as I would wish for you. Let me have what you want most for yourself; let me live the life I choose for myself."

Many tears were shed that night.

In the morning, Miryam asked me to step aside with her. "Blue," she said, "you must talk to my mother, to your Vida. I know she'll listen to you."

I nodded my head but was quiet before I got my words out softly. "Miryam, I have talked to her, and she has listened. She listened to you too. Now it's time for us to listen to her."

"I did listen to her!" Miryam yelled. She crossed her arms and stomped her foot like a toddler. "She doesn't know what's best for her. People don't always know what's best for themselves!"

What could I say? In that moment, I couldn't think of anything. While I was quiet, I saw Miryam's body change with the realization of her own words. *People don't always know what's best for themselves.*

Her shoulders loosened, and her hands went to her face. "Okay! Okay!" she yelled. "I understand that people don't always know what's best and that I am people too."

When she began to shake with sobs, I put my arms around her. Eventually, she left my embrace and took my hand. She gripped it tightly as she walked to Vida. We all sat on the rug that we had sat on together so many times. Miryam looked her mother in the eyes: "I'm sorry," she said. "I'm sorry for thinking I know what's best for you. I realize now that it's impossible for me to know what's best for you." Then Miryam's pace and energy picked up. "But you don't know what's best for you either. And you don't know what's best for me . . . and I don't know what's best for me . . . and that's very, very scary."

"I know, baby," Vida said. "I know."

As those who were leaving prepared to go, and as those who were staying prepared to stay, we all had a little more peace as we realized that accepting that people make different choices for themselves, even ones that affect us, was at least as hard as either going or staying, and that really, all we could do was try to understand for each other.

On the day before our departure, Vida, Suf, Kohenet, and the other women of the harem who were staying in Egypt made a great ruckus as the sun rose. In their hands, each woman held a timbrel—a small exquisitely made drum with carvings of Nile River scenes on the wooden frames and beaded ribbons hanging down with bells on the end. The women shook their instruments and ululated until we had all come out to see what was happening. Then each of the women handed one of the instruments to a woman who would be leaving Egypt. Vida gave one to me, one to Kesher, one to Elisheva, one to May-tal, and a large one painted all blue like the sea to Miryam.

As Vida hugged us, she made us promise that we would be joyful. "You don't need to always be joyful," she said, "but you must remember to *also* be joyful." We cried, and we kissed each other goodbye, and we promised.

The last words Miryam said to her mother were, "If you choose to come later, I will be glad to see you."

The last words Vida said to her daughter were, "You don't need me, but you will always have me. My love goes with you everywhere."

And the last words that my soft-necked friend Vida and I said to each other are words that will always remain just between us.

FIRST

s the first full moon of the year rose, everybody was on edge. No matter the details of what would happen next, everyone's lives would change forever. It was exciting. Scary. Terrifying. Hopeful. Busy, busy, busy. Everyone dealt with it differently. Some people looked like they would pee their pants. Many probably did. Others couldn't stop talking, while some couldn't say a word. Tears were shed; laughs were shared. If anyone in Egypt slept that night, it was only the ones too young to understand what was happening.

We had a large feast that night. We didn't know whether Pharaoh and his army would pursue us, and, if we did manage to be free from him, we also didn't know what was waiting on the other side of that freedom. Of course, everyone had packed baskets and baskets of food—lentils, flour, dried meats and fruits, even vegetables picked at the very last moment just in case we had use for them. But the food was easier to carry inside our bellies than on our backs and heads or even by pulling it behind us in carts.

With so many travelers, we expected the journey to take at least one month, especially since we were not a group of only young and agile travelers but a group with defiant toddlers, weak elders, and infirm loved ones who would need help. And walking and setting up camp, walking again, keeping the animals and the countless people—yes, countless—with us would make our journey take even longer.

We feasted under that full moon until almost dawn. A few people did doze off after their bellies were so full that they couldn't move, but the anticipation kept them on high alert. That was useful, since we needed everyone to be ready once the sun's first light began to peek over the horizon. Miryam, Aaron, and Moses had separated earlier in the night and positioned themselves across the city and in the fields, too, so that they could help lead the people when the time came.

When the night sky showed the first signs of daylight, Aaron raised a ram's horn to his lips and blew one long call: *Auuuuuuuuuuuuuuuuuuuuuuuuuuuuuuuuuu!* Everything else was silent while he blew his shofar, and for a moment after, the absence of the call rang in our ears. Then there was another blast. Moses, who had heard his brother's horn, took up his shofar where he was: *Auuuuuuuuuuuuuuuuuuuuuuuuuuuuuuuu!* When he finished, a third blast came from another corner of Egypt. That was Miryam, who was standing by my side—or, I should say, I was standing by hers.

Miryam—steady, confident, majestic, and strong-lunged Miryam—blew her shofar just as her little brothers had: *Auuuu uuuuuuuuuuuuuuuuuuuuuuuuuuuuuuu!* May-tal looked up at her with eyes wide and body vibrating with the sound of the shofar.

When the blast ended, Miryam inhaled and, without even wiping the tears off her face, blew the shofar again; this time, she sounded off nine blasts in unison with Aaron and Moses. The call resounded throughout the land, and when the last wisps of breath flowed out of the shofars, the first steps forward were taken.

All the children started running, skipping, and jumping toward the land of Israel. They had asked which way it was a thousand times over, so by that morning, they knew. Wheels started rolling, hoofs started stomping, and amid it all, there was a song starting so quietly that it might have come on the wind:

"Happy is the nation who experiences the shofar blast."

Some of us women picked up the song and added our voices.

"Happy is the nation who experiences the shofar blast."

The song grew louder as more people joined in, and the feet of the adults became as light as those of the children. Skipping and twirling and dancing with joy, the Israelites and the mixed multitude of Egyptians who'd chosen to join us were lifted by the music of possibility. The time had come. We were really leaving. Without a word to one another, we women began to reach into the carts that had been so carefully packed and pull out our drums.

We held some fear in the corners of our hearts, but even more so, we were hopeful. Hope is a lighter foot forward; fear holds the pressure of the past, while hope holds possibility. So, on that bright morning, we stepped forward with hope. We couldn't dance all the way to a new land and new lives, but we could start our journey on dancing feet, and as unplanned as it was, that's exactly what we did.

For the whole day, we flowed like a river . . . even if we were a very slow-moving river. When Moses and I had left years before, it was just the two of us and our donkey, and we crossed the land quickly. But such a large group moves forward slowly. Add livestock and everyone carrying as much as they could, and it was chaos like none of us had ever experienced before. But thankfully, that chaos was wrapped in a happy drumbeat and excitement.

We walked in the soft heat of the early spring day, walked and danced and shuffled so as not to step on the people in front of us. And since we had all left at once, it took more than a day before some natural gaps began to appear in our procession. Spirits stayed high as we left the constriction of the pharaoh's world. Laughter was heard often. Many people chatted amicably, while others kept quiet to enjoy their thoughts. Each one of us was a person having our own experience, yet we were with the others at the same time. Each one of us was a drop of water; together, we were the river.

Just days after leaving Egypt, our river of people flowed right up to the Reed Sea. There were many reeds, yes, but there was much more sea. It was wider than the Nile, and we had no way to cross. At first, this seemed like an opportunity for rest. Then it seemed like a small obstacle, something we could figure out with some time. Then we discovered we had no time at all because, as the last of us were arriving at the edge of the sea, Pharaoh's army could be heard coming up behind us.

Seeing the sea ahead of us, Moses cried out and asked, "Why would we take the people to the sea?" He was not talking to any of us but rather to himself or to Yah.

Hur put his hand on Moses's shoulder. "Moses, you did what you had to do. We do not have time to know why. Now, here we are. We will do what we can."

The men among us had weapons, of course, but any battle would lead to losses. Nevertheless, several of the men began organizing a group to meet the Egyptians where they were in order to leave as wide a gap as possible between us and them. We hoped the men could keep the army at bay for long enough to give us a chance to cross the sea.

Eyes wide with fear, Miryam admitted to me that she was glad Vida was not there to be trapped between the army and the sea. While fear spread through most of the crowd, one man got everyone's attention by climbing onto another's shoulders. A few close men circled around him in case he fell, and a wider circle was created to see the spectacle; then all eyes were focused in one direction.

It was Nakshon, brother of Elisheva, who was standing on Hur's shoulders. Hur stood as still as a rock, and Nakshon was able to balance up there even while he yelled. "I can swim!" he shouted. "I can swim!"

Then the men in the close circle took up the chant. "I can swim! I can swim!"

I don't know how many of them could swim, whether they were speaking about themselves or about Nakshon, but they all chanted in unison and were joined by the men who were in the wider circle.

"I can swim! I can swim! I can swim!" The chant continued until everyone else had either joined in or could hear the chant clearly because it was the only sound.

Eventually, Nakshon got down from Hur's shoulders and raised his hands in the air and shouted a new chant: "Praise to the Redeemer of Israel!" Then he ran fast and hard to the Reed Sea and jumped in. He did not swim, but he walked, ran, and pushed his way across. We could see him all the while, even though the deepest parts allowed only his head to show. Elisheva and Aaron followed Nakshon with their children and May-tal and Miryam just steps behind, and the rest of us followed literally on their heels.

Every last one of us crossed the sea. Hur and Moses guided the crowd with their arms raised, directing everyone to enter between them so there would be nobody unseen, overlooked, or left behind. Some of us walked as Nakshon had, but some actually did swim. Some were pulled across by others, and still others sat on shoulders. Forty of the tallest men formed a line from one shore to the other and passed babies arms to arms, above the water, hundreds of times.

Betzalel proved himself, once again, to be a master crafter, quickly adapting some carts to become rafts that men could pull across, empty, and pull back to refill. The tallest women carried jugs full of food and drink on their heads, also making the trip many times. Livestock were led by their ropes, and miraculously, only one baby was born: Nesiyah. I walked across the sea behind six men who carried my father's coffin high above their heads and with a jar containing his scrolls gripped tightly in my hands above the water.

When the soldiers who had gone to meet the Egyptians ran into the sea, they were cheered on by everyone. They had not, it turned out, engaged in battle. They saw that the army was small, and they decided to get as close as they dared to their pursuers and then turn around and run back, hoping to outrun the swords. As it turned out, most of the small army decided not to pursue them the whole way once they saw that so many of us were on the other side of the sea. The men who had gone to stave off our pursuers were the last of us to cross, except for twenty Egyptian soldiers who laid down their weapons and asked Moses and Hur for Yah's protection. Moses and Hur waved them through, then they put down their weary arms that had guided the rest of us and crossed the sea themselves.

Finally, on the other side of the sea, Egypt was behind us forever, and we truly had expansiveness and spaciousness—physical and otherwise—in front of us. Miryam was the first to pick up her instrument again. She chose the timbrel she'd been gifted and had brought along with the promise of using it in joy in our new lives. Miryam, our leader, took the timbrel in her hand, raised it above her head, and began. All the women followed after her with our timbrels and our voices. Her jubilation praised Yah for enabling us to be free of Pharaoh's yoke. And while Nakshon's words had taken us into the sea, we sang a new song on the other side:

"Who is like you among the gods, Yah?
Who is like you, awesome in holiness?
There is none like you among the gods, Yah.
Majestic in glory, a wonder-maker,

Yhhhh Whhhh is, forever and ever."

In an instant, bags were rifled through again, and scores of soaking wet, cleansed women were dancing with timbrels and singing this new song.

"Yah is forever and ever!
Hallelu Yah!
Hallelu Yah!"

IN THE WILDERNESS

IN THE WILDERNESS

n the wilderness, the Israelites and the mixed multitude spread out over the land that was on the other side of the sea. The name of that land was Refidim. Some people, the wearier ones, stayed close, and the stronger went farther. We were no longer crowded like water in a bottleneck, but we were actually flowing this time, as well as spreading out on the other side. The singing and dancing continued long into the night, with each group breaking into its own songs and nobody ready to give in to exhaustion until they had fully felt their freedom.

We camped in Refidim for seven days. Most of that time was spent recuperating. Only the essential tasks were done: putting up tents, pasturing the animals, making quick bread. Many tears were shed, and feet were rubbed. We would not be able to live like that forever, but we lived like that then. Though most of us were recovering, Moses made the journey to Midian to reunite with Tzipporah and his children. He parted on his own with a donkey and supplies and a lad who was not me.

He did not need to walk the whole distance, though. Word of our escape had traveled quickly, and Jethro, the new head of the

Midianites after Reuel died, was already on his way to meet us. He had Tzipporah, Galeet, Gershom, and Eliezer with him. Moses sent his lad back to tell Aaron that they were all on the way. Then Aaron began preparing a feast, and Elisheva came to give us the news and to ask us to prepare to welcome Tzipporah and Galeet.

Kesher, Miryam, May-tal, and I were in an area that had been erected for widows and orphans. Many Israelite women had raised the fear long before we left that they would not be able to travel to Israel without a husband or father to house and clothe them. There were women in the harem who'd had the same concern. The father of their children was the pharaoh, so if they survived leaving him, who would provide for them? Moses, who had shown himself to be a wise leader, reminded us through his response that he was not only righteous but also trained in writing and accounting. He vowed that whatever Israel had, one tenth of it would go directly to widows and orphans. They would be cared for. We would be cared for.

We had a tent area where many of us were still getting to know each other and learning to work together. Nina was among the widows and was there with two of her granddaughters and their mother. I was delighted beyond measure to reunite with Nina and get to know the little girls. Though Tzipporah was not a widow and her grown children were not orphans, we made a lovely place to welcome them.

"Of course we will welcome them," Miryam said to Elisheva, who had stayed to help in the preparations. She, too, wanted to meet the new sister.

We rolled out some of our finest rugs for Tzipporah. These

were two especially long and narrow rugs that were woven to invoke the Nile when put end to end. They were mostly blue, with some white woven in as waves and green for reeds along the banks. There were no crocodiles or hippos depicted, just the peaceful, abundant water. Miryam and May-tal, the sea and the dew, prepared to welcome Galeet, the wave, to the water with them. Until they arrived, we used every moment of that time. Satchels were searched for favorite spices, water was fetched, breads were made, goats were slaughtered, and while we beat the dust off our clothing, the aromas of the stews filled the desert air. And that was just in our corner of the camp.

Moses and Jethro and the men had an even bigger feast. They praised Yah and ate and drank. And we women were all delighted to be welcoming Tzipporah and Galeet into our fold. I was nervous before they arrived, wondering whether Tzipporah would recognize me, and if so, whether she would still be holding bad feelings. I do not know whether she did either, but when she greeted me, she kissed my hand as she did for Kesher, Miryam, and Elisheva. She sat between Miryam and Elisheva on a cushion of honor, and May-tal invited Galeet to sit beside her; Galeet's smile made it clear that she was glad to do so.

Excited to tell stories of Moses to his wife, we had to work not to interrupt each other and overwhelm her. Miryam told Tzipporah about putting Moses in his basket in the reeds of the river and watching him until he was found and pulled out.

In response to Tzipporah's widened eyes, Miryam quickly added, "I knew it would be soon! Don't worry! That was exactly why I'd placed his basket in that exact spot. I'd seen the women bathing there before, and the water was still, so it was only a matter of time before he would cry out and they would hear him and fetch him."

"I remember that day perfectly," I said.

Tzipporah gasped in surprise but quickly quieted herself. I was sure she'd realized who I was then, but I did not want to restart our relationship by hiding myself. Galeet, who clearly had thought I was her age, looked at me quizzically, but she listened to the story about her father.

"A baby never would have escaped our notice where Miryam put him," I said. "Never *did* escape our notice. For me, finding Moses there was equal to finding a new life. That's what it was for him, of course, but I mean for me. It was a way that I got to reconnect with Israelite women. I got to share ancestral stories and speak in my native tongue sometimes."

I put my hand on Kesher's knee while I spoke. Of course, she had been my first connection with my people after I'd returned to the harem, but that story was longer than I was going to explain to Tzipporah on her first day—especially when I was trying to show her that I was no threat to her, that my love for Moses had begun with his mother.

"Even though Moses's mother, Vida, had been born in Egypt," I said, "she'd held on to our old traditions even while adding new ones. It was familiar and embracing to be with my kinspeople." I bit my tongue as soon as I said that, realizing that Tzipporah was in the opposite position: leaving her customs for ours. Even though I knew we had a lot to offer, I also knew the challenge of acclimating and being a stranger in a new land.

Elisheva picked up a different thread when I went quiet. "Moses has been a wise leader," she said. "It hasn't been easy, but he's maintained his patience somehow. He's a very kind man. Thoughtful. He doesn't rush into things. But," she paused, "you're his wife, so certainly you know what a kind heart he has. He and his brother, my husband, Aaron, work well together. They help each other, support each other, and I know they're grateful to have each other. I just want to tell you how grateful we all are to him for helping us get out of Egypt and to the land of Israel, the land of our ancestors."

After a brief silence, Tzipporah told the next story. It wasn't about Moses, though. I thought we might hear about him as a husband and father and shepherd. I'd missed the years of his life in Midian even though I hadn't been far, so I'd wanted to hear about some of those times. I was glad to be together, though, and so glad to have Tzipporah join our circle of women. During all the full moons that we saw while we were in Midian, I dreamt of dancing with her. Finally, at our next full moon in the wilderness, we would sing together. I was eager to get to know her, eager to hear a story about her or Moses or their children.

"I am a mother," Tzipporah said, "like the greatest mother, Newt." She paused to consider whether she should explain Newt to us and decided it best to do so. "Newt is the great goddess who covers the sky with her body. Sometimes she's considered a woman, sometimes a cow, but always a powerful, life-giving goddess stretched on all fours above the earth and below the sky. I have brought children into the world," Tzipporah said, "not with ease, but with strength. Just as Newt did. Does. Every morning, she gives birth to the sun in the east. We see the blood of her pain before the sun rises above, shining its glory on us so brightly that it's a constant reminder of her power. And every evening, she swallows the sun, showing that she is even more powerful by keeping the sun behind her until the morning, when she allows it to be rebirthed."

The only way this was a story about Tzipporah was that it was showing us that she would be polite and talk when it was her turn but not truly share of herself with strangers. As her new sisters ready to embrace her into the family, this was very disappointing, though we tried to be patient.

We continued to host her with the utmost respect and pampering. She allowed me to oil her skin in the ways I had learned in the harem, and she was gracious and genuine in expressing her praise for that. She tasted every stew, every bread, every sweet, and every drink, and she complimented each one. She and Galeet tossed their olive pits into baskets over their heads or from across the rug. To everyone's great entertainment, they never missed. Children and women alike followed their example and took turns doing the same.

During our whole visit, we told Galeet stories about her father and her foremothers. We told Tzipporah stories that praised her husband. They listened, but Tzipporah never offered to tell us anything about him or herself or their children. On the last night of the reunion, Tzipporah did tell us another story. This one was the story of the dung beetle:

"We all know," she began, "that the dung beetle is the most beautiful, the wisest, and also the strongest of all the beetles. It glistens in the light and is a different color every time you turn around to look at it from another angle. It takes the most vile of all things, dung, and rolls it into a perfect ball that it can then move easily to anywhere it chooses. It lays its eggs in there, making a new home for the next generation. It is copying the behavior of the god Kherpi, who does the same with the sun every morning. And my husband, Moses, copies them both."

We didn't know how to react to this. Moses had brought us out of Egypt and away from their pantheon of gods. Now he was being compared to one of them.

"Tzipporah," Miryam said, "everyone, let us praise Yah for the wide variety of people and stories that we get to meet. All these people—all of us—and all these stories are a part of Yah. Let us take them all in with gratitude." Miryam inhaled, and the other Israelite women did too. Tzipporah watched us as we took Yah in. *Yhhhh.*

"And let us remember that everything we are and do becomes a part of Yah," Miryam said. We exhaled. *Whhhh.* Miryam did this a couple more times so that Tzipporah would have a chance to join in, but she didn't. She simply waited for us to finish and then gave us the news I'd begun to think she might deliver.

"Jethro says that Moses must choose. He is either a dung beetle or a shepherd. You are lovely women, but I have many sisters at home. I don't think Moses will leave you all to come home with me, so I don't think we will see each other again." Tzipporah took Galeet by the hand, and the two of them walked out. They spent that night with Moses and his sons.

In the morning, Moses came to us with his head hung low. "I want to do the right thing for her," he said. "I want to do the right thing for my wife and children. They haven't lived in Egypt. They are already home. I didn't choose this path; it was chosen for me. I've tried to reject it, but in my heart, I can't. I want to do the right thing for my people. They are relying on me."

"You can do right by both," Miryam said.

Moses shook his head, though. "Jethro doesn't believe that I can. He says that if I try to do right by both at the same time, I'll fail at both. He is a wise man. He is also my elder and the priest of his tribe. And he will take care of Tzipporah and our children. They are his, too. The land of Israel isn't too far away. I will take you there. Aaron will help—you will help. We will do it. And then, when it's safe and I can be a shepherd of sheep again, I'll come back for my wife and children. They'll come with me then to Israel. My sons will serve our people with the rest of the Levites."

Moses was telling us, not asking. Tzipporah wouldn't be joining our tribe. She'd known that even before she'd laid eyes on us. Jethro was willing to help Moses by sharing his wisdom, but he wasn't willing to sacrifice Tzipporah and her children for this cause. Moses was the leader of the Israelites, not Jethro's leader. Moses felt like there was nothing he could do.

Miryam went to speak to Moses about the matter of his beautiful wife. "She is your wife, Moses. Yours, only. But Yah does not speak to you alone. Yah guides me and Aaron and all those who listen."

Aaron nodded his head in agreement.

"Listen to me now," Miryam said, "and my guidance. You must do the right thing for your wife, Moses. If she is not going with you, if she is to go with Jethro, you must divorce her. Do not make her stay tied to you when she cannot be with you."

Moses began to cry, and Miryam took him into her arms. "Maybe you are not right," he said. "But maybe you are. I wish it weren't so hard. I will divorce her. I will ask her to wait for me for a year, but if I do not come back, she will be free."

REFIDIM

We all left Refidim shortly after Tzipporah did. We hoped we would see her soon, for Aaron and Moses decided that Aaron's son Nadav would wed Galeet when we arrived in Israel. Moses would return alone to Midian and bring his wife, the bride to be, and his sons with him at that time. Until then, and only until then, Tzipporah and the children would wait in Midian, and Miryam would leave the tent of women and children to care for Moses. Elisheva was already taking care of Aaron and their four sons and was busy helping the mothers who were delivering the free generation of Israelites and training more midwives.

However, not all the Israelites were eager to travel again so soon. Many complained to Moses, so he addressed the people. "It is a long journey to our homeland," Moses said. "But there, we will grow our own flocks, build our own cities, and serve our own god. It is our god who brought us out of Egypt with signs and wonders. It is our god who heard the pleas of the Israelites and met me at the base of a mountain with a message to return to help redeem the people of Israel. There I saw a bush, ablaze with color . . ."

There was a collective gasp from the people. Moses had the attention of the tired nation.

"'What is this?' I thought. 'A bush that is burning but not destroyed?' It was at that very mountain that my journey to freedom began, and we will go there together!" Moses raised his hands in excitement. "We will take this journey to Israel together! We will all know Yah!"

After that day, I think Moses began to realize that he was a good leader. His address helped the people move forward with courage and confidence. So, as tired as our feet were, we started walking again. We were no longer dancing, but without the fear of being pursued, each person could now move at their own pace. This does not mean that we walked alone, just that the faster, younger, and most eager were at the front, and the slower, infirm, and elderly, and those caring for them, walked behind.

Elisheva stayed in the back to assist the women who would give birth at any moment. May-tal had been learning from her and was by her side as we walked so that she could listen to Elisheva talk about herbs and be ready when a birth happened. Kesher was slowing down more than I cared to admit to myself. She was the same Kesher I had always known and loved, so it was surprising to see her walking slowly and keeping company with the older women. I had to admit, though, that she was now one of them.

I also walked with the slower women. Not because I needed to, but because Kesher was there and Nina was there. Nina did not need my help. Her granddaughter Amina was by her side for that. But it was such a joy and delight to reunite with Nina that I wanted to spend more time with her. The little girl who had taken my hand had grown into a matriarch. Of course, walking beside the elderly Nina was not the same as when she and I had played with her dolls in Goshen, but the feeling was similar. Traveling with her felt almost like I was fulfilling a promise to Benno.

As we walked, Nina told me stories of my own childhood. She said that Grandfather Benjamin had indulged her with many stories of our time together. I had seen Benno as an old man with my own eyes, yet still it was difficult for me to imagine him as Nina's grandfather. To me, he was always just a little boy. Nina said that to him, I'd always been a little girl. He'd also told Nina that was one of the reasons he'd loved playing with her so much. It made him feel young again.

Nina also graced me with new songs as we walked. She said she made them up easily and that it was more difficult for her to remember them than to think of them in the first place. She sang two songs that were so beautiful we chose to repeat them many times in that day alone. The first one started with a question.

Hope?
Prepare?
Even celebrate?
Do we dare?
Will we really get there?
Trust in Yah, Yah is great, Yah is.
With Yah on our side, we are already there, already here.
Yhhhh, Whhhh.

The second one wasn't an answer, but was about what happened next.

Leaving,
Traveling,
Someplace new,
Goodbye, old home,
We are birds, we've flown.
Hello, new and unknown, waiting to be shown,
Eventually, we will make a better life in a land of our own.

Amina and I memorized those so completely that I can still remember them to this day. I also remember the hidden message inside each of them. At first, I did not realize there was a message. As I said, it was hidden. But Amina saw it right away.

Nina explained, "The words of these songs have one meaning, and the number of words in these songs have another meaning." I remembered how much Nina had enjoyed counting when we'd first met, but I had not heard any numbers in the songs. This confusion probably showed on my face.

"I know what it is, Grandmother," Amina said with excitement. "May I say? Please? I am certain I know."

"Maybe you're right," Nina said, "maybe you're not right. You may still say."

"Each song begins with one word and then one word again. After that, there are two words. Two is one and another one. The next line has three words. Three is two and one. The next line is five words, which is three and two. Each line gets longer and longer because the number of words in the next line is the total of the two lines before it."

Nina's smile was as wide as the Reed Sea, and Amina was so pleased to have put that smile there, so she added more.

"I know where you got that idea," Amina said. "When the numbers go on and on in that pattern, it is the same spiral that pinecones and seashells have, and, of course, the same spiral I have seen you create with colorful rocks many times."

I did not know about these things and was delighted to learn something new from Amina, who was also delighted to have shown me.

We sang these songs together as we walked and also when we stopped to rest, which we did frequently. It was not yet the warmest season of the year, but the sun beat down enough for us to need to find shade from time to time. One morning, even though we had not yet walked until the sun was high, we stopped for a rest. Most of our group was tired often, including those of us who were younger and stronger, for the weight of the others was on us as well.

We had twenty men who were carrying the elders of our tribe in the beds that Betzalel had designed. I was sure that Vida would have hated being in one of those, even though it was less bumpy than being pulled behind a donkey. The men were mostly the grandsons of the elders and were glad that the physical burdens they carried were their own kin, not bricks for the pharaoh; but still, the task took a lot of strength. When we rested, the men voiced their awe and gratitude that we were able to do so without fear of the taskmasters.

During one particular rest, the rest in the late morning before we had walked far, two of the lads spotted men approaching us. They almost ran off into the desert, afraid that the Egyptians had pursued us that far after all, but another lad stopped them from fleeing, saying that we were now rid of them forever. But then two of the elders encouraged all of us who could do so to run and save ourselves, even if it meant leaving them behind.

Korban, one of the grandsons who was carrying the elders, took action: "There is no need to fear. The Egyptians would not wish to pursue us this far. We are safe. And we are free. We can welcome them." He smiled proudly as he went to do so.

We watched from our resting place as Korban approached the men. He bowed politely from a distance, then went to greet them. Two of those men, who we later learned were Amalekites, went ahead of their group toward Korban. They did not bow to him as they approached; they just walked straight to him. Then, one Amalekite kicked Korban to the ground, and the other drove his sword right through Korban's stomach. We all gagged and gasped at the sight. We were stunned to stillness for just a moment but moved to action as soon as we realized that the Amalekite men—those two and the others behind them—were continuing toward us.

"Run," Kesher commanded May-tal. "Run now. Alert our armed men. Run. Then don't come back. Stay with the others."

"But Mother," May-tal said.

Those of us who could had already risen to our feet.

Kesher pushed her daughter and yelled at her. "Run! And don't come back. Listen to my words so that you may have a long life."

May-tal ran, and Kesher called out to her back as she fled, "My love covers you like the dew covers the land. I am always with you! That will never change!"

May-tal waved to us without even turning around and ran for her life—and ours. The two lads who had wanted to escape into the desert followed her, and the rest of us did what we could to prepare to fight in the few moments that we had before the attack. With only daggers, pots and pans, and our bare hands, those of us who could do so fought mostly by joining together to attack one Amalekite at a time. Never had I railed so viciously against anyone, jumping on backs, hitting heads with pans, pulling on a belt around a neck. Elisheva had an oil that burned one man's eyes, but it was only one man, and there were so many of them who had come to attack the weakest among us. Of all the days that I have lived, that was the most horrid. And, of course, worse than the deaths that we caused, were the ones we could not prevent.

All the elders who had been carried, the very same ones who had survived long and painful lives in Egypt, died by the swords of the Amalekites. All our young men were without weapons, and all but three of them were killed in battle. The other three were roped onto donkeys and dragged off with us women and babies.

May-tal succeeded in sounding the alarm and sending help, so before we had gotten too far, we were overtaken by Israelites. Another battle ensued. The Israelites had not had time to learn to be good soldiers, but they had desperation and succeeded in defeating the Amalekites. Forty of our soldiers were killed in that battle. The carnage was terrible and included Nina and two of the pregnant women. Elisheva was able to remove one baby from the womb, and when he let out his first cry, we all wailed with him.

That horrible day ended with a burial. All the Israelites were buried with their feet toward Israel, showing that they had continued their journey no matter what.

AMINA

mina didn't want to carry on with the journey. She said she'd failed to protect her grandmother. She said she should stay by her grave until she joined her in it. All of us, though, were devastated by what had happened.

Kesher, fortunately, was able to persuade Amina to continue with us: "Like Nina, I, too, am old," Kesher said. "I, too, am tired. I, too, struggle to go on. I, too, need help. Please," she said to Amina, "please, walk beside me and let me use your strength. My daughter is not here, yet I need help. I will be able to go farther and need less rest if you will walk with me."

Amina agreed. It was clear that she did not want to, and if Kesher had been merely trying to console her, it would not have worked. Amina was not consoled. None of us were. But Kesher genuinely needed help if she were going to keep moving, and Amina saw that. She could not say no to her.

Those of us who had been through the battle walked to join the others who were waiting for us where May-tal had found them. She was so relieved when we arrived! But all of us, those who had been through battle and those who had not, were overcome with despair. As darkness covered our camp, we paused our journey. Guards created a large circle around us with sentries and fires. And all of us wailed and waited to see what would come in the morning.

It was a sleepless night. Lying on our mats, we created a circle of women to surround Amina to make sure we knew where she was. Her mother was in that circle with her sisters. Kesher and May-tal and Elisheva and I were there as well. Amina's mother stroked her arm. Amina moaned that she should have protected her grandmother better. She should have fought harder. She should have saved her.

"If Grandmother Nina were here," Amina's mother said in a soothing voice, "she would tell you that you did everything possible. She would not be angry at you."

"Well, I am angry!" Amina yelled. She sat up but did not stand to flee. She yelled again from her seated position on the mat: "I am angry! I am angry at the Amalekites! Why would they attack us? Why? We are coming from slavery and oppression and misery! We only want a safe place to travel! Why must we still suffer after finally removing our yokes? We were not even going to stay here!"

A few babies woke to the yelling but were quickly put to breasts. None of the women had been sleeping, and we all felt the pain that Amina was expressing for us.

"There is nothing but desert here!" she yelled. "Can they not see that there's enough room? There's enough room! There's enough room for all of us here! Why would they come and just kill us? Why? We took nothing away from them! Even if we had settled here, there's enough room! But we are not even staying here! We are on our way to our land, not theirs! We just want to live!" Her speech was followed by a long period of sobs, and not just hers.

The morning brought much more yelling. "Why did you bring us out of Egypt only to die in the desert?" This question was asked of Moses and Aaron and Miryam and me and Yah countless times. It could be heard throughout the camp. There were also complaints. "Were there no graves in Egypt? Why could we not have died there? At least we had water and melons and meat!" Though very few people had had those things in Egypt.

Not everyone complained about the harshness of the desert; some complained about each other. Those who were ready to move on called the others a stiff-necked people, accusing them of not being grateful for being out of bondage or not being willing to take the responsibility of people who were no longer forced to serve another. I thought of my soft-necked friend Vida and the women who had stayed behind at the harem. Many had stayed, but many had come. I was glad that I had come. For me, there had never been any question. But it was not easy.

Moses said he would talk to Yah and said the people must listen to Aaron in his absence. Then Moses walked into the hills alone. The people stopped complaining and awaited Aaron's wisdom or instructions. Aaron had not been prepared to give either, but in his studies, he had learned to divert attention. Standing before the people, he took off his shoes, then he took a deep breath. *Yhhhh.* I wanted to ask him later whether this was to receive wisdom from Yah or to buy himself more time, but I forgot to do so. The answer may have been contained in his *Whhhh* as he gave himself to all of us, but I did not hear it.

I joined Aaron in this brief connection with Yah, as did many others. Those who didn't, waited impatiently. When he was finished, he put his shoes back on and spoke. "We no longer need to serve the pharaoh. We now have the honor of serving our own god, YhWh, the god of all. But how will we serve this god? Where will we serve this god? Go home, all of you. Search your satchels, examine your possessions, and begin to set aside the best ones so that we will have the means for our service when it is called for."

This was enough. The people had something to do, direction. There was still a little grumbling, but there was a lot of action. Families retreated to their tents and began looking through their belongings. We did the same in the women's area. As we unpacked, I thought of how wise Aaron had been to send the people who were complaining about what they didn't have to look at the things we *did* have. I found comfort in seeing my familiar cushion come off the cart, and even more so when I saw Kesher's. When we pulled out the beaded curtains that Kesher had made, the very same ones that had impressed me upon my return from Midian, I felt happiness.

I let my fingers run over many of the beads. I took my time and held some in my hand. I then raised some above my head and shook them to hear the gentle music the beaded strands made when they bumped into each other. Then I started looking for more leather and more beads. Some of the women around me began asking me what I was looking for and soon joined me in my quest.

Before long, a group of women had brought out blankets and were sitting in the shade and beading long strands of leather. Others saw what we were doing and brought more blankets.

Some brought more leather and beads and joined us in our creating. Other women brought flour and oils and spices and mixed them together and filled the air with an aroma that lightened our hearts and wet our mouths as we anticipated the flat bread to come. Miryam came with a collection of mirrors, as did some other women who carried even more. They wanted to melt and mold the bronze they'd said, into a bowl for Aaron to wash his feet. Miryam had seen the dirt on her brother when he'd taken off his shoes and wanted to honor him as a leader with something beautiful.

Day after day, we created beauty. Moses was still isolating himself and listening to Yah, and Betzalel and Hur had become leaders among the men. They had groups who were carefully working on our protection by arranging plans and schedules and men who would surround our large camp at all times. Other men were working, as we were, on something that would be ready to honor our god when we could do so. And still others were selecting the best animals for sacrifices. We all ate and drank and slept at the appropriate times. Nobody was overworked, and most everybody's mood was lightened with the new purpose and hope.

One evening, Elisheva suggested that the next woman to give birth name her baby Tikvah, meaning hope. She also said that she had been thinking a lot about this not-yet-born baby. "This baby will be born into a world of hope, yes?" she asked.

All of us around her, our hands busy with work, nodded our agreement.

"And she will be born beyond the reach of the pharaoh's wrath," she added.

We all smiled, feeling so much happiness for this baby we had not even met yet.

"But," Elisheva continued, "she will fall down when she's learning to walk. She will bleed even though her mother will clean her wounds and comfort her."

Again, Elisheva received agreement.

"She will walk to get water, and one day someone will yell at her for not bringing enough, or not bringing it fast enough, or not getting it cold enough, even though none of that will have been her fault," Elisheva said, clearly speaking from experience, and not just her own. "When cooking, she will burn her stews sometimes, but not always, and she will burn her arms, but also not always." Indeed, this had happened to all of us.

"Some nights she will be hungry, and some nights she will be scared. Yet . . . we still look forward to her birth and will rejoice when it happens." Nobody knew who the mother of this baby would be, but we could all feel the hope she would bring.

"I have been thinking about Amina's question," Elisheva said. "She asked why we must still suffer, even now that we are out of Egypt. I do not know the answer. But I have been thinking about it, and it seems similar to a birth. Before a baby is born—like when Tikvah will be born, or when any of us were born—the baby is first trapped in the womb. Then she must squeeze through a narrow space much smaller than what seems can fit a baby. There is pressure to stay in, but she keeps pushing out, and the mother helps to push the baby out through the narrow space.

"Then the baby is born, and we rejoice. She is no longer confined. She is no longer pushing against the narrow space. But still, it is not easy to be outside the womb either. The darkness the baby had lived in all the time is gone, but there's still darkness at night. The wetness the baby was covered in is gone, and now the baby yearns for water—but sometimes there is none. The warmth of the womb is gone, but the heat of the sun burns us. When we are born, we are freed from the limitations of the womb, but we have new obstacles to learn to live with."

Miryam jumped onto Elisheva's idea and kept talking. "And we *do* learn to live with them," she said. "We learned to walk, even though we fell. We wouldn't stop Tikvah from learning to walk, but we would help her learn. And then we would teach her to run. We would not hide the stew pot from her, but we would teach her to keep her clothes far from the fire when stirring the food. And when she is scared, we will hold her, we will do our best to protect her, we will be with her in her fear, we will wipe her tears, we will tell her stories of when we, too, were afraid, and then we will tell her that we will not always be afraid. She will learn, just as we have, that there is a time for fear and also a time for creating; there is a time for crying and also a time for singing."

Inspired by this idea, I started singing. I chose one of Nina's songs so that she could be with us. As I sang, others joined with me. Soon many of us were on our feet, singing and dancing, holding hands or putting arms around each other in a wide circle. The song was soft and quiet, comforting us and reminding us of how good and pleasant it was to be a tribe of sisters together. When I ended up dancing next to Amina, she pulled my arm and took me out of the circle.

"Look what I made, Auntie," she said.

While we had been singing her grandmother's songs, Amina had collected rocks and laid them out on the ground in the spiral pattern that Nina had admired so much and copied so many times.

"That is beautiful," I said to her. "Your grandmother would be pleased, and I am pleased that you showed me."

Amina smiled and let me bring her into the circle where we danced and sang hand in hand.

For forty days, Moses had been letting his people ear rest and listening to Yah in one of the many desert caves. And when he returned, the people were ready to listen to him.

"I have taken to Yah the question of whether we should return to Egypt or move forward to Israel," Moses said.

It amazed me how that question had disappeared from our midst—at least among the women—in all that we had done and been through while Moses was away.

"It is not easy to be our own people," Moses continued. "We will face hardships. We already have. There will be more. But we had hardships in Egypt as well. What we did not have enough of in Egypt was each other. Now, here we are—"

Moses had to stop his address. A noise was coming from the south that made it impossible for us to hear him. It got louder and louder as it approached. Finally, as the sky darkened, we saw the reason: quail. Hundreds upon hundreds upon hundreds of quail flew above us, darkening the sky and deafening our ears.

The quail kept coming. While countless quail flew high above, some came lower. When the lower ones had separated themselves enough from the flock, I could see that as similar as they were, each was different. There were variations in their coloring, their size, and even their sound that was not noticeable when they were in the group. Some of these quail landed in our midst and were quickly caught and killed; others were shot down from the sky. Anyone with a slingshot could hit one, for the quail were so close together that a rock could not have flown between them. No matter what we did, though, the quail just kept on flying overhead for a very long time. When they flew together, they seemed of one mind and one goal. They had a destination, and most of them were set on getting there.

When the noise of the quail finally passed but the people were still in awe, Moses resumed his speech: "What we did not have enough of in Egypt was each other. Now, here we are, the nation of Israel, ready to move as one to the land of Israel. We will not go back together, but forward, together. First, we will go to the base of the mountain, as we had planned. There, we will worship Yah. We will praise and thank our god for taking us out of bondage and leading us to the land of our forebears. Then, we will continue to the land of our forebears. But first, we will feast!"

The quail were roasted, and bread was made. Wine and beer were taken from jugs. Every mouth was filled. Every belly was filled. We all ate and were satisfied.

As our eyes grew heavy and the sky grew dark with night, Aaron called out, "Praise *Yhhhh Whhhh* for the land and for the sustenance!" We all repeated after him before closing our eyes for a peace-full, belly-full sleep.

We had feasted with such abundance that night that when we broke down our camp and left in the morning, we had much to leave behind for the buzzards and other scavengers. While we still held grief and anger over our losses to the Amalekites, it was because of their attack that we moved forward in a new formation. Not only did we move at one pace, but we also had guards who encircled our camp day and night. At night while most of us slept, those on duty kept fires burning around us, and in the middle of the night, a new shift started. Thus, we were assured that the fires never went out until morning. Then guards carried the smoking embers with us during the day so that they could easily make fire for us the next night.

Elisheva proudly told me that it was her older sons, Nadav and Avihu, who had devised a special scent for the smoke of the embers. Because she'd worked with different herbs and oils for healing, she had taught all four of her boys about much of the contents of her midwife's bag; Nadav and Avihu had then shown an interest in making different potions with those contents and noticing the feelings they felt when combining certain plants and burning them at different rates. I knew nothing about these things, but I was quick to praise Elisheva for her and her sons' wisdom and to truthfully say that I enjoyed the smell in the smoke that the embers produced during the days.

This was how we traveled through the desert: protected by fires around us by night and smoking embers around us by day. We never walked more than six days without having a day of rest, and we all helped each other, intent on being like the flock of quail. Only two men left our circle, Hur and Nakshon. To ease our arrival into the land of Israel, Moses had sent the two of them to scout out the best way to enter and to search for Israelites who were already there. They came to me before departing so that I could tell them about the places I had been. I reminded them of Yo-av and Li-av and the other members of their own tribe who had gone ahead of the rest of us. I told them about my mother and her sisters. I told them about my father and his brothers. And for seven days, I read to them from my father's scrolls. When we finished, Hur and Nakshon went to prepare our way home.

While they were gone, I read my father's scrolls again. This time, I invited anyone who wished to come and listen. There were some women who I'd hoped and expected would want to hear the stories. Indeed, Kesher, Miryam, Elisheva, May-tal, and Amina were all eager to hear me read. But to my surprise and delight, many others came as well. The heads of my brothers' tribes—Gaddi from the tribe of Menasse and Joshua from the tribe of Efraim—came and brought all their men and women with them. The head of Benno's tribe was Palti, and he, too, wanted his tribe to hear the scrolls read. Thus it was that all the living progeny of my grandmother Rachel at that time got to hear her son Joseph's stories.

This was how we passed the days between Refidim and the base of the mountain. We read, we created beaded leather and other beauty, and we traveled slowly, surrounded by smoke or fire and a scent that blended with that of our dusty bodies and our livestock. It was a pleasant and predictable routine, and I felt content. When Hur and Nakshon returned, I felt even better.

Hur came directly to me. I hugged him and welcomed him back. "Auntie, I have come to tell you of my night in the city of Jericho."

"And I am eager to hear," I said. "Your mother and sister will want to see you too. Go and bring them as well."

"Auntie, I must tell you—" he started, but he heeded my request and came back quickly with Kesher and May-tal before continuing.

"Jericho is a mighty city a number of days' walk from here in the land of our forefathers . . . and foremothers," Hur said, stumbling over his words. "Well, in the land that you came from. But further north than Hevron and not far from the river. In any case, the walls of Jericho are tall, but the gates are wide, and wider still was the hospitality we found at an inn within. The innkeeper gave us the entire rooftop for the night, along with cushions and blankets for our comfort. I thought of your father's scrolls and his story of the night he'd spent in the closed room when he'd gone to an inn. The hospitality we received was much more generous.

"The innkeeper's wife gave us delicious stew and thick, filling bread for our dinner. Just before we all sat down to dine, the innkeeper introduced us to his wife by thanking her by name publicly.

"'Let us all thank my wife, Shani . . .' he said. Then he paused to catch his breath. He was an old man who could not even rise from his cushion when he spoke. I am not sure he could even see his guests, but it was important to him to thank his wife in front of us, so when he regained his strength he finished his praise, '. . . for this wonderful meal.'

"The innkeeper was an old man, but his wife was much younger, though she was still a grandmother. It seemed that Shani and the other women took care of the inn and travelers and him. He was grateful, and he was very proud of her. After thanking and introducing her, the innkeeper introduced himself."

Hur paused for just a moment, and then, with the wonder he must have felt that night at the inn still in his voice, he said, "Auntie, the innkeeper's name is Joseph."

I gasped.

"I gasped, too, when he said his name," Hur said. "After hearing my gasp, Joseph the innkeeper said, 'It is not a common name, I know. It comes from the tribe of the Israelites.'

"His wife then continued for him. 'Joseph's mother gave him this name because she was from that tribe and because with

Joseph's birth, especially since she was advanced in years, she felt blessed that he had been added to her life.'"

I was still stunned. Hur waited patiently while I absorbed his words. Kesher squeezed my hand tightly.

"His mother?" I asked when I could speak again.

"Yes," Hur said. "When I heard this, I told Joseph the innkeeper that I knew his name well, because I, too, was an Israelite. I told him that Nakshon and I were both from the tribe of Judah. We explained that we were returning from Egypt, where we had been saved by Joseph, son of Israel, and then oppressed by Pharaoh, and that we were bringing Joseph's bones back to his homeland for burial. But I was interrupted, because no sooner had the name Joseph passed my lips than had Joseph the innkeeper reached out and pulled me to his chest and embraced me in a strong hug and called me Brother. He was not a young man or a large one, but his hold was tight."

I felt Kesher's hand grip mine tightly. Hur's words were coming into my ears like a dream, and I thought I was missing pieces of the story, for I could only remember hearing the name Joseph and being in a haze produced by the words *his mother was an Israelite*.

Hur took my other hand in his. It was strong and warm and comforting all at once, and feeling it brought my attention back to him.

Hur looked me deeply in the eyes and said, "Auntie, Blue, daughter of Deenah and Joseph, I shall tell you the whole story that I heard at the inn. But first I will skip to the end so that you may know the answers to two questions you must have: The story is a happy one, and Joseph the innkeeper is the son of your mother. He is your brother."

The sobs that I sobbed cannot be described. Kesher cried with me. After all our years together, I think she felt what I felt many times, and the same was true for me. I was grateful to have her hand to hold and her shoulder to cry on when I received the news that was better than I ever could have dreamt of. When my tears paused, Hur was still sitting patiently. How lucky I was to have him too! He had not grown in my body, but he had grown in my chamber in the harem and in my heart. And now he was a father and a leader and a kind and patient man who was excited with me.

I wiped my face. We breathed together. *Yhhhh*. I thought of all the times I had taken in Yah not knowing that my mother had given me another brother whom I was also taking in. *Whhhh*. I thought of all the times I had put myself back into Yah not knowing that my mother was still receiving a part of me.

"Hallelu Yah," I said when I was calmer.

"Hallelu Yah," Kesher and Hur and May-tal responded.

Then Hur told me the story I had forever longed to hear.

"This is what I learned from Joseph the innkeeper and his wife, though she told most of the story while he nodded," Hur began. "Joseph's father, No'am, was an innkeeper before him. A kind and gentle man, No'am welcomed weary travelers and provided them with shelter and food and a place to bathe their feet before they continued on their journeys. No'am was known in the city for being mild-mannered and quiet and gentle, which was easy to see if you watched him for a while. And that is exactly what No'am's wife had done before becoming his wife: she had watched him for a while.

"Shani, wife of Joseph the innkeeper, said that No'am's mother went by the name Elephant. She had arrived in the city with a maidservant and a cat and a few provisions and had watched the goings on from shadowy corners and crowded markets. When Elephant saw No'am and his gentleness, she watched him more and more, and then, a few days after her arrival in the city, when her food was running low and she and her maidservant had had enough of sleeping in fear, Elephant approached No'am at the gate of his inn. She told him that she and her maidservant, who was called Z, were skilled cooks and weavers and could make his inn more attractive. She asked No'am to give them lodging in exchange for this work, and he agreed. The three of them worked this way—quietly, amicably, respectfully—for more than a month. And then No'am said he would like to make Elephant his wife.

"Elephant said that her father was gone and that she could bring no dowry to the marriage. She told No'am that she had been married before but that her husband had been killed. She suggested it would be better that she continue to work for her keep and remain in her room with Z. No'am was sad, and he did say that if they were to be married, he could bring her a son, a legacy. But Elephant still said she wanted to stay in the position she had. Secretly, she was pleased that No'am didn't force her to choose between marrying him or leaving her work at the inn. This endeared him to her even more, and she felt comfort in his kindness.

"One year after arriving at the inn, Elephant asked No'am if he still wished to marry her. He did. And so, they were wed. And though he had promised her a son, she did not mind not having one. She was content, happy even, with her life at the inn. She loved meeting people from far away, hearing their tales, giving them food and shelter, and then parting with them. She enjoyed that very much. And after many years of this life, she was surprised to learn that she was pregnant and was going to have a child in her old age.

"Elephant was a doting mother and loved laughing with her son, who always seemed to be full of smiles. No'am loved hearing her laugh, and so did travelers who came to the inn. When she laughed, in fact, it was said that she was the most beautiful woman anyone had ever seen. The inn was prosperous with No'am and Elephant in charge, and little Joseph grew to be a happy and hospitable boy, then young man."

I wanted to hear the rest of Hur's story, but I asked him to wait for a moment. It was as if my ears were filled with wind. Whenever I heard Hur say Joseph, I had to listen harder to whatever came next because all I could think was, *There is a man named Joseph who is the son of my mother. There is a man named Joseph who shares a name with my father. There is a man named Joseph who is my brother. There is a man named Joseph who is an innkeeper not far from me.* I closed my eyes and told myself these things quietly before Hur went on.

"When No'am died," Hur said, continuing once I'd opened my eyes again, "Joseph became the innkeeper. His mother continued to help with her cooking and cleaning, laughing and storytelling. But it was after No'am's death that Elephant began to tell her son, Joseph, stories that were only for him. She told him that his unusual name was a Hebrew name and that she came from the tribe of the Hebrews, a people also known as Israelites because they had been named after her father, Israel. Elephant told her son that her own unusual name was one she'd given herself when she'd left her father's home. She said that though she had never seen an elephant, let alone a herd of elephants walking all at once and shaking the ground with their footsteps and filling the air with their trumpeting sounds, she had always imagined them that way and had felt like an elephant with her bold departure from her tribe. She also told him that Z's name had been Zilpah back then but had never told him what her own name had been. Elephant didn't like to talk of her former life. Except that when she was old, she spoke often of her daughter.

"Shani, speaking for Joseph the innkeeper, said that Elephant had a daughter who also had an unusual name: Blue. Elephant had called the girl Blue after a bird with a blue stripe on its wings and because the girl sang as beautifully as a bird—more beautifully in fact."

Hur then interrupted his story about the innkeeper Joseph to tell me that it was at that moment that he had also interrupted Joseph and Shani's story to tell them that I, Blue, was alive and well and not far away.

"'How is that possible?' Hur asked, speaking as Joseph. 'She would be even older than I am, and I have already sent all my teeth to the grave, where I will be joining them any day.'"

Hur explained that he'd told Joseph that he had known me since his birth and that I had not aged one day in that time.

Joseph was surprised, Hur reported, but his toothless smile was wide with delight . . . Hur said that tears had run down Joseph's cheeks and Shani's as well. "'For most of his life, Joseph hadn't known of this sister, and by the time he did learn of her, she had been assumed to be long gone. He never imagined he would meet someone who knew her,' Shani said."

"Then," Hur went on, "Shani told me that when she had married Joseph, Elephant had welcomed her with open arms and a monthly dance under the full moon for just the two of them. Elephant hadn't told her where the dance or song had come from or why they did it, but every month, they took out drums and ate sweets and sang and danced. When Shani had daughters, they were included in the ritual too. And when Elephant was on her deathbed, she had two requests: that Joseph hold her hand and that Shani sing the moon song.

"Shani said Elephant died with a peaceful heart and a relaxed countenance. And then Shani gave me a gift. That is, she gave you a gift, Auntie."

With that, Hur reached into his pouch and removed a long leather strand with red beads strung from end to end. He wrapped it around my wrist twice and then tied the end pieces together.

"Shani had two of these around her wrist," he said, "and she immediately removed one and requested that I bring it to you. She said these were the straps on the sandals that Elephant loved so much that even when the sandals had been worn through, she kept the straps and put them on a new pair of sandals, and then eventually on another pair of sandals. And then eventually, when she was no longer walking through the city or even the inn, she put them on her wrists. In one way or another, she wore these beads for years."

My fingers stroked the red beads. My mother's beads. The tears that fell as I did so were tears of relief. Then they quickly turned to tears of happiness. My mother had lived a good life! A fulfilled life! A happy life! And I had a brother! My joy lifted me into song and dance. May-tal joined me, and I spun her around with me as I sang:

"Joseph, Joseph, Joseph lives!
Joseph lives in Israel!
And we'll see him soon!
Soon we will see Joseph!"

I grabbed my drum, Kesher grabbed hers, and we took the singing outside. May-tal explained to the gathering women that I was singing of a new Joseph, a brother. Before they had even heard the whole story, they raised their timbrels and joined me in a circle of song until the blazing sun forced us into the shade of my tent. There, they listened to me tell them about my new brother and his wife and children . . . and about my mother, Elephant.

YEARS

All the years I had waited to return to Israel had held anticipation and impatience, but learning about my brother made waiting to return even more difficult. Eager to meet him, hold him, and hear from him about my mother—about *our* mother—I considered asking Hur to take me back there. He and Nakshon had gone for a purpose, though: to find a way into the land and make a connection with other members of our tribe there. They had done that and were now making plans with the other men for our journey as a nation. Still, perhaps the lads who had accompanied them could take me while the men stayed here.

Kesher listened as I explained to her my inner conflict about this, for I had never wanted to see my brother; of course, I had never known I'd had a brother.

"Perhaps, I could go first to the land and then welcome the people when they arrive. Or, like Hur and Nakshon, I could go and be with my brother, then return and be with my people. Perhaps I should ask Moses, or Hur. I wish I could ask my mother. Would she want me to meet my brother or stay here? Or maybe both—I could meet him after I stay here. I wonder what

Grandmother Leah would think. She'd kept the secret of Sode but then had wanted to be with her grandson. Certainly Vida wanted her children to be together. She worked very hard for that. I wonder what she would say. Maybe if I asked my father, he would know what to do; he didn't always want to be with his brothers, so perhaps he would—"

Kesher interrupted me. "Blue," she said, "this situation was very unexpected, but none of the wise people you have mentioned are wiser than you are, and none of them are here for you to ask. When you do decide on what is right, even then, you will only be maybe right, maybe not. Perhaps you could stop wondering for a few days, as it's tiring and keeps you away from what is around you. Or if you are eager to know, then ask Yah."

Indeed, I had been eager to know. So much so, in fact, that I had thought there must be a quick way to solve this problem so I could choose one way or the other and feel better. Suddenly, it felt like this was the most important question of my life. Of course the answer, like all others, was with Yah. I thanked Kesher and then moved to a quiet cushion in the shade so that I could ask Yah.

With my eyes closed, I took in all the people I had wanted to ask for help. I breathed in their wisdom and their love. *Yhhhh.* Then I gave of myself to my brother, who was not so far away, and anyone who might go with me to meet him. *Whhhh.* I did this a few more times, but I was not able to settle my thoughts. I tried singing to myself in my head so that I could still take in Yah and give myself to Yah. I sang the songs of my ancestors that I had learned from my mother and grandmothers. I sang the songs of my childhood with Shirli and Mangeena. I sang Nina's songs that were on the lips of the women around me. I breathed. *Yhhhh. Whhhh.* Still, I could not settle my thoughts.

Though the sun was hot, I took a rug outside to lie down beneath the sky. With my eyes closed, I was not able to feel the Oneness with Yah. With my eyes open, taking in the wonder of the blue sky above me, I still could not feel myself being a part of it. What I felt most acutely was a small rock poking my shoulder through the rug. I sat up to move the rock, and when I did, I paused to examine it.

The rock fit well in my hand. It had many bumps, but it was not sharp. Though it was mostly red—if I had to say it was a color, I would say red—it clearly had lines going across it, or maybe around it. The lines were blue and gray and white. These lines were thin and separated red from red. I thought the rock looked like a tiny little mountain. I was so big that I could hold a little tiny mountain in my hand, so tiny that it was just a rock.

I placed that rock on the hard ground beside me and began to gather others. I put the first two that I found in front of the first one. Those two rocks were my parents, and the first one I'd found was me. I looked for and found three more rocks. These would be my grandmothers Leah and Rebekah and Rachel, even though I had never met Rachel. I put those three behind my parents. Soon I'd found five rocks to add to my pattern, my five children: Hur, Miryam, Aaron, Moses, and May-tal. I could see the spiral beginning to emerge on the ground and was excited to add eight more loved ones. Benno and Geeborr, my first friends; Habibti, who had been my friend when my father had first made a place for me in the harem; Kesher, my first connection to my people when I'd returned to the harem; Vida, my soft-necked friend; and

Suf, who had helped all of us and was still helping Vida. I placed a rock for Kohenet, too, who had also done so much good, and one for Elisheva, the little girl with the broken water jug who had become a midwife, a messenger, and a sister.

However, these were not the only people who had been woven into my life and who had accepted me as threads in theirs. Eager to show my expansion, I gathered the next thirteen rocks more quickly and less carefully than I had the first ones. I named each one as I set it with the others. The first was for Elisheva's brother, Nakshon; then one for his father, who knew how to swim; his Israelite mother; and his Egyptian mother. Another rock was for Massoot, the midwife who had helped save him, and two more were for the brave midwives Shifra and Pu'a, who had defied orders to save so many babies. Betzalel and his sister Ra'ayva and his Israelite mother Ra'ayon and his Egyptian mother Eemo each got a rock. And another was for Amram, who hadn't lived to leave Egypt. The thirteenth stone was for the pharaoh, for even he had a place in my life.

I could imagine Nina looking over my shoulder, the shoulder that had been poked by just one rock only moments before, and smiling. I imagined her smiling as I was inspired to add even more rocks. Sarah, the matriarch of us all was the first one placed in the next row. I added people from generations before me as well as rocks for my own three brothers, one right next to the other: Menasse and Efraim, who would never make it to our homeland, right next to Joseph the innkeeper, who had never left it. I kissed a rock that was for Nina and put one for Amina right next to it. I placed rocks for Tzipporah and her children, who I hoped I'd get to know, and one for Reuel, her father, who had been the son of a friend of my father's. I placed a rock for Lo-Mukar next to a rock for someone I knew would be kind to him: Bilhah.

The spiral grew so large that I could no longer give names to every rock. These were not people I knew well, but they were all around me. They were on this journey with me, and I, with them. I continued to grow my spiral until it finally ran into a tent and I had no more room. I looked up to see that the sun was setting and a crowd had gathered. I had the answer to my question: my place was here, and I would stay.

TOGETHER

Together, we traveled to the base of the mountain where Moses had seen the flaming bush, heard the call to return to Egypt, and felt his brother's arms around him again after so long. It was Moses's hope that visiting this landmark on the way to Israel would not only provide a resting place but also a place for the people to connect with Yah.

Traveling with so many people and animals, it took us much longer to get there than it had taken when it was only me and Moses. We also encountered heavy rains that forced us to camp only one day away from the mountain. When we arrived, the bushes that had been a stretch of bright yellow and orange beside the wadi when we had been there last were now green with fresh leaves. The wadi itself was also no longer a wadi at the base of the mountain, but a river. Water flowed in abundance that we hadn't seen since leaving Egypt. Of course it was nothing like the Nile, but there was plenty of water for all of us to bathe ourselves and wash our clothes. Word spread quickly that there were no crocodiles or hippos in this water, and soon it had more people than fish in it.

Little children squealed with abandon, and many adults joined them in their joyful noises. A group of boys began shouting, "I can swim! I can swim! I can swim!" while splashing each other and playfully jumping on one another's backs. We all let the dust and dirt that had been caked on us over the last many weeks wash away from us. With it, we also washed away tension and fear. We laughed and cried. We scrubbed each other's backs and pulled tangles out of each other's hair.

As our clothes dried in the sun, I asked Kesher whether she would like me to put oil on her newly clean skin. She immediately accepted, so we went to get oil. Miryam overheard and made the same offer to Elisheva, and before we had even unpacked the oil, every woman in the camp had caught on to the idea and was ready to be pampered and feel renewed. Perhaps the men, too, felt this way, though we did not know what they were doing in their area. In ours, large oil jugs filled smaller jugs. Herbs were brought out and put in the oil much later than usual, but it was enjoyed anyway. The children who got hungry that night had nothing but dried barley cakes for dinner. We were all too relaxed to even get up to eat ourselves.

When we awoke in the morning, we were refreshed. For many of the women, it was the first time in their lives they'd felt that way. We were able to prolong our luxury with thanks, once again, to the water. The animals could drink until full, and no troughs needed to be filled. And once again, no food needed to be prepared. While we had slept, the ground had been covered in mushrooms. For as far as we could see, the brown desert floor had turned white.

We ate mushrooms until we were satisfied without even needing to prepare anything.

"Praise Yah for the land and the sustenance!" May-tal shouted. We all did. And then, some of us went back to the river for a second day of playing and bathing. Some used the oils again. Some sat in circles and sang. Some slept under the sun. We all had smiles on our faces, food in our bellies, and faith in our god. Even Pharaoh's birthday celebrations in the palace had not been as joyful as the three days we spent at the base of the mountain.

On the third day, when we had eaten our fill of mushrooms, bathed until every speck of dust was gone, oiled ourselves and each other, cleaned our clothes, danced, sang, laughed, and slept, light flashed across the sky. Thunder crackled above the mountain. Somewhere, horns sounded. Then again. Light! Thunder! Horns! Then again. Light, thunder, and horns all together! Again! The ground shook. The mountain lit up with light. People started rushing toward it. Moses and Aaron stood at the base, warning them not to go up. The slope was slippery, and the night was dark except when the light was blinding.

"To go up there like this will mean your death!" they warned.

So, the people stayed together at the base of the mountain. We looked on in awe as the horn blasts changed sounds. We listened in awe as the light sang. We felt the thunder through our feet and our hearts that took on the beat. As one, we breathed in the wonder. *Yhhhh*. We kept Yah inside us until Yah was too big to fit and insisted on bursting out and returning to the mountain, forcing us to breathe ourselves along. *Whhhh*.

"Hallelu Yah!" Moses shouted.

"Hallelu Yah!" we called back, again and again and again, a hundred times, long into the night.

Then, Moses stopped. The silence that followed was sudden and complete.

Then Aaron filled it, addressing us all. "Listen, Children of Israel," he ordered. "YhWh is our god! *Yhhhh Whhhh* is the One!" He held up his hands above us all, his grown man hands, still with his fingers different from ours, not afraid to show his difference. He continued to speak directly to each one of us. "*Yhhhh Whhhh* blesses you and watches over you! *Yhhhh Whhhh* shines His face upon you and shows you the way! *Yhhhh Whhhh* lifts up His face to you and makes you whole!"

We were all drenched. Not from rain, for there had been none, but from our own sweat and tears of ecstasy. By the time the dawn broke, most people had fallen asleep. I had been one of them. I woke to the sound of a woman crying not far from me. When I sat up, I saw she was being held by other women. I rested my head again but could not sleep. Nor could I stop hearing the woman's cries. I went to see what was happening.

"What's wrong?" I asked her.

"Nothing," she said. "Nothing at all is wrong."

I learned that her name was Noa and that the four women with her were her sisters. They were not comforting her but were holding on to her as she cried in relief.

"Nothing is wrong, and nothing will ever be wrong," Noa said. "After all the years of struggle in Egypt, I've been shown that I am not a piece of trash to throw away. I am not an animal to work into the ground! I am holy! I am a part of a nation of priests just because I live. I have a god to watch over me! I deserve to be clean! I deserve to be cared for! I deserve to have clean clothes and rest and joy! I deserve to have this holy experience!"

Noa stood and continued, her voice getting stronger with every word. "Being here now, I know that I am holy because Yah is holy! That is all, and that is enough! I just need to *be* in order to be worthy. I am so grateful for this day! If I die tomorrow, it will be enough because nothing can ever take that away from me! Nothing can remove Yah from me! Nothing can remove my holiness! I have been shown my own worth! Everybody around me can see my worth! Yah sees this worth in me! I am nothing like what the Egyptians saw in me. I am nothing like what they tried to get me to believe that I was. Even when I was filthy, I was not filth. Even when I did not satisfy them, I was good enough. I truly am someone who deserves to be part of a holy nation, someone who is clean and who gets to have a personal audience with Yah! Nothing can ever take that away from me! Nothing can remove Yah from me! Nothing can remove me from Yah! Nothing can remove my holiness! Nothing can ever be wrong again!"

Once Noa had said all of that, she cried in her sisters' arms and succumbed to sleep. She and her sisters curled up like kittens on the blanket and slept long past the sunrise, as did so many others. People woke up groggy but were still moved from the night before. If anyone else found the words to say how that night had changed them, I did not get to hear, but I think Noa's experience—even if not her exact words—spoke to the collective feeling in the camp.

OUT OF EGYPT

We had been out of Egypt for a year when Kesher stopped being able to walk on her own. Every step left her gasping for air. This was difficult for her, but no special accommodations had been needed because we weren't walking anywhere. We had been camped at the base of the mountain for months and showed no signs of leaving. After that night of revelation, we had all felt our unity. But when we recovered from the experience, many of us were surprised to find that unity did not mean being of one mind.

The first time we learned this was when twelve men, the heads of the tribes, went to Moses and said that they did not want to go to the land of Israel before first having someone from their own tribe scout it out. Only Hur and Nakshon, that is, only Judah's tribe, had been on the earlier mission. The heads of the tribes thought that should be rectified, and because they were the heads of their tribes, they kept everyone from moving forward until they had given their go-ahead. Moses felt he had no choice but to agree.

This time, the men did not need to hear from me about what to expect because they could hear it from Hur and Nakshon. But there were two who chose to come directly to me anyway: Joshua, son of Nun, from the tribe of my brother Efraim, and Satur, son of Mikhail, from the tribe of Asher. Both of them addressed me as Auntie, but in different ways.

"Auntie Blue, daughter of Joseph, it is an honor," Joshua said. He kissed my hand and sat at my feet to learn.

"Auntie Serrah, daughter of Asher, it is an honor," Satur said. He kissed my hand and sat at my feet to learn.

While the others were with Hur, I told Joshua and Satur what I knew, then I asked them to bring back word of my brother or my mother's sisters. But they did not do so. When the twelve scouts returned forty days later, ten of them reported that we should not enter the land. They said it was too dangerous. They said that it, indeed, was a land flowing with milk and honey. They praised the size of the grapes, describing them as big as melons. But, they said, the men there were as powerful as giants and would kill us like grasshoppers if we tried to go in. Only two, Joshua, head of the tribe of Efraim, and Caleb, head of the tribe of Judah, came back ready to enter the land.

Hearing the warnings against continuing our journey, the people got scared. It was as if the thunder and lightning at the mountain had been forgotten. As if the crossing of the Reed Sea had been forgotten. As if leaving Egypt had been forgotten. As if being oppressed in Egypt had been forgotten. Neighbors and kin quarreled endlessly about whether or not to move forward, each person certain that they were right and certain that their opponents were supporting a plan that would get them killed.

All of them forgot that there *were* no opponents, only fellow weary travelers who wanted the same things: to live their lives with stability and peace. It was just that some thought completing our journey to our homeland was the path to stability and peace, and others thought that returning to life in Egypt was. Unable to move forward or backward, we were still camped at the base of the mountain on the night of the full moon that marked one year of having left our bondage.

That night, we reminisced about the grand exodus we had made. We told each other stories about it, about where we had been and what we had been doing and thinking and feeling on that day and during the time leading up to it. We remembered what it had been like to be strangers in a strange land. We remembered, too, the yearning for our own land. I thought that surely we would set forth again soon. But we did not. Even the remembering brought quarrels, disagreements, and blows when not all the stories were the same, and a storm of freely slung hatred blocked our path forward.

Kesher never arrived in the land of Israel but was buried with her feet pointing in that direction at the base of the mountain. Except for the time I had spent as Moses's lad in Midian, Kesher and I had been connected every day since Kohenet had let her into my chamber. We had grown more mature together, though only she had grown older. Her death was an enormous loss for me. I sat in mourning with Hur and May-tal and Miryam, Aaron, and Moses. For seven days, we were together. We did not get up from our mourning.

It was difficult for me to imagine life without Kesher. I did not *want* to imagine life without Kesher. Or even live life without

Kesher. I had lost so many people. But I did not share this grief with my children. I did not want them to think that they weren't enough for me. I loved them completely, but I also started dreading the day that I would need to bury them, lose them, part with them. Without Vida and Kesher, I was the only elder among us. Just as Grandmother Leah had mourned that for herself, and just as Grandmother Rebekah had mourned that when she was in the same situation without Deborah, I began to mourn it. I felt alone, even when I was with others.

I cried with my children who were no longer children, and together we consoled each other as much as we could, though I cannot know what thoughts they did not share with me, just as they did not know what I withheld from them.

However, our time together was not only sorrowful. We also found time to smile and laugh together. We shared memories of Kesher. I soon found that I was telling the children stories about Kesher that they didn't know. Though they had been there in the harem with us, they had been young. Then they had grown up, and Vida's children had lived with Suf, and Hur had married and gone to live in his own quarters with first his wife and then his children. Eventually only May-tal was there with us in our shared quarters.

I enjoyed telling stories about Kesher, even though I did not enjoy her absence. Miryam wondered aloud whether Vida and Suf were still alive. It had not been that long since we'd seen them, but we had faced danger, and maybe they had too. We would never know. Naturally, we began to tell stories about them too. They lived on through our stories. We all did. I was sorry that they were not there to enjoy it, but I don't think Kesher or Vida would have begrudged me for having a lovely reunion with our children even though the two of them were not there.

Moses said those seven days of mourning was the longest amount of time that he'd had without a question or a petition or a complaint in a long while. He did have some quiet time when he went up the mountain to listen to Yah, and ever since the scouts had returned, he'd been imparting rules and laws that he'd heard in his Yah ear. The Israelites no longer served Pharaoh, but without learning to serve Yah, they would be lost. So, Moses taught them how to serve Yah. He always had a long line of people asking him for guidance or to interpret a law or to settle a dispute.

Moses said that many times people came to him asking about things he had already said. He felt that this took time away from others who had questions he hadn't heard and made him frustrated and less effective. When he asked Yah what to do about it, Yah said to speak to the Children of Israel and tell them to make fringes for all the generations to put on the corners of their garments and that one of the fringes should be blue. That way, the Israelites will see these reminders and remember to do the commandments. Moses thought the blue one was perhaps for me. He said I was the memory of our people. I did hold all the stories, and I told them as often as possible.

But many of the Children of Israel continued to forget. They continued to both complain to Moses and seek his direction, even with the fringes. And we continued to stay in the wilderness. While we were there, Betzalel designed a beautiful tent of meeting so that we might have a place to make sacrifices and perform rituals. Anyone who wished to could contribute to this Tent of Meeting. I gave all the beaded leather I had made, and other women shared theirs too. We continued to bead strands when we learned that if we made enough of them, we could cover the entire tent with this special leather and get to see the sunlight bounce off the beads. We were in the wilderness long enough for the Tent of Meeting to go from a plan to a real tent. We were in the wilderness long enough for Betzalel to make plans for a temple to build when we settled in Israel.

We were in the wilderness long enough to feel like we had actually settled there. We made our meals. We carried water and babies. We made sacrifices and had fests. We were there long enough for fights and rebellions. We were there long enough for Aaron and Elisheva to become grandparents and long enough for their first two sons to tragically die in a fire. After that, Elisheva passed her midwife bag to May-tal, who took Amina as an apprentice.

We wandered many years in the wilderness. Setting up camp in one place, staying for a long time, then moving on. It was the way shepherds traveled the land. There was enough room, yes, but it was not our land; it was still the wilderness. We wandered long enough for Nesiyah, the baby who had been born at the crossing of the sea, and Tikvah, our little baby of hope born on the other side, to become married women. And we were there long enough to say goodbye to Aaron, Hur, and Elisheva. They had grown old, though they were still younger than I was, and I'd had the privilege of loving them since they were children. That they did not get to live in the land of Israel was deeply disappointing. To bury them was devastating.

Miryam's funeral was at once the most heartbreaking and heartwarming of them all. She had made it clear when we parted from Vida that she had not wanted to be alone in her old age and at her death, and she was not. Moses and May-tal and I were by her side for days as she struggled to take her last breaths. What used to be Elisheva's midwife's bag had been gifted to May-tal, and she lovingly used its contents to ease Miryam's pain. We sang to her and told her stories and sat quietly with her hand in ours or our tears on her face.

On one of her last days, Miryam gave a soft laugh.

"What is it?" Moses asked her.

"Once, I was named Yam for the sea of love I was born into. Then I became Miryam because of the bitterness of being separated from my mother." Her voice was quiet, but determined. "Soon I will die, just like my mother. Maybe I will see her again. Maybe the bitter water of my tears will dry, and I will become Yam again, without bitterness."

Miryam's departure felt bitter to those of us who loved her and would miss her. But her death was not a private departure. When the other women of the camp heard that Miryam was dying, they began coming to her to thank her. She had been their inspiration, their hope, and their leader, and they had not forgotten that. In fact, they came to show her that they actively remembered it.

The first visitor was a mother with a young daughter who was missing all her front teeth. The mother gently kissed Miryam's hand, then said, "This is my daughter, Mayim. I gave her a name meaning water so that she would always be reminded of you, Miryam."

Miryam smiled at the mother and daughter. The mother bowed before backing out of the tent, but the girl came forward and kissed Miryam's hand gently. Having never borne a child,

Miryam's heart filled with pride that someone in the next generation would remember her.

We soon found out that it wasn't just some*one*, but many little daughters of Israel who would carry the memory of Miryam forward. Countless women and girls of all ages came by to say that they or their daughters were named Miryam. Still more had names about water: Ma'ayan, to remember the springs of life and hope that were found in the wilderness; Peleg, because of the little tributaries of water that lead to patches of lushness; Be'eri, because the girl was a well who was always with her mother, always sustaining her. All these names and more were for Miryam, daughter of Vida, who had been more of a leader of women in Egypt and the wilderness than she had even known.

Even after Miryam's death, even after we buried her with her feet pointing toward the land of Israel, as if she were still walking and would arrive there soon, we still wandered in the wilderness.

Eventually, I had been patient long enough, so I went to Yah and asked, "If this is what it's going to be like, why am I even here? Was I not there to help my tribe return to the land of my grandfather? If not, why was I given this extraordinary life?" I did not want it anymore. I vowed that when the next full moon came and went, if I was still in the wilderness, I would go to the land of Israel, even if I had to go alone.

When I returned from talking with Yah, May-tal asked me what I had learned. I told her about my vow. "You will not go alone, Auntie," she said. "Wherever you go, I will go." Other women immediately chimed in with her. I had not known any of those women back in Egypt, but they had traveled with me in the wilderness. They had aged while I had not. Yet they were not afraid of me, and they did not ask me if I was real. Not all of them embraced me or sought my company or counsel, but enough did that many of them planned to also leave with me.

The morning before the full moon would rise, I went to sit by the Tent of Meeting so that I could see Moses. While I waited, I admired the beauty of the tent: the copper wash basins, the beaded covers, the glistening gold. I was accustomed to the smells of the sacrifices. Those blew with the wind and were always a part of the camp, though they were much stronger here, where I was closer. But I smelled something else that morning. It was warm and pleasant, though faint. I could not name it, so when Moses approached, I asked him.

"I smell something here; it's very faint, too faint to travel on the breeze like the others. It's a spice, but I cannot detect which one. It's very nice, warm, special. Of course, you spend much more time here than I do. Do you know what it is?"

"Auntie, I am sorry," he said, truly looking remorseful. "When traders came through, I immediately bought several large sacks of it because of your father Joseph. I was going to tell you, but I forgot. Please, wait for me. I will come right back with some."

True to his word, as always, Moses came back shortly with a satchel of spice that I could smell before even opening it. He reached in and took a pinch and spread it on my wrist. It was a dark red-brown spice that quickly filled my nostrils and heart with joy.

"This is cinnamon, Auntie," he said. "I read in your father's scrolls that he had once received and loved this. So, as I said, when I saw that some traders had this spice, I bought it. I love it as much as he did . . . as much as you do."

I truly did love it. And I loved that it was used in the Tent of Meeting. And I loved Moses. Still, I was determined to leave the wilderness. I told him then about my vow, and I told him that there were many women prepared to leave with me. We would be going home. He could come with us or not. I understood that he would know from Yah what he must do—just as I knew what I must do. Moses said he could help, and he asked me to meet him there in the morning. I agreed and went back and told the women that I would get help from Moses in the morning.

That night, we had a large celebration under the full moon. Eye cookies were baked out in the open and exchanged with the traditional words, "This is an eye." We saw each other. And we were free. So when we gathered in a circle that night, I reminded the women of how that tradition had begun.

"Long ago, when we were slaves in Egypt," I said, "the Israelite women had to stop the tradition of singing and dancing under the light of the full moon. The overseers would not allow it. They tried to oppress us in every way, even by removing our celebrations. But they could not stop our joy. The wise women changed the celebration so that it would be on the new moon, in a blanket of darkness that could protect them. But the women could *see* each other, even in the dark. They saw each other's love and beauty, creativity and strength, nurturing and joy. They baked eye cookies to remind their neighbors that they were seen. And there was a secret ingredient baked into those cookies. So secret, that even the women themselves forgot what it was: they would greet each other with the phrase 'this is an eye' because it was a phrase that had been adapted from a traditional song: '*This is a day that Yah has made, so we will rejoice.*'"

That ingredient had, indeed, become a secret not only from the Egyptians but also from the Israelite women. Whether the elder generation had forgotten to tell the younger ones, or whether they had omitted it to protect them is the new unknown. But now that the code had been revealed, it would never be hidden again.

"From now on," Noa shouted, "we will remember that this is a day that Yah has made. We will not only rejoice, but we will also be glad in it!"

Noa was the first to take out her drum that night. She still held within her the worthiness she had felt at the bottom of the mountain, even after so many years. Her sisters and daughters and nieces took theirs out right after her, and many other women followed. One woman hushed her, though, telling her not to tempt Yah into punishing us again, but she was not able to dim Noa's light.

"You should certainly celebrate quietly," Noa said to her, "if that is what you feel you should do. After all, Yah not only created this day, but Yah created this you. I will rejoice and be glad in you being you!" She hugged the woman and kissed her on both cheeks before adding, "And I am the only one in this whole wilderness—in this whole world—who can be me. Yah created me! It would be an insult to Yah's own creation if I were to act like you and have nobody acting like me. In being myself, I honor Yah's creation."

That night, Noa was eager to celebrate and was excited to know that we would soon be in the land of Israel. In no time at all, the excitement spread, and the women, dancing with their drums and timbrels, followed Noa as she sang her song. We rejoiced and were happy under the moon on that day that Yah had made. For some, that meant greeting each other and quietly eating their cookies and then sleeping well before a big journey. For others, it meant singing and dancing. That night, we successfully honored Yah and each other by loving each other as we would love ourselves, doing what we chose, and letting others choose for themselves. My choice was to sing and dance with Noa. We, and the other women who danced, danced the whole night long.

MOSES

oses came to my tent just as the first light of the morning announced that the sun would soon rise. He usually didn't walk through the camp since he couldn't get three steps without being stopped with questions or comments or complaints. But the barely starting predawn light gave him the privacy to seek me out and ask me to walk outside the camp with him. May-tal was not on her mat when he arrived at our tent. She often was out helping with a birth. I saw him place something there for her to find later, then he and I left the tent together. It had been so long since we'd had any time alone. It was a treat to walk with him in silence.

Finally, when we had gone far enough, we sat on a rock in the shade, and he opened a conversation.

"I'm going up the mountain again. Alone, again."

"You've done it before. You know you can do it."

"Yes, and I know how difficult it is." He paused. "And yet, this time does feel different. Still difficult, but different. I'm scared."

"Were you not scared the other times?"

"Of course I was."

"And Yah was there with you. And all was well."

"Better than well," he corrected. "But it was still difficult."

I looked at his face, so worn, wrinkled, and tired. Still, I could see the round cheeks of his babyhood hiding beneath his gray beard. His brown eyes still had a mischievous twinkle, even when tired. I looked into those eyes and reached out both hands to his ears. I pulled gently on the tops and down the sides before giving a firm, loving little yank on the lobes. I did it again, and he smiled.

"I don't have the words," he said, "to tell you how much comfort your presence has brought me during this journey. To have someone with me, even in the crowd, someone who knew me as a little boy and as a young man, someone who knew my parents, someone who knows where I came from and what it was like—Auntie, thank you."

"Moses, look me in the eyes."

He did. He looked, and we looked, for a long time. Though he was younger than I was by three generations, he had been a constant in my life for longer than anyone else I now knew. Whether he realized it or not, he and May-tal were the only ones left who knew the me of before.

"Moses, I hear your gratitude for my presence, for my assistance. I will tell you three very important words, and you must believe me."

"I always believe you, Auntie," he said.

So, I told him, slowly dwelling on each word as I continued to hold his gaze and his hand: "You are welcome."

We sat in silence together, and I hoped and trusted that he understood my full meaning. It wasn't just a polite phrase—

it was offered as a gift. Even a leader such as him must sometimes be told that they are welcome to have support and love. And when I said the words aloud to him, I knew they were true for me, too, and so I repeated them to myself under my breath: *You are welcome.*

"Auntie," he said. "I know why we have not yet entered the land."

I waited for him to continue. He sobbed for a long time and took off his shoes before saying the next words.

"It is because of me, Auntie. I am not to enter. Yah has told me."

This made me cry. After all Moses had done, he would not enter the land. I had accepted that this might happen for me, but I wanted better for him. Before I had a chance to ask why he wouldn't enter, Moses went on.

"I was the leader who helped the people leave Egypt. They are a different people now. They need a different leader. It will be Joshua. He's prepared."

We sat in silence. We had been camped so close to the land by that point that we had all wondered why we had not yet entered. This helped me understand. We breathed together in our quiet space. *Yhhhh. Whhhh.*

Finally, Moses said, "You have buried so many people, so many loved ones."

"Yes."

"Does it get easier with practice?"

Of course, he knew the answer from his own experience, but I voiced it anyway: "No."

"And now," he continued slowly, "now I may even need to ask you to bury me."

"If it needs to be done, I will do it."

A tear left the corner of his eye and found a wrinkle, became a rivulet, then found a path to his cheek and another to his beard, where it got caught and was soon joined by other tears—bitter, salty water. It really never did get easier, but we sat with it, together.

"Before you climb this mountain, your last hill," I said, "I would like to give you a blessing."

He sat up straight, both serious and excited at once.

"As you take this next portion of your journey, to a place that Yah will show you, remember our forefather, Abraham. Neither of us met him, but he, too, followed Yah. His path led him to wealth, stature, and legacy. Along the way, he had many experiences of honor, challenge, joy, sorrow, and even shame. And yet, he was a blessing. You, too, are a blessing, my dear boy. May you know in your heart, in your soul, and with all that you do, that all that you have done—and all that you have been—has been and will continue to be, a blessing."

Moses's body shook, and he gasped for breath as the sobs left his throat. I held his right hand as his left wiped his face. When he calmed, I saw that he was going to speak, but I had more to say, so I continued.

"Would you like a special story?" I asked him. "And a song just for you?"

His face lit up, and he smiled as big as he had when he was an energetic wild little boy running around the palace. I was glad he still viewed this as a gift to him, because for me, it felt like I was indulging myself. I felt that we would not see each other again after this, and I was not ready for our final parting. I was so filled with love for this boy that I could have blessed him for days to come, but I knew our time was limited. So I did what I could to have a little more.

He laid his head in my lap—with his people ear listening, of course—and I removed his head covering and stroked his hair. It looked like a scene of tenderness between a grandparent and grandchild. That I was the elder and he the younger was not apparent by the looks of it, but he did not mind that my skin was still as soft as it had been when I'd first arrived in Egypt, my legs just as strong. He did not mind that I would outlive him. He was as grateful for me as I was for him.

"Ready?" I asked.

He nodded in my lap.

"Once," I began, "there were three children of Israel wandering in the wilderness."

Moses bolted out of my lap and looked at me. "Three Israelites wandering in the wilderness?" he asked. He was nearly shouting. "Three Israelites? Only three Israelites? Not countless Israelites? Three? No sheep shitting everywhere and cows trying to wander away? Only three Israelites?" He repeated it over and over: "Three? Three?" He began laughing so hard that his words became almost unintelligible. "Three? Three!" Moses clutched his side and rolled on the ground laughing. "Three Israelites!" I had not meant to make him laugh, but I was delighted by his joy.

We had privacy where we were on the outcropping, though we could still see and hear the multitude. We were too far to distinguish who was gathering twigs for fires and who was pounding tent pegs back into the hard ground. We couldn't tell whether the smell of smoke was from birds being brought to sacrifice or goats. We didn't know whose babies were crying or whether their parents were yelling after them or singing to soothe them. But we could see, smell, and hear the presence of the countless bodies that had been our constant for all these years, so when I heard Moses laughing about the absurdity and delight of a story with only three Israelites in the wilderness, I joined him. The two of us laughed until our sides hurt and our faces were washed with tears and the sun was high above us and all those many, many people.

"Oh Auntie, that was the best story I have ever heard in my long, full life! And I know there is more, but right now, I cannot imagine anything better than the gift you have just given me. Please, please, let me sleep with this feeling, with you, here in this quiet and relief, and know that I can look forward to more when the evening is cool."

So, we lay side by side in the shade. I could not refuse his request, nor did I want to.

When the sun was lower, we were both so much more relaxed and free than we had been in a long time. Looking at our nation from a distance, I whispered, "How beautiful are the tents of Jacob."

Moses nodded his head and added, "Your dwellings are lovely, Israel." Together we looked at the camp in awe and wonder.

When I started the story again, the opening words, "There were once three Israelites wandering in the wilderness," brought a little giggle, but I was able to tell the rest.

"The first one was Miryam." I thought of the very first time I'd ever laid eyes on her, that brave little girl who had saved her brother and brought three children and my soft-necked friend into my life on the same day. I paused to wipe tears from my face. The bitter water leaving my eyes made me feel as though Miryam were with us in a way. I took a deep breath and continued my story. "She was brave and strong and nurturing. She helped her parents to save her baby brother. She became a caregiver for him and for so many others. She became a leader of women. She showed them how to flow from fear to bravery. She showed them how to flow from oppressed to strength. She showed them how to flow from suffering to joy. She herself was the water that helped them move from bitterness to sweetness. Miryam showed the women how to love others the way she wanted to be loved, even when it was difficult. She showed them how to rejoice, even when there was sorrow."

Moses nodded his head in agreement and whispered, "Thank you, Miryam."

"The second one was Aaron," I said. I put my fingers together the way Aaron's had been so that on each hand, my first and second finger became one and my third and fourth became one. I held my hands up for Moses to see, and he smiled. Then I rested one of those hands on my knee and one on Moses's. In that way, it felt like Aaron was almost with us. "He was resilient and loyal and had a sense of humor," I said. "He went with his mother to a new life, and then with another mother to a newer life. He watched out for his little brother and anyone who was in harm's way when he was there. His fused fingers reminded him every day that he was different, and he reminded his fingers that even when different meant difficult, he was loved. He did things people didn't expect. He showed them possibilities. He was by his brother's side during the most difficult times, and the loyalty didn't end with his brother. Aaron performed rituals on behalf of all the Israelites, making great sacrifices to do so. He, too, was a leader."

Again, Moses nodded. Then he said, "Thank you, Aaron."

"And the third Israelite," I said, both of us knowing it would be him, "was just a boy. Not a boy born of a god, like Ra-moses, but just a boy, Moses. He grew up like any other boy. He had joyful times and sorrowful times. Over time, he did things he was proud of and things he felt ashamed of. He was a regular boy; and he was different from all the other boys, just like each of the other boys were different from him and from each other. Moses," I said, deciding to speak to him directly, "you have spent your life pursuing justice, for yourself, for your father, for your wife, for your people. You, too, have been a leader, even when you didn't want to be. Maybe the leader could have been anyone, any boy or any girl. But it wasn't. It was you."

Below us, we could still see and hear the so-many-more-than-three Israelites. Above us, the sky was declaring that it would be dark soon. We would both need to leave the mountain, need to leave each other. He would go up on his own, and I would go down and rejoin the group going to Israel. He said as much, then added that he was glad that even though he would never set foot in my homeland, I would. I squeezed his hand and asked whether he wanted one more song before we parted. I hoped his face would light up, but knowing that it was his last song from me, he accepted with gratitude, but not excitement.

"There is no other in Israel,
A prophet like you,
Who has heard Yah's voice
Always in their ear."

I sang this seven times, then we stood and faced each other. I loved him. I saw that he loved me. I breathed Moses and that love and Yah into my body. *Yhhhh.* And then, myself into all. *Whhhh.* Moses did the same. He took it all in, would take it with him up the mountain. *Yhhhh.* He released what he no longer needed. *Whhhh.*

Then I spoke: "As you go up your final path, know that Yah is blessing you and watching over you. Yah is shining the light of Yah's own face upon you and is gracious to you. Yah lifts Yah's face to you, making you whole. You are never without Yah, and Yah is never without you."

We embraced. We held each other long enough for me to repeat the words directly into his people ear as he did the same for me, and just a little bit longer. Then Moses walked up Mount Navo and never came down.

NEW

The new leader prepared our camp for travel. Moses had been right. With him now gone, we could move forward. I was going home. After lifetimes of waiting, we were going home. When the Children of Israel were about to finally enter the land of Israel—after so many years—the horn blowers rose early in the morning and took their places at the head of the line. The twelve of them looked over the crowd.

The tents were packed, and the donkeys were loaded. The shepherd boys stood by the flocks, and the soldiers stood at the fronts of their tribes. There were many men. Just about every one of them old enough to grow a beard took up arms and prepared to conquer the people of Canaan. Or maybe be conquered by them. The fear was palpable. Still, they were ready to march and do what they could to be able to live in their promised land, all the while protecting the women and babies, the elderly and feeble, and the Tent of Meeting in the middle of their formation.

The children and the women who had families stood throughout the dismantled camp. Some women had babies wrapped on their backs in addition to the hard crackers and water jugs they carried. Some shed tears of sorrow for the sons they felt they were about to lose. Some steeled themselves for attack and capture . . . and worse.

The twelve horn blowers looked at each other, then raised their trumpets to their lips. There were still shofars throughout the camp, but time in the wilderness had made it possible to make so many things. These trumpets were made of brass and made flashes of light bounce through the desert, some of which caught fleetingly on brown rocks or dusty bodies. But the sight didn't distract them. In unison, the horn blowers blew a long, steady metallic alarm. *Auuuuuuuuuuuuuuuuuuuuuuuuuuuuuuuuuuu!* It was one note with no interruptions that told everyone: get ready. It was to be followed by the nine short blasts that meant: here we go! But before the men could blow the next blasts, there was a different sound.

All at once, the children, the youngest generation, everyone still growing teeth, even down to the toddlers, called out in unison:

"Listen!"

"Listen!"

"Listen!"

And the camp went silent. The elders had been too busy the night before to know that the young ones had been conspiring their own plan. Now it had been pulled off perfectly. Everyone was attentive. As one voice, those children, here and there, all throughout the multitude, looked at the adults who were lead-ing them to the promised land—to the land their ancestors had come from and to the land *they* would inherit, with all the corresponding honor and responsibilities—and reminded the soldiers and everyone else of the most important thing:

"Listen, Israel!"

Everyone listened as the children took a deep breath in. *Yhhhh.* The camp grew bigger, expanding with the collective intake of air and courage and support. And then we exhaled: *Whhhh.* Relaxation, release, reliance. *Yhhhh. Whhhh. . .*

". . . is our god!" they shouted.

Standing on the brink of the unknown, the reminder brought the Israelites back to ourselves and to each other. Pausing to say The Name cut into the fear and made room for possibility. This was the best thing that could have happened. It was what the children had hoped for. They breathed again. First, bringing Yah into their bodies, *Yhhhh*, the whole nation joining along with them this time. Then, they all put everything they had and were into Yah on the exhale. *Whhhh.*

". . . is one!" the children shouted.

And on that cue, the twelve horn blowers blew the nine short blasts of the alarm and marched into the land of Israel. They were followed by soldiers, priests and Levites, children and young families, goats, sheep, cattle, and dogs. The dust that was kicked up by so many feet moving in one direction was tremendous. But one person stood by, watching it all in awe.

Blue, daughter of Deenah and Joseph. Serrah, daughter of Asher. Me. Sister, Mother, Daughter, and Friend. The one who held the memory from the beginning of the Israelites. The one who was going to uplift Israel. The one who did uplift Israel. I stood toward the front, waiting for everyone to pass me. I would see this journey to the end this time. I would see that every last

Israelite left the wilderness, those who had been born into the tribe of my grandfather Israel and those who had chosen to join us. We were such a fruitful nation that most people just walked past me, but those who were meant to see me, did.

Joshua, Moses's successor, descendant of my brother Efraim, who marched right behind the horn blowers, bowed his head and kissed my hand before being the first to cross the shallow river into his new land. There was no time to stop now. Now was, finally, the time to go. The men behind him who marched along the side that I stood next to were treated to my humming as I watched them go. They may not have realized that I was the source of that soft sound, or even that I had made any sound, but the sounds of the footsteps changed as they passed. They became more energetic, more purposeful, more hopeful, and more in rhythm with each other. The soldiers stood a little taller as my eyes and smile showered them with pride.

Noa walked by me. She was no longer a young woman, but a new grandmother. I still recognized her from the radiance she maintained after her experience at the base of the mountain. She and her four sisters walked arm in arm into the land of Israel. They were clean and proud and accepting of their worthiness to inherit the land of their forebears. Then I saw them pause on the other side of the river, reach into their bags, and raise their timbrels. They must have been little girls when we'd left Egypt, but now they were the elders. With their voices raised in song, it was clear that they were ready.

Little Nina's granddaughter, Amina, was a grandmother too. I saw her walk by with her family, and I quietly whispered a thank-you to Kesher for having convinced Amina to keep going after Nina was killed. When Amina saw me, she separated from her husband and children, took one little toothless granddaughter by the hand, and brought her over to me.

"Auntie," Amina said, "look what Benno made. This is Dorit." Amina kissed my hand, and Dorit did the same. "From generation to generation, Benjamin's tribe has grown. I wish we could show him, but I'm glad I can show you."

"I can show you too," Dorit said. "Look at me, Auntie!" Dorit did a little dance in front of me, twirling and skipping and leaping. She was a vibrant little girl who had never known the oppression in Egypt. Dorit took me by one hand and Amina by another and had us lift her up off her feet to help her jump so far forward that it was as if she were flying. I could not stop smiling, though my arms had started to tire from lifting her.

"Dorit," I said, stopping the game but not letting go of her hand, "that was a wonderful dance you showed me. I loved watching you. Soon I will watch you walk into the land of Israel. I will love that very much. When you are there, if you don't see me but you wish for me to see what you can do, you may call to me."

I squeezed Amina's hand and said, "When you were a child, you used to like to show me what you could do. And when your grandmother Nina was a child, she liked to show me what she could do. But it's not just children who want—and need—to be seen. If you make a pattern or sing a song, if you're hurt or scared, if you plant onions in the land of Israel and watch them grow tall and watch the children grow taller yet, you might want to share that with someone. In those moments, if you wish to, you may call to me. It doesn't matter if you call me Auntie or Blue or Serrah, but you may call to me. Ask me to look, and I will not only look, but I will delight in seeing you as much as I delight in seeing you today."

Amina promised that she would, and little Dorit did too. Amina and I hugged. When we separated, she was surprised. "Auntie, you . . . you have wrinkles by your eyes."

I had smiled countless times, and it was starting to show.

"Go," I told her. "Cross into the land. I will watch you cross into the land, and I will see everyone else go as well. I will see it happen." She hugged me again, then she and Dorit caught up with the others, and I watched those women and girls from the tribe of Benjamin, Benno's descendants, cross into the land where we had been born.

More people passed me. So many more. They were hard to count—like the stars in the sky and the sand at our feet. Even that day, another baby was born. She was called He-naynu, meaning *here we are*. She crossed the river in her mother's arms, the youngest one to enter. Soon, a new generation would be born on the land.

May-tal was the one who had delivered He-naynu. She had helped deliver hundreds of babies from other women's bodies, though none from her own; but that was not what we talked about when she saw me through the wave of Israelites.

"Auntie," she said through tears, "I have never seen you look this way."

"Do you mean radiant with happiness?" I asked, jokingly.

She smiled. "I mean older," she said.

"Do I look as old as you?" I asked.

"No," she said, "just older than you did before. But"—May-tal reached up and moved my head covering back—"you have a few gray hairs."

There were still Israelites passing me, still sheep and goats and donkeys with carts. But I could just see the first soldiers that were at the back of the line.

"I believe I will make it, then. Maybe," I said, "maybe I will see everyone go home and also get to go myself."

"We can go right now, Auntie," she said. "Let us walk into the land together."

"No," I said, "I want to see everyone go, not just some."

"Then I will wait with you, and we will cross together." I thought about that for some time and agreed that we could wait and watch together. My youngest child and I would be the two women—who had chosen our own lives—that would witness this miracle. We stood side by side, our gaze at the wonder before us only occasionally interrupted by May-tal checking to see whether I looked different. Finally, we watched all the soldiers but one walk across the river and onto the land.

That last soldier was Caleb, head of the tribe of Judah, one of only two scouts who had thought we should have done this years ago, had placed himself at the end of the line. He wished to personally see that everyone crossed safely. When he reached me and May-tal, he said, "Aunties, take my hands, and we will cross into our homeland."

My feet were beginning to ache. It was no wonder that Vida had not wanted to make this journey. Nevertheless, I wished to cross alone, just me and Yah, and I knew I could still do so. So I said no. This surprised him.

May-tal took my hand then and said, "Auntie, let's walk in together." But I still said no. I would see this happen, including watching her go in. Imagining my thoughts, May-tal added, "You do not need to go alone. And when we get to the other side, if you find it difficult to walk, I will stay beside you. I will help you. I will be with you." I hugged her. She knew that was not what I wanted.

"I will not be alone," I said. "I will be with Yah."

"Aunties, we must go now," Caleb said.

"Go," I said to May-tal. "I will enjoy watching you. You have important things to do; there are babies waiting to be born on the land of their matriarchs. They need you. I also have important things to do. I will discover what they are after I walk back home. Love me the way you would love yourself." Then I turned to Caleb. "And you go too," I said.

"Auntie, who are you that you speak to me this way? Surely you know the struggles we have been through in the wilderness. Now we leave that behind."

"Indeed, I know the struggles," I said. "I have weathered them all. I am Blue," I told him. "Daughter of Deenah and Joseph, known in Israel as Serrah, daughter of Asher."

"But . . ." he stammered. I already knew what he was thinking: Asher and all the sons of Israel had died so long ago, even before we'd left Egypt. Maybe he had heard rumors about me, maybe not, because how could I be Asher's daughter? But he said none of that. He only asked these words: "You're real?"

"I am real," I answered. May-tal kissed my very real hand and my very real cheek. I embraced her with my very real arms and left some very real tears on her neck. Caleb bowed his head to me, then I watched him follow May-tal across the river. And thus, I saw every Israelite enter the land.

WORDS AND THINGS

WORDS AND THINGS

These words I write now tell of things that happened after the Israelites returned to the land of Israel. Like the rest of my scrolls, I am writing this from inside the besieged city of Jerusalem. Rabbi Yohanan is no longer here. He was snuck out of the city about two months ago in a closed coffin—alive, but thankfully uninspected. He carried with him a Torah scroll, that is, *The Five Books of Moses*. He also took my other four scrolls, this being my fifth. He and Ezra, the student who has been helping me all these months, had worked devotedly for seven days and nights to copy the scrolls so they could be sent out. I trust that the rabbi is safe, and my story with him.

Since the rabbi's departure, Ezra left the dormitory where the young men stayed and took over Rabbi Yohanan's apartment. He has been not only my scribal assistant, ink and parchment acquirer, and meal preparer but also my companion. We share the small space, which feels cozier now that I've taken down the privacy curtain. He still brings me food, though now that my task is complete, I have also been to the market with him. There is little food to be found there. We have seen some of Rabbi

Yohanan's other students when walking. None of them recognize me when we're out because I have begun to age. It isn't happening as quickly this time as it did before, though. I look like I could be Ezra's mother, though he says he doesn't mind. Soon enough, my feet will start to ache and my shoulders will crouch, and I will be mistaken for his grandmother. He might mind then. We will see.

It was only the first time that I walked with Yah that my aging happened so quickly. I wonder if it was connected to the drastic change of the Israelites not leaving Egypt after my father's death. Maybe Yah knew I could no longer fulfill my purpose in that time and needed me to leave. But like so many other things: I don't know.

When May-tal and Caleb set foot in the land of Israel, I took off my shoes and walked across the river. The cold water felt good on my feet. I could tell they were sore, but still strong. I placed one foot and then the other on the land of my birth. I was filled with awe and gratitude, joy and relief, wonder and appreciation. All of this was bursting out of me so forcefully that I thought I might fall down if I didn't stop to lie down. So I did exactly that. I stretched my body out on the same rolling hills where I had first laid down next to Benno. I didn't expect to grow taller than any onions. But I expected that I would grow old there while I slept.

I did grow old there that night. So much so, that when I rose in the morning and was examining my strength and senses, a shepherd approached me and asked after my health. "Auntie, are you well?" he asked. "Why are you out here alone? Do you need help?"

I was there alone because I had let my people go before me. I would walk with Yah alone, so I was there alone. I hadn't considered whether I'd needed help, because I hadn't thought I would be there. But if I were to walk with Yah again, it seemed that it was not yet.

Though I had not planned them, words came out of my mouth. "Yes," I said, "I wish to get to the city of Jericho. Is it far?" I put my sandals back on and brushed off my tunic.

The shepherd whistled, and two lads started walking toward us with a donkey. "It is not far at all. You can arrive before the sun kisses the top of the sky. My lads will take you there." He looked around for any belongings I might be carrying and saw none. "Please, take these figs with you for the journey."

"What is your name?" I asked him.

"Auntie, I am Hamed, son of Abuyi. I know this land well, and so do these lads. They will take you safely to the city."

"Hamed, son of Abuyi, I have nothing with which to pay you," I said.

He bowed before me. "Auntie, I am not helping you for your coins. Allah will reward me with praise in this world and the next."

"You are an Ishmaelite," I said. It was a statement, not a question. "Thank you for your kindness to a stranger. I am also a descendant of Abraham. We share this custom."

Hamed kissed my hand and bowed again with respect. Then he helped me onto the donkey, and the boys took me to Jericho, where, as promised, we arrived before the sun was above it. They helped me dismount at the city gate before returning to Hamed. I had no plan, but I walked slowly to the shade of the city walls.

My bones were feeling older, slower, and stiffer, and I didn't think it was from the donkey ride. But I didn't mind moving slowly. I didn't even mind stopping to rest. I leaned against the wall inside the gate. While I took in the scents of the city, a kitten walked over my feet and rubbed against my leg.

I looked at this little brown kitten and began to laugh. "Are you from Barley?" I asked her as I picked her up into my arms. She didn't answer. "I'm from Deenah," I told her. "Also called Elephant." The kitten rubbed her face against mine then wiggled out of my grasp to jump to the wall beside us. I watched her climb up and walk across the edge of the rooftops. Looking up, I saw what was surely my destination: a house with an open window and, hanging out of it, a long string of red beads. Just like my mother's beads that I'd worn on my wrist for years. My first thought was that my brother might also have my unique timelessness. Tears immediately welled up in my eyes at the thought of not being the only one. But, I remembered, my mother had died. And Hur had reported long ago that my brother was already an old man. In fact, once our journey had been delayed again, I had assumed and accepted that I would never meet him. Still. Maybe. Maybe I would meet my brother, and maybe he would be like me.

I rushed to the house as quickly as my aging body would allow and entered without a knock or invitation. All the eyes in the room turned to me. I thrust my arm in the air to show the beads I wore there, and while nearly everyone stared in confusion, the innkeeper herself ran toward me and took both of my hands in hers. She held my newly misshapen fingers delicately and used one of her fingers to cautiously touch the beads. Then she looked into my eyes, hers as wet as mine, and smiled.

"Auntie," she said, leading me further into the inn, past the other patrons and to a private room, "please, sit." When she saw to it that I was comfortably settled into a large cushioned chair, she turned to a little girl who had followed us in. "Go and get Mama," she said. "Tell her that our auntie has arrived. Quickly. After you tell Mama, go round up the others."

When we were alone, she offered me wine and fruits but could not stop staring at me long enough to bring them. My curiosity was more thirsty than my mouth, so I did not mind. And I didn't need to wait long to have it quenched. The woman admired the bracelet again and bowed her head onto my hand, then kissed it. "I am Rahab," she said. "I am the innkeeper here. I am the daughter of Peelpeelon, who you will meet in just a moment. She grew up on the knees of her grandmother, Shani, wife of Joseph. We are descendants of Elephant and her son, Joseph. You must be a descendant of Elephant and her daughter, Blue. You have the bracelet." Her fingers wandered back to my beads as she said that, and her hand was on my wrist when her mother walked in.

It hurt my neck to raise my gaze from my wrist to see Peelpeelon as she walked through the door. Her face held the wrinkles of many years in the sun and also the creases of countless smiles and laughs. When her eyes met mine, I saw Grandmother Leah. But it was not my grandmother who came and kissed my hand and who surely endured pain in her knees as she placed them on the ground so that she could fully embrace me. No, this was a granddaughter of my brother. He was not like me. He had lived a long life, aged, and died. I would never meet him. But he lived on in his granddaughter in ways that I could not imagine. "We are so glad you're here," she said to me between sobs. "We have waited for you."

As we held each other, the room filled with more and more of my mother's descendants, old women and young women, children and babies. My mother, Deenah—Elephant—lived in all of them—in this one's eyes and that one's hair, and surely in the way they wove their blankets and seasoned their stews, and even in the legends they told. I breathed them all into me. *Yhhhh*. Peelpeelon stopped our hug and sat beside me. She held my hand and inhaled everything in as well. Together we released ourselves—gave ourselves—to our tribe. *Whhhh*.

Everyone sat. Everyone breathed. The room ebbed and flowed with our breathing. The knowledge that we had all been sharing ourselves with each other all this time—but from so far away, and now, from so close—caused the hair on my arms and the top of my head to prickle and dance. The silence as we connected was broken when a girl of about my age, that is, the age I had always been, pulled a younger boy into the room.

"Look, Joseph," she said, "our auntie has returned. She is a descendant of our forefather's sister, Blue."

"Auntie, you must be eager to hear our stories of Elephant and the son she had late in life," Rahab said. "I am certainly curious to hear stories of your foremother, Blue."

"I am not a descendant of Blue," I said. The room filled with confused silence. My voice was slow and quiet. It was difficult to speak, but I had three more words to share: "I am Blue."

This surprised them even more. But soon they began to move. Peelpeelon kissed my right hand, and Rahab my left, the one with the bracelet. Then the two of them were hugging me. Soon many hands reached out to touch me, even more lovingly than any oiler, on my arms, my legs, my back, my head, and my face. The last thing I remember is all my wounds being cleansed by the tears of my sisters. Then, I walked with Yah.

When I first came to Jerusalem, I didn't know where I was. Or when. I was alone in what I soon learned was King Solomon's court. I had a moment to assess myself. I was once again wearing the tunic I had worn when I was running away from the famine and toward Egypt and my father. I immediately checked my wrists and saw that I was not wearing my mother's red beads. It's funny that this was my greatest concern.

Right now, hundreds of years after the destruction of the temple that I helped King Solomon build, my greatest concern is for Ezra and the other people under siege in this beautiful city. In just the few months since my arrival, the moon has grown and shrunk and renewed itself without any singing or eye cookies, but with much pain. The food is mostly gone, the water, withheld. The Romans are waiting for the Israelites—the Jews, as they now call themselves—to die. And whether it's by their swords or from starvation or the sicknesses that are plaguing so many, it does not matter. The rabbi's students have referred to their captors as Amalekites as often as they've called them Romans.

I wish I were here to lead my people out of this confinement and out of this suffering to wider places and new beginnings, but there is nowhere to take them. There are Romans from here to the sea, to the east, to the north, and down to the Negev desert and beyond. It isn't only in Jerusalem that they've taken over the land of Israel, but in other cities, in villages, in the fields, and in farms everywhere.

Each time I prepare to walk with Yah, it seems that my body ages more slowly than the last. It is happening again now. I will be gone before the city falls. There is nothing I can do about it. It is already Ezra who writes these words for me so that I can rest my stiff hands. He says he does not mind. He says that doing so is his honor and that I may tell him as many words as I wish. However, parchment is not easy to get. I know he has been reusing some, and I'm grateful that my scrolls have already been copied once and have been sent out with Rabbi Yohanan. I hope they will be copied again.

Now, I would rather spend the little time I have left sitting in the sun with Ezra and listening to the Levites sing on the Temple Mount while they still do, while they still can. So, these will be my last words. I have known since shortly after my arrival in Rabbi Yohanan's class that my purpose here was to write the story of the Israelites' journey from the land of Israel and back again. I take pride in what I have accomplished. I have done my job. My joy this time here was to be loved and supported by Ezra and respected by Rabbi Yohanan.

The first time I was in Jerusalem, my purpose was to help King Solomon build the First Temple. My joy then came from the time I spent with Michal, a princess and a queen and a woman whose name means brook—possibly another Israelite named for Miryam. We shared countless stories, songs, and dances, and lots and lots of laughter. And my joy came from the tour that the king himself arranged for me when I started to age. I did not see all the land of the twelve tribes that had come from my grandfather and grandmothers, but I traveled as far north as Tishbi, where I saw open expanses, beautiful fertile ground, and possibility farther and wider han I had ever imagined. Those are stories that could fill scrolls of their own. Perhaps I will write them one day. Perhaps somebody else will.

Tonight, there will be a full moon: the first one of the new year. This is the day on which, so long ago, I left Egypt. Ezra tells me that the Israelites still mark this day every year. Before the sun sets this evening, he will invite all those who are hungry to come and eat. There isn't much more than bitter herbs, but eating that will remind them of the bitterness of slavery and the miracle of our exodus. And he will open these scrolls from end to end and invite all who are interested to come and listen to the words that tell of when I left Egypt. With his help, they will hear my story. They will hear my song.

AUTHOR'S NOTE

It has been a joy, a privilege, and an adventure to write *The Desert Songs Trilogy*. The characters in these books have welcomed me into their lives in ways I never could have imagined just a few short years ago. They've inspired me, guided me, and kept me company in my life through many changes that have happened since we started this journey together.

I'm grateful to Deborah, Joseph, and Blue for letting me tell these versions of their stories. I've enjoyed getting to know them and to see the world through their eyes. And I'm also grateful to some of the other characters who popped up for me to unexpectedly fall in love with. Atsu, Benno, Deenah, Elisheva, Esau, Keturah, Leah, Nina, Vida, as well as other "supporting" characters jumped into my heart with full force and now have a permanent place there. Writing this series also opened the door to new, powerful, and meaningful ways for me to experience God through many names—YhWh, Yah, Elohim, Oneness, The One Here, and more.

People often ask me how long it takes to write a book. My response is that it takes a lot longer to not write a book than to write one. I wrote the first drafts of *The Scrolls of Deborah* and *Seventeen Spoons* in about six months each. I worked on *The Song of the Blue Bird* for more than four years. Most of that time was spent not writing because I was stuck. I had a hard time connecting with the scenes and with Blue herself. Having lived for so many generations, she had more wisdom than I could fathom and such a unique life that I couldn't figure out how to write it down. The best I got was a chapter here or there. When that did happen, I shared the stories with Robin.

At this time, I want to sincerely thank Robin, a wise bird in her own right, for listening to the early versions of the Blue stories. Robin is a widowed octogenarian who spent her first years of life in a Japanese internment camp in California. She grew up to be an educator who brought her compassion, humor, and wisdom to countless students as well as her friends and family. She married a Jewish man named William Joseph, and together they doubled the amount of discrimination they faced. They did the best they could to heal from their personal and generational traumas and bring goodness into the world. The two of them raised his two sons and the daughter and son they adopted together. All four of these adult children are compassionate people who are working to create a kinder world for the next generation. Robin has been a role model and a patient, supportive ear—especially during the slow parts of the process.

It was my amazing, brilliant, creative editor Gina Frangello who helped the process move along. With her guidance I was (finally!) able to get unstuck and go from trying to write this book for years to doing so in a one-month somewhat frenzied overhaul that turned into the rough draft for this book. Now I feel like I have done some justice to Blue's life story, though I believe that she would be the first to point out that it's impossible to include every event, every perspective, every thought . . . By necessity, a lot has been left out of her scrolls, just like a lot was left out of Deborah's scrolls, Joseph's scrolls, and Moses's scrolls. Just like a lot would be left out of mine or yours.

As Blue told her story, she did so in five books that share the same names as the *Five Books of Moses* in Hebrew. For example, while the second book is called Exodus (actually a Greek word) in English, it's called Names in Hebrew because that's the first word in that book. Similarly, the chapter names in this book come from the first word or an important word or phrase in the first line of each new chapter, which is the way the Torah portions are labeled. The time frames covered in each of Blue's books and chapters don't correspond to Moses's.

Included in this book, and in this whole trilogy, are lots of songs. As always, it's Shira Gura's compositions that provide the soundtrack for my days, my writing, and my imagining. She has even created original music to some of the words that I wrote, including the tune for "Joseph Lives" in this book. Also in this novel are scenes inspired by the music of Miriam Margles, whose song "Ashrei HaAm" (Happy is the Nation) helped me transport myself into the moment of leaving Egypt; Elana Jagoda, whose song "Holy Sister Miriam" played on repeat on my phone for months; and Dorothy Richman, whose song "Enough Room" is so true and calming and also expresses Amina's beliefs, though she shouted them out in frustration after the attack from the Amalekites. When the women danced with their timbrels, following Noa as she sang her song, it was a nod of gratitude to Debbie Friedman.

I want to thank four excellent teachers whom I've had the privilege of learning with in the last few years. Thank you to my three Torah teachers, Rabbi Shira Levine, who holds space for all ideas, Rabbi Avi Strausberg, who brings extensive resources, and Yael Unterman, who runs excellent Bibliodrama sessions and has taught me how to do so as well. And thank you to my former Arabic teacher and current friend Tahani Abd Al-Halim, who was always patient in slowly enunciating the Arabic words and names that I asked her to help with.

Thank you to Eli for many things and, specifically, for helping to visualize the timeline of Blue's life. Thank you to Mia for many things and, specifically, the laughing matter that was a part of this journey. Thank you to all the people who have engaged in conversation with me about the Garden of Eden—especially Daria, Josh, Shlomo, and Zev—which ended up being a much smaller piece of this book than I anticipated but still a large portion of my thought process.

In writing this series, I have felt the power of having a tribe. Someone to laugh with, someone to sing with, someone to cry with, someone to complain with, someone to discuss ideas with, someone to celebrate with. I often long for the physical proximity of the extended family (received and chosen) that it seemed like these people of the past had. However, even across land and sea, my tribe has been all these things and more, and my gratitude for that is immeasurable. Thousands of thanks to my tribe, to my sisters, mothers, daughters, and friends who have supported me in this trilogy and in life. This includes all the people above and also Adi, Devora, Fran, Gila, Henya, Iris, Jan, Jay, Julie, Lori, Naomi, Natanel, Netta, Nili, Patti, Sandy, Sarah, Sophie, Tom, Yosi, and Zeev. The list is truly longer than that. Sometimes a tribe is so big that it's impossible to thank everyone.

Sometimes a tribe is so big that it's impossible to know everyone. I want to thank the MOTs who showed up for me online when I put out a request for suggestions for water-related names that could honor Miryam. I received many more names than I could use because so many women offered ideas.

Thank you to everyone at Row House Publishing who contributed to the process of making these stories into a trilogy of books, including Meghan Rollins Wilson for the close read and excellent editing, Rebekah Borucki for loving these books even before they were finished, and V. for making sure all the pieces of the process got finished. Finally, Dear Reader, thank you for picking up this book and for traveling with me to far off places and times. If you enjoyed *The Song of the Blue Bird* or any of the books in The Desert Songs Trilogy, please leave a positive review online and recommend it to anyone in your tribe who you think would like it too.

Thank you,
Esther

Keep breathing.
Keep dreaming.
Keep singing your song.

ABOUT THE AUTHOR

Esther Goldenberg is a sister, mother, daughter, and friend who loves looking at the moon. No matter the night, it reminds her that everything is just a phase. In this phase of Esther's life, she's reminding herself to keep breathing, keep dreaming, and keep singing her song. Her work is inspired by her lifelong love of daydreaming and her short excursions into nature. *The Song of the Blue Bird* is the final installment in The Desert Songs Trilogy.